Tempting
Eden

Tempting Eden

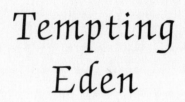

MARGARET ROWE

HEAT / NEW YORK

THE BERKLEY PUBLISHING GROUP
Published by the Penguin Group
Penguin Group (USA) Inc.
375 Hudson Street, New York, New York 10014, USA
Penguin Group (Canada), 90 Eglinton Avenue East, Suite 700, Toronto, Ontario M4P 2Y3, Canada
(a division of Pearson Penguin Canada Inc.)
Penguin Books Ltd., 80 Strand, London WC2R 0RL, England
Penguin Group Ireland, 25 St. Stephen's Green, Dublin 2, Ireland (a division of Penguin Books Ltd.)
Penguin Group (Australia), 250 Camberwell Road, Camberwell, Victoria 3124, Australia
(a division of Pearson Australia Group Pty. Ltd.)
Penguin Books India Pvt. Ltd., 11 Community Centre, Panchsheel Park, New Delhi—110 017, India
Penguin Group (NZ), 67 Apollo Drive, Rosedale, North Shore 0632, New Zealand
(a division of Pearson New Zealand Ltd.)
Penguin Books (South Africa) (Pty.) Ltd., 24 Sturdee Avenue, Rosebank, Johannesburg 2196, South Africa

Penguin Books Ltd., Registered Offices: 80 Strand, London WC2R 0RL, England

This book is an original publication of The Berkley Publishing Group.

This is a work of fiction. Names, characters, places, and incidents either are the product of the author's imagination or are used fictitiously, and any resemblance to actual persons, living or dead, business establishments, events, or locales is entirely coincidental. The publisher does not have any control over and does not assume any responsibility for author or third-party websites or their content.

To Laura Bradford, for absolutely everything, especially MORE

Copyright © 2010 by Maggie Robinson.
Excerpt from *Any Wicked Thing* by Margaret Rowe copyright © by Maggie Robinson.
Cover art by Alan Ayers.
Cover design by George Long.
Text design by Laura K. Corless.

PRINTING HISTORY
Heat trade paperback edition / June 2010

Library of Congress Cataloging-in-Publication Data

Rowe, Margaret.
    Tempting Eden / Margaret Rowe.—Heat trade paperback ed.
        p. cm.
    ISBN 978-0-425-23431-0
    I. Title.
    PS3618.O8729T46 2010
    813'.6—dc22   2009053825

PRINTED IN THE UNITED STATES OF AMERICA

10 9 8 7 6 5 4 3 2 1

Prologue

When he was done, she'd be the greatest whore in all Christendom.

If they'd been in London, her body would have already been sold to the highest bidder in the Marriage Mart. He'd have had to dower her for some chinless earl to take his pleasure in her innocence. Since London was out of the question, and a ton marriage was not on her horizon, there was no better man than he to teach her. She was destined to be a prim little prude if he didn't intervene.

And she might prove more capable than her mother in providing him with an heir. No one would dare question him and live to tell the tale.

Baron Ivor Hartford carefully watched his stepdaughter Eden as she sat across the gleaming mahogany dining table. He'd planted the seeds patiently, and soon it would be time for the harvest.

Her pale plain face was flushed. She giggled.

Excellent.

She was not usually a giggler, but rather a serious girl. Earnest. Clutching her dead father's dusty books to her ripening bosom with fervor, she had long surpassed the learning of the governess who was abovestairs with his younger stepdaughter. But Ivor would soon further Eden's education beyond her wildest imaginings.

Now he saw her attempt to rise from the table and sway. The footman rushed to catch her.

"I'll take care of her, Henley," the baron said.

All night he had signaled Henley to refill Eden's glass. They had been quite alone at dinner. His wife was upstairs recovering from yet another miscarriage, deep in her laudanum dreams.

When Eden had placed her hand unsteadily over her wine goblet, Ivor had teased her. "Why, Puss, you're a grown woman now. Eighteen. If you were in town, you'd be drinking champagne and whirling about the dance floor with the young bucks. You might even be married and a mother yourself. A little wine won't hurt you."

He had cajoled and flattered, and she had drunk.

He picked her up now and carried her up the stairs. He sent her maid, Mattie, away to fetch some headache powder. No doubt Eden would have need of it.

Hartford placed her on her bed. Her arms were still around his neck. He disentangled her, brushing against her breasts, then settling his hands firmly on each luscious mound. Her eyes flew open in surprise.

"So beautiful, Puss," he whispered. "You've bewitched me. I cannot help myself." Then he bent to kiss her full on the mouth. As her lips opened in protest, his tongue took advantage.

"Mm. You taste like spring wine. Delicious. Sleep well, Puss, and dream of me."

Chapter 1

Eden Emery was well and truly ruined. In all senses of the word.

She didn't resemble the sort of female that one would even *want* to ruin. She was as thin as a wraith, having lost her appetite for food and most other things quite some time ago. Her tightly braided schoolgirl plaits, shadowed gray eyes and pale skin made her unexceptional, perhaps even unappealing, in every way. But one man had not thought so, and he lay dead in her bed.

Somewhere down the long hallway her sister Jannah coughed. Eden couldn't turn to her for help. Jannah would expire from shock knowing the lengths that Eden had gone to keep her safe. Warm. Fed. Untouched.

Eden turned away from Ivor Hartford's body and washed herself thoroughly, scrubbing the sin from her skin with an almost vicious vigor. Her own body now repelled her because it had so compelled him. Her mother had not been in her grave a day before the man had come back to her bed. He'd ridden her hard to prove his dominance, and she had let him, as she let him do everything.

He had trained her well. He'd said and done things to her to weave her into his web, as helpless and mindless as a fly. She had even betrayed her own mother without much remorse when the woman was alive. How foolish Eden had been, thinking the baron might leave her alone once there was no one to trick.

What a selfish, naïve idiot Eden had been. Jealous, at the heart of it. She had a beautiful, stupid mother, and she was an ugly, smart daughter. She'd been every bit as stupid as her poor mother. More so.

How simple it was to fall into their old routine once her mother was gone. With one flick of an eye or raised eyebrow, Eden knew what was expected of her, and knew the consequences if she refused.

Not that she would think to do so.

At least Ivor was a man of habit. After he had established his unquestionable mastery over her once again, he had slept in her bed-chamber Saturday nights, the better to torture her in church Sunday morning with his pious façade, and had spent Sunday evenings cel-ebrating his own peculiar brand of religion. Occasionally he varied from this routine, just to keep Eden sufficiently off-kilter. In fact, tonight was Wednesday.

She dressed herself in her most severe black woolen gown, a left-over of what seemed like endless years of mourning, twisting her braids into an unbecoming bun, neutralizing her womanhood with studied care. Holding her breath, she cleaned her stepfather as best she could and struggled to get him back into his dressing gown. She no longer had the need to keep her tongue and told him in plain and vulgar language how he had robbed her of her future, even if in her long-ago childish vanity she had been more than complicit.

She spoke of her late father, a surprisingly ecumenical country vicar, who'd named his children for the paradise of different cultures.

Elysium, her beloved brother Eli, had died at Waterloo. Jannah was dying down the hall. Eden herself had shrunk in size as she grew in sin. There had been no heaven on earth for any of Vicar Emery's offspring. However, there was no doubt in her mind that Lord Hartford was going to Hell, no matter what it was called. And she would soon follow.

When Eden was satisfied that every button was buttoned and all traces of his wicked pleasure were gone, she straightened Ivor's body on the bed and rolled him off, and he landed with an unpleasant thud on the carpet. She stripped the bed and stuffed the soiled sheets in her wardrobe, then smoothed the coverlet over the bare mattress. The room needed airing as well. Shivering, she opened both windows into the night. The candles flared. Lord Hartford had always insisted on light, the better to see her humiliation and ultimate compliance. And sometimes, he used the candles for altogether different purposes.

She arranged an open book on the floor near her chair, neatly placing her magnifying glass on the side table. She then sat down and counted to one hundred, listening to her heart race, composing her thoughts. Should she ring for the servants? No, that implied she was in control of her emotions. And she certainly was not that. She wondered if they could be trusted to keep the manner and location of Lord Hartford's death quiet. He had used them with as little charity as he had his stepdaughter. She rose, closed the windows and flew out into the hall.

"Help!" she cried. "Help! Lord Hartford has fallen ill!"

No doubt Jannah would awaken. There was no help for it. Hopefully Mattie would not let her get out of bed.

After an agonizing wait, Kempton, Lord Hartford's bleary-eyed valet, shuffled down from his room. Several other servants clustered outside Eden's bedroom door, unwilling to look at their master's form on the floor.

"I was reading," Eden gasped, having no difficulty summoning a note of panic to her voice. "He must have felt unwell and seen my light, come to me for help. I think—I fear—he is dead." She shuddered. This was no act.

Reading. Ha. Milo Kempton had not been in the baron's service long, but long enough to know the prim and proper Miss Emery must be turning cartwheels while she played the sorrowful stepdaughter. It hadn't taken him but a few weeks to figure out there were strange things afoot in this isolated house, for all that the other servants kept their mouths shut. Knew what side of their bread was buttered, they did. It was hard to come by employment up here. The baron was a right bastard when he felt like it, but that hadn't bothered Kempton none. Kempton needed a job, too. He'd been an army man, and after a few months begging on the streets, he had been ready to work for the devil himself.

He bent and turned the devil over. Lord Hartford's eyes were open, his lips tinged blue. There was no question he was dead. Kempton glanced up at Miss Emery. Her dark eyes slid to a corner of the room. Guilty as sin. And he was glad of it. Maybe something good would come of his employer's demise after all, for both of them.

"I'll take care of him, miss," he said, straightening up. "He told me before he went to bed he wasn't feeling up to snuff. I'm only sorry he bothered you instead of calling for me." He winked at her, quite broadly, so she couldn't miss its implication. He was ready to lie for her, and ready to lie *with* her if it came to that. She was a plain, skinny thing, but those were sometimes the ones who were most surprising. She must have had some mysterious hold over her stepfather for the old goat to be regular as clockwork in her bed. "Perhaps you should go downstairs. Get Mrs. Washburn to fix you a cup of tea. Or a tot of brandy. You've had a nasty shock." He smiled and patted her shoulder. She stumbled backward at his touch.

"Yes," Eden said faintly.

My God. Kempton knew. That smirk. The overly familiar press of his fingertips into the fabric of her dress. What would it take for him to keep silent? Eden made her way downstairs, only to realize that she was still barefoot as she reached the cold flagstones of the hall. She closed the library door against the hushed grunts and grumbles of the servants above as they laid out Lord Hartford in his own bed. He had been a large man, and his dead weight made moving the body difficult. Eden had reason to know.

Why had she chosen the library instead of her mother's cheerful pink parlor? The library was Hartford's room, smelled of him, his books, his liquor, his cigars. Here she had spent hours on the leather couch, posing for his artistic fantasies, fearful one of the servants would enter the deliberately unlocked door. Touching herself at his precise directions and unraveling in shame. Bending over his desk as he entered her from behind, one of his hands muffling her cries while the other snaked around, forcing her sweet agony. Standing mute and shackled as he struck her bottom. But his brandy was at hand. Eden poured a staggering amount and drank it down, trying to control her shaking. A tap at the door, and Mrs. Washburn entered, bringing her hot, strong tea and a plate of biscuits. She set them on the empty desk.

"I'm so sorry, Miss Eden. This hasn't been a happy house for you, has it? First your poor brother, then your mama. Miss Jannah

sick. And now Baron Hartford." The older woman smoothed
her skirts, as though she were smoothing the wrinkles out of her
thoughts. "We, all of us staff, hope the new baron is a better man.
You've suffered enough."

Eden looked at the housekeeper. Mrs. Washburn's face betrayed
nothing, but her little speech hinted otherwise. If they had suspected how Lord Hartford had used her, they hadn't lifted a finger.
Well, how could they? It wasn't their place or their business what the
"quality" did. They needed the shelter as much as she and Jannah
did in this remote corner of the kingdom. Eden felt the first tears of
the evening sting her eyes. "I'm not sorry he's dead," she whispered.
"But I didn't kill him, I swear it."

"Nonsense, love! Not for one minute did I think that," said Mrs.
Washburn, sounding shocked. "It was well past time, the old bastard. Sit down. Drink your tea. Charlotte is making up the yellow
room for you to sleep in tonight. I'll go help her. But ring if you
need anything else."

Eden swallowed the hot tea without tasting it. What she needed
could not be supplied by a dozen Mrs. Washburns. But she'd have
to make the best of it. At least the past four years had trained her
for something.

"Make sure Jannah is all right. I'll come up to her as soon as I
can."

"You worry about you. We'll take care of your sister."

The housekeeper left her alone after lighting some lamps. Eden
must write to Ivor's solicitor. He'd know how to get in touch with
the baron's heir, some nephew she had never met. And she had to
find out what provisions had been made for her and her sister. She
knew her mother had brought nothing to her marriage but her
vague beauty and three hungry children. Eden felt sure her mother

married Ivor simply for their security, for who could love such a villain?

Well, Eden had. At first. Fool that she was. And when she had finally come to her senses, Ivor had threatened to turn to her younger sister for comfort. So they continued their devil's bargain. Eden was as well trained as any courtesan and had come cheap besides. He had only given her the one gift, a loathsome reminder of his mastery.

And now the bargain was over. Eden and Jannah were to be at the mercy of another lord. Eden searched through the baron's drawers for correspondence and found the address of his solicitor. She set to writing a sanitized version of this night's work, refusing to allow her hope and fear to take hold and blossom. Jannah was too sick to leave Hartford Hall. Eden only hoped the new baron would permit poor relations of his uncle's to remain. So she could not flee, not yet.

When she was done, she tore the silver collar from her throat and threw it in the fire.

*   *   *

The next day, Jannah had been soothed, more letters written, the service organized, the menu discussed with Mrs. Burrell and Mrs. Washburn. Surely some in the tiny village would make the trek to Hartford Hall after Reverend Christopher did his best to induct Ivor Hartford to the afterlife, if only out of curiosity to gain entrance to the house. The baron had refused visitors after both his stepson and his wife died.

Eden had waited impatiently until the body was removed to the church before searching Ivor's bedroom. Kempton had mercifully gone with his master, riding alongside the cart, his last official act as valet. She had not forgotten the wink he had given her last night, or failed to notice the man's sneer as he had deliberately brushed against her in the hall this morning. Her fleeting feeling of relief was now replaced with dread. She must dismiss him before Ivor's heir arrived. She had very little in the way of coin, but perhaps Kempton would be satisfied to raid the baron's possessions and help himself. No price would be too high for his silence. Once Jannah was gone, it wouldn't matter. For all she cared, Kempton could announce her sins to the world at Hyde Park Corner.

Eden wiped a stubborn tear from her cheek. It was pointless to succumb to self-pity when she had to find the book. Methodically, she searched through every drawer in the dressers, every trunk in the dressing room. She even struggled with the mattress, tipping it to the floor and dragging it back up again.

Could Ivor have hidden it in plain sight? It would be like him to do so, or so she had thought as she stared at the ceiling after Mrs. Washburn put her to bed last night. He had a reckless streak, risking all behind unlocked doors or garden hedges. The more anxious Eden became at the possibility of being discovered, the more satisfied he was.

After a sleepless night, Eden had skimmed the shelves in the library at daybreak. She found nothing but dust and a few salacious drawings of herself tucked between some volumes, which she had torn and burned. She must find his leather portfolio as well. The original drawings for the book were just as damning as the book itself. Ivor had been a skilled artist. There would be no mistaking the model for anyone other than herself.

Eden curled up in the window seat, the glass cool against her back. She closed her eyes against the bright blue October sky. How beautiful it was here, and how false. She was exhausted, but until she found *something*, she couldn't rest. *Patience*. Hartford Hall was not so very big that she couldn't search it top to bottom before the new baron came. She had at least a week, and probably more. If he couldn't be found, winter would come soon, no matter what the calendar said, and make travel impossible. She and Jannah might be safe for months.

And really, where could Ivor have hidden the book? He had shown it to her in the library late yesterday afternoon, taken an early dinner with her, come to her bed before she'd even had a chance to undress for him. The book had to be close by. She would find it. And his artist's case was too large to hide easily. Ivor had sometimes sat right here on the tufted cushion and sketched her as she lay on his bed.

She shot off the seat and lifted the hinged lid. The leather case was in the dark square, quite alone. No book. But Eden was thrilled just the same. The hearth was cold, but a neat pyramid of firewood was laid. Soon she was feeding the pictures into the flames, watching the edges blacken and curl, fly as hell-born sparks up the chimney. The fire was the first step to purifying her life. The last of the paper crackled when she felt the hand on her back.

"What are you about, Miss Eden?"

Kempton. The voice was soft, but she heard the menace within. Eden rose from her knees gracelessly. "The room was cold."

He chuckled as if they were friends. "Aye. I didn't want to roast the old man before he's buried. He'll be seeing the heat soon enough."

She saw Kempton take in the open leather case at her feet and held her chin high.

"I didn't expect you back so soon."

" 'Twasn't much to do. Vicar and his wife took care of milord. I thought *you* might have need of me, miss."

He was leering at her. No deference to her station or his. She had to get rid of him. Today was not soon enough.

"I thank you for attending my stepfather. But now that he is gone, we have no need of your services. I shall see to it that Collins gives you an excellent reference," she added, referring to the butler. "And—and severance pay. I will speak to the new baron about it."

Kempton gave a harsh laugh. "Not good enough, Eden. Your new man won't be here for a while. What'll I live on? I'm sure you can find something for me to do until he comes."

He called her Eden. No longer "miss." Although she had sensed his purpose, this was happening too fast for her. Eden took a step back as Kempton advanced. Another two steps and the back of her black skirts would be singed by the open hearth. "Take what you want from this room then and leave." She stood stone-still as his blunt fingertip traced the hollow of her cheek.

"It's you I want. I bet you could teach me a trick or two or have fun trying."

Eden's eyes locked on his. Kempton wasn't unpleasant to look at. But she had not made one escape to be caught again.

"No doubt I could." She tried a smile. "But it seems I have found my conscience at last."

"Conscience won't keep you warm at night."

She felt his breath on her cheek. He would not be satisfied with a hasty kiss, and despite everything she'd ever done, she couldn't bring herself to contemplate more. "Very true. Nevertheless, I should like you to leave after the funeral. Name your price."

His eyes swept slowly from hers to her waist. "Don't think you've got it. The baron wasn't a warm man, was he?"

Stingy, more like. His estate was in order, but he didn't spare much on anyone's pleasure but his own. The library alone was worth a fortune.

"The books."

Kempton snorted. "Those filthy things? I won't get a bob for a stack of them."

"No, some of them are very valuable. Rare." She'd seen the bills herself.

"Won't be easy to sell, Eden. Not for a man like me." Kempton turned away and walked toward the bed. Eden swallowed as he stretched himself out, his boots leaving a trace of dirt on the coverlet.

"I won't," Eden whispered.

"You will unless you want me to tell the new baron what you've been up to since your mother died."

Kempton didn't know what had come before. He had only been employed by Ivor for the past year. That, at least, was something.

"Tell him then," she declared brazenly.

"I'll tell your little sis, too. It'll break her heart."

Eden spun to Ivor's dresser, picked up the carved African mahogany box that held his watches, cuff links, and other valuables. "You have a key to this, do you not? Take the contents. I'll see that you get money."

"And have me arrested for a thief? I don't think so." He patted the space beside him, laughing when Eden shuddered.

"I promise that won't happen. Give me your direction and I'll send you payment for your discretion." At least until Jannah died.

Kempton raised himself up on one elbow. "Don't see what the baron saw in you anyway. You're not much to look at and stick thin, though your bubbies look a treat. I'll see them now, and think on your offer."

Eden pitched the box at him. He caught it deftly and shook it. The jangle and tinkle competed for the thudding in Eden's ears.

He shrugged. "All right. But I'll have you in the end. You won't get far with Major Stuart Hartford, I reckon. I heard all about him in the army. After his men all the time to keep their flies buttoned up right and tight, as if a bloke doesn't deserve a bit of fun after almost getting killed. Like the village priest, he was, but he's not apt to forgive *you*. And who will hire you for a companion or a governess when I tell them you're just a dirty little whore?"

Eden shut her eyes to his triumphant face. There was no hope for her, just a delay to the devil. But time was what she needed, for Jannah.

"Please go. I'll speak to Collins."

"Tell that old buzzard to fix me up right and proper. He'll know where he keeps the best household silver."

"There must be an inventory—"

"Bugger the inventory! Stuart Hartford won't miss a few candlesticks. I mean to make you pay, Eden. And pay some more. You'll be hearing from me when I've got a place."

Before Eden's hand touched the doorknob, he had grabbed her, squeezing a breast, his breath hot on her throat. "You won't get away from me so quick." He gave her a rough, sour kiss. Eden bore it as she had borne so much. She had now been kissed by two men, a paltry amount at her advanced age, but she had other, darker experience. Kempton was right. There really was no better name for her than whore.

Chapter 2

"Sweet Jesu. It's the back of beyond, Hart. Whatever will you do to occupy yourself?" Major Henry Desmond of the 1st Regiment of Foot studied the map before him, measuring the mileage from London with his thumb and forefinger. With Bonaparte safely in exile on St. Helena, army life and maps had somewhat lost their luster, but Des was manfully attempting to enjoy his London posting by amusing himself at the tables with his cronies and in every available youngish widow's bed. Now Stuart Hartford, his oldest friend and fellow Grenadier guard, had sold out and would soon be lost to the wilds of a substantial Cumberland baronage.

"His death was not unexpected," Hart said, reaching for another celebratory splash of cognac. "My father always said his brother would meet him in Hell sooner than later. The two of them were rather infamous in their prime. I'm only sorry I missed the funeral to make certain he's truly dead."

Des knew Hart's father had gone to his reward some time ago.

His uncle, run out of town years ago for an unknown infraction, was supposedly reformed, but neither Hart nor Des had ever been entirely convinced. The elder Hartford men had been notoriously wicked in their tastes. Des had known Hart's father too well, heard too much of his uncle and held his tongue. No man, whatever his personal convictions, cared to have his relatives criticized.

And Hart had personal convictions aplenty. Rebelling against his elders in his own way, he had striven to be such a pillar of moral rectitude his twenty-eight years that he had been called "Holy Hartford" behind his back, and sometimes to his face. He had used his family's history as a hard lesson of what not to do. Des doubted that he'd even sown any of the wild oats to which a handsome young army officer was entitled. If he had, not a word had passed his lips about it. Hart was discretion itself, which was somewhat disappointing. The man was much too young to be such a dull dog.

"I thought your uncle had settled down in the country with a widow and her brats." Thunderstruck, Des clapped a hand over his mouth. "Surely you're not expected to provide for them, too!"

"Ah. There you have it. One of the brats has written to me. She is, I believe, now an aging spinster with a sick sister. What sort of brute would I be to toss them to the wolves? I've talked to the solicitor. Uncle Ivor left them nothing, not even a sterling teaspoon. It's very odd. He was their stepfather for a decade at least."

Desmond scowled. "A rum business, Hart. Even with your blameless reputation, you're not the proper sort of chaperone to two maiden ladies."

"Indeed not. That's why I've enlisted my aunt Juliet."

"Good Lord." Des leaned back in his chair, hand over his heart. *Juliet.* A most managing female, even if she was easy on the eyes.

"Desperate times, needs must, et cetera. She will join me on my journey north at the end of the week. I'll settle my affairs up there and be back before you know it." Hart rose, his golden head burnished in the blaze of the club's candlelight, a silver saber scar dueling with the impudent crease on his cheek. Des might have been jealous of such manly perfection had he not liked Hart so well.

"That's if the Mad Matchmaker doesn't drive you over a cliff," Des replied, forgetting his vow not to defame his friend's relations.

"Nonsense, Des. She's been saddled with that romantic name, after all. She just has my best interests at heart."

"She wants you to *marry*," Des said in disgust. "As though we survived hell on the battlefield so we could be chained to some hen-witted debutante."

"Well, I expect we'll both be leg-shackled eventually. Better to marry than to burn, don't you know. And I have a duty to my title now," said Hart with a grin, his blue eyes dancing at Des's obvious dismay. "Perhaps one of the orphans will do. This Eden seems a bit desperate and might be very accommodating."

Des made a face. "Eden? What sort of a name is that? I expect she really ought to be called Hortense or Calpurnia."

Hart laughed. "I shall let you know if you are correct. No doubt she's as above reproach as Caesar's wife. But just at present, I'm off to burn. Care to join me at Mrs. Brown's?"

Des was momentarily speechless. Mrs. Brown ran the most exalted and exclusive brothel in all of London. The annual membership fee to partake of such amusement could feed a small regiment for some time, and soldiers were known to have healthy appetites. Furthermore, a plump purse was no guarantee Mrs. Brown would open her door to you. It was said her admittance standards were more rigorous than the most prestigious gentlemen's clubs. There was a waiting list as long as two or three arms, too. Des rather wondered how Hart had finagled his way into the madam's good graces so swiftly, but then, Hart was Hart. And lord knows, he deserved some fun after all they had been through.

"You've bought a subscription?" Mrs. Brown's girls, all named for Greek and Roman goddesses, were no doubt worth every penny, but Des had lately suffered some reversal at the tables and couldn't imagine coming up with the scratch for even a week's worth of sensual delight, much less a year's.

"Indeed I have."

"By God. Membership there is too expensive for my blood," Des said, attempting a careless indifference. But he knew that members could bring a guest now and then, and his spirits and other aspects of him lifted. "Why did you do it? It's most unlike you. You have ever railed against debauchery like my old governess."

"Why not? I'm Baron Hartford of Hartford Hall now, with pockets of pounds, not plain Stu Hartford, scrounging about on His Majesty's payroll. Even if I dower the girls, there will be plenty left over."

Des felt a bit foxed. "Dower the girls? Mrs. Brown might have something to say to that."

"No, no, you fool. The orphans. The spinsters. The Emersons. Nay, that's not right. The Emerys. Calpurnia and Hortense. My poor relations."

Des stood and clapped Hart on the back. "Well, that's all right then. If you insist, I shall be pleased to accompany you to Mrs. Brown's Pantheon of Pleasure. I hear there's a new Athena. Bryson's got his eye on her already. She's very tall and," said Des, pausing for just the right word, "refreshing."

"The ideal female," laughed Hart. "I confess a spot of refreshment shall be most welcome." And long overdue. Hart could scarcely remember the last time he had bedded a female, and nearly wondered if all his parts were in working order. He was a man of hard-won abstemious habits. It had not always been easy ignoring his baser urges—the urges of his father and uncle. He had controlled himself admirably in the battle against the French and the battle for his own soul. Places such as Mrs. Brown's had been quite above his touch and usual interest. They provided precisely the sort of expensive entertainment that had ruined his father and sent his uncle packing to the country.

No one had been more surprised than he when he approached Mrs. Brown as a kind of lark and she accepted him. No doubt she wanted to know if the Hartford blood ran true, despite his every effort to deny its heat. But he was ready to lay the burden of his virtue temporarily at the white feet of one goddess or another. In the coming months, he would test his capabilities in a first and last fling while he waited for his aunt to find him a wife. Then his brief experiment in sin would be erased by a return to duty and sobriety, a wife and children.

But not tonight. The men ambled down the stairs into the street and hailed a hackney, determined to take their pleasure no matter the price.

* * *

Several days later, Hart was grateful for that pleasure, for none was to be found journeying with his aunt Juliet. His mother's younger sister by a decade and a half, she was not so very much older than Hart himself, yet she wielded her auntship with the ferocity of an ancient society tabby. Hart was treated to the pedigree of every eligible miss of Juliet's acquaintance, and a great portion of strangers as well. He wondered how his cousins Raphael and Sebastian would weather her matchmaking determination once they came of age, and was grateful the woman was merely an aunt and not his mother.

But his mother, that poor lady, would have had little reason to recommend marriage. Mrs. Hartford's wayward husband had not made her particularly happy, and she had died when Hart was still at school.

Juliet, on the other hand, had made a love match and was anxious that all share her good fortune. Her husband had not lived long enough to be found continuously at fault, or boring, or inconsequential, as undoubtedly he would have been if he'd reached portly middle age. Rafe and Seb would probably never reach his pinnacle in their mother's eyes, but they were safe at school, away from her interference. Hart, however, was sitting opposite her in a well-sprung carriage, which was beginning to feel like a plush torture chamber.

Juliet Cheverly was not wearing an inquisitor's uniform, however. In fact, she looked every inch the supremely-wealthy-if-not-titled lady she was, swathed in furs and ruby velvet, a diamond pin on her hat vying for attention with its feathers and braided trim. Hart knew beneath her kid gloves too many fingers were beringed. In the event the lure of a new carriage and all her baggage was not enough temptation, he and his outriders were all heavily armed in case some unlucky highwayman caught a sparkle emanating from her person and thought to take advantage. He hadn't been to Hartford Hall since he was a child, but it was unlikely it had changed sufficiently to be as fashionable as his young aunt. She was bound to be disappointed. And overdressed.

"Tell me about these girls, Hart," she asked for the umpteenth time.

Hart sighed. "I've already told you, Juliet, I've never met them. My father and my uncle had a falling out, as you know. I've not been to the Hall but once that I remember, and that was many years ago. I gather their mother was the local parson's widow. A renowned beauty, as I understand it. Uncle Ivor took a fancy to her and married her. There were three children. The brother died at Waterloo, Lady Hartford not long ago, and the youngest girl is very ill. Some lung disorder, I believe. She stays abed most days. Miss Emery writes that the doctor has given up hope."

"How sad. All that death." Juliet shivered despite being cloaked in her furs. Her husband, Thomas, had been gone five years and Hart knew she missed him fearfully still. "Poor Miss Emery. Losing her blood family and then the protection of her stepfather. Do be kind to her, Hart. A woman alone is at such a disadvantage in this world."

Hart reached for her hand and squeezed. "There's not a person alive who can get the better of you, madam. Perhaps Miss Emery is made of the same stern stuff." Lord, he hoped so. He was quite counting on his aunt taking the girl to her bosom and getting her out of his way. He had no objection to supporting Miss Emery and her sister financially, but he'd never be able to call Hartford Hall a home if he had an unmarried woman underfoot once the sister died. And whatever his plans for his estate were, they did not include falling prey to some compromising situation.

His aunt smiled sadly. "I may look brave on the outside, but I shall always suffer from my loss."

Hart winced. Once Juliet started touting the virtues of her late husband, there was no stopping her. Diversion was essential.

"I daresay you might help Miss Emery and her sister with their wardrobes. Even if they're in mourning, there's no reason for them to be frumps. I can count on you to help them, can I not?"

"Certainly! I shall be most happy to bring out two young ladies when the time comes. Of course the poor sister—what is her name? Jenny?"

"Jannah."

"That might be a bit of a challenge if she's bedridden. But no doubt Miss Emery can benefit from my expertise. I wonder if there are adequate modistes to be found in the vicinity." Juliet peered out of the carriage window as if she expected to see a row of shops pop up rather than the harrowing roads and the misty peaks of the Pennines. "If worse comes to worst, my maid might be prevailed upon to exert herself. She's very handy with a needle. Perhaps I should have brought fabrics from London. Oh dear. I wish you'd spoken of this earlier." Juliet prattled on, oblivious of the fact that her nephew was no longer listening.

* * *

Not three miles away, Eden Emery was inspecting her toilette, which would never in this lifetime have passed muster with Juliet Cheverly had she been consulted. Eden and the maids Charlotte and Mattie had refurbished her best mourning dress. Even Jannah had stitched a bit of ribbon on a cuff. The new baron's valet and former batman, McBride, had arrived several hours earlier on horseback, informing them that Lord Hartford and his aunt would be along shortly. Eden was grateful there was to be an aunt as chaperone. She never wanted to find herself alone with another Baron Hartford. If he was anything like his depraved uncle, she would wish to follow Jannah to the grave as soon as possible. When Ivor was in his cups, he had often told her of his youthful exploits with his brother, counting on the tales to shock her. The son was probably cut from the same cloth.

She cast a worried glance at her sister, who was dozing again.

Jannah had been in high spirits over news of company, and had made numerous suggestions as Mattie arranged Eden's wavy brown hair into a smooth bun. But the fun of watching her older sister dress up had worn her out. Eden slipped out of Jannah's bedroom and into her room, to stand in front of her own mirror.

She was not a vain woman. Since her stepfather's death, she had filled out some and was no longer her scarecrow self. God had not seen fit to grace her with any particular attributes save an overgenerous bosom, which was presently tamed by rigorous lacing. Her eyes were as large as they needed to be, her thick dark brows straight. Mattie had done a rather creditable job confining her hair, but Eden saw a pale specter in black before her. That would never do. She'd need every negligible charm to persuade Lord Hartford to let her stay here with Jannah until the end. After that, it didn't matter. Perhaps she could turn governess or companion if Kempton could be satisfied. She shut out from her mind her true calling.

The letter from Kempton had arrived yesterday, as though he knew exactly when the new baron would arrive. There was no return address, nor did he name the figure he expected for the next installment of extortion. He meant to keep her off-balance, just as her stepfather had. Once Stuart Hartford settled his affairs and left, she would scrape together whatever she could for Kempton. But she would not give him her body. If she ever bedded a man again, it would be by her choice.

Kempton might even have the book, although he had made no mention of such a bargaining chip. Eden's search had been fruitless, though she hadn't quite given up hope. The new baron's visit would interrupt her methodical sweep of every place a devious mind like Ivor Hartford's could have chosen to hide it. She'd gone so far as to pick apart seams of sofa cushions and remove rear panels of furniture, unlikely as it was for Ivor to have had time to conceal the horrible thing in such a way. If anyone came upon it—if the new baron found it—her position here with Jannah would be in jeopardy. She could not imagine trying to explain the drawings of her wickedness to a stranger.

She could not explain it to herself. She had *needed* to submit to Ivor in a way that would always bring her shame. Of course, it had all gotten well out of her control, given Ivor's nature. What had initially thrilled her had become a living hell.

Eden pinched her cheeks and bit her lips, but she still looked pasty and ill. She found her mother's rouge pot, somewhat congealed after all this time, and set to smoothing a bit on her face and mouth. Not enough to shock. Her mother had been a very beautiful woman, beautiful enough to overcome her humble birth as a farmer's daughter and catch the eye of a serious young curate, and then, more exaltedly, a baron. Beautiful enough so that neither man seemed to object to her lack of mental acuity. Eden didn't want to catch anyone's eye, nor did she want to look a fright. This new Lord Hartford was an unknown entity, but most men liked a pretty woman. Eden might never consider herself pretty, but now at least she looked presentable.

She heard the commotion in the drive. The baron's dogs set to barking hoarsely and Collins shouted at them. The hounds were both toothless things, but they were too old to remember their shortcomings. She went to the window and stared down at the golden-haired man in a greatcoat who bent to them, stroking their heads with both hands. An exquisite blond woman remained in the carriage, leaning out the window. Eden had never seen such finery, even if it was just from the shoulders up, and immediately she felt deflated. That red hat must have cost as much as Eden's yearly clothing allowance.

Of course, her stepfather had balked at spending money on clothes, when he much preferred her out of them.

No. She must not think of Ivor. He was dead and her servitude was over. She had survived it with her reputation intact thanks to the loyalty of the staff, save for conniving Kempton. She had forgiven her sickly mother for being too distracted and drugged to notice that her husband had formed an unhealthy attachment to his impressionable stepdaughter. Though her body had betrayed her time and time again, she had almost forgiven herself for responding to the calculated manipulations of an experienced seducer. Eden had never planned to marry anyway. Her stepfather had merely robbed her of a useless membrane and her dignity but had not stolen her soul. In time, she might even retrieve some of her heart.

She met the traveling party in the entryway. A massive number of boxes and bags were being carried in, and the servants the new baron had brought with him were orchestrating their disposal under Collins's direction.

"Welcome to Hartford Hall, my lord." Eden curtseyed quickly, her eyes lowered.

"Come, come. We are cousins of a sort, are we not? Please call me Hart, as my family and friends are wont to do. You must be the older sister. Cousin Eden, I think."

Eden had to look up. She was tall, but Baron Hartford was much taller. His bronze gold hair curled beyond his collar, the tanned skin around his blue eyes crinkling as he smiled. The smile revealed healthy white teeth set between full, firm lips. Her lover's lips.

Eden felt the room tilt. Hartford was the image of his uncle, much leaner of course, the debauchery washed clean, the hair not faded with traces of silver. She never fainted. Never. Not even when she pushed her dead stepfather off her own exhausted body. But her last conscious thought was that there was a first time for everything, and she fell to the floor in a wrinkled black heap.

"Good heavens! You've frightened her to death! Suzette, my vinaigrette," Juliet called to her maid. "Quickly. Do step back, Hart. The poor thing is done in. Miss Emery. Eden. What an unusual name, dear. Wake up. He shan't bite, you know. He is rather large, but quite gentle beneath all that hulk." Juliet patted Eden's cheek with her ruby kid gloves. "Perhaps some water, Suzette. See if someone here can fetch it."

Juliet was in her element, ordering and commanding. Hart moved to a corner of the hallway, keeping out of the way. He looked around, not remembering much about this house. To his knowledge, he'd only visited once. His father and uncle had spent the week arguing and very likely inebriated, although he hadn't recognized the signs as a young boy. His mother had not come and he was left to his own devices. He walked the land with some scruffy dogs and befriended the farrier's son. Idly, he wondered if the boy was now a man somewhere on the estate.

The house itself, while not architecturally imposing, was handsome. It seemed well maintained, the interior scented with the usual beeswax and lavender. He glanced into the double parlor, finding the furniture simple yet gleaming, although the walls were covered in a most unfortunate pink paper. A fire crackled in the rose marble hearth and a tea table was being set up by a maid.

Perhaps Miss Emery was merely hungry. Young women were known to skip meals to slim. Lord knows she was a scrawny thing. Or maybe an overzealous maid had laced her mistress too tightly. Miss Emery had seemed rather wooden as she walked down the stairs, her eyes focused on her slippers. Everything about her had seemed tight, from her scraped-back hair to the long sleeves of her ugly mourning gown to her solemn lips. Her voice though—now, that was not wooden. It was low and soft and quite possibly the most fascinating thing about her.

The sooner he could send her away with Juliet, the happier he'd be. Of course, that meant that the poor girl upstairs—at least he presumed she was upstairs—would have to die. How very uncharitable he was being. He was sure he wished Miss Jannah Emery a long life indeed.

"Oh! I do beg your pardon. I'm not usually prone to such behavior."

Evidently, Juliet had met with some success. Hart turned to the musical sound. A viola, perhaps. No, a cello. Mellow. Soothing. So sensual and so at odds with Miss Emery's appearance.

Juliet fussed at her charge. "You've had a dreadful time of it, my dear. Losing your stepfather so suddenly and worrying about your sister. All the excitement of our visit. I promise you, you shall not have to lift a finger to keep us entertained. Hart! Come help me move Miss Emery into the parlor."

Hart smiled. At least his brawn was good for something other than frightening a plain virgin. He noticed Eden shudder as he took her arm, and had to stop himself from tucking a glossy strand of chocolate brown hair back into its pins. Her face was as white as the starched linen on the tea table, save for two perfectly round spots on her cheeks. Rouge! Miss Emery had planned to make a conquest of him then. He'd have to tell her she could stay at Hartford Hall as long as she liked so she didn't go to further trouble. Black was not her color, and virgins were not his style.

Eden felt his fingers at her elbow, burning through the bombazine. Her stomach roiled with fear at his touch. Mattie and Charlotte hovered near the tea tray, their concern for her clear. "Thank you. I am fine now, Lord Hartford. Lady—?" She looked quizzically at Juliet.

"Mrs. Cheverly, but Juliet will do nicely, my dear."

"Surely you both will want to freshen up before we have our tea. I'm a dreadful hostess." Eden colored. "I am not actually your hostess, am I? This is Lord Hartford's house and I am here on sufferance."

"Don't be silly. This has been your home for half your life. My nephew is not going to throw you out in the cold." Juliet laughed. "And I'm perfectly ready for tea. Even something stronger, if you have it. It is terribly chilly and dreary up here, is it not? However do you stand it?"

Eden thought that Juliet didn't really expect an answer, certainly not an honest one. And it was true; Juliet Cheverly looked ready for tea, ready for anything. She was as neat as if she had stepped from within a fashion plate. Eden watched as she removed her furs and tossed them casually on the back of the sofa. Her maid Suzette was quick to remove them and scurry upstairs after the men and the baggage.

"Silly girl. She could have taken my hat and gloves, too. I shall make myself at home." Soon the jeweled hat and gloves were laid next to her. Juliet's buttery curls frothed in elegance around her face. Eden had never seen such a beautiful woman save for her mother, whose darker coloring had been very much like Eden's own. "I do hope you are not offended that I have come to you in scarlet," Juliet chattered. "There was not time for new mourning clothes, although you may rest easy as I have some in my baggage should you require me to wear black for propriety's sake. While I never met your stepfather, you can be assured I am very sorry for your grief. I know what it is like to lose someone you love—"

"Juliet," Hart interrupted, "which would you prefer? Sherry or brandy?"

"Brandy will be lovely. I'll put a drop or two right in my tea. Hart, do say you'll join me. I expect you'd like a brandy, too, after being trapped with me in a confined space for so many days. No doubt I've driven you to distraction," she said cheerfully.

Eden nodded at Charlotte, who disappeared down the hall to the library where her stepfather's liquor was kept. She had drunk quite a bit of it lately herself in her fruitless quest for sleep. "Mattie, my sister might wake at any moment. Why don't you go upstairs and sit with her?"

"Yes, Miss Eden."

"How is your sister, Cousin Eden?" Hart asked.

His concern appeared genuine, but Eden found herself unable to look him in the face. He was too handsome, too much like Ivor for any sort of comfort. "One day is much like the next, my lord. She has an inflammation of the lungs. Incurable, or so the doctor says. She has been ill these past two years."

"The poor dear," whispered Juliet. "How old is she?"

"Just sixteen. She is the baby of the family." Eden gathered her courage. "I hope, my lord, that you permit us to stay at the Hall until—" She swallowed hard, unable to complete her sentence.

"There is no need to say more, Cousin Eden. Of course you and your sister are welcome to stay here. This is your home. I shall endeavor to treat you with the kindness and comfort that my uncle did."

Hart reached for her ice-cold hand. She shrank back against the sofa, unable to stop the tremor at his touch. He must have known it was unwelcome, and he quickly released her, giving her a puzzled look. He was trying to be kind, but she wanted nothing more than for him to get back into his shiny new carriage and ride away.

"And when the time comes," Juliet said firmly, "I shall take you to London so you may experience a season. You've been quite buried up here, have you not? A bit of town bronze and some pretty dresses and I have every expectation you'll catch yourself a husband!"

Eden nearly choked. The woman meant well, was trying to be kind, too. But Eden had no intention of ever falling prey to any man again. She might lose herself forever, and this time not live to feel regret. "I will never, ever marry, ma'am. It is my intention to seek a position as a governess or a companion."

Hart frowned. "That won't do. People will say I'm a cheese-paring ogre for turning a young woman out to fend for herself. You are family. I'm responsible for your welfare."

Eden sat stiff with pride on the sofa. "I am not so young, my lord. Two and twenty. And you are hardly any relation at all. Thank goodness," she added softly.

Not softly enough. Juliet gasped. She was prevented from de-fending Hart, as she surely looked prepared to do, by the appearance of Charlotte and the brandy. Juliet glared at Eden in disapproval. "Hart, I believe we all deserve some spirits. Do the honors, if you please."

Hart rose, tamping back his own irritation. He had been pre-pared in good faith to do right by his uncle's stepchildren, al-though there was no compelling legal reason to do so. The man had thought little enough of them, not even providing a modest portion upon which they could live. Perhaps Miss Emery had been equally ungrateful toward his uncle, prompting him to teach her a very valuable lesson in humility by leaving her destitute. It did not seem fair, however, to include the ailing Jannah in any sort of retribution.

"Cousin Eden," he began, in a voice known to strike fear in the hardiest of his troops, "surely you must know my uncle left you penniless. Whether it was an oversight or a deliberate snub, I have no idea. But I shall not stand aside while you ruin yourself as you choose a life of ignominious servitude rather than my protection. I forbid you from seeking employment."

Eden's face leached of what little color it still had. Her inept attempts at beauty once again stood stark upon her cheeks. She gazed at the baron, astonished. "You f-forbid me, sir?" she managed.

"I do. If you care so little for yourself, think of my reputation. I had hoped that you and my aunt might deal together. If you are seeking to be a companion, you need look no further. She would not make you her drudge or drive you mad with demands. And if you're bound to be a governess, I wish you well dealing with my young cousins. They'll cure you in a heartbeat!"

"Hart, you're too unkind. Raphael and Sebastian are lovely boys, Miss Emery. And you would be more than welcome in my home."

Hart glanced at his aunt. Juliet was probably now not so sure she wanted this grim, prim miss anywhere in her bailiwick. Then Eden stood, a mottled flush on her parchment white face.

"I thank you for your concern, my lord, Mrs. Cheverly, but I assure you it is misplaced. And while I am fl-flattered by your offer, I have already secured a position in London, a very nice position, to be held for me until I am able to undertake it, should I choose to accept it. Until then all I ask is to be allowed to care for my sister."

"Well, of course," Hart began, but she rambled over his words nervously, her hands working themselves into a fever.

"We shall keep to our rooms and be of no trouble to you. You won't even know we are here. Mrs. Burrell is an excellent cook and Mrs. Washburn, the housekeeper, will do everything in her power to make your stay here comfortable. Pl-please enjoy your tea. I must go check on Jannah." She nearly sprinted out of the parlor and up the stairs.

"Well!" said Juliet.

"No wonder Ivor left her in the lurch. She's the most awkward thing. Ugly as an old boot besides." He swallowed a healthy dose of Ivor's brandy and poured another.

"Hart! It's not like you to be so unkind. She is not one bit ugly, although her dress is not quite de la mode. Her looks are no more above average, I grant you, but it seems she's had a hard life. It is very primitive here. Perhaps she just doesn't know how to get on in society. To be sociable."

"An understatement, my dear aunt. She's just plain rude."

"You certainly are not used to a woman who does not fall at your feet. For all your aloofness, you are very much in demand by the fairer set." Juliet laughed. "Let me amend that. She did fall at your feet, but apparently it was not because of your male beauty, my lord Hartford."

"She loathes me. I could see it in her eyes. I told her she could stay," Hart grumbled. "It's not as if I have any intention of taking over here. She can continue to run things as she pleases."

"She's done a remarkable job, you must admit. The house seems in good order, even to my high standards. Perhaps she's overwrought about this visit, about making a good impression."

"Well, she's failed on that score." Hart took a deep swallow.

"Tsk, tsk. It's not like you to be so ungenerous. There's the worry over her sister, too. Let's give her time to adjust to our presence. I'll make inroads, I'm sure. And you have estate business to occupy you. In a week or two we'll be back in London and you can get on with your life. And find a *wife.*" Juliet looked amused by her own poetry.

It certainly would not be Eden Emery, thought Hart, remembering his conversation with Des. He was not in such self-denial that he wished to embroil himself in a marriage of total inconvenience.

Juliet chattered on as Hart consumed a fair amount of the contents of the tea tray. He wanted to make his own good impression on the staff—they had certainly made one on him with the substantial spread. Stuffed to the gills, he was anxious to stretch his legs after being cooped up in the carriage.

And escape his aunt's incessant marital advice.

When she paused from her benevolent diatribe to nibble on a biscuit, he excused himself to take a walk outside. A bit of fresh air and quiet—that's what he needed. One of the old dogs lifted his head from his slumber and decided to amble after him in decidedly arthritic fashion.

Hart was a man of property now, a country gentleman, he thought with some amusement. He even owned half-dead hunting dogs, one of which was wheezing loyally behind him. Each leaf of copper ivy climbing up the house belonged to him, each brick, each dark glass pane of window, each blade of browning grass. He noted the flowerbeds along the path had been ruthlessly pruned and mulched. Hart knew nothing about gardening, but expected Eden Emery had a hand in readying the garden for the winter. One frosty stare of hers could wilt the hardiest flower. She looked as if she enjoyed chopping things down, him included.

He knew he was being uncharitable. Her guardian had died, and her sister was very ill. Her life had turned upside down, and now she and her sister were homeless save for Hart's goodwill. Eden didn't seem to be able to swallow pride easily, and she'd already begged on behalf of her sister.

Perhaps he should make more of an effort with her despite her prickliness. He could try to charm her—she might even be an easy conquest. She was an awkward, backward sort of girl, obviously un-used to male company.

He found an opportunity to begin again with her as he rounded a corner of ragged boxwood that marked a small square garden. Eden was perched on a bench within it like a black crow. She had been viciously picking apart a leaf to its veins, no doubt imagining she was tearing Hart limb from limb, when he entered the gap in the shrubbery. If the French had been unable to kill him in ten years of war, he was not about to let some country girl succeed.

"Oh!" She stood up immediately, leaf bits dropping from her skirts. She had washed the ridiculous rouge from her cheeks and looked now like a black and white sketch. Something depress-ing, he thought rather cruelly. He could see his presence was still unwelcome—her dark eyes glittered with tears that she quickly blinked back.

He couldn't help but stare. Her eyes were her best feature, so deeply gray they appeared black, and fringed with thick, straight lashes. Just now they glistened with tiny diamonds of moisture. He watched as she wiped them away with the back of an ungloved hand.

"I did not mean to disturb you," Hart said, and meant it. Now was not the time to exercise his flirting skills. He felt like an in-truder in this private garden room. Even if the house was now his, it had been Eden's far longer. Of course she held him in aversion—he had disturbed her narrow, orderly little world. But that was the way of entailment. Since his uncle had made no provision for her, the entire situation was most irregular, and Hart was curious enough to get to the bottom of it.

"It is I who am disturbing you." Eden adjusted the heavy shawl she wore against the cold desolation of the garden. "I imagine you want to inspect your property. It's only n-natural." She looked around her, anywhere but at him. "The garden was quite lovely once. Before my mother took ill, it was her pride and joy. She was a farmer's daughter, you know. This is not the right time of year, of course, but I'm sure you can bring it back to life. I've done the best I could."

He was impressed by the number of words she had strung together, although she still wouldn't meet his eye. Was she so shy of people that she had no social graces? She was far too old to behave like a child still in the schoolroom, uncertain and uncomfortable. How could she think to become a governess when it was clear she needed one of her own to smooth away her edges?

"Is there no gardener?"

She shook her head. "There hasn't been for some months. Mr. Tilney retired, and your uncle did not plan to replace him until next spring. Now—it will be up to you."

"Maybe you can recommend someone. I noticed your handiwork as I walked the grounds, and I thank you. The household seems well run inside, too. I assume that's your doing."

There was a flare of surprise in her eyes for a precious moment, and then she faded back to her nervous agitation. He smiled to reassure her, which only made her stumble backward into the stone bench and flush in embarrassment.

"The staff is small, but they're very hardworking. Loyal." Her hands twisted, and Hart suppressed the urge to get her another leaf to rip apart.

"My uncle did not spend much on his household, did he? I had a cursory look at the books with his man of business in town."

Eden shook her head. "He was not an especially—*domestic* man. B-but we were cared for well enough."

Hart doubted it. Her dyed black dress was years out of fashion, the jagged edge of the shawl mended with tiny neat stitches. With a little effort and some coin, he supposed Eden Emery could be made passably attractive. He should be grateful so little had been lavished on her. His uncle's parsimony meant more money for him to spend in the long run. And no matter what Eden Emery said now, Hart was prepared to spend some of that money on her and her sister. She was his responsibility as much as Juliet and her boys were. At least she didn't prattle on like Juliet—getting her to talk was like pulling teeth.

"Sit out here with me for a while." He turned his smile upon her again. Hart's smile was dependably dazzling. It usually had the desired effect on ladies, and had fooled an enemy or two, but he could see Eden was not going to allow herself to be at all smitten. Her lips were pressed tight, and she rubbed her hands together as she had earlier. She wore her misery like the old shawl clutched around her. He listened to her stammer on about the chill and the damp and her obligations to her sister, but she finally sat down again at the very edge of the bench.

He wasn't sure why it was important for him to do so, but he had a few days to win her over, and he would. Starting right now in the bleak brown garden. Impulsively, he removed his greatcoat and put it around her shoulders. "There. That should keep you warm enough for now while we get to know each other a bit." He eased down, leaving a more than proper distance between them.

"But no! That is, I'm fine," she said, looking stricken, trying to pull the coat away. He placed a gloved hand lightly on her bare one to stop her.

"Really, Cousin Eden. Allow me to be a gentleman."

"But you'll be cold!"

"Nonsense. I'm a soldier. Or was until I sold out recently with my sudden good fortune. Will you believe me if I tell you despite my recent London posting, I'm still not used to being comfortable in warm dry clothing? I'm a pretty hardy fellow, accustomed to being shot at and sleeping in ditches. A little brisk weather is nothing to me." He realized he still had her hand trapped beneath his and let it go.

She had nothing to say to the weather, the most prevalent topic of conversation in England, nor did she quiz him on his service, which was a relief. Hart was not one to revel in his supposed glory days. To break the silence, he picked up a fallen branch and tossed it into the air for the dog. Unimpressed, the animal just snorted beside the bench, keeping his great head on his paws. Even the dog was impervious to his charm offensive, Hart thought ruefully.

Just when he was beginning to think that Eden was like one of the stone statues he passed on the alley, she turned to him.

"My brother died at Waterloo." Her voice was not much more than a whisper.

"Yes, I know. I'm very sorry." He waited for her to say more, but she was concentrating on a silver button on his coat, twirling it between two long fingers. "I was there. We lost far too many good men."

"Eli was just a boy."

"One grows up rather fast in the King's Army."

"I suppose you're right." She let the button go before she worried it off. "It's all he ever wanted to do. Join the army."

"Sometimes we must be careful what we wish for." Hart shifted on the damp bench, not liking the direction of the conversation. The army had been a lucky escape for him from the ignominy of being a Hartford when he was her brother's age, but Eli had not fared so well.

Hart cleared his throat. "I shan't be underfoot here too long, Cousin Eden, so you'll get everything back to normal soon."

"Nothing will ever be normal again."

Well. She was certainly direct. And bitter. Befriending her would be a challenge. His uncle had had peculiar notions all his life. He had obviously stinted on his ward's education and deportment in this backwater. And perhaps as a farmer's daughter herself, the girl's mother had not been much help either. Hart would make sure the Emery sisters wanted for nothing. Hartford Hall might be remote and a touch stark, but he meant to make it a proper home for himself eventually. By then Eden Emery would be off in London with his aunt, or perhaps married if he could find a man who was not too fussy to do the job. Someone who wanted to be glared at for the rest of his life. "I know you feel that way now. But I've only been here a few hours. Give me a chance to prove to you that I have no intention of interfering with your routine at Hartford Hall."

"You say that now, but you're a *man.*"

Hart couldn't help laughing. "You make me sound like a leper. I confess to being of the male gender, and acknowledge you females might suffer a bit under the current laws of the kingdom. But surely you know a woman's stealthy power over a man. You probably could have me eating out of the palm of your hand if you but tried."

Eden's mouth fell open. Perhaps he'd gone too far in his teasing. She hadn't had the exposure of a London season to sharpen her conversational skills. But at least she was looking at him now, her dark gray eyes stormy.

"I shouldn't like to feed anyone like that. It sounds frightfully— messy."

"My word, Cousin Eden. I believe you've made a joke at my expense."

"I believe I have," she said, a measure of wonder in her voice.

"Let it be the first of many. I'm a worthy target. I hear tell I'm considered to be a bit of a stuffed shirt." His men had called him Holy Hartford, and he supposed he'd gone out of his way to be good. Sometimes *too* good.

"A perfect gentleman."

"I *have* tried. It gets tiresome, but I have my family reputation to live down. Perhaps you didn't know, but my uncle Ivor was considered to be rather wicked before he came to live here."

Her eyes widened and he wondered if he was being fair to the old boy. But perhaps if she knew his uncle's true nature, her mourning might be somewhat shortened. The world really was a better place without the infamous Hartford brothers in it.

"It's true. I don't wish to speak ill of the dead, but he and my father were a pair of ne'er-do-wells. I've gone out of my way to reverse the family curse. I'm always kind to orphans and animals, that kind of thing."

She lurched up from the bench, his coat falling from her shoulders. "You d-don't have to be kind to me. I'm not some—*project*. I'm fine. Perfectly fine. I need to get back to my sister now." She disappeared before he could say a word to stop her or rise as any gentleman should.

"Huh." Hart bent to scratch the old dog's ears. "Put my foot in it again. Your mistress is a mystery, isn't she? I've always loved a puzzle, and I've got plenty of time to solve her."

Chapter 3

"What's he like?" Jannah's dark eyes were glassy, a sure sign she was feverish again. Eden put a cool hand on her sister's forehead and bit her lip.

"Kind to orphans and animals by his own account," Eden said dryly. "But underneath, he's rather dr-dreadful. Forceful. Used to getting his own way, I expect, on the battlefield." *And in the bedroom.* She had not missed his flirtatious smile in the garden. Stuart Hartford possessed a golden radiance that would be hard for most women to resist, but she would have no trouble guarding her heart. She didn't have one anymore. "He ordered me about like I was one of his foot soldiers, telling me what I must and must not do. He forbid me to—" Oh, she couldn't tell Jannah of her plans to seek a job. Her sister would know what *that* meant. "He told me he wouldn't make any changes here, but I don't believe him."

"Oh, dear. I thought he might be nice." Jannah sighed.

"Nice!" Eden snorted. "He's the image of Lord Hartford."

Though he had been her stepfather for ten years, he had never encouraged a more informal address. Even when she was on her knees before him performing the most intimate of acts, he insisted she call him by his title. Relished it, in fact. Reveled in his perverse power over her.

Jannah giggled. "He *is* Lord Hartford, Edie. He must be handsome, then. Our step-papa was."

Eden's skin crawled in response. Though he'd threatened to, Lord Hartford hadn't bothered with Jannah much. He'd been far too occupied seeing to Eden's subservience. "They won't stay long. We'll have the Hall back to ourselves before winter comes."

Jannah's brows knit. "They?"

"There's his aunt. I told you she was coming."

"Oh, yes. Is she an old dragon?"

"Oh, no. Quite the opposite. Very young and very pretty. Too young to be a grown man's aunt." Eden had an astonishing thought. "Perhaps she's really his mistress."

"Scandalous! Please let her visit me. It may be my only chance to meet a fallen woman," pleaded Jannah.

One stands before you. Eden shook her head. "I'm not sure you're up to company, love. I believe your fever's returned."

"I'm always too hot or too cold. If we wait for me to be just right, I'll be dead."

"Hush! Don't say such nonsense," Eden said, bringing the patchwork quilt to her sister's chin.

Jannah pulled it down again. "You must face facts, you know. I have. There isn't much time, and I can't see the world or her people if I'm forever stuck in this room."

"Oh, Jannah."

"And don't tell me I'm so brave. I'm not. What I am is bored. All

I do is sleep and read books I've read too many times already. Please bring this anti-aunt to me. Is she very wicked?"

"You are far too eager to encounter wickedness, miss. She seemed very nice. When I fainted—"

Jannah sat up a little straighter. "What? You never faint."

"I think Mattie must have laced me too tightly," Eden lied. "I've grown a bit stouter since I wore this gown for Mama's funeral." That, at least, was true. In the past few weeks, since her stepfather's death, she had begun to taste her food again. Mrs. Burrell had noticed and each meal was piled high with Eden's childhood favorites. "Anyway, Mrs. Cheverly—Juliet—took charge. And she drinks brandy, too."

"Oh!" Jannah clapped her hands. "She *is* wicked! Please brush my hair and bring her up."

"Right now?"

"This instant! I haven't coughed once. Please, please, Eden."

Eden tidied her sister's hair with a silver-backed brush. It was as lustrous as a mink's pelt, longer and darker than Eden's own ordinary brown strands. Jannah was the image of their mother, a discomforting fact her stepfather reminded Eden of every time he felt the need to coerce her to do his bidding. If Eden didn't cooperate, he'd move on to the prettier, younger sister. "Shall I put it up so you look like a proper young lady?"

"Don't bother. I'm sick of being proper! Please fetch me Mama's bed jacket. I shall look *comme il faut*."

Eden left her sister fussing with the lace ruffles and stepped down the landing into the guest wing. She had put the baron's aunt in the second-best room, its walls covered in French blue wallpaper and the bed draped with matching toile curtains. The new Lord Hartford was next door. Eden hoped he didn't mind that he wasn't given the master suite, but her stepfather's personal effects were still scattered throughout the room. In the weeks since his death, Eden had simply been unable to bring herself to go through them, once she'd burned the pictures. The book, however, was still nowhere to be found. She took a deep breath and knocked on Mrs. Cheverly's door.

"Come."

Juliet was seated at the rosewood desk, sheets of her own personalized vellum spilled from their stack. Suzette had helped her change already from her ruby red magnificence into a shimmering gold silk dress. Topaz drops dangled from her ears and encircled her slender throat. She planned to dress for dinner, too, although the routine at Hartford Hall left much to be desired. But while she was here, she would not abandon those poor girls to the poverty of their upbringing. Surely a little gaiety, even in the face of death—or perhaps because of it—was necessary.

Mindful of her pledge to soften Miss Emery up, she managed a welcoming smile. "Do sit down, Miss Emery. Eden. May I call you Eden?"

"You may call me anything you would like."

Well, it was barely a concession, but Juliet decided not to take umbrage and waved a white hand over her correspondence.

"I'm writing to my boys. They're at school together, but they fuss if they have to share one letter. So I am required to write to each one of them individually. I mustn't repeat myself, either, because they compare letters. It's most vexing. I shall tell Sebastian all about our trip and Raphael all about his new cousins."

"I do not mean to impose on you, Mrs. Cheverly—"

"Juliet, dear. Please."

"Juliet, then." Eden gave a slight smile, transforming her face significantly.

Juliet realized with a start that this was the first smile she had seen on the young woman's face since their arrival. She rather wished Eden would do it more often. Hart wouldn't call her an old boot if he could see her now.

"My sister would very much like to meet you. We don't receive visitors often, so this is an exciting event for her. But—" Eden twisted her long fingers together.

Juliet laid her pen on the tray. It was so obvious Eden needed comforting, but she had seen the girl's aversion to physical contact when Hart had touched her. "You don't want her to get *too* excited. I understand. Is she very badly off?"

Eden nodded. "Our mother died just a year ago, and now Lord Hartford. Even though his funeral was very quiet, it's all been too much for Jannah. Her condition is worse by the day. And she knows it."

"Then I shall be a dull old aunt. If I must."

Eden's lips twitched at Juliet's jest. "Oh, no. It is precisely because you are so young and vibrant that Jannah wants to see you. She must find my company dreadfully flat."

"I imagine you want what's best for her, and that means saying no often, does it not?"

Eden blushed, bringing welcome color to her cheeks. "You are very wise for being so young."

And now an actual compliment. Perhaps Eden was not so impossible after all. She studied the girl for a moment. Some judicious plucking of those fierce straight eyebrows and a smile or two might make Miss Emery a taking thing. Her figure, what Juliet could see of it under that ghastly black dress, was more than a bit too slender, but that could be improved upon. Eden's hair was healthy and shiny, although it was pulled back into an unbecoming knot. Juliet, though she loved her boys quite desperately, had always wanted a girl to fuss over. Miss Emery might be a little long in the tooth to play dress-up, but Juliet could envision a project that might keep her occupied in this isolated house.

"I'm delighted to make your sister's acquaintance. It's been an age since I've had the pleasure of the company of young ladies. Tell me what you do for amusement here in the country."

"I'm afraid you'll be disappointed. We are very dull here compared to what you're used to in London. The village is not much, as you know. The gentry neighbors are miles and miles away, and my stepfather was not fond of them in any case. He kept us very much to himself. When Mama was up to it, we attended church, of course—Mama always insisted upon that although she found the new vicar's sermons quite lacking in comparison to my father's. Baron Hartford was much preoccupied with his business affairs. And his library and art."

As soon as she said the last two things, Eden wished she could call the words back. Juliet Cheverly didn't look like she ever missed a trick, like a bright yellow bird that spied each passing bug and butterfly. Eden hoped the woman would not inquire too closely about her stepfather's interests. The baron's leather portfolio had contained lascivious renditions of Eden, some of the dismissed maids and, shockingly, her own mother, which Eden had destroyed. What remained in the library was a scandalous and valuable assortment of naughty prints and books, which some gentlemen might find titillating. Ivor certainly had. Eden wondered what the new baron would do with them.

"Are there no young people in the neighborhood?" Juliet asked.

"No. We are rather remotely situated here. And as I said, Lord Hartford—my stepfather—was not sociable. My sister is not only my sibling but my dearest friend."

"Take me to her then. Wait. I have a gift for her. Well, gifts for you both." Juliet opened a drawer and removed a misshapen parcel tied with twine. "These are the very latest from Hatchards. I trust you are both romantically inclined?"

Juliet's smile was so joyous Eden did not have the heart to tell her she would rather poke out an eye than read a ridiculous romance. She knew perfectly well there were no heroes or happy endings in this world. But Jannah would welcome them as she'd read her old books so often the pages fell from the spines.

"You could not have chosen better for my sister," she said with perfect sincerity. "Jannah will adore them *and* you."

They found Jannah propped up by plumped pillows, her face shining.

"What a pretty child you are!" exclaimed Juliet.

It was true. Eden thought that despite her pallor, Jannah looked as fetching in a confection of rose pink lace and ribbons as her mother ever did.

"Oh, Mrs. Cheverly, I'm scarcely a child. Were I not plagued by this indisposition, I should likely be making my come-out soon and catch myself a marquess!"

"Ah, a girl with ambition, I see. But why not a duke?" Juliet teased. "I was one such young miss myself, but then Mr. Cheverly chanced by and all thought of being Lady So-and-So flew right out of my head. A title is lovely, of course, but the man more important. Don't you agree, Eden?"

"I am scarcely in a position to judge. The only titled gentleman of my acquaintance was my stepfather."

"Well, he was not a candidate for marriage, was he? When you come to London with me—"

Eden was not one bit pleased with Juliet's interference. The very last thing Jannah needed was an exhausting trip. She glowered under her famously bushy brows, a silent warning to Juliet and her runaway tongue.

Jannah clapped her hands. "London! Oh, how marvelous! Do say we can go, Eden. I should so like to see the sights I've read about."

"I don't think it's wise, love. The trip alone would tire you out terribly."

"Perhaps I misspoke. I'm sure your sister knows what's best." Juliet rushed on. "Hart says I am an incorrigible matchmaker. Pay me no mind. I'll save my exertions for my boys when they're a bit older. And my nephew, of course. It's high time he wed. A gentleman needs the guidance of a good woman. Why, Mr. Cheverly hardly knew how to dress before he met me."

Eden and Jannah were then treated to a treatise on the eminent Mr. Cheverly for the next quarter of an hour. By then, even Juliet noticed she was losing her audience. Jannah had suppressed a few yawns and Eden could not stop fidgeting with the ribbon rosette on her cuff. Finally excusing herself to go finish her letters, Juliet left the sisters alone.

Jannah gave Eden a cheeky grin. "Well! Not so very wicked then. But she's very beautiful."

"She's very meddlesome. No doubt her husband died just to escape her endless chatter."

"Eden! It's not like you to be mean. It's obvious she still mourns him. I wonder why she doesn't see it's she herself who needs a husband." Jannah plucked at the lace at her neck. "But perhaps you *should* go back to London with her."

"I'll not leave you alone. I have no wish for a husband, either, so there's absolutely no point in falling into Mrs. Cheverly's matchmaking clutches."

"Why are you so opposed to marriage? I can understand you rejecting Mr. Oliver. You'd die of boredom and all his brats. But there might be a nice man for you somewhere if you'd but look. You haven't been spoiled for choice here."

"Mr. Oliver was really looking for a governess rather than a wife. I don't believe he even cared when Lord Hartford forbade it. Anyway, my place is with you," Eden said with firmness that brooked no further questioning.

Jannah sighed, and a cough escaped.

"There, that's enough conversation for you today, sweet. Shall I read to you awhile?"

"Please. One of the new books."

"Very well. Perhaps some poetry. That shouldn't take so long and you may rest." Eden found a beautiful slim leather volume and began to cut the pages. Before she had finished, Jannah had drifted off to sleep. Eden decided she'd better tackle the talkative Mrs. Cheverly before the woman said or did anything else to upset her sister.

* * *

Hart had concluded his interview with the bailiff, John Pinckney. All in all, the operation of Hartford Hall and its environs was very sound. The solicitor in town had provided Hart with a list of his uncle's investments as well and introduced him to his uncle's young man of affairs, Mr. Calvert, before he left for Cumbria. For the first time that he could remember, Hart felt perfectly safe. Safe from war, niggling debt, and, just at present, his aunt Juliet, who was closeted upstairs with the other females in the household.

Hart leaned back in the library chair, taking in the almost oppressive masculine atmosphere of the room. His uncle had been a most indifferent correspondent. The breach with Hart's father had leached on over to Hart himself, and Hart felt that if the Hall had not been entailed, he might not presently be sitting pretty in this house, all of his financial burdens eased. His army career had not lent itself to material gain or even much glory. True, he'd been a popular officer and had done his duty. He'd served with some distinction but had done everything in his power to erase the last decade's horror from his mind. It was a vast relief now to know he had his own home and comfortable income. Half pay and econo-mization were now a thing of the past, far sooner than he'd ever expected.

His uncle had not been so very old, after all. He might have married again had he lived. It was surprising given his predilec-tions that he had married a vicar's widow in the first place. *And* been saddled with three children. But Lady Hartford's beauty must have been legendary, if the portrait of her over the mantel was any indication, although the beauty certainly had not been passed to her eldest daughter.

Juliet had been most informative during their private dinner to-gether last night. True to her word, Miss Emery had not joined them. But Juliet had been full of details of meeting both sisters, and of the frosty dressing-down she'd received from Eden after she somewhat imprudently invited the girls to London.

"London! Surely the youngest one isn't up to such a journey," Hart had replied, tucking into a saddle of lamb roasted to perfec-tion.

"Your carriage is extremely comfortable. We could make fre-quent stops."

"Out of the question." And that was that. Hart refused to be con-fined with both sisters *and* his aunt. He'd go mad or murderous.

He supposed, though, he ought to meet Jannah and see for himself the state of her health. If she suffered from consumption, there was no hope, but he knew there were other lung ailments that responded to certain treatment. A warm climate, for example, far from the damp cold of the fells. Even her sister looked like she could benefit from a holiday to put some real roses on her cheeks and flesh on her bones.

Pushing himself away from the desk, he rose and looked out the mullioned window. The steep snow-topped crags of the Pennines hemmed in his boundary. His uncle's property—his property now—was beautiful yet bleak at this time of the year. The leaves had fallen and the cold had settled into the bones of the house, no matter how many roaring fires were blazing in the hearths.

What had kept his uncle here instead of the snug town house in Mayfair? Surely whatever the old scandal was was old news. But Hartford Hall would not hold Hart long. He and Juliet had better return to civilization before true winter set in and they were trapped in snowdrifts.

Hart's father had claimed Ivor was even more wicked than he himself was. Hart did not care to discover that particular truth, as Charles Hartford had been wicked enough for ten men. The army had been Hart's family for so long now he had nearly forgotten the disgrace of being Charles Hartford's son. The one good thing his father had done was to purchase him a commission in the army. Bonaparte had been a great equalizer. No one cared that Charles Hartford lay drunk in a gutter after a night of whoring while his son Stuart Hartford led a victorious charge.

Ivor had removed himself from town under duress a dozen years ago, married and had become, if not respectable, then more restrained in seeking his pleasures. His estate was solvent, his only folly a rather exorbitant bill for his library. Hart didn't begrudge the man his reading. He was fond of reading himself, and now would have more time to do it.

Hart left the window to peruse the bookshelves, finding the usual fare of a country gentleman. He took down a book on animal husbandry. He now owned a vast quantity of sheep, about which he knew absolutely nothing, save that they tasted delicious and their wool was warm.

But wait. Hart's mouth twisted. The old devil. Beneath the hand-tooled leather binding was a volume that spoke little to the necessities of a farmer but more to the desires of a satyr. True to the title, animals were involved, and a whole host of other creatures. Hart snapped the book shut. Returning it to the shelf, Hart skimmed more volumes. Book after book shocked Hart, and he had thought himself unshockable. When he unfolded a paper that fell out of what certainly was not *The History of Lancashire*, he had to sit back down before his knees gave out.

It was a charcoal sketch of Miss Emery. Eden. Fingerprints had smudged the lines, but there was no mistaking her straight brow or the look of unexpected ecstasy on her face. Her body was sin incarnate. She held her sex open for the artist with her elegant hands, splaying her legs.

Her full breasts, tipping to each side as she reclined against a spill of pillows, were rendered in exquisite detail, the nipples shaded and erect.

The same pillows, he recognized with a jolt, that were piled on the leather couch before the fireplace in this very room. Hart closed his eyes briefly, feeling guilty for—what? trespassing? The library and all its contents were his now. He would never have dreamed the virginal, shrewish, skinny Miss Emery to be capable of such a pose.

Then he looked more closely, trying to make sense of what he was seeing. The expression on her face, transcendent. The languid lushness of her body. He found the artist's signature, cleverly entwined within her feminine curls, branding her. *Ivor Anthony Hartford.*

Surely this drawing was not merely speculative. It was the work of a lover, one who knew every smooth inch and nuance of pleasure to be found on his partner. Hart was ashamed to feel his own manhood responding to the wanton vision before him. He crumpled it up before it burned *him*, and threw it into the fire.

My God. What was he to do with a harlot in his house? All her starchy reserve and hesitant mumbling was a ruse. She was no more innocent than the women at Mrs. Brown's. She'd be better off there than here at Hartford Hall, a daily reminder of his family's debauchery. Even though his uncle was dead, he'd left a poisoned thorn behind.

Hart would uproot Eden from his garden. A woman with a body like that would find a protector with little difficulty. Perhaps he would suggest just that avenue for her.

Hart ran his fingers through his hair. Deuce take it. There was the sister to consider. And perhaps he was jumping to conclusions. By all accounts, his uncle had been no saint, and she was too thin now to match the plush curves he'd just destroyed.

It was time to have a talk with Cousin Eden.

* * *

The little party was upstairs in Eden's mother's sitting room, a brightly patterned space that gave no quarter to the illness that had pervaded the past. The tea tray had been sacked, its few crumbs attesting to the superiority of Mrs. Burrell's cooking. Jannah had been allowed to dress and get out of bed and was now quite full of lemon curd tarts, sitting next to Juliet on the little divan, the two of them poring over a week-old gazette from London. Eden was engaged in the more mundane task of mending stockings, one stern eye fixed upon her sister and her companion. Thus far Juliet had made no further mention of London or marriage. She had, however, offered her maid's assistance in the restyling of both Emery sisters' hair and had offered to pluck their eyebrows herself. Eden had heard that in the last century women actually removed every bit of hair and pasted on mouse-skin eyebrows, but Juliet assured her it wouldn't come to that. Eden was willing to give the procedure a try. Jannah had always teased her that her bushy brows made her look grouchy even when she was smiling.

So when Baron Hartford begged admittance some time during their beauty strategy session, he was briskly turned away by his aunt. He found the female laughter within unsettling, and chose instead to take the dogs for a walk.

They were not the dogs of his youth, but they were still too old to keep up with his long stride and soon lost interest. He hiked up a hill and turned to look down upon Hartford Hall in the thin autumn sunshine. The vines were turning rusty on the gray stone façade, the glass windows dark, framed by bright white paint. One day these hip-roofed rectangular boxes set at a right angle would feel like his country home, the home of his future children, should he finally acquire their mother. He expected he'd have to relent and let Juliet do her worst once they returned to town. Perhaps he'd been hasty applying to Mrs. Brown's. A year was a very long time to postpone the inevitable. He couldn't hold out against Juliet's interference, no matter how surprisingly entertaining he found membership at Mrs. Brown's.

For one thing, he'd discovered to his relief that he was not like his father or his uncle. He was not interested in anything out of the ordinary, not that the goddesses could ever be called ordinary. The delicious taste of sin had not turned him into a glutton. Hart had feared all his life that if he gave in to vice, he'd soon be in its viselike grip. But he was merely a mortal man, finding pleasure in pleasurable things after years spent in self-denial. Someday he hoped to find equal or surpassing pleasure in the arms of a wife.

But what to do in the meantime. There was the vexing problem of the Emery sisters. Maybe he could send them away. Italy. Greece. Somewhere warmer and far away and beyond temptation. For Hart was tempted, and he did not want to be.

He shook his head, trying to clear the image of Eden from his mind. There had to be an explanation for the wanton sketch he had found. Perhaps in his dotage, his uncle had suffered from an overactive imagination.

But the man was not past fifty, hardly elderly enough to fall prey to the vagaries of senility. Hart hoped when he reached that age he'd still be in full possession of all his faculties and manhood besides.

He sat on a conveniently flat rock to contemplate his future. The life of a gentleman of leisure had its appeal after ten years spent at war. He might even sell the small house in Mayfair if the market was good, or let it again for the season as his uncle had. Hart didn't have much interest in balls and routs and such foolishness. If he could find a serious, virtuous young woman, he thought married life might even be tolerable. They could build a real family together and wipe out the stain of the Hartfords for the coming generation at least. One could always hope. But a bit of prayer might be necessary as well.

Chapter 4

It was now dusk and rather dim in the library, but even in the flickering glow of the lamplight, Hart had to admit his aunt had performed a minor miracle. While she was still gowned in severe black, Miss Emery's face looked more open, relaxed. Juliet had given an arch to each of Eden's brows and her hair was arranged becomingly with some loose tendrils lending an air of near frivolity. She still avoided his eyes, but her modesty wasn't as effective as she might have wished. Now that Hart had seen Miss Emery in her natural state—at least on paper—he wouldn't be tricked by her nervous virgin act.

"Thank you for agreeing to see me," he began. He leaned back in his uncle's comfortable leather desk chair. The library had seemed the best place to conduct his business with her, but she seemed acutely ill at ease. He suspected he knew why. "Please sit down. I have ordered dinner in an hour. Would you care for some sherry?"

"No, thank you, my lord," Eden said, prim. "And I shall not be joining you for dinner. Your aunt was very kind today, but I'm afraid she tired my sister out. I shall take dinner in Jannah's room."

"Suit yourself," Hart said with some annoyance. "I do hope you allow me to at least meet with Jannah once before I leave. I assure you, I'm not a dragon. I wish to see for myself her circumstances and how I might help her."

"You can leave us alone!" Eden blurted.

Before I discover your secret. But it was too late—he knew already. Not the details, but he would soon ferret them out.

"Now that I cannot do. I feel responsible for you, no matter that you seem to hold me in such aversion."

"I'm s-sorry to give you that impression, my lord." She spoke the words, but Hart heard no true apology in her voice. "It's just that Jannah is so frail. A change in her routine upsets her."

"I have a proposition for you." Hart watched as Eden became even more rigid in the chair. "Not that kind of proposition, Cousin Eden. Really, you do have a very low opinion of me. I wonder what has given you reason to distrust me so?"

He waited for her to respond—to call him a *man* again—but she merely shrugged and fiddled with her hands. He squelched his impulse to reach across the desk and still them. She'd wear her skin right off if she didn't stop.

"I should like to send you and your sister somewhere more clement for the winter." He held up a hand to stop her from objecting. "Before you speak to me about routines and changes, consider. The damp weather here cannot be good for anyone with a lung condition. My aunt Juliet is willing to act as chaperone. I spoke to her this afternoon and she thinks it's a capital idea. You needn't traipse all over the Continent, either—rather I can procure a villa for you in some quiet spot. Imagine flowers and warm breezes."

* * *

He rambled on, smiling at her, deepening the crease on his cheek, a veritable travel guide for lush holiday spots.

Stuart Hartford was a handsome man, far more handsome than his uncle. Now that she sat across from him, she realized their resemblance was superficial. Stuart's eyes were larger, more blue green than ice. His nose was narrower, although its bridge had been broken at one time. He had a rakish saber scar and a charming smile. She had to look away. She was thinking like an infatuated schoolgirl, and she knew too well where that led.

If only. If only Ivor had died four years ago. Stuart Hartford might have been the answer to all her prayers. Any girl's prayers. He was, as she had noted, a perfect gentleman. But it was too late now, because her imperfections had doomed her chances for any sort of respectable life.

"I don't think it's possible," she said at last, when he finally paused for breath. "There has been blood in Jannah's handkerchiefs. She's tried to hide them, but the maids have come to me."

"I'm so sorry."

"Dr. Canfield told me months ago it was just a matter of time. So you see, L-Lord Hartford," she said, tripping on the name, "your offer comes too late."

"What *can* I do?"

"I wish I knew." Eden felt the lump in her throat. She could not cry in front of this stranger again. Would not.

Somehow he'd come around the desk and placed a large hand on her shoulder. She looked up and was lost.

"Let me get you a sherry. I insist." He went to the well-stocked drinks tray.

Her stepfather had not stinted on the quality or quantity of his libations, and had at times used alcohol to make her more pliant to his demands. Even before he had taken her virginity, he had urged the footman to keep her glass full at dinner. "You're a young lady, now," he'd say, winking. "Why not enjoy yourself?"

Her mother often took a tray in her room, claiming a heavy meal before bedtime upset her stomach, so Eden would dine alone with Lord Hartford while Jannah was upstairs in the nursery. Often she was dizzy from the wine and disoriented by the conversation, and he would help her upstairs. He'd brush against her private places, seemingly by accident. In her embarrassment, she'd felt somehow at fault. He would kiss her good night. A first, just a fatherly kiss on her temple. He'd cup her cheek and stare down upon her, his cool blue eyes assessing. When he knew she was ready— more than ready—he kissed her on the lips.

"You taste delicious, Puss," he'd said. "Like spring wine."

Hart handed her the delicate sherry glass. Eden made a pretense of sipping from it. She'd learned long ago to avoid spirits in the company of a man. She dared not lose her head again or loosen her tongue. Every word she uttered in Stuart Hartford's company cost her.

"Thank you, Lord Hartford." She placed the glass on the desk. She fisted her hands in her lap, wondering when she would be allowed to leave this interview.

"I fear we started off on the wrong foot, Miss Emery."

Thank goodness there was no more "Cousin Eden" nonsense. Eden inclined her head and nodded. She could barely cobble together two words in his presence.

"I am rather used to giving out orders. Perhaps I overstepped my bounds trying to make arrangements for you, but I am concerned. I will of course respect whatever choice you make, but I wish to reiterate that my family is at your service should you require assistance. I should hate to think of you slaving away to earn your bread. I am sure that had my uncle lived longer, he would have settled your future in a more satisfactory manner. He could not possibly have known his time was so short."

He had stopped speaking, evidently waiting for a response from her. Eden was convinced his uncle had known precisely what he was about. His lack of a bequest was his parting shot to let her know how very little he had valued her. At the end, she was just chattel, like his poor old dogs, collared and cowering.

Think, Eden. But she had lost whatever malleability she ever possessed and remained stiff in her chair. She wondered where the book was. She'd searched throughout the house for it, frantic. She'd found the sketches, thank God, but the book was still missing. Could Kempton have it? She'd never be free of him if he did.

When she didn't find it in her stepfather's room, she'd left everything as it was. There was nothing incriminating about brushes and cravats, watch fobs and boots. But the hair on the back of her neck prickled every time she returned to the scene of her many crimes. The book was here in the library somewhere, she knew it. The sooner Lord Stuart Hartford left, the sooner she could begin her hunt again.

"I know I must face the future, but I don't wish to talk about it anymore. I've made plans. But thank you." She began to rise.

"Very well. Let's talk about the past, then."

Eden's breath hitched. The new Lord Hartford seemed a stubborn man, reluctant to let her go when it must be so obvious she wanted to fly right out of the chair. She sat back down and gripped her shaking hands.

"Perhaps you might tell me a little bit about growing up at Hartford Hall. I only recall visiting once, though I know I was dragged off to church by the housekeeper. Mrs. Kenny, was it? I believe I must have heard your papa, but I'm sorry to say his oratory was probably wasted on me."

For a moment his crooked smile revealed the boy he had been. In all likelihood she had been there that Sunday morning so many years ago. Perhaps she was wearing her best starched white pinafore, her hair neatly braided beneath her chip straw bonnet, her little gloved hands resting solemnly in her lap. Her mother would have been beside her, jiggling a squirmy Eli in her arms. But in her mind's eye, Eden saw only the shadowy transept, the leaded glass behind her papa as he exhorted his faithful to do the Lord's work. The mischievous boy in the Hartford pew was nowhere to be found.

"Mrs. Kensit. She was housekeeper here until my mother married Lord Hartford."

"She's no longer working here. Has she passed?"

"No. M-mama and she did not see eye to eye, so Lord Hartford pensioned her off. She's still in the village." Eden neglected to mention that the old woman gave her the cut direct every time their paths crossed.

"You were born here?"

"Yes. Not in this house, of course, but at the vicarage."

"How old were you when you came to live at the Hall?"

"Almost twelve." Eli had been ten, and Jannah just six. Hartford Hall was quite a change from what she was used to, and Lord Hartford very different from her father.

"Did you get along with my uncle?"

"P-pardon?" Eden was beginning to feel like she was taking an examination for which she had no correct answers.

"Perhaps I'm overly curious. My father contemplated another marriage after my mother died, and I was not enthusiastic. It came to nothing in the end, but I was vastly relieved. It's difficult for children to make adjustments. Then, of course, when I was older, I thought the woman had got the better bargain. My father was not an easy man to live with. Was Ivor a good father to you?"

Feeling the hot color wash over her cheeks, she took a swallow from her previously untouched sherry. It was time to end this test before she failed it completely.

"Y-yes. But I never, ever thought of him as a father. I was nearly grown when we came to live here, as I said."

"Twelve doesn't seem so old to me."

"My own father had died, and my mother was never very . . . strong," Eden said, picking her words carefully. In truth, her mother had been addicted to laudanum and her mirror. Her understanding, never acute, was insufficient to deal with three children on her own. "I assumed a lot of the responsibilities for my siblings."

"Then you must understand how I feel about your present situation."

"I'm not a child any longer, my lord, and I can make my own way, I do assure you. If you will excuse me, I must sit with Jannah. She is usually in better health in the mornings, so if you would like to visit with her after breakfast tomorrow, I shall tell her."

She left in haste, her ugly dress crackling. Hart sipped his brandy and gazed into the fire. He'd not gotten far with her, but it was a start. She was hiding something. Getting her to admit to it might prove difficult, but Hart had never been known to resist a challenge. And there was something about Eden that made it impossible for him to do so.

He closed his eyes, and the image of the sketch came unbidden but not unwanted. He may have tossed it into the fire, but he could not toss it out of his mind. What would it be like to see Eden soften before him, shed her hideous dress and show him her greatest secret?

Bah. What had come over him? He was lusting after her like a virginal schoolboy. It was more than time to head back to Mrs. Brown's and relieve these inconvenient urges. Hart poured himself another glass and waited for the dinner bell.

* * *

A good father! Stuart Hartford's probing words echoed in her head. Ivor Hartford had ignored her until she belatedly grew breasts, then pursued her with a determination that she was ill-equipped to resist. Eden looked out Jannah's window. It was pitch black now, the last of the dusky purple and gray that had crowned the mountains long gone. Her sister lay sleeping fitfully, a frightening rattle in her chest every time she breathed. It had been so bad at dinnertime that neither of them had eaten much.

Eden blamed the new baron, both for her sister's decline and the disquieting thoughts that swirled within her. If only he'd stayed away and not come to upset them. Hartford Hall had been here more than one hundred years and wasn't going anywhere. They didn't need Stuart Hartford strutting about, even if he did own the place.

He did make a fine figure of a man, however. She'd have to be blind not to notice his powerful physique. Even if he no longer wore the uniform, he was a soldier from top to toe, back straight, shoulders squared, a rather fierce gleam in his blue eyes. His body was honed from riding and swordplay and all the other things military men did to keep fit. Bedsport, for example. Eden was sure the new Lord Hartford had never suffered much from the lack of female companionship. Just like his uncle.

She let herself wander, picking at the scab of the past that never quite healed over. She needed reminding of the betrayal of trust, both her stepfather's and her own of herself.

One evening not long after Ivor Hartford put her to bed and kissed her in a most extraordinary fashion, he did not leave her at her door, but entered with her. He stood behind her, holding her in front of her mirror, his hand idly slipping beneath the bodice of her new gown. A gown he had ordered for her himself. She had felt very grown-up in it, although Mattie had clucked in disapproval, called it cheap and said it displayed too much of her bosom, which had finally, miraculously, appeared.

"Nonsense," Eden had said airily. "My stepfather has excellent taste. It came all the way from London!" And she tugged it down an extra inch when her maid left the room.

Her stepfather looked down approvingly at the expanse of flesh Eden had so rebelliously exposed to him. "Look at yourself, Puss. Look at us. You know I cannot help myself."

Eden's eyes widened as his hand delved deeper. She felt him warm and large upon her breast. He bent to kiss her neck, watching for her blush and shiver in the mirror as he did so. Their eyes met.

"I should go," he said softly. "But one night I hope you will ask me to stay."

He left before her words could come. "Stay," she whispered.

Shortly after that, she begged him and completed her ruination. She'd done it to herself, by herself.

Eden's stomach interrupted her misery with a rumble. Mattie had taken the tray away hours ago. Eden was—impossible to believe— hungry. Acutely and shamefully so, when she had so many more things to worry about than a hot meal. But since her stepfather's death, she was awakening to the taste of food again.

And to the taste for an attractive man.

Oh, but she was a fool. She hadn't learned a thing, not one. The lonely, awkward girl was still inside her, clamoring for attention. She would not seek it from Stuart Hartford, no matter how valiant and heroic he seemed. If she was lucky, she could avoid him for the rest of his visit and pray she never clapped eyes on him again.

It was her turn tonight to sleep in Jannah's room, and she was already in her nightgown. However, there would be no sleep unless she did something to feed the monster that was her belly. Eden tiptoed to the bedside. Jannah was fast asleep.

Her unwanted guests were abed, too. The house was dark and still, the clocks ticking rhythmically. Eden picked up the taper and padded down the carpeted stairs in her bare feet. The flagstone kitchen floor would be cold on her toes, but the sooner she got downstairs, the sooner she could come up. She knew Jannah could have a crisis at any time.

The kitchen hearth had been banked, but the room still glowed with golden warmth. Eden set the candle down on the table and headed for the sideboard. Mrs. Burrell always left a loaf of bread, a crock of butter and a pot of raspberry preserves out. It was sometimes the only thing Eden could get Jannah to eat. Jannah loved her raspberries and could no longer pick them herself. Years ago, before the illness, before the baron, Eden and her little sister roamed the estate, filling pails, gorging on the juicy fruit until their lips were stained as red as their mother's rouge.

Eden cut a thick wedge of bread, slathered it with jam and was about to cram half the slice into her mouth when the kitchen door swung open. She was so startled she dropped it, leaving a sticky trail of scarlet down the front of her white night rail.

"Blast!"

At the same time Stuart Hartford uttered a rather more explicit curse.

"I do beg your pardon, Miss Emery. I did not mean to frighten you and deprive you of your midnight supper. It seems we had the same idea."

Eden stared down at herself in dismay. Her hair was unbound, flowing to the small of her back, but her front—she may as well have been standing nude before him with a bright red stripe leading him to her sin. The thin batiste nightgown had been washed so many times all her dark bits were visible to a discerning eye. And Lord Hartford looked very discerning indeed. She scooted down to pick up her bread, wrapping her arms around herself as best she could.

"I'll come back later. When you're done." He sounded regretful. And hungry.

"N-no. This is your house. I'll leave."

"Nonsense. We both live here for the time being, and I'll not deprive you of your dinner. I'm a gentleman, remember, not some ogre. Mrs. Burrell tells me neither you nor your sister touched your tray."

Was he checking up on her? Spying? She felt herself flush. "My sister took a bad turn."

"I'm sorry to hear that."

She looked at his shadowed face. Even in the dark of the kitchen, he seemed sympathetic. How she would like him for a friend, but that was inconceivable.

He waited a beat for her to say something, but she couldn't find any words.

"Carry on then," he said, his voice clipped. He turned on his heel and disappeared through the door.

"Wait!"

His head popped round the woodwork. "What is it?"

"I-I can cut another slice. For you. Mrs. Burrell put up the preserves this summer. They're very good."

"I don't think that's a good idea, Miss Emery. Think of how this encounter would look should a servant find us. Or worse, my aunt."

He gave her a slow smile. "We are both not dressed," he explained patiently, seeing her confusion. "Think of the frightful scandal."

Absurd. He was still in his linen shirt, breeches and boots, although several buttons of his shirt were undone. For a proper young gentleman like Stuart Hartford, he probably considered himself near naked in the presence of a lady without a jacket, tie and waistcoat. She cast her eyes away from the crisp curling golden hair she glimpsed on his exposed chest. She was no lady.

"Oh. You're teasing me. But you're right."

"Of course I'm right. I'm always right. But I really am hungry. Scandal be damned. I warn you, though, I won't marry you, no matter if we *are* discovered at our clandestine midnight supper."

Eden lifted her chin. "If you recall, I told you I will never marry."

"Then we are in total agreement." Hart swung a long leg over the kitchen bench and folded his hands on the pine table.

"I suppose you expect me to wait on you."

"You *did* offer."

"A jam sandwich, then?" Eden asked.

"I actually had my heart set on ham." He grinned up at her and she could not have denied him anything he asked.

She knew her way around the kitchen, and soon presented him with a thick sandwich, pickles and a wedge of cheese. As she put the plate on the table, she detected more than a whiff of brandy. No wonder Hart was so relaxed and playful—he was half-foxed.

But Eden preferred him like this to the way he'd looked at her earlier. As if he knew *everything*.

That was impossible. He'd had nothing to do with his uncle for years. And if proper Major Stuart Hartford *had* known what she was to his uncle, she would not still be standing here. He would have given her marching orders as soon as he walked through the door.

She watched as he took an enormous bite, his eyes closing in ecstasy. "Um. Still can't get used to it," he said, his mouth full.

"Did they not have sandwiches in the army?" she asked tartly.

"It's not just the sandwich, dear girl. Or the pickles. It's everything." He gestured vaguely toward the stove. "This is my kitchen."

"All the pots and pans are yours, it's true, but you best not bother Mrs. Burrell or she'll take a knife to you."

"You are making another joke at my expense, Miss Emery, but I don't mind. I never much thought about the succession here, you know. I always supposed Ivor would have children of his own."

He'd certainly tried with her mother. Baby after baby had been lost, each one taking more of her mother's tenuous grasp on reality.

"Well, Hartford Hall is all yours. Will you bring Juliet and her boys to live here with you?"

"Lord. I hadn't thought about that. The boys are perfect little devils, just as they ought to be."

Hart launched into an illustrative account of their mischief, describing a recent trip to Astley's Amphitheatre. Eden found herself laughing out loud, something she hadn't done in months, perhaps longer. That thought was so quelling, she spent the rest of the time in silence, peeking at Hart through her eyelashes.

He was so perfectly, utterly charming, which only caused her old tension to return. She ate her own sandwich slowly—with food in her mouth, he wouldn't expect her to talk. Perhaps he'd run out of questions to ask her. She was about to rise when he reached across the table and patted her hand. A ripple of electricity sizzled through her.

"Could I trouble you to make me a cup of tea? It's damned cold in this house, isn't it?"

Eden was sure he was staring at her nipples through her night rail. Her feet were bare and frozen to the floor. She could use a cup herself, but she would make tea for him and then flee the kitchen.

"I'm a little drunk, you know. Need something to warm me up and clear my head. That library. The atmosphere. It's a bit unsettling. You know how it is. I saw how you were in there tonight. It got to me, too."

Eden's lips felt frozen now. "I don't know what you mean." She got up and put the kettle on.

"Ghosts. Oh, I didn't see any—I'm not completely cracked. But if you wanted to tell me anything, anything at all, I'd listen."

And you wouldn't like what you'd hear. "There is nothing to tell," she said, trying to keep her voice from shaking. "How do you take your tea?"

Hart put both elbows on the table. "I'm not your enemy, Eden."

"Of course you're not. I have no enemies," she lied.

"What about friends?"

"Jannah is my friend. And I've been down here much, much too long. I'm afraid you'll have to make your own tea."

"I'll manage then. Good night, Eden. Pleasant dreams."

How she wished for an unspoiled night, but she deserved every nightmare that was visited on her.

* * *

Hart watched her run away. Did the woman not own a dressing gown? She had been almost as exposed to him in the candlelight as she had been in his uncle's drawing room. If his aunt had appeared, Hart would have found himself procuring a special license in the morning despite his declaration, for he had surely seen enough of Eden Emery to make him guilty of compromising her.

Not that she had any virtue to compromise. He was almost sure of that. When he'd surprised her, she had looked a perfect wanton, her head tilted back in blissful anticipation, raspberry jam on her already crimson lips, her slender body outlined beneath that flimsy shift in the dying firelight. His inconveniently aroused cock twitched in remembrance. He could imagine her taking pleasure in everything he might offer.

She'd invited him to stay in the kitchen with her—so shy and blushing. Did she not know the picture she presented? No doubt she did, and was attempting to trap him somehow, although once he'd agreed to join her, she'd become mute. It wouldn't work. She could not alternate between her repressive reserve and artless coquetry and think to seduce him. It might have worked with his uncle, although the man had not rewarded her for her efforts in his will.

He would meet her sister tomorrow—today, now—and get the hell away from Hartford Hall before his uncle's improbable mistress cast any more dark gazes his way. She would not be compromising *him* and all he had striven toward.

The sooner he got back to London—the sooner he got back to Mrs. Brown's—the happier he'd be. Perhaps membership there had opened the Pandora's box of his lust, for surely he should feel nothing but contempt for his uncle's mistress.

She should not entice him. She was too skinny. Stern and standoffish. Socially awkward.

But when she smiled, it was as if a rare moonflower bloomed at midnight. And when she laughed, he quite forgot to be suspicious of her.

He put himself to bed without that cup of tea he'd so desired. But not all desires could be ignored. His cock firmly in hand, he sought relief as he had done so many times over the years. This time he didn't imagine dark Spanish beauties or pink English girls, but a tall young woman whose legs were spread, her folds parted, her ripple of brown hair spread upon his pillow. She touched herself and wordlessly invited him to do the same. There was nothing she would refuse him. Her cutting tongue could be persuaded to gentle his shaft before she guided him into her tight wetness. He would plunge into her again and again until—

His seed spurted on his belly. If she were here, she'd lick him clean and he would let her. She'd be the perfect whore, despite her futile attempt to disguise her true nature. Hart reckoned his uncle had been a lucky man, Eden Emery at his side, the two of them tucked up here away from civilization and reveling in mutual decadence in the library.

But a life like that was not for him. Never for him.

* * *

Some hours later, Jannah was up with the birds, had breakfasted lightly and now was wrangling with her sister as to what she should wear to meet Baron Hartford.

"He's just an ordinary *man*," Eden said, exasperated. "And you may *not* wear your blue dress. We are in mourning for Mama and his uncle. What kind of hoydens would he think we were if we were to cast off our blacks?" Privately, Eden loathed the thought of wearing black in honor of Lord Hartford for the next year. It was just one more way he'd keep control over her, even from the grave. He had robbed her of choice, of dignity, of *humanity*. The marks he had left upon her body were only just beginning to fade.

Through the years, she had managed to hold herself together in front of Jannah. At times Eden felt like two people—the bossy big sister and the subservient slut. The duality had been tenuous at times. Even now she expected to be summoned to the library for her ritual punishment.

It had not begun on such a low note. At first, her stepfather had been gentle, almost boyish.

"That dress I gave you," he said, *as they walked hand in hand to her room one night. She leaned into him, hoping to catch another kiss.*

She looked up at him and smiled. "I love it. Besides being beautiful, you gave it to me, my lord."

Her infatuation was so blazing she saw him take a step backward. Steady. She'd not scare him away by seeming desperate. She wanted to do the thing with him properly. Although proper had nothing to do with it.

He shook his head sorrowfully. "It doesn't show you to advantage, Puss. I don't think it fits correctly."

"What do you mean?"

"I made a mistake. Comes of being cut off here in the country, I expect. I hear a lower neckline is all the rage now in London. Your—your breasts"—and here he looked down, as if embarrassed—"should be peeping from the bodice. Spilling out to be caught by a lover's hands. A man should see what he's paid for," he whispered.

That sounded wicked. And quite wonderful. "Mama would notice." Not very likely. But Mattie would.

"Then you'll have to give me a private showing." He lowered his voice so that Eden could barely hear him. "I dream of suckling your nipples and making you come."

"Come where?" she asked, stupid girl that she was. He had laughed and chucked her on the chin.

"The night you finally let me make you mine, wear that dress. Fix it so I can see you. All of you. Shock me."

Eden felt the familiar surge in her lower regions. She knew what he wanted; she wanted it, too. More than anything. She kissed him hungrily, her mouth aching for the tangle of his tongue.

"Don't make me wait too long, Puss," he warned.

Eden shook the thoughts from her head. Her stepfather had been a very clever man. She might almost admire him for his skill had he not ruined her so completely.

"If you don't hurry up, it will be time for your morning rest. Here," said Eden, bringing a plain black gown to her sister's bed. "This will do. I shall give you Mama's ruby bracelet and my paisley shawl."

"Oh, very well." Jannah allowed Mattie and Eden to dress her as if she were a doll. Truthfully, she did not really feel up to meeting anyone, especially such a handsome man as Juliet Cheverly had described. She'd had a bad night and troubled dreams. When Mattie left her to fetch breakfast, she'd spat the blood into her washcloth, then buried it underneath the old schoolbooks in her painted chest at the foot of the bed. But fit or not, she needed to see for herself the man Eden might be forced to depend on. Her sister had seemed so unhappy since Mama died. Even, she had to admit, for some years before.

At the stroke of eleven, the baron was ushered into the late Lady Hartford's sitting room, the site of yesterday's beautification project. While it welcomed the morning sun, the curtains had been drawn to protect Jannah's reddened eyes, which were sensitive to sunlight. Jannah could never have managed the stairs today. She was breathless just sitting in her mama's favorite chair.

When Stuart Hartford entered, she felt a momentary rush of pure calf-love. Now here was a hero come to life! He was romantic perfection. His military bearing mixed with the undeniable warmth in his smile would have been the downfall of girls far less vulnerable than she.

But he was not for her. He might be the answer to one of her prayers, however. How splendid it would be if he fell in love with Eden. Then her sister could stay right here instead of going off somewhere to earn her living. How could Eden resist him? Jannah was determined to show her sister to be irresistible herself. It was past time for Eden to have a life of her own, not always taking care of her or Mama or at their stepfather's beck and call. She would sing her sister's praises until Stuart Hartford would be overcome by duty and do the right thing.

Hart took her hand in his and kissed it. "It is a pleasure to meet you, Miss Jannah."

Hart did not have the disadvantage of watching a young girl in the bloom of youth fade incrementally day by day. For those who loved her, the changes had been gradual. But from his quickly mastered expression, Eden saw that he recognized that Jannah was not long for this world. Her skin was translucent, each blue vein visible. Against her white face, scarlet patches stained her cheeks. Her dark eyes were already searching for a distant view.

Hart was charming, gently solicitous, asking seemingly innocuous questions. Jannah was far more forthcoming than Eden had been. In her innocence and illness, Jannah seemed unaware how damning her answers were. Despite Eden's efforts to alter the conversation at each discomfiting turn, the picture of her life at Hartford Hall must have been becoming clearer.

"My sister is quite a scholar, you know," Jannah said. "I believe she was quite instrumental in helping my stepfather organize his library. He was forever seeking her out for her assistance. He depended on her as if she were his very own daughter."

Eden felt her breath leave her. The new baron had been here three days and had spent a great deal of time in the library. Surely Lord Hartford had already inspected some of the volumes. She had dared not warn him earlier of their content. In this and so many things, Eden had wished to appear in oblivious ignorance.

"Indeed?" Hart raised gold-tipped eyebrows in surprise. "Are you a great reader, Miss Emery?"

"My stepfather's collection holds no interest for me." Eden searched her mind, trying to remember if there was in fact any sort of order to the books on the shelves. "I'm afraid my contribution consisted of straightening the volumes and dusting. Lord Hartford expressly forbade me to acquaint myself too closely with his books. He told me some were very r-rare." Would he know she was lying?

"Surely one of the servants would have been better suited to that task," he replied.

"As I said, the books were considered valuable. It was no hardship. Jannah, love, I fear we have overstayed our welcome. It is time you rested a bit before luncheon." Jannah's last words had been mere wheezing. Eden kissed her sister's reddened cheek and opened the door, looking pointedly at Lord Hartford.

As they walked the hall together, Hart put his hand on Eden's arm. "Thank you for letting me meet with your sister. I am sorry if it was too much for her."

Eden stopped short and stepped back, removing herself from Hart's hold. "You know it was."

But perhaps now, his curiosity satisfied, he would leave them both alone. He could have no objection to her spending the rest of the day with Jannah. But he stood rooted to the carpet, looking her over with his stormy sea blue eyes.

"It's a puzzle, you know, about the contents of the library."

Eden tried to brazen it out. She lifted a newly sculpted brow. "In what way, sir?"

"Surely you became curious in all your years of 'dusting.'"

She could hear the sarcasm. "If you had known your uncle, Lord Hartford, you would not think to cross him." That was close enough to the truth. "He told me not to open the books. I did not."

"I wonder. There is an enormous unpaid bill for a book I cannot seem to find. Perhaps you would help me search for it. You may already know where it is."

"I-I-" Eden stammered. Could this man be any more vexing? But perhaps his request could be turned in her favor. "If you tell me its name, my lord, I can search for it once you and your aunt are on your way back to London. It's a shame to lock yourself indoors when the autumn days are so fine." *Idiot.* The sun had not shown its face for much more than an hour at a time since his arrival. He had certainly set her on edge. If she dared, she'd push him out the door this very minute.

"Come downstairs with me to the library. I will find the printer's bill."

Eden closed her eyes for a moment. He said himself the library made her uncomfortable. For her it was torture. More time spent in that room with this man. More time to remember. Surely he had learned all he could about the estate by now and could leave? He'd seen Jannah's condition for himself. He had met with Mr. Pinckney and all the servants. The vicar, too. But she followed him down the stairs to the back of the house.

Hart unlocked the desk drawer, where he had neatly stacked the outstanding tradesmen's bills. "Here it is. From an Arthur Griffin of Gryphon Press. No doubt he thinks he's a clever one with the play on words. *The Education of a Young Lady.* I thought perhaps it had been ordered for you or your sister. Have you seen this particular volume?"

Eden remembered the gryphon perched over a book on the

frontispiece, its talons sharp. The title on the bill was not quite accurate, but there was no need for her to elaborate. "I do not recall it, but I shall make every effort to look for it once you're gone."

"You seem in an awful hurry to get rid of me, Miss Emery."

"My sister is ill. Surely you can see that now that you've met her. The disruption to her routine is not good for her."

"Should she stay locked up in her room, then, alone? Just waiting to die?"

"How cruel you are! And she is not alone," Eden said hotly. "Mattie and Charlotte are with her constantly. I am there with her as much as I am able. Now that Lord Hartford is dead—" She broke off.

"You have a bit more time to spare for your sister. How very generous of you," Hart said, unmistakable coldness creeping into his voice. "While you and my uncle engaged in licentious behavior, your little sister had to fend for herself with the maids."

"How dare you!"

"Can you deny it? I found the proof in the library with my own eyes!"

So he had found the book! All this business about ghosts and the bill was just another means to torture and trap her. "Where is this proof?" she said, willing calm to cloak her. But she saw her guilt reflected in his eyes. His lips thinned and she could feel the chill of his disapproval wash over her.

He knew, or thought he did. It was useless for her to try to explain. What had Kempton called him? Holy Hartford. He would never understand. She barely understood herself. She waited for her world to come crashing down again.

*   *   *

He'd awakened with a pounding headache and the shame of semen on his bedcovers. All night Eden had darted in and out of his dreams, her sheer night rail, then her naked body enticing him into one lurid fantasy after another.

He'd lost patience. She was guilty as sin, her hands contorting in their nervous dance. He had gambled confronting her openly. So his assumption was fact. A pity. He could forgive much, but never this. His uncle was beyond his reach, but Eden Emery was a beautiful thorn which he would remove no matter how much she tempted him.

"I burned it. So you are safe. Unless there are more."

"It was the only one," she whispered.

"How lucky," he said in disdain. "That charcoal sketch I found tucked into a book was most singular indeed." Ignoring Eden's look of confusion, he continued. "You realize, of course, that your admission changes everything. My aunt and her boys are everything to me. I cannot allow a woman such as yourself anywhere near them. You have done enough damage to your own family. Once your sister—" He paused, softening his words. "When her time comes, you will leave this house. Don't worry. Unlike my uncle I'll make some financial provision for you. For services rendered, so to speak. Perhaps he did not feel he got a good bargain in the end. But you are to stay away from my family and my home."

"Very well, my lord," Eden said. "I shall be glad to be done with anyone named Hartford. May you join your uncle and the devil!"

She left, a blur of black muslin. Hart couldn't believe it. The trollop had seemed furious with *him*. He wondered how long it was after her mother died that she seduced his uncle.

Dutiful sister or not, the woman was morally questionable when it came to sex. Allowing herself to be drawn in such a damning way, it was obvious she was indiscreet, and that could be dangerous. He'd found out about her easily enough. If his aunt planned to give her a London season, who knew what she would do, and who with, teeming as the town was with rakes and rogues who would scent her unmistakable sexuality. Scandal could wreck a family, as he very well knew, and he'd not let his well-intentioned aunt get swept up in wickedness. Juliet and her boys should be free of the Hartford disgraces. He didn't want to be a prig, but he had a duty to his family. Eden's presence was a provoking reminder of its failures. And the very last thing he needed was a repeat of last night's sensual debauchery picturing Eden Emery as he stroked himself to ecstasy.

Chapter 5

Eden longed to throw something, but she knew a shower of broken china would attract the attention of Mattie at the very least. Every item in her room belonged to the odious Stuart Hartford anyway. No doubt he'd send her a bill once he sent her packing. So she made do by pounding her bed pillow until her fists felt as if she'd gone a round at Gentleman Jackson's.

It was pointless to try to explain her circumstances. She couldn't even explain them to herself. And her shame really was unbearable. She had been a smart girl; her papa had always said so. She *would* have been interested in Baron Hartford's library had he had anything in it that resembled real literature and history. But there was nothing except false titles on the bindings and sin within. And she had been forced to read every one.

Surely now the baron would leave. He held her in complete antipathy. He was right to hate her. She hated herself for her first mistake and the many thereafter.

Her mother and Jannah had left for a fortnight to visit Jannah's godmother. Eden had been invited, but at the last minute backed out, blaming her monthlies.

"I cannot possibly ride all that way in a carriage, Mama. I shall die. In fact, I wish I were dead right now," Eden cried dramatically.

"Hush, dear. A woman suffers so she might one day bear a child. Children are such a blessing."

Her mother's pupils were huge from the drug. Eden wondered if her mother could survive the journey herself, but Eden had helped her pack the necessary vials of poppy. Jannah was twelve, old enough to be resourceful, the same age as Eden had been when she was relieved of the duty of running her little family, when her mother remarried. Eden felt some guilt, but not enough. If her mother had not been so determined to provide Lord Hartford with an heir, she might have paid more attention to the children she already had. Tonight Eden would take her mother's husband into her bed and into her body. She had left the letter on his desk. There could be no mistaking her intention.

Dear Lord Hartford,

I have decided not to accompany Mama and Jannah on their trip. I do not want you to sleep all alone in this house. I look forward to having dinner with you this evening in my room. I have asked Mrs. Burrell to send a tray up at seven o'clock because I am sick. She will not think it odd that you keep me company, because you care for me.

With love, your Puss

She began dreaming and dressing hours earlier than necessary. Thank God Mattie had gone with her mother and could not criticize her appearance. She had altered the lovely red dress Lord Hartford had given her so that the rosy tops of her nipples were exposed. She knew he'd like it. He'd asked her to do it.

That had been weeks ago. She had been frightened of her feelings, but she was

*ready now. She left her hair down and tossed a woolen shawl around her for pro-
priety in front of the servants.*

*The tray was delivered promptly, and Eden removed her shawl. Ten minutes
went by, then twenty. Mrs. Burrell had sent brandied wine up to help with Eden's
"female troubles," and half the small decanter was already gone. Eden fastened the
shawl around her dress once again and rang for the butler, Collins.*

*"Lord Hartford was to join me for dinner because I am unwell," she said.
"Could you see what is keeping him? I shouldn't like Mrs. Burrell's good cooking to
get cold."*

*Five minutes later Collins returned and told her Lord Hartford would be un-
able to join her.*

"I don't understand."

*"He said to tell you he'll look in on you before he goes to bed, miss, if it's
important."*

*Important! It was a very matter of life and death! Did the stupid man not un-
derstand what she had planned? No, he was not stupid. It was she who had somehow
ruined her evening. Perhaps he had gotten tired of waiting for her to make up her
mind and had lost interest. He had seemed cooler of late, hadn't he?*

*"Wait. Please take a note to Lord Hartford. It shan't take me but a minute to
write it. And take away the tray. I'm too ill to eat. Perhaps you should leave the
wine."*

*She had spent hours on her original note, but she had no time now to be clever.
She simply wrote,* Come to me tonight, I beg you. *She didn't seal it but folded
it so many times it resembled a paper lump.*

*Collins looked disapproving, as though he wanted to say something to her. Some-
thing like "Don't drink so much. And don't sleep with Lord Hartford." It was
probably plain to all who had eyes she was madly in love with her stepfather, and
she was not one bit ashamed. After years of awkwardness, she was a woman grown
and knew her own mind.*

Eden sat by her fire, finishing the rest of the wine. She arranged and rearranged

her breasts. She tried to read and couldn't concentrate. When she at last heard the tap
at her door, she felt a stab of fear. And forbidden thrill.

The thrill had faded long ago. An empty routine of obedience
had taken its place. But Eden would never obey another man again.
Not as a lover. Certainly not as a wife.

She went to her little writing desk and pulled out the crumpled
letter from Kempton. He would get no satisfaction from her now.
Hart knew the truth, or at least he thought he did. He had heard it
from her own lips.

It was time to mend fences. Eden had fallen out of touch with
the few friends and relations her mother had. Years ago, when
Eden's mother, Marjorie, had married John Emery at the age of
fifteen, she was living with her older brother George and his family. George was happy to see the back of her. Spoiled and cosseted
by their late parents, Marjorie was far more ornamental than practical. And George's wife was understandably jealous of a beautiful
young girl, while she was fading. When the young curate came,
Marjorie's family felt God himself had sent him to remove their
burden.

Marjorie could barely manage a household. Eden's father would
laugh as he remembered the ruined dinners and lumpy stockings.
But he loved to look at her across the breakfast table, as long as
someone else was stirring the oats. He had trusted Eden to help her
mother. How disappointed he would have been to know how badly
she had failed.

Then Eden's father had died suddenly. She, all of eleven years
old, assumed responsibility for her family. Baron Hartford had recently returned to the neighborhood and released her from her fa-
milial duty once he was introduced to her mother, who made a very
fetching picture in her widow's weeds. The marriage, well before the

proper year of mourning was up, would have been more of a scandal if the parish had not been secretly relieved.

The baron had not been looking for a helpmeet, Eden realized, but someone decorative he could dominate. Marjorie had not been enough of a challenge. She was without much imagination or understanding. How bored he must have been until he remembered there was another female in his household ripe for debauchment. It was a wonder he had waited as long as he did.

Reliving the past would get her no closer to her future. Eden began her letter to her dreaded uncle George and his wife. She let them know that Jannah was very ill and dropped a hint about her own uncertain future. Then she wrote to Jannah's godmother as well, a cousin of her mother's who had married a man of property and was now a widow. Mrs. Stryker was a keen traveler. Perhaps she needed a companion for her adventures.

If Eden could get to London, she might also seek employment through an agency. She had lied to Lord Hartford about having secured a position, but she knew now employment was more essential than ever. She'd not touch a penny of his money. She'd rather starve. She had years of practice.

* * *

The weeping woke her with a start. Eden knew before she put a foot on her floor what had happened. She didn't even bother with her dressing gown.

There was just enough gray light of dawn to see her way to Jannah's room. She turned the door handle and found Mattie sitting on the bed. Mattie, Charlotte and Eden had taken turns sleeping in Jannah's room on a cot for the past few weeks. Now Eden wished she had spent the night in her sister's room instead of writing letters and wishing both Barons Hartford to the devil. At least she had shared a plain dinner with her sister, during which she'd endured listening to Jannah wax poetic about Hart the handsome army officer. The man's visit had probably hastened her death, Eden thought bitterly. Jannah had been so enervated she'd coughed for what seemed like hours into the night.

"Oh, Miss Eden! I was about to come to you. She's—she's gone."

Eden embraced Mattie before looking at her sister's pale form. Jannah seemed peaceful at last, not gasping for breath. Eden pulled the linen covers up, but hesitated before covering her sweet face.

"I closed her eyes," Mattie said, her round face red from crying.

"Did she say anything?"

"Not that I could understand, miss. I was asleep when she made a little noise. By the time I got to her, she had passed."

"Best go downstairs and tell Mrs. Washburn and Collins. They'll know what to do. I'll stay with her."

Eden watched as Mattie belted her robe about her buxom figure. The maid didn't bother tidying her hair, but moved quickly. Eden thought her haste was unnecessary; Jannah was quite beyond help. But she sat on the soft feather bed and held her sister's cooling hand.

She had been six when Jannah was born. A baby sister at last, to make up for her vexatious brother and the other children her mother had lost. Jannah had danced after Eden like a merry little shadow. They had been inseparable until Eden had been seduced and the wall of secrets rose higher and higher.

She looked up to see Stuart Hartford on the threshold. He was already dressed for riding.

"I am sorry," he said. "May I come in?"

Eden was suddenly aware she sat in her threadbare nightgown again, her nipples bristling in the chill of the room.

She nodded. She was too heartsick to argue. "Perhaps you could see to the fire." Usually it was kept blazing all night, but poor Mattie must have been so exhausted she'd fallen asleep.

He said nothing as he efficiently set to coaxing the coals to flare. After laying a few logs down, he removed his jacket and handed it to Eden.

"You must be cold."

The jacket held warmth from the man's body. Carried his scent. Eden flinched away. "If you could fetch my dressing gown, I would prefer it."

"As you wish."

Hart walked down the hall, not quite certain which room was hers. A door stood open at the end of the corridor. The bed was rumpled, a severe gray woolen robe tossed across a chair. It certainly was not designed to entice a gentleman. In fact, nothing in this room exhibited any form of passion. It was nearly as spare as a monk's cell. The only adornment was a pair of Canton Ware vases empty of flowers on the chimneypiece and a framed pencil portrait of a woman and child he supposed to be Eden's mother and sister. Hart had only seen the one charcoal sketch by his uncle, and the subject matter was markedly different, but it was obvious he had been the artist here, too. Whatever his uncle had been, he had talent. The oil painting in the library of the late Lady Hartford was very well done, too. She had been a great beauty, far more lovely than her daughter. Odd that Eden compelled him as strongly as she did when there were so many beautiful girls who possessed qualities she lacked—like morals.

When he returned to Jannah's room, the servants were clustering around Eden. Someone had thought to wrap a blanket around her. He gave her the robe and excused himself.

Damn. He had been determined to leave Hartford Hall tomorrow with Juliet. Now it seemed his first formal performance as Baron Hartford would be as host to a funeral. And if he knew softhearted Juliet, she'd want to get her hands on Eden Emery and make her a protégée. Hart couldn't permit that.

He went out to the stables, finding activity already, although the sun had not yet risen. From the looks of the sky, he might never see it when it did. As he saddled his horse, he discovered that the stable hands had already been informed of Jannah's death. No doubt they thought him a cold man for keeping to his usual routine, but a ride always helped him think, and think he must.

Eden had looked starkly attractive this morning, with her loose hair cascading around her. She had shed no tears, but her pain was evident, as was the lushness of her breasts through the transparent night rail. No wonder his uncle had been tempted, as he himself had been tempted the other night. Perhaps she was not entirely at fault for what happened between them. His uncle had been a libertine in his prime, and the books in the library proved he had not lost his taste for sin. The isolation of Hartford Hall was enough to turn anyone slightly mad. It was even affecting Hart, infusing his brain with improper thoughts of a girl who had just lost her sister. Eden had somehow invaded his dreams *and* his waking hours. Her sensual voice, her wide dark eyes, even the tilt of her prideful chin warred with what he knew of her.

Hart found he had traveled the same path on horseback that he had hiked the other day. He turned to face his home, and for the first time felt a spark of belonging. In the spring, the hills would be dotted with his sheep and lambs. His eyes searched, and he found the tidy home farm in the distance, its neat fallow fields resembling a child's board game. The acreage was too steep to plant much more than would supply the needs of the tenants and hall, but he could not complain of the hearty fare he and his aunt had consumed during their visit. He could be happy here. His own corner of Paradise. Once Eden Emery removed herself.

She had spoken of employment in London. There she would go, as soon as arrangements could be made. If absolutely necessary, she could ride back to town with them. Hart could spend the days riding alongside the carriage.

Or he could send the women ahead. He had men to spare to escort them. With his newfound riches, he'd employed a couple of ex-soldiers who felt the loss of Napoleon and the funds to foil him quite keenly. He'd never been called a coward, but Hart was uncertain he could stand to be in Eden's presence for the lengthy journey. He'd speak a few blunt words to her about confiding in his aunt. There was no reason to drag Juliet into the mire.

With the Eden problem settled to his satisfaction, he gave his horse its head on a flat stretch, enjoying the wind in his face. He felt it would be the last bit of freedom he'd experience for the foreseeable future.

* * *

The late baron had thought his neighbors quaint provincials. He deigned to visit them only on rare occasions, but did not reciprocate by inviting them into his home. He did sometimes entertain a friend from London, for whose amusement Eden had been asked to perform, much to her mortification. Lord Blanchard had sat like a spider in a corner as Ivor demonstrated his power over her.

But on the whole the Hall had been very quiet. Eden was pleased to see neighbors who remembered the child she was, sitting quietly in church listening to her father's every word. They could not come for her mother or brother, would not come for Hartford, but they were there in force for Jannah.

When at last the pillaged platters of cold meats and pies and salads were returned to the kitchen, Eden was left in the drawing room with Juliet and Hart. Eden had begun to think of him as just Hart, as it was a vast relief not to keep calling him Lord Hartford. Juliet had been kindness itself the past few days. After the funeral, she had pressed hands and charmed complete strangers. Eden imagined Juliet knew more about the neighbors now than she herself did. After years of isolation under the baron's thumb, she was truly alone now without Jannah.

Hart had said nothing of any substance to her since their disagreement the day before Jannah died. She wondered when he would expect her to leave. She was already prepared to go, having organized her few possessions in the idle moments she had as Juliet took charge of the household. It might be weeks before her letters bore fruit, too late now in any case. She needed to go at once.

"Are you tired, dear?" Juliet asked solicitously. The candles cast long shadows in the room, but Juliet still looked fresh as ever. From her myriad trunks she had unearthed an exquisite mourning gown. With its jet beading catching the firelight, she was impossibly chic.

"A bit." Now was as good a time as any. "I want to leave Hartford Hall as soon as possible. There is no longer any need for me to postpone my employment."

Eden glanced at Hart. He displayed no emotion. He'd been quite concerned over Eden's future at the start of his stay, and Eden hoped Juliet would not notice the change and quiz him on it.

"I do understand. You must find the atmosphere gloomy now.

My nephew and I have not discussed it, but I presume we shall be leaving in a few days ourselves. Surely you may travel back to London with us. You can stay with me until you finalize the details of your position. You've never said, Eden. Whom will you work for?"

"Jannah's godmother," she lied. For now. She hoped in time it might be true.

"She resides in London?"

"Yes, ma'am."

"Perhaps we can do a bit of shopping before you plunge into your job. Have some quiet entertainment." Juliet patted Eden's arm. "I know you are grieving, but I should so like to send you off after you have a bit of fun. You deserve it."

Involuntarily, Eden looked over to Hart again. His cold eyes met hers, and she felt her face go hot and her tongue thicken. "Th-that's very kind of you, Juliet, but not necessary. The sooner I accustom myself to my new circumstances, the better." She twisted her mother's bracelet around her wrist. She had hidden it from Kempton, but perhaps it could fetch something at a jeweler's. It was studded with tiny rubies, a bride gift from her stepfather. He had not been an extravagant man.

"Mattie should come along," said Juliet, surprising Eden. "The poor girl is fagged to death. She needs a change of scenery, too."

"I doubt Mrs. Stryker will expect me to come with a lady's maid," Eden said doubtfully. The woman would be shocked enough when Eden turned up on her doorstep.

"Of course not! We shall send her back here by and by. Or she may decide that London has more opportunities. Give me a week, Eden. I should so like to introduce you to society—nothing untoward, I promise. No balls or cotillions. We could take tea at my young friend Althea's. She's still in mourning for her mother and would welcome the diversion. And I believe Hart should accompany us. Althea would make him a perfect wife."

"Who is this paragon?" he rumbled.

And he would require a paragon, thought Eden. Insist upon it. Someone pure and virginal and untouched by scandal. He and this Althea or someone like her would raise blazingly blond giants in this house and exorcise the demons unleashed by his uncle.

"You remember Lady Dorr?"

"Gad, yes. What a witch."

"Althea is her youngest daughter. And lucky you. Your prospective mama-in-law is already with the angels."

"More likely she's an imp of Satan. Old Scratch must be sorry he won her soul by now."

Eden felt uncomfortable listening to their teasing exchange. She didn't belong here. It was time she excused herself. She rose from the sofa and Hart followed suit.

"Juliet, we'll discuss the afterlife and my matrimonial prospects another time. Eden, I should like a private word with you in the library before you go upstairs."

Damnation. Hadn't she suffered enough today? Eden nodded and followed him along the corridor.

"I shan't keep you long," he said, gruff. "Please sit." He turned his back to her and went to poke the fire.

She remained standing, prideful. "I know what you wish to say."

"Do you?"

Eden ticked the impromptu list off her fingers. "I'm fully aware my presence is anathema to you. You don't want me to take advantage of your aunt's hospitality. If it were in your power, you'd send me straight to Lady Dorr."

"*Still* making jokes at my expense. Very amusing. Perhaps Hell does not hold its gates open for you just yet, but you must realize how insupportable it is that you make your home with my aunt for any length of time."

"Are you afraid my sin will rub off? I assure you, sir, I'm done with the so-called pleasures of the flesh. I want nothing to do with any man."

"A pity you weren't so circumspect earlier."

Eden choked back her retort. Hart was a wall of propriety she'd never be able to scale. "I would prefer to go to London on my own. But as you are aware, your aunt is most persuasive. She does not appear to take the meaning of 'no.' What am I to say to her?"

Hart sighed. "She is too kindhearted by half. No doubt if you told her the truth, she'd just feel you were an innocent led astray by a lecher."

"And is that so impossible to believe?" Eden asked, already knowing she would not get the answer she hoped for.

"I saw the picture, my dear," Hart drawled, his tone dripping in condescension. "You were hardly unhappy with your circumstances. Your face, your fingers— Do I need to go on?"

The wretch! Had he not seen her humiliation, page after page? Or perhaps he had as little respect for the female sex as his uncle. He just didn't share his uncle's particular methods.

"Did you read it all?"

Hart's brow wrinkled. "What do you mean?"

"The book," Eden said impatiently. "*The Education of a Young Lady*," she said, her voice dripping acid.

"I'm not talking about the missing book, but the picture that was *inside* a book. Of you. Touching yourself like a wanton."

Eden swallowed. So he had not found it either. She must have overlooked one of Ivor's loose drawings. If just one sketch had driven him to this measure of disgust, imagine what would happen if he found an entire book filled with them.

"What is it you want me to do, my lord?"

"I see no way around it. You'll go back to London with my aunt and my men. You may indulge her for a day or two with jaunts around town, but then I want you gone. Understood?"

"Perfectly." Eden's lips thinned. How self-righteous he was. He probably believed Eve was responsible for the fall of mankind. "Will you not be returning with us?"

"No."

Her own imp whispered in her ear. "Why not? Do you find me too tempting?"

Before she knew it, she was in Hart's iron grip. His blue eyes stormed above her. "Have you no shame?"

"Why should I?" Eden asked, trembling. His closeness was overwhelming. The clean scent, the heat of him disordered her senses. She looked up into his furious face, mesmerized by the twitching muscle in his cheek. "I am what God and your uncle made me," she whispered. "You may argue with them, but I fear it is too late."

Hart watched her mouth move. A mouth made for sin. Too wide for fashion. Too red against the pallor of her face. She was right; she tempted him beyond bearing. And she was no innocent. "Made for sin," he muttered aloud. Knowing he would regret this until his dying day, he captured her lips with his own, drowning her in his anger and desire.

* * *

She was trapped in his arms. Trapped again. She knew how it would end, and forced herself from her willing surrender, clawing at and tearing the veils off a hidden memory to break Hart's spell. She had read Ivor's version in the book, every word, knew now what had really transpired that night four years ago when her step-father had taken her maidenhead. The beginning of her end.

He told her he'd be quick, "To get the pain over with." And in truth he could not have held back. He'd written he was as randy as a schoolboy. He rutted inside her, careless of her comfort, gratified to feel how wet she had become waiting for him all that time. Months, really. He'd taken a risk, but it paid off. The sooner she knew that his pleasure was paramount, the better. Begin as you mean to go on.

"Now, Puss," he'd said, as she had swallowed her sobs so as not to wake the household, "we've accomplished the rudimentary. There's no point in spilling tears for your useless virginity—you're mine now and always will be. And if I know any-thing, you were made for this. Made for me. Made for sin. A man can only stand so much temptation. You made me kiss you, didn't you, always finding a way for us to be together. You've let me fondle you without one word to stop me. You loved it and made me love it, too. You know you're a wicked little whore." He kissed her nose, as though he had complimented her. "Why, I believe you've wanted to fuck me ever since I married your poor mother."

She had wondered then if his words were true.

"You were desperate to find out . . . something." He held her chin and looked into her eyes. "And now you have. Puss, remember it was by your express invitation that I came to your room tonight. You bared your breasts for me like a common harlot. You didn't cry out when I entered your room, now, did you?"

She shook her head. She had risen from her chair and flown into his arms.

His thumb traced her swollen lips as a tear streaked down her cheek. "I've caught you in my library where you had no business being. They say curiosity killed the cat. Well, now you know, Puss, and you're still very much alive. Look at yourself. Wild and wanton. You're no longer my little girl, but my woman. I shall teach you tricks, and soon you shall be begging me for more lessons."

"Never," she whispered.

"Liar." He chuckled and rose from the bed. She lay curled up into herself, shaking. He went to her dresser, pulling a tangle of stockings from a drawer. Within minutes her arms and legs were lashed to the bedposts.

"Do you ever touch yourself there?" he asked, inserting a finger within her curls. "I've wondered. I've imagined you in here in your room, all alone. Waiting for me to come. Wondering what's taking me so long."

He was very sure of himself. He had every right to be. Her face reddened; she bucked but couldn't escape his probing. He took a corner of the sheet and wiped the smear of blood from her center. "I see I was right. You've wanted a proper fucking. Needed it. You've been after me like a bitch in heat. You think what we just did was the end of it? I promise you, it will improve. Whatever you've tried to do with your own hand, it's even better with a real man, Puss. A man who can do this." He settled between her open legs and began to lick, suckle, kiss. She closed her eyes and he took her to the place she'd almost been, the place he had always known was within her. She shook, this time not with fear but with an orgasm so intense she thought she would die of it.

He mounted her again. This time the penetration was eased by his semen and her own honey, and he took his time, sliding in and out with deliberate control.

When his hand slipped between them, she felt the tingle of pure desire. Lust. He rubbed and tugged as he pumped within her, and she unfurled again in an unconscionably short period of time. She would never forget his triumphant look as he spilled within her again, or her cry of ecstasy. He was the devil, and she his handmaiden.

With all her might she broke Hart's kiss. Were it not for the dismal reminder of her undoing, she would never have wanted it to end. The kiss was hot and dark, wholly without equal. In a way, she felt as though it was the first time she had ever been kissed properly. But there was nothing proper about it.

And it was bound to end in heartbreak for her.

She had at first thought to struggle. Felt she *should*, but it would

have been for show. Hart's hands had banded her arms tightly as
he drew her to him. Her helplessness spoke to her innermost need.
Eden felt an incandescent flare of passion, far different than what
she had felt with his uncle. Then she had been young, confused and
so very hasty to lose her innocence. But for Ivor Hartford, she had
been nothing but a controlled experiment, born of his boredom.
Convenient. Concupiscent.

Hart's fingertips seared her through the fiber of her sleeves. She
felt sure each pad had left its mark, not as a bruise but a blessing. To
be held by a man who didn't intend harm to her—

How foolish she was. Naïve. *Still*. Hart was like all men. He
might not intend to hurt her, but nor did he wish to help her, save to
pension her off like an old retainer. He thought her the basest sort
of woman. And yet she remained uncomplaining in his arms. Like
a love-starved child.

"Let me go, my lord." It had taken all her will to say the words.
To be safe in Hart's arms was a near miracle. And she'd not regret
a single second of it. She felt alive for the first time in years. She
had walled herself off for so long, but perhaps her heart was not
dormant after all.

That was dangerous.

Although her lips now brushed his cravat, Hart wouldn't let
her go. Couldn't. What had come over him? He realized ruefully
that his manhood was thrusting into the folds of Eden's mourning
gown. No matter how very far she had strayed from respectability
in the past, her sister had been buried in the churchyard today. He
was a complete cad to take such advantage. But he continued to hold
her in his embrace, feeling the racing of her heart through the layers
of fabric between them.

Her hair had fallen from its clips, a slippery curtain of

mahogany. Her dress gaped in the back, where his fingers had unconsciously sought the sweet relief of her naked skin. He knew if she stepped away, her gown would reveal the ivory swell of her breasts beneath her cotton shift. He refastened her hooks with reluctance.

"I apologize." He set her away from him and swiftly sat behind the desk, but she wouldn't need much imagination to figure out what he was attempting to conceal. "That was unforgivable."

"Surely not," said Eden, with a wobbly smile. "It was just a kiss, after all. And my entire fault. I provoked you."

Hart could not think of a civil thing to say. Yes, she was provoking. She was a strumpet, pure and simple. And she had felt perfect in his arms, as though a piece of him had been missing and was found. She stood before him, disheveled, her lips twitching in amusement as he absently rubbed a small bronze statue.

He looked down at the statue and quickly pushed it away. No doubt she was wishing he was rubbing *her* in the very same spot. She was wicked. And he was ridiculous. This entire situation was wicked *and* ridiculous.

There was not a doubt in his mind that he wanted her. Wanted her beneath him and above him. Wanted her to pulse around his cock and cry his name, over and over. He was bespelled and bedeviled and as hard as a rock. The girl who had seemed so unappealing just a few days ago now made his blood thrum. But she was not for him. Could never be for him.

"If that is all, my lord, I wish to retire."

"Yes, yes," Hart agreed. How soon could she and her aunt be made ready to leave? Tomorrow was probably too soon. Juliet would never make a good soldier; she had imported half of London's finery with her and it was strewn all over her bedroom. But he had to give her credit. She had even packed several mourning gowns, telling him she never traveled anywhere without them.

"For you never know, Hart, when life will take an unfortunate turn," she had said.

He was very much afraid his just had.

Chapter 6

It was raining in earnest by the time Eden walked the four miles and reached the village, a stinging assault to her senses. It was too soon for snow, but not, apparently, for the needle-sharp sleet mixed in with the driving rain. The weather had reflected her own mood perfectly as she clutched her woolen cape closer as it billowed in the wind. She'd given up trying to keep the hood on her head, so the lovely curls that Juliet's maid had coaxed into being had long washed away.

She was on a fool's errand. A sentimental fool. Tomorrow she would leave Hartford Hall for good, if Juliet and the servants were ever able to pack all the woman's belongings back into her trunks in time. Juliet's possessions seemed to have grown exponentially through the duration of the visit. Hart's fashionable aunt had changed her clothing several times a day, despite the fact there had been no one to impress. Hart had given his aunt the departure ultimatum yesterday at breakfast, some twelve hours after The Kiss, and had disappeared for the remainder of the day.

Eden touched her lips. Her mouth felt no different today than it ever had. She knew better.

The vicarage gate creaked as it had done the past twenty or more years. Eden could remember it heralding visitors when she was just a tiny girl. And sure enough, before she had a chance to knock, Mrs. Christopher, the vicar's wife, opened the door and embraced her.

"Come out of this rain at once, child! Whatever were you thinking, to go out walking on a foul day like this?"

When she had left the hall, it had just been misting. Eden supposed she could have ordered a carriage, but she had not wanted to find Hart, who so obviously wanted to remain hidden from her, to ask him. He'd been assiduous in avoiding her company. But before she could say a word, she was swept away by Mrs. Christopher's chatter.

"Mr. Christopher is out in all this nastiness himself. Old Molly Robshaw has taken a turn for the worse. Frances! Brew some tea please. Eden, dear, let me take your cloak and you go sit by the fire in the kitchen. It's much warmer in there if you don't mind. Frances and I have been baking."

The kitchen was just where she wanted to be. She followed the vicar's wife through the narrow hall and smiled at the maid-of-all-work, Frances, who was wiping flour-dusted hands on her apron. Once done, she hugged Eden quickly and then hefted the kettle from the hearth and poured the boiling water into a simple blue china teapot. Frances belonged to the vicarage as much as the furniture did. She'd served there all her adult life.

Eden sat back on the plain wooden chair. Fresh loaves of bread cooled on racks on the worktable, delicious evidence of the women's labor. The warmth and smell of the whitewashed room brought her right back to her childhood, although her poor mother would have burned whatever was in the oven. But Frances had been there then to save supper.

"My nose tells me the ginger biscuits are done, too, Frances. How lucky for us!"

"How are you, Frances?" Eden asked.

"Just the same as ever. You're looking much better, dearie, if I can be so bold to say it. Plumper. Healthier, and I want you to eat all the biscuits you want. No more of this slimming nonsense."

"Indeed not. You are fine just as God made you," agreed Mrs. Christopher. "How are things up at the Hall? If you need any help with Jannah's room, you need but to ask, you know." Mrs. Christopher opened a tin of fruitcake and began to cut thin slices from the dense, dark loaf. She set three plates upon the scrubbed pine table for the impromptu feast as Frances lifted the cookies from the tin to cool.

"Charlotte and Mattie will take care of it, thank you. I have already told them to bundle up the clothes and bring them to you. I am sure you know who could best use them." For a moment Eden thought of Jannah's favorite blue dress. She should have let the child wear it that last day when she was so eager to impress Hart. Instead, Jannah had been buried in it. "I've come with some news, though. Mrs. Cheverly has invited me to stay with her in London before I begin my employment, and we leave tomorrow."

Mrs. Christopher poured Eden a cup of strong tea and brought it to her before the fire, joining her on the chair opposite. "Frances, butter some bread for us, too, please."

"Oh, really, no," said Eden. "I'm not even hungry." She had been refusing kindly Mrs. Christopher's treats for so long now, her response was automatic.

"Nonsense. We all need to stop and eat something. You'll be doing us a kindness if you join us. So you really are leaving."

"I must. But I stopped to say good-bye, and see this house one more time."

"It's not much compared to the Hall."

Eden looked around the homely kitchen. "No, it's much better! It's the first home I remember. And Frances was right there, teaching me to roll out dough."

Frances grinned. "You was always in the way. Had to make use of you. Don't suppose Mrs. Burrell even let you in *her* kitchen." She cut into a fresh loaf and spread butter on each slice.

"No, she didn't. She really isn't very patient with children. Her own grandchildren live in terror of her and she drives the poor kitchen maids into fits." *When I got to an age when Mrs. Burrell might have tolerated me, I didn't have time,* Eden thought. No free time to learn anything but her stepfather's lessons.

"Luncheon's ready." Frances had added a bread-and-butter sandwich and a ginger cookie to the fruitcake on each of the plates. The women joined her at the gateleg kitchen table.

"Lord, bless this food to our bodies and us to Thy service. In Jesus's name we ask it. Amen," Mrs. Christopher said softly. "Now, tell us, where will you be working?"

"Jannah's godmother, Mrs. Stryker, has need of a companion. She wrote of a trip to Italy." Of course that had been months ago. Perhaps she'd already gone and come back.

"Italy! How very exciting!"

Eden spent the next hour in comfortable conversation. And she did eat her fill and more. Despite the fact that Mrs. Christopher urged her to stay until her husband came back with the gig, Eden took her leave amidst a tear or two and set off down the muddy road. The temperature had warmed and the rain had lessened, but it was still an unpleasant journey. When she heard the rumble of hoofbeats behind her, she hopped over the ditch so she wouldn't be run down, then stood still.

Blast. It was Hart, greatcoat flapping and face scowling. He reined in his horse, looking down at her, his blue eyes as icy as his uncle's. "What the devil are you doing here?"

To hell with him. She was done being judged. She held her spine stiff and lifted her chin. "Good afternoon to you, too, sir. I wanted to say good-bye to the vicar and his wife. He was not at home, but Mrs. Christopher had me to lunch. Go on to the Hall. I'll be along shortly."

She heard him mutter an oath, quite a wicked one. "You may ride up with me. You're a drowned rat."

"You have such a pretty way with words, my lord. I am perfectly fine." Unfortunately, her chattering teeth belied her assurance.

"Don't be a stubborn fool." He dismounted and walked toward her. "Come. I'll catch you as you jump over."

Hart opened his arms to her. Arms that had held her so close two days before. How could she possibly survive, pressed up against him all the way to Hartford Hall?

She shook her head. "I think not. I do not wish to inconvenience you."

"It'll be a damned inconvenience having to bury you next to your sister when you catch your death."

She felt the color drain from her face. The starkness of his words reminded her of just how alone she was.

His voice softened. "I'm sorry. That was crude. Forgive me."

He looked perfectly sincere, a golden angel of mercy. At least she thought so through the haze of tears. She took a blind step forward, then slid down into the ditch, where her bottom landed with an ignominious squelch in the mucky mess.

"Bloody hell! Can you stand up?"

Eden shifted, trying to get her boots untangled from her skirts. She reached up to Hart's gloved hand.

"You're not going to pull me in there with you?" he asked, a half-smile forming on his handsome face.

"I should. It would serve you right."

"I *am* sorry, you know. For everything."

So he regretted The Kiss. She could not. She placed her hand in his, feeling the comforting warmth of his palm. He tried to pull her free with one strong yank, but one of her feet was sunk to her ankle.

Eden wiggled it in vain, allowing more cold mud to seep between her toes. "I believe my boot is stuck."

"Can you remove it?"

Eden bent over, trying to unfasten the mud-covered buttons with numb fingers. The hems of her dress and cloak were so soaked and heavy with slime she fell again.

"Oh, dear." Not really the words she wanted to say. She had never felt so clumsy in her life.

"I believe you'll have more success if you take off your cape."

Eden knew he was right. It was not as though it were keeping her warm anyway, just weighing her down and holding in the chill that was permeating her core. Once she was free of the cape, she remained seated on it and played with her boot buttons. She opened enough of them so she could slide her foot out.

"There. Stand up and lean over the bank with your arms outstretched."

After several ungainly attempts, she did as asked. Eden felt his hands under her armpits, pinching. She certainly wasn't heavy, but the position was awkward. He gave a great tug and dragged her over the hump, then helped her to her feet.

Her cape and one foot-friendly old boot were lost to her forever. Eden looked down. The front of her dress was crusted in slime and debris.

"Oh, dear," she repeated.

Hart was removing his greatcoat, which was splattered with mud but nowhere near as disreputable as her dress. He held it between them like a curtain, closing his eyes.

"Take off your dress and put this on. Hurry. The sooner we get back to the Hall, the sooner you can set yourself to rights."

He must be joking. He expected her to remove her dress in the middle of all outdoors? She examined the sodden material that enveloped her, clinging to every curve. The stench of the ditch water assaulted her nostrils. Perhaps he was right. She could barely stand to breathe the noxious aroma herself, and he surely didn't want to. She hastily untied her dress and dropped it on the ground. Even her shift and petticoats were damp in places. She shivered and wrapped the greatcoat around her in gratitude.

His eyes narrowed. "You're quite blue."

"I *am* cold," she acknowledged. Suddenly she was in his arms again as he rubbed her roughly to warm her up. It was not at all sexual. She was reminded of the first time she saw him, patting the old dogs that had come out to greet him the day he arrived. She began to understand why they now followed him everywhere.

She thought if a stranger had chanced upon them in the road, he would have remarked that he had seen two lovers in a shocking state of undress, their wet hair plastered to their heads, their bodies melting into each other in the mist-shrouded lane. The girl's eyes were half-closed, a look of pure contentment on her face. The tall gentleman was a little more difficult to read. His face showed a combination of pain and pleasure. But when he bent to kiss her, his intentions were so clear any decent man of Christian piety would have been forced to avert his gaze and continue his journey.

* * *

He needed to get her out of the rain. He needed to stop kissing her. He needed her.

Hart had allowed his lust to overtake his judgment once again. He was quite helpless to resist. Her lips beneath his were at first tentative, shy. His urgent tongue sought the sweet haven of her mouth and soon was layered and parrying with her own. A sigh of surrender escaped her, encouraging his hands to sweep beneath her borrowed cape to the rim of her wet bodice. Her marbled nipples met his gloved fingers. He had to feel her, skin to skin. He wondered what she would do as he released his hold and stripped himself of his gloves, dropping them to the mud. But his lips still claimed her, and she pulled on his jacket to bring him closer. An arc of searing heat jolted from his chest to his groin. His hands returned to her breasts, freeing them from muslin and linen. She was cold as ice, yet brought his fingertips to flame.

He lowered his mouth to suckle at one pale breast. To bring her warmth. To bring the fire of his body to hers. She cried out as he scorched her with his kiss. He felt her stumble beneath his hands as she shivered from cold and desire, and he realized that in one more minute they'd be rutting in the road, oblivious to the weather.

Or his conscience.

He pushed his practical, sensible thoughts away and drew her nipple farther into his mouth, the pebbled tip trapped between his teeth and tongue. Her fingers threaded through his hair as her breathing became ragged. Glancing up at her, he saw her eyes closed, her lips parted in the smallest of smiles. Suddenly he wanted to widen that smile, make her lose herself utterly under his touch.

He dropped his hand to her belly.

"Oh, no. Don't."

She said it with so little conviction. And apparently he had lost his as well somewhere back along the road. In moments she was bunching her petticoats between them. She wore no drawers, and his fingers buried themselves in her folds. She was hot and wet and felt like heaven itself. What would he give to replace his fingers with his cock? He was afraid the price would be too high. He tilted her toward him as he licked and suckled at her swollen lips, held her close against him, skimmed her bud with his thumb until her honey burst forth on his hands. Her responsiveness shattered him. It had taken so little effort or time to bring her to completion. She had come so quickly, almost *too* quickly, as though she'd been Sleeping Beauty waiting to awaken just for him. He knew that wasn't true. A woman like that—

A woman like that was not for him. Could never be for him. He wrapped his arms around her and held her as she shook.

"We've got to get back," he ground out as he finally broke away. His arms felt unbearably empty when he let her go.

*   *   *

Eden nodded. Of course they did. She was drenched and half-frozen and hysterically happy. She allowed him to place her on his horse, a monstrously tall beast that had waited patiently while his master ravished her.

And she was ravished. Totally enraptured. Her lips and breasts were swollen with kisses, her center weeping. She had barely remained on her feet as he swept into her, surprised her, shocked her with his skill. He had sheltered her womanhood with his hand, making her feel safe. Cared for. She'd had no time for thoughts or regrets as his fingers and lips performed their magic. When she left tomorrow, she would not regret today.

Hart threw himself up behind her, clutching her so close she could feel the evidence of his arousal at her back. He spoke not a word for the ride ahead, but held her as though he suspected she might turn to mist herself.

When they arrived at the Hall to the dismay and exclamation of Juliet and the servants, she was surprised to see his shuttered face and hear his expurgated version of the events. She limped away on one boot, feeling like a fool.

But had she expected him to declare his intentions? Court her? Marry her? She was unfit for marriage, unfit to be anything but a casual dalliance on the road. His uncle had seen to that.

After building an enormous fire in Eden's room, Mattie and Charlotte raced up and down the stairs with hot water, towels, Juliet's special French milled soap, tea with brandy and everything else they could think of to save their mistress from an ague. Eden was then ensconced in the steamy tub, more than a little tipsy. Her hair was still wet, but now it smelled of roses. She casually wrapped it in a loose turban, then leaned back.

Somewhere else in this house, Hart was being seen to. She wondered if he was in his own bath, stroking away his frustration. Her fingers slipped beneath the water and into her curls. She was still slick with need of him.

Perhaps if she could tell him the truth, the whole of it, he wouldn't hate her so.

She closed her eyes, allowing her own hand to substitute for Hart's. Imagining his tongue again, the grazing of his teeth, the hard length of him finding her wet for him. Of course she was wet, submersed in the porcelain tub, her nipples ruched, her pale skin marbled in the flicker of the fire. Light and shadow. Unexpected. Unequaled.

She pressed harder and felt the edge rise up to meet her. To be with a man she could respect, give herself to with no reservations or aversions. No coercion. She spiraled forward, catching her cry, pushed herself once again over the edge until she could bear no more pleasure for today.

When she opened her eyes, Hart stood before her, his hair still damp. He was wearing a clean shirt and breeches and an expression of severity. Behind him the panel to the hidden staircase stood open.

"Wh-what are you doing here?" Eden asked, sitting up abruptly and slopping water onto the rug. Realizing she was exposed to him, she slipped back down, covering her breasts.

"There's no point in hiding yourself. I have been standing here these past five minutes." His face was flushed, angry. "It wasn't enough before, was it? It will never be enough for a woman like you."

She'd heard nothing but her own mewls of pleasure. Her closed eyes had only seen an imaginary Hart, not the furious warrior who now looked at her with contempt. But with desire as well. He was fighting with himself, but Eden knew which side of him would win. "Why are you spying on me?"

"I wasn't quite sure where I'd end up when I found the passage," he drawled. "Believe me, I never expected to find myself in your room, watching you frig yourself."

It was Eden's turn for fury and embarrassment. "Go away!"

"Not until I've had my say. How convenient that there was a connecting stair from your room to my uncle's library. Odd to think no one bothered to tell me about it. That must have spared your family and the servants from finding out what you'd been up to."

Eden remembered when Ivor Hartford had told her to move from her old bedroom to this one. No longer would she be right next door to her sister. She could visit him without being detected. At first it had seemed like wicked fun, a kind of house party game. But the end result had been sleepless nights and tortured days.

"You don't understand," she began.

His face was all hard angles in the play of the flames. "I believe I do. Did you think to trap me, too? I won't marry you, any more than my uncle could have. You know the laws of consanguinity do you not? No man can marry his stepdaughter. The Church forbids it. So your plot was as pointless with him as it is with me. No matter how desolate and pathetic you appear. No matter how many times you kiss me."

"*You* have kissed *me*, you horrible man!" Eden reached for a towel to cover herself. But no. Let him see her. Let him see every inch of her. She climbed out of the tub and stood before the fire, dripping on the hearth, unwinding the towel from her hair.

"Do you like what you see, Lord Hartford? So did your uncle. From the age of eighteen I was his mistress. Or perhaps I should say he was my master." She gave a broken laugh. "You know of the Indian sexual arts, do you not? If you somehow have missed them in your world travels conquering England's enemies, there is a most informative book in your library devoted to obtaining power over women. Your uncle was very inventive and wished to replicate as many of its positions as possible." She dropped on all fours, her voice shaking, and exposed her buttocks to him. "If a man mounts a woman like a dog, holding her waist, and she twists around to make eye contact in submission, it is called the position of the dog. The names alone are very amusing. And if you cannot read, there are helpful illustrations."

"Stop this at once." His voice was sharp enough to quarry rock.

"Why? You believe you already know the truth. How can it hurt to hear it?" She combed her Medusa-like tangles with her fingers, ruffling up her thick, dark hair. "Your uncle loved my hair. He'd wrap it around his fist as I took his member in my mouth. If I didn't perform to his satisfaction, he'd pull it, sometimes slap my face. He could be quite cruel."

"For God's sake," Hart whispered. She was tormenting him, her words, her body such temptation that he could not understand. She was shameless and reckless and made him feel the same.

She dropped to her knees in front of him, tears streaming down her face. "Shall I show you what I did?" When Hart was silent, she reached for the placket of his breeches.

Hart felt frozen. Stricken with horror, and unwelcome desire. Her fury and her beauty blended into an intoxicating cocktail of sin. How simple it would be to let her do to him what she had done to his uncle before he sent her away. But Hart came to his senses before her hand touched his flesh.

"Get up. Get out," he barked. "When you get to London, go see Mrs. Brown. She employs whores like you. You should do very well."

Her eyes glittered, her mouth twisting in a ghastly smile. "But this is *my* room, Lord Hartford, at least until tomorrow. I earned it on my back and on my knees and bore the beatings. At least my sister died a virgin."

He couldn't listen to her ravings one second longer. He turned, slamming the door behind him.

She would hear the panicked thudding of his footsteps as he fled down the secret stairs. She would think she had driven him away in disgust, when in truth he really wanted to stay. *Coward.*

But if he gave in again, he would be no better than his uncle. Shivering with cold, he returned to the library and poured himself a brandy, then locked himself in the room. It would be a long night.

Hart did not know what had come over him this afternoon. He had felt impelled to taste her, touch her, put his mark upon her and drive the memory of his uncle from her body. Even as the freezing rain sliced down his collar, he had been alight with heat for her. He had nearly convinced himself he had been struck by a temporary madness. She was leaving tomorrow and good riddance. But watching her come apart again in her bath had made him want to cover her fingers with his own. To kiss her fluttering eyelids and lick the pearls of water from her breasts. To haul her out of the tub and sink into her. He'd been stiff with need all afternoon, and was harder now. What was happening to him? He had never behaved in such depraved fashion in the whole of his boring, virtuous life. To make love to her with his hands and mouth in the middle of the road—it was insanity. But the truth was, he'd simply had no choice. None.

Fate. It was his greatest fear—to follow the path of his uncle and father because there was no other available to him. He'd fought against it with all the fervor of a character in a Greek tragedy, but in the last act, the predictions always came true. How ironic if after a life of virtue he was brought to his knees by a woman whose name promised Paradise but who would lead him to Hell. He was as torn as if a French bayonet had ripped his soul. Somehow he had to piece himself back together. Put the past few days out of his mind. Find what was left of it.

Hart drank deep from his glass. He would challenge the gods and rewrite his ending. There was a first time for everything.

Chapter 7

CUMBRIA, NOVEMBER 1818

Juliet had whisked Eden and her maid away at first light three days ago. Hart felt enormous relief. What he and Eden had begun was so wrong on so many levels, it didn't bear thinking about. Despite his futile vow to push the unwelcome memories from his mind, he revisited each moment.

He had kissed her, not just once, but several times. Had done much more and yet not enough. Wanted what she had offered on her knees, tears coursing down her cheeks and tangling in her dark lashes, her intentions sinfully tempting before he had the sense to push her away. He had put a stop to a fate that would destroy them both.

She had come to him the morning that she left, covered from chin to boot in black. He had sat at his desk, stony-faced, while she stuttered out an apology and tried to explain whatever Byzantine relationship she'd shared with his uncle. He'd raised a dismissive hand almost at once to save them both from further embarrassment, then gone back to his account books. He would not soon forget the hopeless look in her dark eyes as she stood shifting from foot to foot. But he was right to send her away, if only for his own sanity.

He had actually wondered if he should stay in the country all winter in order to escape her in town, but he ultimately decided against that. He needed to find a wife. And Eden needed to be wed or employed before her history was revealed. Before he might be forced to wed her himself. If this job she spoke of did not materialize, Juliet could find some poor fool to take her even if she was still in mourning. God knows, the dowry he intended to provide should bring out every fortune hunter in England.

She was not for him. She had been his uncle's whore. He'd burned the proof, but he had it from her own lips. In unvarnished detail she'd told him of the years she'd spent with the man, each detail more shocking than the last. She'd seemed proud, too, despite her tears. When she tried to win him with her luscious mouth, his temptation had known no bounds.

Enough. He gathered up bills and papers to take back to town with him. Improbably he now had a "man of affairs" in London to see to the petty details of his newly idle life. Mr. Calvert was a clever young man, but Hart would feel useless if he left everything up to Calvert. After more than a decade spent in the army, Hart could never get used to being a gentleman of total leisure. Calvert had been with his uncle for a year and had been given complete reign over everything in London, since Ivor was evidently too busy in the country fornicating with his stepdaughter.

Hart would wait here a few more days, then return to London. Heaven forbid he encountered Eden on the road until he could make himself think clearly. What had she meant by that last hysterical outburst?

Hart toyed with the ring of keys that his uncle had left in the desk drawer. He had no idea what they opened, but hopefully Collins would know. It was past time he gathered up whatever valuables Ivor had and disposed of them. One of the first things to go would be the hellish "library." More than half the books were beyond the pale. He knew because he had gone through each one, assuring himself that there were no remaining pictures of Eden to reveal what had transpired at Hartford Hall. He wondered how young Calvert would relish the prospect of finding a new owner for the volumes, for that was certainly something Hart had no interest in doing himself. He'd thought of burning them, but after going through the ledgers, he knew he'd be immolating hundreds of pounds' worth of perversion.

Ringing for Collins, he poured himself another glass of port and stared into the fire. The house was quiet, something Hart was not used to. For years he'd been surrounded by the noise of men and war, animals and machinery. Until the other day, his aunt had flitted about the hall, laughing and teasing, trying to cheer Eden up. He could even imagine Eden's melodious voice responding.

Collins entered the shadowed room. "Shall I remove your dinner tray, my lord?"

"Yes, in a minute. Do tell Mrs. Burrell it was excellent, as usual. But that is not why I called for you." Hart reached into his pocket and held out the keys. "Can you tell me what these unlock? I'd like to make sure I inspect everything before I leave."

The old butler fished a pair of spectacles from his coat and examined the ring. "These two are to the wine cellars, which you've already seen."

Hart nodded. His uncle's cellars were on a par with his books. Only the finest vintage had been purchased.

"I believe this one is for the box on the dresser in Lord Hartford's bedroom. Kempton would know, but he's left us." Hopefully Ivor's valet was now miles and miles away. Collins knew Eden had given him the contents of the box and most of her savings. At her direction he had packed a small trunk of valuables for the man before he sent him off with a ridiculously false glowing reference.

"This key unlocks the safe in the wall." Collins walked across the room, fiddled with the hinge on a picture, and exposed a good-sized square cut into in the paneling. It was intended to be secret, hidden behind the boring pastoral painting of sheep. But not much got by Collins, including the clandestine staircase and the very inappropriate way his late master used Miss Eden.

He still suffered some remorse for not stepping in. He rationalized he had been protecting his daughter Charlotte, who for a frightening while had garnered the baron's attention. He'd done the best he could. He suspected if he'd known all the actual details of the relationship, he might have had an apoplexy, or consulted with Mrs. Washburn and Mrs. Burrell on which herbs might be used to hasten the baron's end. The total reality was still Eden's secret, but what he thought was bad enough.

God only knew what the reprobate had in his safe, and Collins didn't want to be present when the new Baron Hartford discovered whatever filth he might find. "If that will be all, sir." At Hart's assent, he carried the tray out of the library and down into the kitchens.

Mrs. Washburn, Mrs. Burrell, Charlotte and Billy, the new footman, were just sitting down to their meal. A place had been laid for Collins. After the hustle and bustle of the past few days, he thought the kitchens seemed a touch eerie. Almost too quiet. Hart's rough young soldiers had added some life to the Hall, and Charlotte in particular had had her head turned. She was also jealous that Mattie had been plucked away by Mrs. Cheverly to see the sights of London. Collins would do his best to smooth his daughter's feathers. The care of his young daughter was almost too much for a man his age, but he'd been unable to resist her mother. An old man's folly.

"More work for me," she was grumbling as he entered the staff dining hall.

"Don't be silly, Charlotte. Soon we'll have the house to ourselves again. The baron will be leaving within days," Collins said, placing a strip of linen across his paunch. "We'll close up most of the rooms and live like kings. And queens," he said, winking at his daughter.

"What's his nibs doing upstairs?" asked Billy, shoveling a wedge of mutton pie into his mouth.

"I'm sure I couldn't say," said Collins repressively. "He did ask me to tell you, Annie, that everything was excellent as usual."

His daughter was not the only one to have her head turned. Mrs. Burrell turned pink with pleasure. For all that she was a grandmother many times over, working for Stuart Hartford had made Mrs. Burrell as besotted as Charlotte.

"Please pass the carrots," said Collins, bringing her back to earth.

"Certainly, Charlie," she said, lifting the white ironstone bowl in her capable hands.

* * *

Hart wondered what treasure he'd find. A bag of guineas? Some diamond stickpins? A few naughty snuffboxes? All of the pertinent deeds and ledgers and shares were tucked away in the bank, with copies at Calvert's offices. The key fit smoothly into its lock with a satisfying click, and the wooden door popped open.

He felt a moment of disappointment. Instead of a pile of bank-notes, he found a single leather-bound book. Hart took it from its resting place and put it on the desk. It really was too dark to read in the cavernous library unless he lit another branch of candles. Deciding to bring it and his unfinished glass of port upstairs, he extinguished the lighting. Another one of his uncle's "valuable" books, no doubt. It might make for entertaining bedtime reading, and help dispel the sexual tension he was plagued with.

He'd sent his valet along with the women, so he prepared himself for bed without the hovering McBride's assistance. Turning the lamps up, he sat by the fire in his banyan and studied the spine. *The Education of a Young Lady of Doubtful Virtue.* So here was the *truly* valuable book. The bill for it had astonished him. He wondered if the illustrations were painted with gold leaf. It was not especially thick, so it would make quick reading, if in fact there were any words accompanying what were bound to be dirty pictures. His uncle's collection was probably the finest of its dubious kind.

The pages had already been cut, yet the book seemed quite new, hardly as dog-eared as some of the other volumes Hart had looked at. Somehow that gratified him. He didn't care to be reminded of what his uncle had probably been doing as he perused each one.

The frontispiece had the gryphon trademark and the book's title. The author was Lord H.

Hart got a sinking feeling in the pit of his stomach. And when he turned the page, his worst fears were confirmed.

This couldn't be. With clumsy fingers, he flipped though the book. There was only one model for the artist, yet many illustrations, each one progressively more graphic and tortuous than the previous picture. And she had stopped smiling long before the midpoint of the volume. His uncle had captured the hunted look of a woman, a girl really, who knew her choices were limited, none of them good.

Hart closed his eyes, but he still saw a collage of Eden's images, her beauty bare, her eyes vacant. This was what she had alluded to, and he had been too obtuse to understand.

He forced himself to return to the first page and began to read the words that Ivor had paid so much to have printed.

* * *

*T*hey *lay naked on a blanket under the hot sun. He had lapped wine from her belly and retrieved the strawberries he'd placed in her cunt.*

"You are red. And sticky." She laughed, placing a finger in the corner of his mouth. He had quickly suckled at her finger and watched the haze of her longing transform her playfulness into quite something else.

"Wash me, Puss."

She straddled him, her heavy breasts falling to his chest. Her pink tongue darted and she licked his lips, the place beneath his nose, his chin.

"Mmm. You taste delicious."

He raised a sandy eyebrow. "Are you still hungry?"

"Always." She looked at him shyly, then scooted down and took his manhood in her mouth. He lay back, watching the clouds scud across the sky.

He was bored. The little whore would do anything now. Yesterday he fucked her right behind the hedge, with her mother reading in an iron chair just yards away and the snicking sound of the gardener deadheading roses in the background. He was even getting careless with the necessary precautions. But then, it would not be too awkward or unwelcome if he got a child on her. His wife seemed useless in that arena. She could simply be persuaded to pretend her grandchild was her son. His stepdaughter would have no say in the matter if she knew what was good for her.

It was time to bring the girl to her next natural step. She was so eager. Like a puppy. It was hardly a challenge to get her to spread her legs, or her lips. He had not asked for her arse; he was far too finicky for that. Unpleasant memories of his own youthful subjugation had ruined that particular vice for good.

She was cheerful, obedient. She loved him, or thought she did. Perhaps it was the secrecy and shame that spurred her on. She really was a consummate little slut. The plain ones were always so grateful, although her body was better than most by far. Absently, he tangled his fingers in her hair.

Her mother was sickly and stupid. Once the girl had been broken to him, she seemed not to give her mother a thought. But it was so handy her having a younger sister. One mention of the child's name and the girl was putty in his hands.

*   *   *

*H*e had not come to her for two weeks. Avoided her eye at the dinner table. Returned her carefully worded notes unopened.

The girl would think she had displeased him. But how? She had done everything he asked. Everything. True to his word, he had taught her tricks she'd never dreamed existed, and she performed them to perfection. Held her jealous tongue when she caught him kissing her mother. Laughed as he teased her little sister. Loosened her hair, lowered her necklines, hovered outside the library door. He knew the ache between her thighs was driving her to distraction. She must be spending her nights in fevered dreams, twisting her body around in imaginary ecstasy.

She knocked at the library door, then turned the handle. It was locked.

"Who is it?"

"It is I, my lord. Puss."

"I'm afraid I'm busy."

"Please, my lord, I won't take up too much of your time."

He opened the door and looked at her with deliberate disdain.

"What have I done?" she cried. "Why won't you see me?"

His hand shot out and he pulled her into the library roughly. "Come in before someone overhears you."

He locked the door again behind her. She stood in the center of the room, head bowed, eyes downcast, a picture of misery. Perfect.

He sighed. "This has been wrong. We cannot continue. I've allowed you to seduce me. I'm being devoured alive with guilt. I deserve to be punished. Beaten."

"It's not your fault," she said, rushing to him. "Punish me. It's my wickedness that drove you to it. I am a whore. A slut." She looked around the room wildly, eyes settling on a riding crop that had been thrown on a chair. "Strike me, my lord, and then love me again. I cannot bear it!"

He shook his head. "I could not. You may have brought me to sin, but I cannot harm you."

She tore at her clothing, then knelt on the carpet, presenting her bare bottom. "I deserve it. I deserve everything you could ever think to do to me. Do it. Do it now."

In her distress she didn't see the gleam of satisfaction in his eyes. He picked up the crop and tossed it back and forth between his hands. "Very well. I can deny you nothing. You are my undoing."

He hit her five times with the crop. Not particularly hard. That would come later. She uttered not a cry, not a whimper. Brave, foolish girl. The welts rose against the pure white of her bum. Delicious.

"Oh, Puss, I am so sorry. Forgive me."

"Fuck me, please, my lord. I am going mad without you."

He entered her from behind, where he could enjoy the proof of her devotion. She was drenched from her first true taste of his domination. They came together in a furious rush; she relieved, he exultant.

* * *

She sat unusually still at the luncheon table. Her little sister and governess were present. Even her mother was there, pale and ethereally beautiful.

"Some wine, my darling?" he asked, signaling to the footman.

"Just a drop," his wife slurred. He knew she couldn't bear to eat, but never turned down the wine that continued her disconnection.

All this food. Course after course. He had outdone himself for the special celebration. His wife had forgotten the date.

He looked at the girl and smiled. He knew precisely why she looked like a statue. Before escorting her into the dining room, he'd inserted a dildo in her cunt and told her she must keep it within her at all costs. It wouldn't do to have the thing go rolling around the under the table. She was to exercise her vaginal muscles around it. Imagine that it was his cock inside her. If she was a good girl, after lunch, it would be.

He turned his attention to his stepdaughter.

"Yes, my lord?" she murmured.

"Some wine? It is your twentieth birthday, after all."

His present was uncomfortably lodged within her. How was she to learn if he didn't guide her? Wine would take some of the sting away if later on things went awry.

* * *

She was as light as a feather now, just a bag of bones. He untied her ankles, spreading her legs wide. He thrust three fingers roughly inside her.

"Wet. My God, what a whore you are." He grabbed his sketchbook and sat on the edge of the bed. "I shall want to remember this night, Puss. You look quite beautiful. Almost as beautiful as your mother." He pushed her knees up so she was exposed and fanned her hair out on the pillow, then raised her bound arms until they were over her head. He knew he didn't have to tie her to the bedpost. She would not move unless he instructed her to.

He was an excellent artist, but it seemed this evening he was dissatisfied with his efforts. Page after page fell to the floor. He stretched her legs so wide, he thought she'd crack open. The drool from the gag dripped relentlessly down her neck.

"Something is missing." He took the oil pencil and wrote on her stomach.

From her position, she could not see what he had done, but he told her.

* * *

*H*e had beaten her today. Spanked her, really. There was no point to her being melodramatic. He'd found the pessary inside her and pulled it out in fury. He'd turned her over his knee as he'd never done before and blistered her so hard with his own hand she wouldn't be able to sit comfortably for a week. He'd fucked her after. She couldn't possibly have mistaken it for lovemaking. But he knew she'd enjoyed it anyway. She'd begged him to stay the night but he laughed and said he was growing old. That perhaps she was too old for him as well. Now, her sister . . . her sister was a ripe morsel, enough to make a mature man feel like a lad again. She had thrown herself around his knees and cried. He'd let her pleasure him with her mouth but withdrew to splatter his semen on her body. She had wiped up the wet with her hands and licked them clean, then licked and sucked his cock until he hardened again.

* * *

*I*t was Sunday evening. She lay in his arms. She wore a new silver collar around her neck, just tight enough so that every time she swallowed she was aware that it was there. The exterior was brushed silver, but inside it had been engraved with her name. Not her given name, but her real one. It was the most beautiful gift he had ever given to her. He had forbidden her to remove it, not that she ever would.

"I may have to go to London for a few days. I don't suppose your sister could spare you," he said, wrapping a strand of her hair around his finger.

She shook her head. "But must you go? Cannot your man of business attend to whatever it is?"

He pinched a nipple. "Not this time. Will you miss me then?"

"Of course. You have never left me."

"I have a surprise. For you. But I must handle it personally."

Her hand went to her throat. "But I already have this beautiful necklace."

"Collar," he corrected.

She blushed. She knew its significance. He owned her. She was his property. Like one of his old dogs.

"I'll leave day after tomorrow. It's a pity I cannot take you with me. I would *like to show you off. There's a gentlemen's club I used to belong to which we'd both enjoy."*

"I thought ladies were not allowed in gentlemen's clubs."

"This club is different. And you are not a lady. You are my whore. You are slave to my master. There are others who share our proclivities. The discipline. Wouldn't you love to stand before a room full of men, wearing only my collar? All those pricks at attention?"

If it made him happy, she'd do it. It was not as though she had never been watched before. Lord Blanchard had visited a few times. But he had only observed, never participated, save for when he pinched her bottom and told her what a fine little doxy she was.

"I want only your prick, my lord."

"And so you shall have it, Puss."

* * *

Hart rubbed his eyes. He had been reading in fascinated dread for what seemed like hours. At first he had read only Ivor's smug words, but soon he pictured what was in Eden's mind as she endured one degradation after another.

Ivor was the ultimate unreliable narrator. Eden had not liked but had somehow endured what he had done to her. The passages were so graphic there were times when Hart simply had to stop, then skip forward. Reading each word had poured acid on his soul. What a pious fool he had been. Eden had been robbed of her innocence by a master of deception. A monster. The proof was in black-and-white, handsomely illustrated, and in his hands.

There was one thing remaining. Pasted to the back cover was a piece of parchment paper. He unfolded it carefully, recognizing his uncle's own elegant copperplate. It was dated on the day he died.

It described Ivor's thrill of holding this very book. He'd given it to Eden to read. Hart could feel her understanding and despair emanate from the evil of its pages.

He'd had a blinding headache all day. But his excitement was palpable. It had come. Finally. The months of waiting were over.

He untied the wrapping paper and string from the book. It was beautifully bound in red morocco; that had been a prerequisite. With trembling hands he tried to cut the pages, but he was simply too excited. He'd have to send for her.

Eden came in quietly, and without a word disrobed as she had been instructed to do always. She sewed all her clothes herself now, making them as easy to remove as possible. He was not pleased when she fumbled and delayed his pleasure. There was a drawer full of underthings for show, but she never bothered with them.

She sank to her knees and kissed the toe of his boot.

He nearly stopped her in his impatience, but she was too exquisite. The marks he'd left on her body never failed to move him. The image of her earnestly poring over their book in the nude was far too tempting.

"You may stand, Puss."

She rose to her feet unsteadily. He handed her the paper knife. He could see the flash of fear in her eyes.

"You misunderstand," he drawled. "I have a surprise for you. But first you must prepare it. You may sit."

She seated herself before the fire. She was cold. Her nipples were hard and her milk white skin was covered in goose bumps and long blue bruises. She made quick work of her task. The volume was not thick but large.

She read the title out loud. The Education of a Young Lady of Doubtful Virtue. *She began to turn the pages.*

Her face flushed. She skimmed the book. She recognized herself, on her knees with his cock in her mouth, on her back, a knowing smile on her face. Her round bottom, striped from the crop. Bound and gagged. Pages and pages of their perverse pleasures.

He stood behind her, a quake in his deep voice. "It's not only the pictures, my dear, but I wrote the prose, too. This tells the story of our union. How I turned you from schoolgirl to slut. My very own little love slave. And how happy you are to discover your true nature and obey my every command."

"I don't understand."

"It's a private printing. The publisher didn't want to do it at first, the prig. But my money talked some sense into him. Cost me a fortune. We'll have to consider later how you'll thank me for immortalizing you. Here, read a bit."

She went back to the first page. She was seventeen here, clothed. He had noted she had finally filled out, and despite her plain face, he was determined to seduce her. He was bored with his dull wife, buried in the country, so he set little traps.

That was the year of her confusion. The next year was clearer. She had walked into those traps with her eyes wide open and her heart fluttering.

Her enslavement had all been planned to the smallest detail. The techniques he had taught her and their order. The increments of her subjugation. How he mastered her every aspect, even without a word. How she begged for him. How he collared her.

"Trained you like a good little bitch," the baron said, smirking, "and no one's the wiser. You're a loyal and faithful whore. Why, if I told you to suck off an elephant, you wouldn't think twice! A pity this can't be mass-printed. I'd make a killing. It's quite the best textbook on seduction and sexual slavery I've ever seen. Well, Puss, what have you to say?"

"Thank you, Lord Hartford."

"You'll have to do better than that, Puss. Words are all very well, but I want action. Pick something from the book for old times' sake."

She of course conceded, pointing to a picture of herself on her knees.

It excited him to see her utter submission. It had taken four long years, but she was his absolutely. He would come to her bed tonight. It was only Wednesday, but he wished to glove himself within her, watch her glow, feel her rise beneath him.

"Braid your hair tonight like a schoolgirl," he said.

Hart imagine his uncle looking at the book in the firelight for a long while. When the bastard was satisfied that everything within was to his specifications, he wrote this short addendum and affixed it to the back of the book.

Then locked it in his safe.

Hart knew he could never sleep. Rising from the chair, the book falling to his feet, he began flinging random belongings into his bag. Dawn could not be too far off. At the first shaft of light, he'd return to Eden and try to make everything right.

At the very last moment, he picked the book up from the carpet and placed it in his bag. He needed to pay a visit to Mr. Griffin of Gryphon Press. He knew now what Eden had meant when she said, "It was the only one." He just had to make sure for both their sakes. It was crystal clear to him now what his duty was. And for once, duty might twin with his desire.

Chapter 8

Wearing cotton gloves and a smock, Juliet was arranging hot-house flowers in enormous crystal vases on a canvas-covered table in her conservatory. She had been nattering on about getting Eden to help her, but Eden thought she might be ill from the cloying sweetness and begged off. The scent of earth and blooms was nearly overpowering. Juliet's home, while lovely, was a riot of odors and colors which Eden found overstimulating. She longed for the simplicity of her childhood parsonage.

They had been in town just two days, long enough for Eden to write again to Mrs. Stryker. She was hoping to hear from her this morning. But when the butler brought her a silver salver, there were two letters. Eden quickly pocketed yet another grubby note from Kempton. How could he know she was here unless he had been following her? She thought back to the stops they'd made along the way to London. Juliet Cheverly and her armed entourage were hard to miss. Eden may as well have paraded naked on a

white charger. She broke the seal on the other message and wanted
to cry.

"Why the long face?" Juliet put her shears down in concern.

"It's a message from Mrs. Stryker's housekeeper. It seems she's in
Italy for the winter."

"Capital! Now you shall have no excuse not to stay with me."

Oh, she had every excuse. Kempton could come for her, spoiling
any chance she had of respectable employment. If he had the book,
there was no escaping what she had allowed herself to become. And
Hart would arrive in town any day now. He would be angry to find
her still sponging off his aunt. He couldn't find her here. And more
important, Eden could not trust herself to see him again. Her dis-
play of long-pent-up emotion had terrified her and horrified him.
No doubt it was a consequence of being so starved for affection
most of her life.

No one had loved her but her father and sister. Even her brother
Eli had been too army-mad to act as brotherly as he should, and her
mother, to put it charitably, had been limited. Hart was impossible
to ignore—noble and charming and handsome. And so very far
above her. There was no point in fancying herself enamored with a
man who held her in utter contempt, even if his kiss was the most
deliciously wicked thing she'd ever tasted.

Hart had somehow achieved hopelessly heroic status in her
eyes. It wasn't only his looks, but his principles. Principles that
she had perverted time and time again. She could hardly blame
him for wanting to protect his family from the likes of her. But
his rejection did not dampen her reawakened desires, and had been
almost more hurtful than what she had endured with Ivor. How
lucky Hart was honorable and correct at all times—except, of
course, for that amazing aberration on the frozen, muddy road.

The very traits that so attracted her to Hart made it impossible for him to accept her.

It was easy for him to be good while it had been all too easy for her to be bad.

Perhaps her attempt to become respectable was futile in any case. Why should she offer herself up to domestic service when her true calling lay elsewhere?

What had Hart said? *When you get to London, go see Mrs. Brown. She employs whores like you. You should do very well.* Mrs. Brown. That was the name. A name so innocuous. So conventional. She smiled inwardly. Kempton would never think to look for her in such an establishment. It was almost too amusing. She would be hidden among the hidden, sinning among the sinners. How could he ruin her reputation when she ruined it herself? Eden wondered how she could find out how to contact this Mrs. Brown without giving herself away. Who in this household was apt to know the direction of a house of ill repute?

Ha. Juliet probably would. For all Hart's attempts to "protect" his aunt, Eden had found the woman to be quite astonishingly liberal. The journey to London had been an eye-opener, filled with titillating gossip. Juliet seemed to know everything about everybody, and was not one bit shy about sharing information.

"I'm grateful to you, really, but I must find employment."

"Why?" Juliet asked, resuming her snipping. Bits of greenery flew unheeded onto the brick floor of the conservatory. "I know Hart will offer you a handsome competence and a dowry besides once he gets his affairs in order. He was most particular that you and your sister be well settled, and now that she, poor lamb, is gone, it will be even more important to him. He's a very honorable man, you know, my nephew. Sometimes *too* honorable."

As Eden was all too well aware. "I know. It's just my stubborn pride. My papa always cautioned against it, but I seem unable to come to terms with it. Do you know of any employment agencies?"

"I always used Lytton's when I needed a new governess. Which, I'm sad to say, was a frequent occurrence when my boys were little. I suppose you might register there," Juliet said doubtfully.

Eden pretended to think. "I believe some of the servants at Hartford Hall talked about a Mrs. Brown's."

Juliet pealed in laughter. "Oh, my dear, *that* is not an employment agency."

"What is it then? One of the maids who left us said she was going there."

Juliet removed her work gloves, took Eden's hand and pulled her to the wicker sofa. "I should not speak of Mrs. Brown's to you. A young virgin. Well, youngish anyway," Juliet amended, her eyes twinkling, taking the sting out of the insult.

"I am not so innocent as I look, Juliet. How am I to make my way in London if I am perceived as a green girl?"

"I assure you, *no one* will dare speak to you of Mrs. Brown's. And I should not."

Damn. Now was not the time for Juliet to hold her tongue. "Please tell me. I cannot bear a mystery."

"Well . . ." Juliet moved closer and lowered her voice. "Mrs. Brown's is a sort of place where some gentlemen go to amuse themselves."

"Like Brooks's or White's?" Eden asked, hoping to keep a straight face.

"Not quite." Juliet sighed. "It is a pleasure house. Actually, I believe the correct name of the establishment is the Pantheon of Pleasure. I'm afraid, my dear, your maid went off to be a whore."

"No!" said Eden, feigning shock.

"It's true. I hear it is the most exclusive and expensive of places of that kind. Was your maid very pretty?"

Well, at least Hart had not totally insulted her. He thought she belonged in the best whorehouse in London, the wretch. "She was quite lovely. I cannot bear to think of her in such a situation. I must find her."

"Out of the question! No doubt it's much too late. She's probably very happy there, and, anyway, you could never visit such a house, even with a platoon of footmen in your wake."

"Well, no, of course not. But perhaps I could write to her. Do you know the address?"

Amazingly enough, Juliet did. She told Eden in a delaying morsel of gossip that one of her dearest friends had waited outside Mrs. Brown's very doors in a carriage for a full week spying upon her negligent spouse. He had not failed to turn up punctually each night as she sat grimly underneath her fur cloak, sipping a flask of hot tea laced with brandy for sustenance. They were now separated and Lady Katherine was enjoying a forbidden and very satisfactory fling of her own.

"Good for Lady Katherine, but where exactly is the place?" Eden asked, tamping her impatience.

"I believe it's just off Arlington Street. Quite an exclusive neighborhood. Mrs. Brown inherited the property upon her lover's death, much to the very great chagrin of her neighbors. But I've heard she is the absolute soul of discretion, as are her customers. There's never talk of drunken revelry on the street or any such nonsense. Of course I do not know the house number. But one of the footman will be sure to find it should you wish to send a note to this girl. They'll probably all fight over which one of them is to deliver the message just for a possible glimpse of a flock of fallen women. Are you certain you wish to get entangled in this business? There is absolutely no hope that your maid has remained untouched, you know."

"Quite sure. Just how far away is it?"

"Oh, not far at all. Part of its great success is its location, you know. Handy to the grandest homes and clubs. And if I know my footmen, they'll be sprinting all the faster so they might spend more time on Mrs. Brown's very tempting back doorstep."

"If you would give me the direction of Lytton's, I shall write to them as well."

"Eden, you've become very dear to me in the short time I've known you. Please don't do anything hasty. Can you not wait for Hart to return to town?"

Why? To be compromised by Kempton and his threats and endless demands? So Hart could cast her aside again? He'd already deemed her one of the fashionably impure. She may as well make it true. Resolved, she shook her head. "It's best I don't get too accustomed to all this luxury," she said, waving a white hand at the tropical splendor of the conservatory. "You know my mother was a farmer's daughter. I don't really belong here."

"Eden! You are as much a lady as I am. Your stepfather saw to it you were raised as a gentlewoman. You have all the accomplishments, do you not?"

You have no idea what I can do, Eden thought.

*   *   *

It was done. The notes, both of them, had gone with two strapping young footmen. Eden decided impulsively to cast her fate with whichever message received the first response. With her luck, she was not at all surprised to find the purple-sealed vellum come back within the hour. Mrs. Brown would be delighted to invite her for tea this very afternoon if it would be convenient.

Eden swallowed. She had not anticipated such an early encounter. But what was the point of putting it off? She might lose her nerve and find herself under Hart's baleful glare again. Or Kempton's body. Time was of the essence. The sooner she went, the sooner her life could begin. She tossed the note into the fire.

One of the footmen, Robert, had blushed and stammered but had given Eden the directions. How to dodge Mattie, though, was another affair. Juliet had an afternoon engagement, but Mattie took her duties guarding her mistress in the wicked city quite seriously. Eden told the maid she was exhausted—that much was true—and encouraged her to go out with one of Juliet's maids to the shops for some ribbon. Green ribbon. Just the color of new grass.

Mattie frowned. "You'll not be able to use it for a year, Miss Eden."

"I know, but I shall look at it and think of spring," Eden replied. Inspired, she described other frivolous necessities, just to ensure that Mattie would not return before she did. Pressing nearly the last of her coins into her maid's chubby hand, she went upstairs to "rest."

Eden examined herself in the pier glass in her pretty room. Her dress had once been light blue, but it had been dyed black three years ago for Eli's funeral. She didn't have time to change. Pinching her cheeks and chewing on her lips, she only succeeded in making herself look like a bedlamite. Well, she felt like one. Going to Mrs. Brown was perhaps the most foolish act she had ever committed, even worse than what Lord Hartford put her through, because she was making a fully conscious decision.

She was no longer a hesitant virgin flattered by the improper intentions of a consummate profligate.

She was no longer the naïve girl awash in first-wakened passion.

She was no longer the passive slave waiting for the word or the whip.

But she would be free forever of Kempton, for how could he hurt her when she would hurt herself?

She wagered she knew how to use her body with greater skill than most. And she knew she was capable of feeling. Too much feeling. She must never allow herself to fall under the spell of any one man again. Hart was as forbidden to her as a trip to the stars. Perhaps she could erase his lingering touch once and for all. She had spent her last night dreaming of his hands and his mouth on her body. Her last night imagining the feel of his browned skin against her own, each point of contact a lick of welcome flame. Her last night wondering how it would feel to have his cock inside her, gliding her to a glory she had never experienced with Ivor.

And she knew somehow that would be true. Hart would be as good in bed as she had been trained to be bad.

In one last desperate attempt to suit fashion, she pulled a strand of hair from her blameless coiffeur to coil to her shoulder. Shrugging into her black velvet cape, she covered her head and made her way down the back stairs and into the garden. She unlatched the gate and turned toward Arlington Street.

The dampness of the day prompted her to walk quickly, and by the time she arrived at the imposing mansion, she was flushed and anxious. Squaring her shoulders, she marched up the marble front steps. Before her gloved hand could touch the brass knocker, the butler opened the door.

"Miss Emery?"

"Yes. That's right." For a moment she wished she had given a false name.

"Right this way, miss. Madam is expecting you."

He led her through a maze of connected rooms, stairs and cor-
ridors, all fortunately empty at this time of day. When they reached
a carved oak door, the butler relieved her of her cape.

"Miss Emery is here, madam," he said.

Eden entered, schooling her features. Whatever she had expected, this was not it.

* * *

Mrs. Brown examined the girl who stood stiffly before her in
her private parlor.

Well, she was hardly a girl. Miss Emery was not in the first
blush of youth, nor had she made any effort to appear so. She wore
an unbecoming gown which had obviously been dyed black and was
years out of date. Her hair was pinned neatly into a coronet. One
errant strand rested upon her shoulder, its crimp loosening with
weight. If this was Miss Emery's attempt at appearing seductive, it
fell sadly flat.

Mrs. Brown was an astute businesswoman, and Miss Emery did
not appear to have much to recommend her for that business at the
moment. But Mrs. Brown had been intrigued by the letter, with its
neat penmanship, and was in desperate need of another girl just at
the moment. No one so far had been quite right for the next Flora.
She relaxed back in her cream-striped chair. Everything in her parlor was pale and understated, the better to showcase its mistress.
Mrs. Brown's own silvery hair and white, revealing clothing shone
like sparkling beacons of elegant sin.

"Do sit, Miss Emery. May I offer you some tea, or perhaps
ratafia?"

"No, thank you." Eden eased herself onto a straight-back gilt

chair, the most uncomfortable piece of furniture in this unexpect-
edly serene space. The rooms she had been led through had prepared her for quite another vision, although nothing at Mrs. Brown's
was vulgar. Quite the contrary. The public rooms had been opulent
without being ostentatious, the lewd pictures on the walls depicted
a wide variety of the pleasures of the flesh, but the paintings were ex-
ecuted with some delicacy and skill. Mrs. Brown herself was dressed
in the first stare of fashion, although her dress was more suitable for
a Cyprian's ball than a daytime tea party. And she was exquisitely
beautiful, her throat encircled with a simple strand of diamonds
that were probably not paste.

"What has brought you to me, Miss Emery? Or may I call you
Eden? Such a lovely name. It would be a shame to lose it." All
Mrs. Brown's girls were named for Greek and Roman goddesses
of mythology. Mrs. Brown herself was Iris, goddess of the rainbow, a messenger of the gods. She had spread her message far and
wide throughout the ton, enabling her to live quite comfortably.
The fact that Iris was alleged to be a virgin goddess had always
amused her.

Eden swallowed, then raised her chin. "A gentleman of my acquaintance told me this was where I belonged."

"Indeed." Mrs. Brown had not expected such a brazen declaration. It was hard to imagine this young woman in the throes of
passion, although it was clear even draped in black, she had a very
creditable bosom. The rest of her needed some fattening up, though.
There was none of the tease or coquette to her. Most men preferred
a bit of froth. Eden Emery exuded an unsettling stern rectitude.

"Just how many lovers have you had, Miss Emery?" she asked
with a smile.

Hart's kisses and caresses didn't really count. "Just one, ma'am, but I am experienced. Well trained. There is nothing that shocks me."

"And who was your teacher, my dear? I confess you do not look the voluptuary."

"My stepfather. The late Baron Hartford. I'm sure you are aware of his reputation. It was well deserved."

Mrs. Brown could not stifle a gasp. The current Baron Hartford was known to her now, as his uncle and father had been before him. Of course young Hartford was nothing like them. He had become a fixture for a few weeks before he left to settle his uncle's estate. He had a healthy, quite normal sexual appetite. The same could not have been said of his relatives.

"Forgive me, Miss Emery, for doubting you. I was a little acquainted with the late baron. This house has been in operation for some time, although I am not quite as old as you may surmise. My hair was every bit as silver when I was twenty as it is now. Some people thought me a bit of a witch, and I tried not to disappoint them." She laughed, giving lines to her smooth face for the first time. "Ivor was a frequent habitué before he left town for good so many years ago. I was glad to see him go. A matter of self-preservation, as I'm sure you're aware."

Eden knew very little of her stepfather's London life. She could only imagine. She inclined her head in feigned understanding and let Mrs. Brown continue.

"I am most particular with my girls. Many young women come to me in hopes of establishing a better life for themselves. Some are without much learning or prospects, victims of abuse far worse than even you may have endured. They have not had your educational advantages. Usually considerable effort is made to acquaint them with their duties. Some polish, a sort of finishing school, if you will."

She poured herself another cup of tea and to Eden's astonishment dropped in five lumps of sugar. "In your case, perhaps such schooling is superfluous. I'm not without influence. If you are seeking a protector, I'm sure something could be arranged."

Eden shook her head. "I should get bored submitting to the will of one man. 'Variety's the very spice of life, that gives it all its flavor.'"

"Cowper, although I doubt he had this profession in mind," murmured Mrs. Brown. "You hardly look the submissive sort, but then one can never tell. Surely your late stepfather made some provision for you. Especially considering—"

"He did not. And I shall not take the charity of the Hartford family. I wish to be completely independent."

Mrs. Brown sipped her tea, appearing to choose her words carefully. "A whore is hardly independent, Miss Emery. You must answer to the needs and desires of the gentlemen you service without flinching or distaste. Indeed, with unbridled enthusiasm," she added dryly. "I have a reputation of having a select clientele, yet invariably there is someone who may wish to bend the rules, as your Lord Hartford was wont to do." She leveled her silver gaze upon Eden.

"And you must answer to me. I'm known to be fair, but I am strict. It's true I've had a few gently bred girls in my house at one time or another, but frankly, you seem better suited as a governess."

Eden flushed. "I realize my appearance is not pleasing. But I had thought you might help me with that."

"Tsk. It is not so bad as all that. Indeed, you are attractive in your own way. Miss Emery, are you quite certain this is the life you should choose? Are there no friends or relatives you might seek? I am sure the new Baron Hartford would be horrified to know you're in my sitting room begging for employment."

"It was he who sent me here," Eden said, her voice barely more than a whisper.

Ah, there it was. The answer to the knotted problem of Miss Emery's grim determination to prostitute herself. There had been a lover's tiff. The girl was out to thumb her nose and every other part of her body at the baron. Could it be she had no knowledge that the man had become a patron here? Or perhaps Eden was a sly minx who hoped to encounter and win Hartford back under Mrs. Brown's very own roof.

It was clear she needed to know more about the relationship between these young people. Perhaps she could facilitate a reunion of sorts. For all her apparent wickedness, Mrs. Brown was quite a romantic at heart. But a shrewd businesswoman first, and she would see how Eden's fall would benefit her own coffers.

"Take down your hair, Miss Emery."

"Pardon?"

"I wish to see what I have to work with. Remove your dress as well." Seeing Eden's embarrassment, she admonished her. "If you're missish with me, how can I expect you to dance naked before some drunken young lord who wishes to share you with his best friend? You must lose some pride, Miss Emery. It will not serve you well in this profession."

Eden pulled the pins from her hair and slipped them into her reticule. Her dark hair fell to her waist. "I shall need assistance with the fastenings. Certainly I could not bring my maid to this interview."

Mrs. Brown laughed, then rose and obliged. "This dress is fit for the burn pile. I assume you have no appropriate clothes for your new experiment. You will be an expense to me."

She stepped back, noting the very plain chemise and stays Eden wore beneath her black gown. "Hmm. I believe our last Flora was your size, or close to. She left us a little while ago to become the particular friend of a certain peer. She was dark like you as well. The goddess of flowers, also known as Hebe or Chloris. The name Flora is so much prettier, however. How will that suit you?"

"First Cowper. Now mythology. I am surprised by your knowledge, Mrs. Brown."

"I would not have risen as high as I have if I were an empty-headed nitwit. Did you not know? All my girls assume a new name and identity when they come to me. My benefactor considered himself to be a scholar of the classics. It was his fancy to install Greek and Roman goddesses right here in the heart of town instead of Mt. Olympus or some looted temple. And drive his toplofty neighbors mad in the bargain," Mrs. Brown chuckled. "My girls are noted not only for their beauty and skills, but for their conversation as well. Some have even found their way into the highest social circles. Of course, their gentlemen are most generous to me. And a time or two, I've even arranged a marriage."

As Mrs. Brown spoke, she was pulling Eden's shift this way and that. Eden felt a blush creep from her barely covered chest to her cheeks. She had never been inspected so thoroughly except by her stepfather, and he was hardly this dispassionate. She was startled to feel the woman's fingers unlacing her corset.

"You won't be needing this unless some gentleman requests it. Raise your arms."

In seconds, Eden was naked save for her stockings. She was awash with gooseflesh and mortification.

"Too thin, but still lovely. Your breasts are really quite impressive. We shall teach you to use some cosmetics here"—Mrs. Brown's fingertips brushed Eden's pale nipples—"and, of course, on your face. Some kohl for your eyes. You'll be shaved below, of course, and those lips rouged, too." She laughed. "Some of our gentlemen are interested in our pleasure as well, and we wish to make it easy for them to grant it. You know of what I'm speaking, I presume?"

Eden nodded. Her stepfather delighted in her coming apart for him, although he knew how greatly she resisted. But when she was bound and exposed to him, resistance was futile.

She must be mad to set upon this course with Mrs. Brown. But she was a whore already. It was time to embrace her base nature. She had already fallen so far there was nowhere else to go.

Mrs. Brown went behind the Chinese screen and retrieved an embroidered silk wrapper. "Put this on, Miss Emery—Flora. We shouldn't want you to catch a chill."

Eden wondered if Mrs. Brown had lost count of how many other girls had been inspected and instructed to wear this flimsy robe. She turned to her side, exposing the fading marks across her back and buttocks.

"I see the late and unlamented Lord Hartford did not change during his sojourn in the country. But if you permit such use, there are plenty of men who would employ you, although I generally discourage such practices."

"It doesn't matter." Eden had knotted the belt tightly and held one hand over her exposed chest. False modesty personified. Here she stood in a bordello being inspected by a madam. She had better come to her senses quickly or this new position was doomed to failure for both of them. If she retained any maudlin hope that her life would ever be normal, that she'd have a loving husband and children, she needed only to remind herself of the existence of her stepfather's book and all that was within. There was no use crying over spilled milk and lost innocence. She had thrown her innocence away, flung it so far it was as distant as a glimmering star. Soon it would burn out, and there would be nothing left of Eden but a dark void. No, nothing really mattered anymore.

"I trust you'd like to see your room? The sooner we get you settled in, the sooner you may begin your lessons."

"You want me to start immediately?" She had imagined that she would return to Juliet's and then somehow disappear in the next few days. But it was probably better this way. She was wearing her mother's ruby bracelet and had left nothing of real value at Juliet's. She could send a brief message. There would be no fooling Mattie again.

"Why not?" Mrs. Brown smiled. "But do not think you will be entertaining customers this evening. We have a great deal of work ahead to make you ready."

"But I'm hardly a virgin," Eden said. "And I daresay I could teach *you* a thing or two."

"I should like to see you try. You were taught to please one man. You will need to learn how to please many. Some girls detach themselves and pretend, but I suspect you enjoy the sexual act or you would not have come to me. That's a most rare accomplishment for a woman. You will be a great success here if you can find pleasure as well as give it."

Eden twisted her hands. "I am unnatural."

"What nonsense! God has given you a great gift."

God! Eden shuddered. What sort of woman was she to take pleasure from being tied and abandoning herself to sin? She had felt so deliciously wicked at first, doing and loving everything Ivor asked of her. But ultimately he became bored by her submission and sought ever more cruel and callous games. By then she was in so deep there was no way out. She, the daughter of a clergyman, was a harlot, pure and simple. Her stepfather had recognized it and cultivated it. Hart had condemned her for it. But Mrs. Brown seemed to admire her, and here she would stay until she could burn Hart's touch from her memory.

She followed Mrs. Brown up the stairs to Flora's bower, an overblown room of flower-and-vine patterned wallpaper and the strong scent of attar of roses. As soon as they entered the chamber, Mrs. Brown had handed her a vial and told her she must use it. It was always Flora's signature scent, and no doubt Eden would get accustomed to it as she applied the oil to her every nook and cranny.

Seated on a chaise, Mrs. Brown was discussing the litany of sex acts in the contract as casually as if she were preparing an Oxford Street shopping list. With every weary nod of Eden's head in assent as Mrs. Brown quizzed her on her experience, the woman seemed more pleased.

"Within the week or sooner, you'll be ready join the Pantheon. And I'm delighted you are perfectly sanguine about performing fellatio on your gentlemen, too. That particular act is an acquired taste," Mrs. Brown said, smiling at her own little joke.

For Eden, it was business as usual, particularly after her mother died. There was no longer any chance of passing off a child she and Ivor might create as a sibling. She recalled her introduction to her stepfather's greatest pleasure.

"Puss." Lord Hartford stood in the doorway of her mother's sitting room. Eden had chosen to read there in the brightness of the afternoon sunshine. Her mother and sister had gone to the village. She had begged off, hoping her stepfather would seek her out. Willing him to. And here he was. She smiled up at him. "I will have need of you in a quarter of an hour in the library." He disappeared down the hall.

The warmth pooled in Eden's belly. The words of her book swam before her eyes.

She counted the minutes by the little timepiece on the mantel. When she stood to go downstairs, she felt the rush of liquid between her legs.

"I am wicked," she said to the empty room. "He is right."

Her stepfather was sitting negligently on the leather sofa, his legs spread. "Help me with my falls, Puss."

Ever obedient, Eden leaned over to unfasten his trousers. His cock sprang large and lusty from its confines.

"I always find," the baron drawled, "a bit of anticipation heightens the pleasure. Would you agree, Puss?" When Eden in her embarrassment failed to respond, he pulled her down. "On your knees, Puss. It's time for another lesson."

Eden knew at once what he wanted. The shelves of his library were now at her disposal. Indeed, the baron insisted she spend her free time acquainting herself with his collection. She licked her lips nervously.

"That won't do," he chuckled. "Your tongue belongs in quite another spot. Lap me from base to tip, cradling my balls in one hand while you hold my shaft in the other. Not too tight, mind, or you'll be punished."

Eden concentrated on her task. His taste, his scent, were somehow already imprinted upon her. When confronted with a glistening jewel of fluid at the tip, her tongue swirled and licked it without thought.

"Gad, you're a wonder" was all the baron said.

It was so natural to take him whole in her mouth. She sucked reflexively, letting him slide deeper into her throat. Her tongue worked him. It was effortless and strangely exhilarating. She felt her power over him, knew precisely when he was ready to spill his seed. She hesitated.

"Stop at your peril," he growled, holding her head still. "And swallow every drop."

The warm spurt splashed against the back of her throat. She struggled at first but obeyed. She'd always obey. The baron knew her weaknesses.

When he was done, he gathered her up in his lap. "Not a hair out of place," he teased. "Did you enjoy it?"

"Yes, my lord," Eden answered honestly.

"Let's see how much." Lord Hartford's hand disappeared under her skirts and into the slit of her drawers. "You are sopping, Puss. It seems a shame to waste all this." With a few hard strokes he brought her to completion and gave her his fingers to lick clean. "Run along now. I will come to you tomorrow night if you're a good girl. I've promised tonight to your mother." He grinned wickedly. "I shall be thinking of you as I perform my husbandly duties, Eden. Your mother pales in comparison. And is not half so biddable. She would never get on her knees for me. But you, my little slut, you delight me. I much prefer to fuck you."

He kissed her then. Eden was not so fond of his kisses as she was of the other things he did to her, but she liked them well enough. He tasted of stale brandy today. When he disengaged, he held her neck tightly and bit her, drawing blood. "Marked. Mine," he said in satisfaction. "What have you to say to me, Puss?"

"Thank you, Lord Hartford," Eden whispered.

"Louder, Puss, or I shall be cross."

"Thank you, sir."

"Who owns you, Puss?"

"You do, my lord."

"And you'd best not forget it. You may tell yourself you serve me to protect your sister, but we know differently, don't we?"

Eden swallowed her shame and confusion. "Yes, my lord."

She went upstairs to her bedroom and stared into her looking glass. The bruise on her neck could be covered with a scarf or a ribbon, but she could not erase the knowledge in her eyes. She was eighteen. Her stepfather was a mere five and forty. Although his twin brother had died recently, Hartford might live forever. She would be in his thrall for years to come, until he tired of her and turned to Jannah. As he surely would. Every day her little sister grew into her beauty. Her brother was of no help to her. Lord Hartford had promised to buy him a commission once he was done with school and Eli would disappear onto the Continent the first chance he got.

Eden could never go to her mother now. She doubted the woman could even un-

derstand in her addled state. *Eden had betrayed her with very little compunction. Her mother's husband had flattered her, excited her, enthralled her, and she had thoroughly succumbed, fallen so readily into his games of flirtation.*

It had started, she realized now, years ago. A fleeting touch here. A knowing look there. A breath behind her neck as he came upon her unawares. His lips brushing hers instead of her cheek as he bid her good morning. A whisper in her ear, the promise of pleasure. Of danger. She had been in a kind of trance while she waited nervously for him to make his move and come to her. As she knew he would. As she wanted him to. It had been months of torture, waiting. But he hadn't come to her until she had asked. No, begged. And now the torture was tenfold as she writhed beneath him, waited eagerly for his summons, bore his brand as though she were his slave. He had enflamed her senses and extinguished her conscience.

And she hadn't been able to do without him until that very last day. She started from her reverie as Mrs. Brown spoke to her.

"Tomorrow, my dear, we shall cease prattling and start performing. No, not with patrons just yet. I shall bring my three top girls as a sort of vetting committee. You will show us what you are capable of."

"You wish me to make love with other women?" She had seen pictures, of course.

"Not at present, although such activity has much to recommend it, as you shall no doubt learn in the future. Some of the girls find their pleasure solely from such diversion, although their gentlemen would never know that, so proficient are they in their pretense." She winked one smoky gray eye at Eden. "No, Athena, Ceres and Juno will observe you at your leisure. A whore is a bit of an actress, you know, and it's essential to perform to a gentleman's expectations. We shall provide you with some assistance, but how you choose to entertain yourself will be very informative." She rose from the chair, folding the signed contract of employment. "No doubt you are tired. It has been a day of much adjustment, and tomorrow will be challenging. I shall send Francie up with a tray. Perhaps some wine to relax you. Eat and drink every bit or I shall hear of it and be vexed with you. We will begin early in the morning with your toilette. Get some rest."

Eden was left alone in her vibrantly floral room. She crossed the carpet to the wardrobe, where several scandalously sheer and low-cut dresses hung, a garden of spring colors decorated with flowers and beads. There were no clothes in the empty drawers save a transparent nightgown, but an array of cosmetics was spread neatly on the dressing table. A silver-capped jar of familiar-looking sponges was tucked behind a vase of dusty paper flowers. Ivor had supplied her with the preventatives until he decided she might be more efficient than her mother in providing him an heir. She thanked God nightly, and daily, too, that she had escaped that fate. On impulse, Eden turned the door handle. She was locked in. Just as well. This was where she belonged.

Chapter 9

A different young maid knocked on Eden's door quite early. The rest of the house was hushed, most of its inhabitants having earned the privilege to sleep until noon. The maid, a pretty little slip of a girl with taffy-colored curls tumbling from her mobcap, set a heavily laden tray at Eden's bedside and opened the fringed curtains to let in the pale autumn light.

"Good morning, Miss Flora," she said, bobbing her head and bringing Eden a tissue-thin wrapper.

Breakfast in bed. What luxury. Eden could not remember a time when she had been so pampered, save when she had the croup as a little girl. It was she who often brought breakfast to her mother and sister in bed.

But this meal was a far cry from the hearty yet plain fare at Hartford Hall. The maid, who said her name was Josie, uncovered dishes of hothouse strawberries swimming in cream, a fluffy omelet studded with interesting flecks of green, brioche, brown toast with raisins, ham and two kinds of sausage. There was honey *and* jam, tea *and* coffee.

"Monsieur don't know what you like, Miss Flora. You've just to tell him and he'll fix it. Madam says you're to eat every bite."

"If I eat like this every morning, I'll not be able to squeeze into the clothes in the closet," laughed Eden. "Nor appeal to any gentleman."

"Oh, a man likes him some meat on a girl's bones. At least my da always said so. Madam says when I'm older and fill out a bit she'll take me on, give me a try. I keep pesterin' her. I'm rarin' to go, I am. All those pretty gowns and jewels," Josie said with a dreamy expression on her face.

Eden covered her dismay. Who was she to judge? It was difficult to imagine this girl thought being a whore was preferable to being a maid. But then, she thought ruefully, it was equally difficult to believe she herself had signed a contract with Madam yesterday when she could have been safe and bored as an elderly lady's companion.

"How old are you, Josie?"

"Thirteen, miss."

"You're just a child!" Eden said, nearly choking on a berry. "Surely too young for—"

"Oh, I ain't a virgin, miss. My da put me out on the streets when I was ten. Madam saw me one day and took me right home with her. She's got a regular little army of us now. She's taught us to read and everything. By the time I'm sixteen, she reckons I'll be ready to become a goddess. Until then I'm keepin' me eyes open and me mouth shut. A very superior establishment this is, miss." She stopped for a moment. "Madam says I've got to work on me el-elocution. I keep fergettin'. You sound cultured, you do. I wonder if you'd help me?"

"Of course." Eden had no idea where to begin such a lesson, but couldn't refuse the eager little maid.

"Eat up. Madam is sending Mr. Anton, the hairdresser what takes care of the girls, in to see you in half an hour. He'll fix your hair. You know." The girl grinned cheekily, pointing downward. "And he's ever so clever with the hair on your head, too. Then you'll have your bath."

Eden swallowed. She hadn't really expected a man to do the shaving, but then she should have. He could give her practice for presenting herself to her future patrons without embarrassment in compromising positions, she supposed. She wondered if he enjoyed the view as he worked on Mrs. Brown's girls. She herself had been quite ignorant as to what she looked like "down there" until her stepfather had done a series of drawings that left nothing to the imagination.

She had made considerable inroads on her breakfast, tidied herself up and was nervously pacing her bower when she heard the knock on her door. Expecting to see Josie, she was surprised to find Mrs. Brown herself, accompanied by a benign-looking middle-aged man who didn't seem to have a single strand of hair upon his shiny head. He carried a large satchel, doubtlessly filled with the instruments of his trade.

"Flora, may I introduce Mr. Anton? Tony, darling, here she is, our new Flora. Is she not just as lovely as I described?" Mrs. Brown was looking radiant herself in a gown shot through with silver threads and spangled with crystals. Eden was sure it could not be much past ten in the morning and wondered if Mrs. Brown was ever to be found in a plain gray day dress and apron. She thought not.

"Hmph." Mr. Anton sniffed and walked all around Eden, who

was feeling nearly naked in her wrapper. "I don't know, Iris," he said in a faintly accented voice. He looked positively mournful.

"Come, come. You'll scare the poor girl."

"Those eyebrows."

"They've already been plucked!" exclaimed Eden. And hellish it had been, although she allowed that Juliet had achieved remarkable results.

"So you say, but they are not to my standards." He stepped forward, weighing a length of her hair in his hand. "Not bad. The color, it is dull, though. Are you sure we do not do something?" he asked Mrs. Brown.

"I believe it will do. But it is too long."

Eden could not remember the last time she had trimmed her hair. The baron had liked it long, the better to control her with it.

"I shall think while I take care of the other. Lie down, Miss Flora. Iris, I shall need hot water and towels." He spied the remains of Eden's breakfast. "Have Josephine take this away and bring me some chocolate. Perhaps a croissant or two. Henri knows what I should like. The peach jam, not the marmalade."

"Tony fancies himself quite an artist and I indulge him. For a very moderate fee and all he can eat, he visits the house thrice weekly to attend to the needs of my girls." Mrs. Brown smiled and left as directed.

"I am in Iris's debt for so favorably establishing my niece with a young marquess," the barber confided, rummaging through his satchel. "And I bring her *ton* gossip from the more—shall we say—respectable women I beautify. We will share a sherry later before I leave to conceal Lady—" He stopped himself, the soul of discretion. "A certain duchess's bald spot with false hair and glue."

Eden climbed upon her bed and lay stiffly. After he had been presented with a bowl of water and a stack of pristine towels, Mr. Anton asked Eden to raise her nightgown.

"A jungle" was his verdict, as he created lather in a small bowl.

"I'm not certain why this is even necessary," complained Eden, eyeing with some aversion the scissors and deadly razor that the man had laid on her bed.

"Hygiene, Miss Flora. It is Madam's trademark. You will be clean and smooth. After your interlude with one gentleman, you may easily accommodate the next. Lie still please."

He pushed her legs apart and began to soap the area. He was brisk and professional, with nary a hint of desire. He might have been an ordinary barber attending to any reputable gentleman.

Eden closed her eyes and willed herself to relax. The scrape of the razor was the only sound in the room for a very long time.

"But what is this?" Mr. Anton cried.

"An—an accident."

"Iris must be consulted. It is too bad." He pulled down her nightgown and left her.

It had been no accident.

They sat at the dinner table, just the three of them. Her sister rambled on about the darling kittens in the stable. Eden poked a fillet of chicken around her plate. It would be removed uneaten, just as her last course had been.

"Pussies," the baron said, winking at her. "I like kittens. They are so much fun to teach."

"Don't," she mouthed, her color rising.

"If you catch them young enough," he continued, "they'll do anything you want. Even go against their natural inclinations. I daresay I could get one to bark like a dog!"

"Oh," her sister laughed. "My lord, what a tease you are!"

She stopped suddenly, as if she was ashamed. Just a few weeks ago their mother had died. She hurriedly swallowed some watered wine. "Edie, do say you will play the piano for us this evening. It would do my heart good to hear one of Mama's favorite songs."

"Your sister does not feel quite the thing, little one. I believe she needs to go to bed early tonight," replied the baron.

"You're ill? Why didn't you say something?" Jannah's beautiful face was full of concern. Eden could barely meet her eyes.

"It's nothing, love. I'm just tired. Perhaps Mattie will play cards with you." She rose from the table and went upstairs.

He entered her room some time later without knocking.

"Take that disgusting thing off."

"Yes, my lord." She unbuttoned the buttons that had taken her shaking fingers so long to do up.

"You know," he said, "no matter how much distaste you show me, I'll have you anyway. In fact, it only makes my victory the sweeter."

She said nothing.

"Cat got your tongue, Puss? Your little sister's eclipsing you daily. While you're shriveling up like an old prune, she's bursting like a ripe fig. What is she now, fourteen? Fifteen? Not much older than you when I married your mother and you set your cap for me. I resisted as long as I could, but you lured me to your bed. Oh, don't protest. You were so hot for me a bucket of cold water would not have doused your ardor."

"Do not touch her."

"I won't need to if you come to your senses. There's absolutely no point in you behaving like a skittish virgin. You are mine and have been these past three years." He advanced toward her, his pale blue eyes noting that he'd hit home.

"Why do you torture me so?" she asked desperately.

"Because you want me to. It's your nature. There is nothing you will not do, isn't that right, Puss?"

"Stop it."

"If I told you to fall to your knees, you'd do so. If I told you to kiss your own breast, you could easily manage. And have." He laughed shortly. "If I told you to lie still so I could carve my initials into your skin—"

In shock, she called him by his first name.

He slapped her across the face. "I have never given you leave to call me by my Christian name, Puss. Apologize."

"I am sorry, my lord," she whispered.

"I see my little idea has surprised you. But no one need know save you and I." He removed a small silver knife from his pocket. "Lie down."

"Please, my lord, I beg you—"

"The more you beg, the more determined I am."

She climbed on her bed, folding her hands protectively over her mons pubis.

"I see you have divined where I shall mark you. Don't worry. Your sin will be buried beneath your nether hair. In the unlikely event you ever give yourself to another man, he'll not even notice that I was there first. Must I tie you down, or will you submit?"

She closed her eyes and said nothing, did nothing. How lucky that I and A and H were simple straight lines. The pain was nothing to what she had permitted him in the past.

"There." He went to her washbasin and came back with a damp cloth, gently wiping the blood from her body. "That wasn't so bad, was it?"

"No, my lord," she said dutifully.

"There is no question now that you belong to me. You're a good girl." He patted her head in a fatherly way and made to leave.

She sat up on the bed. "Are you not staying?"

"Do you want me to, Puss?" He had probably never really intended to leave, but it always amused him to see her resolve crumble to dust.

"Oh, yes," she said.

She wouldn't find her own satisfaction, but that was unimportant. She was unimportant. He'd taught her that.

Eden's heart began to pound. Surely she wouldn't be turned away from this place, now that she'd finally made her decision? She sat up to try to see Ivor's initials, but was interrupted by the return of Mr. Anton and Mrs. Brown.

"Look. It is insupportable what that man has done to her," said Mr. Anton, a tremor in his voice.

"Don't take on so, Tony. She survived it, did she not? And he is mercifully dead now, quite beyond your disapprobation. Flora, my dear, how would you feel about having a design painted right there?" A cool fingertip touched the disfigurement. "A flower—a rose, perhaps, in henna. If it suits you, we might seek a permanent tattoo to cover up your little problem. Later Selene might show you the cunning little moon and clouds she has in just such a place. There was an unfortunate birthmark, you see."

Eden swallowed. "All right. But who will do it?"

"Why, Tony, of course! It was he who painted most of the lovely artwork displayed downstairs. One blossoming rose will be but a trifle to him."

The hairdresser smiled. "It is true. I studied art in Vienna. Madam is one of the few who have recognized my talents. We shall remove your underarm hair first, however, and deal with your coiffeur. And those wretched eyebrows. Iris can send someone to my lodgings to obtain my brushes and stains. We shall have a little fun, no? And Iris, the breakfast tray? I am so very peckish."

*   *   *

Eden had been transformed. Mr. Anton had cut her heavy dark hair to release some waves that fell about her shoulders. The image of a full-blown rose had been painted in henna on Eden's bare mons to conceal Ivor Hartford's marks. Her nipples and lips were rouged and her body dusted with golden powder. She was a glowing Flora, goddess of flowers and the season of spring.

And she had "proven" herself. Eden had been required to demonstrate her sexual techniques using a variety of props and positions. Completely nude, of course. Her eyes, now sloe-eyed with kohl, had closed as she unself-consciously masturbated before Mrs. Brown and three of the girls. And why not? She had done this so often for her stepfather, and for herself, it was perfectly natural. As she did so, this time she thought only of Hart, although her audience did a distracting running commentary on her facial expressions and the sounds she chose to accompany her exertions.

When she had exhausted herself and passed inspection, the women left her, save for Ceres. Mrs. Brown had been sufficiently impressed with Eden's—now Flora's—carnal skills. But there was one act between a man and a woman of which Eden had claimed ignorance, and that must be remedied with all due speed.

Eden examined the large marble "he's-at-home" the girl handed her. She ran a finger over an amazingly lifelike vein, cupping the balls in her other hand. The carver had textured the base with a simulation of fine hairs. "I believe it's quite impossible."

"Not at all," Ceres said cheerfully. "You'll find it feels ever so good up your arse if you put plenty of oil on it. You'll go off like a rocket if you touch yourself, I guarantee it."

"But why would a gentleman choose to place his member *there?*" She could not recollect any of Lord Hartford's books showing this particular activity. Perhaps it was not to his taste.

Ceres snorted. "They bugger each other in those fancy schools they go to. Sometimes they'll even want you to strap on a cock and ride *them*. The bum passage is much tighter, you know. Those that's got little rods prefer the feeling, and there's no worries they'll sire a bastard on a whore. It's my personal specialty, which is why Madam wanted me to instruct you. You're to practice on your own, then watch me tonight."

"Watch?" Eden asked faintly. She remembered the occasions she had performed for her stepfather's friend Lord Blanchard as he had watched, his face flushed and eyes glittering. She wasn't sure she would enjoy being on the other end of the equation.

"Oh, you won't be in the room with us, never fear. Lord Regan is a pervert but not in that way. There's a peephole in the cupboard. He'll never know you're there. And it's not a nasty dark closet, either. Madam keeps a comfortable chair there and all the champagne you can drink. Well," amended Ceres, "that's probably only for the subscribers. But the chair *is* nice. You can get right comfy and enjoy the show."

Ceres rose from the chaise longue, her cap of scandalously short red curls framing her piquant face. She wore what all the whores wore in their time off, a sheer peignoir that left nothing to the imagination. Mrs. Brown was a firm believer that all her girls should be ready to service a gentleman no matter the time of day. At the enormous membership fees she charged, a gentleman could expect to get his money's worth whenever it suited him.

Ceres had the slender body of a prepubescent boy. Her nonexistent breasts were noticeable only because of her large strawberry-hued nipples. Gentlemen who in truth preferred boys but were too high in the instep to acknowledge such a thing enjoyed her flat white bottom and flat white chest enormously.

"Use plenty of oil or unguent, mind, and take it slow. It's apt to be a trifle uncomfortable at first, but trust me, you'll enjoy it."

Eden held the cold marble in her hand. Surely she'd freeze within. Slowly she rubbed sweet-smelling rose oil on its surface, warming herself and the object to the task. No doubt there was a peephole somewhere in this room, too, and Mrs. Brown just waiting to see if she were obedient.

Eden lay on her side, willing herself to relax. She wondered if Hart had ever done such a thing, or even wanted too. Surely not. He would be too pure. Pouring oil into her hand, she rubbed her bottom. Slowly she rotated the tip of the dildo around her back passage, feeling a frisson of wickedness. It slipped in, inch by inch. She felt stretched, not so much in pain as deliciously from being full. Pushing gently, she felt her lubricated body absorb the invader quite easily until the root was buried within her up to its stone balls. She turned carefully on her back, hoping not to dislodge it.

She was completely depraved, there was not a doubt of it now. Her stepfather had known her nature long before she did. Remembering Ceres's advice, she rubbed her clitoris until her cries could have woken the dead Lord Hartford in Hell. She had discovered the one thing he hadn't taught her and swore that before the week was out, she'd not be satisfied with just a marble replica.

In the next room, Mrs. Brown had indeed watched her protégée come undone. The girl was the most purely sensual creature she'd ever encountered. She would drive any man happily to a conflagration. No wonder young Hartford had been frightened of her. No doubt she ignited the very nature he had sought so long to repress. The two of them would be explosive together, and Mrs. Brown began to plan for Flora's unveiling.

* * *

"That's it, lad, that's the way," said Lord Regan, a portly young earl who sat naked on a chair holding Ceres's head between his knees. She bobbed up and down obediently, purring, lapping.

His fingers twisted in ecstasy in her short curls, and Eden could see what role Ceres played this evening.

The girl had opened her door to the earl wearing skintight breeches and nothing else. Her torso had been powdered to diminish some of the brightness of her nipples, but her face was scrubbed clean of makeup. Eden had to acknowledge Ceres made a very fair boy. She was still wearing her pants, but Eden could see she would not be for long.

The earl grunted, his eyebrows drawn together as if he were struggling with a difficult mathematical problem.

Ceres paused in her ministrations. "Now, sir?" she asked, pitching her voice low.

At the sound of a second grunt, Ceres rose, turned her back and unfastened her pants. It wouldn't do to have Lord Regan notice she was missing his favorite requisite equipment and lose his will. He was here with a group of friends and appearances were everything.

Ceres had already oiled her back passage. Back to, she slid herself down on Regan's hard prick slowly until she rested in his lap. He was buried as deep within her ass as he could go. Eden watched Ceres's face slacken and her eyes go dark.

"Ah. God, but you're tight. Hot."

"God's got nothing to do with this, my lord. You feel so good. You fill me to the brim." As Ceres spoke, her voice husky, Regan's hands grasped her slender hips and drew her up, then down. Their dance was slow, deliberate. Ceres wrapped one arm behind her, holding the earl's head as he passed his own hand down her flat chest to her belly. To preserve his fiction he didn't stray any further south than her navel. When at last he spent himself, he cried, "William! William!" which bothered Ceres not at all. She merely turned in the direction of the peephole and gave Eden a wink.

Chapter 10

Mattie had dissolved once more into tears at Hart's blistering questioning. Juliet was doing her best to calm the girl and had become quite weepy herself.

"Hart, that's enough. It should be clear to you she knows nothing." Juliet had arrived home from a very pleasant card party to discover her house in an uproar. Hart in all his travel dirt had terrorized Eden's maid because Eden had gone missing.

"I'm sure she'll turn up, or get word to us. She's probably just visiting a friend. I admit, it's careless of her not to notify us—"

"It's been hours since anyone's seen her," he snapped.

"She asked me for ribbon," Mattie sobbed. "And a paper of pins. Black buttons. We had a lovely time walking the shops and stopped for a warm apple turnover. But we weren't gone long!"

"Mattie, dear, go wash your face and see if you can help Suzette do something. You're excused." Juliet shot Hart a quelling look.

"I know I've been a brute. There's a reason."

"There's always a reason, or you men think there is. I'm sure there's a perfectly good explanation." Surely Eden would not have been so foolish as to try to visit her wayward maid. Juliet didn't want to tell Hart that she had even discussed a bawdy house with the girl. "I wonder. She had written to Lytton's. The employment agency, you know. Perhaps she went there and has been hired."

"Oh, God. This is all my fault." Hart ran a hand through his disordered hair.

"Now, you know she expressed a desire to get a job. And the woman she was to work for, Mrs. Stoker—no, Stryker—is out of the country. Eden was quite distressed. I told her she could stay here as long as she liked—"

"Oh, but she couldn't. I'd forbidden her," Hart said bitterly.

"What do you mean? What have you done, Hart?"

"I don't have time to explain now. Where is this Lytton's?"

"I wager they'll be closed at this hour." She watched him fly down the stairs, then rang for her butler.

"Gerrard, could you please find out who took Miss Emery's letters? Send them up to me."

In a matter of minutes Robert and Steven were standing before her. They were brothers, both tall and well favored. Steven had the potential to rise to butler someday, Juliet thought. He had presence even now. Robert, on the other hand, was terribly shy and stuttered over the simplest sentences.

"I am wondering. Did Miss Emery receive replies from her letters?"

Robert nodded his head in the affirmative. He'd waited in Mrs. Brown's kitchen, which looked no different from the kitchen of any superior household he'd ever been in. There had not been an inch of ankle or bosom to be seen, just a French chef who had barked at a very scrawny kitchen boy and a cluster of maids who were too young to diddle. The room had smelled delicious, though, and he'd eaten three flaky rolls waiting.

Steven spoke up. "The business was shuttered for lunch when I got there. I left the note in the postbox."

"Did Miss Emery speak to either of you? About her plans, that is?"

Both men said no. Even if he could get his blasted tongue around the words, Robert was not about to tell his mistress he'd told Miss Eden how to get where he'd been. He'd be fired on the spot. And anyhow, she wouldn't have gone *there*. She was not that sort at all.

* * *

Hart came back within the hour. He needed a drink. Hell, he needed an entire bottle.

Eden was still gone. Mattie had told Juliet only her black cape and reticule were missing from her wardrobe. It was dark. She was a stranger in London. Almost anything could have happened to her.

At least she couldn't be ruined, Hart thought wryly. His uncle had already seen to that. He washed in the guest bedroom that had been prepared for him and readied himself for Juliet's onslaught.

He found her in her overly Egyptian drawing room, gazing like a sphinx.

"I thought we'd dispense with formality. I've ordered dinner to be sent in here."

"I'm not hungry."

"I am not either. It is difficult to think of one's stomach when one has lost one's houseguest, but my cook will be a crosspatch if all her efforts go to waste. You'd better tell me."

"It's not my story to tell." And it was far too sordid, he thought.

He had to protect Eden's reputation, even from his aunt, whose compassionate understanding might be strained by such depravity. "I made a mistake with Eden. I was hoping to rectify it."

"And you rode hell-for-leather to apologize to her."

"Yes. And to ask her to marry me."

"Marry!" The shock was evident on her face. "Her mother grew up on a farm, you know. She made a point of telling me."

"Do not tell me she's unsuitable. She has more bravery than I do." Hart poured himself a dram of whiskey and swallowed it in one gulp.

"I agree she's shown herself to be strong through all her losses, and she's a lovely girl, but that is no reason to offer marriage. You barely know her. You're a peer now. You have your family name to consider."

"Damn the name! Damn my family. They are not fit to wipe her boots. I want to spend the rest of my life making up for the hell she's been put through."

Juliet's blue eyes narrowed. "Have you compromised her?"

"I wish I had," Hart said bleakly. "I'd never have let her go."

"You cannot be thinking clearly."

"I'm as clear as I'll ever be. I must get married anyhow. Why not Eden?"

"*Why* Eden, Hart? You cannot claim to love her."

No, he could not. Whatever he felt, it was not what he thought love was meant to be. His aunt was right—he barely knew her, knew only what his uncle had done to her. He would lose whatever standing in society he had should the truth come out. All the years of resurrecting the Hartford name from the abyss—for what purpose? So he could follow his uncle's footsteps in the most literal of ways?

Maybe it was just as well Eden had disappeared. His need to

play savior might dissipate given time. But he didn't think he'd ever forget the taste and the feel of her. And he didn't want to.

* * *

Hart had not slept but for a few hours last night, and those hours had not been restful. Page after page of the book had invaded his dreams until he scarcely knew what was real and what was imagined. He wished he'd never seen his uncle's artwork, yet it compelled him in the most shameful way. No, he didn't want Eden to submit to him in his uncle's fashion, but he could not deny that he wanted her in any way he could have her.

Some could receive no pleasure unless they were humiliated. Was Eden such a woman? Did she need beatings and restraints to come? He thought not. She had melted in his arms that day in the rain, covering his hand with her artless response, as though she had been starving for his touch.

As he was now starving for hers. What had happened to him? He was most unlike himself. Where was the rational, responsible officer? The man who delayed gratification, bore hardship far worse than the absence of a woman he desired? He thought of the anxious machinations of her hands, her inability to look him in the eye, her stumbling over words. He should not want anyone so jittery. She was like a long-tailed cat in a room full of rocking chairs, waiting for the inevitable hurt. He understood now why she had been so ill at ease, and wondered how or if she could ever change.

There were still a few things he could do to help her, even if she had vanished. An early morning visit to Lytton's had resulted in failure. No one there had ever heard of Miss Eden Emery, nor had there been any young lady matching Hart's description who had asked about employment yesterday.

Hart had returned to his aunt's guest room. He went to his saddlebag and pulled out the dark red book. He would not open it again. He sent McBride for paper and twine. When his valet returned, Hart sent him home. They would not be spending another sleepless night under his aunt's roof. Hart wrapped the book, tying it a bit haphazardly since his hands were shaking. No doubt McBride could have done a better job, but this was something he had to do himself. With the package tucked under his arm, he then journeyed across town to the handsome offices of the Gryphon Press.

After a short wait, he was ushered into Mr. Griffin's chamber, a dark-paneled room with floor-to-ceiling bookshelves along one wall displaying the company's publications. Framed sepia illustrations from said books were hung at regular intervals, but there was no trace of anything remotely resembling Hart's uncle's artwork. Behind the far wall the actual business of printing could be heard and felt, a muted clacking and thrum of the presses. A coal stove set into a marble fireplace threw heat into the space, enough so Hart felt a sweat break out upon his brow. A gentleman of indeterminate years but evident prosperity rose from his desk to greet Hart, his fingertips stained a permanent gray.

Despite the fact he was the publisher, there were still some printing jobs Arthur Griffin had to do himself. He was very much afraid he knew what was under Lord Hartford's well-muscled arm. He extended a hand, but the young lord made no attempt to take it.

"Please be seated, then, Baron Hartford. I believe I know your intentions."

"I doubt it, or you'd not be sitting behind your desk but running for your life."

"Come now. You are not the first man to threaten me, nor will you be the last," Griffin said mildly. He'd not been successful in business as long as he had without being an astute judge of character. He was in no physical danger from Stuart Hartford, but he did expect a blistering set-down. And who could blame the chap? Having such a relative must have been a trial. Griffin attempted to soothe him.

"If you wonder if I'll be discreet, you can be assured I have been. I've been doing limited editions for the peerage for years and have not earned my reputation unjustly. No one shall learn of your uncle's peculiarities from me. The man is dead, and his secrets buried in the grave with him." He paused, examining his stained hands.

"I was not anxious to take on his commission, you know. Usually my most arduous task is to print a few vanity tracts of rubbishy poetry for some young blade to impress silly girls. Iambic pentameter and idiocy. Now and again, I've published an old man's diary that probably is more fictional than factual. Reproducing your uncle's artwork was most difficult, a task I handled personally. As per his request, the plates were destroyed and his drawings returned to him. And I was relieved to do so. A very unpleasant subject matter. Unpleasant for the young lady in particular, I should imagine."

Hart laid the book on the desk. "Then this is the only copy?"

"Indeed it is. And the bill for its production is still outstanding. I expect payment in full will follow this discussion. If you wish to receive a receipt, I'm sure my clerk can furnish one for you."

Hart gritted his teeth. "I'll see to it immediately. If I find you have lied to me—"

"I am a gentleman of my word," Griffin replied with some annoyance. "Really, young man, everyone's family has a few loose screws. Look at our poor king, may God and His Majesty forgive me. How a man chooses to amuse himself is his own business. Surely you knew of your uncle's reputation. The contents of this book should not have come as a complete surprise."

"My uncle and I were not close. Until recently, I was serving in the army." Wondering if he should risk it, Hart had to ask. "Did my uncle confide in you as to the identity of the young woman?"

"That he did not. I assume she was a servant. No decent woman would consent to such things. It may surprise you, my lord, but I merely set the type. I did not pay close enough attention to read every word. I did not *want* to read every word."

Hart allowed himself a brief hope. "Then no one else has seen this."

"Have I not just told you so? My pressmen and their apprentices are God-fearing souls. I should not wish to disturb their sensibilities." Griffin looked at his hands again, then placed one upon the wrapped parcel. "I have three sons at Oxford, my lord. A set of twins and their brother. They are very expensive. Their sisters even more so. Your uncle made it difficult to turn down this job. I did it with the utmost reluctance, but I did it. And I have no wish to see the results ever again." He pushed the book back toward Hart.

"Then we are in accord. Would you mind very much if I burned this in your office?"

Griffin's mouth twitched. "Not quite the fires of hell, but it will do. Be my guest."

Hart crossed the room and knelt before the stove.

"Would you care for a brandy while you wait? I'm sure you will feel more comfortable when you know it's nothing but ash. That may take some time."

"No, but thank you."

Hart wondered where Eden was, wondered if he'd ever see her

again to tell her she had nothing to fear. The future was a mystery, but the past was now in flames.

* * *

He was taking tea with his aunt when he really wanted to drown himself in the deepest bottle. She was fretting over yesterday, going over and over her interviews with Mattie and the footmen, and he almost missed the remark about the wayward maid.

"What did you say?" Hart asked, sitting straight up in his chair.

"Do listen. I know you think I am a chatterbox, but it gets tedious when one has to repeat oneself constantly. Eden wrote a letter to a runaway maid, a girl she believed to be residing at"— Juliet dropped her voice—"Mrs. Brown's. Robert took it. There was a reply, he said, but it wasn't with any of the things she left behind."

Hart was aghast. "You directed her to Mrs. Brown's?"

"Don't be absurd. I expressly forbid her to go. Eden was naturally anxious for the girl's welfare, that's all. She would not be such a fool as to go there herself. I told her she would be much too late to save the poor thing's virtue in any case. And even if she had tried to seek out the girl, Eden would certainly have come back home by now. It's not as though Iris Brown would think to make a protégée of her. Oh, Hart. What if she left to take some air and was kidnapped? I have not been able to sleep a wink."

Hart put the china cup down. "I have to go."

"Where are you going?"

"To Mrs. Brown's."

"Why? Eden can't possibly be there."

Hart wanted to hit something. If he had felt guilty before, it came down upon him now like a lightning bolt. He had sent Eden to Mrs. Brown every bit as much as if he'd escorted her there himself.

"I'll speak to the maid, Juliet. See if she knows anything."

"Oh." Juliet's face brightened. "Perhaps that is a good idea. Do let me know, won't you?"

By the time Hart reached the house off Arlington Street, he was disheveled and out of breath. The butler gave him a frosty glare but asked him if he had any particular goddess he wished to see. When Hart told him he wished an audience with Mrs. Brown herself, the butler left him cooling his heels on the parquet floor.

Eventually Hart was allowed to sit in a tiny green-papered room off the foyer. He imagined the butler took his break here between openings of the door. Mrs. Brown soon joined him, wearing a champagne lace dress and good-quality pearls. She curtseyed.

"Lord Hartford. I'm afraid you've come at a most awkward time. I can give you but five minutes." She had come from Flora and the young housemaids, arranging a schedule for their tutoring sessions. Josie had prevailed upon Flora's good nature, and Mrs. Brown's latest novice seemed most eager to instruct them. Flora's background as a gently reared young woman could not be overlooked and would work to the benefit of all. Five minutes was quite enough time to discern this man's intentions toward her newest goddess. Perhaps Flora had somehow even contacted him herself. Iris was not prepared to be cut out of any transaction between them.

"I am looking for a girl," he began.

She smiled at him coquettishly. "Then you certainly have come to the right place."

Hart was frowning, not one bit charmed. Iris thought another tack might be necessary. "No, you misunderstand. You may have someone in your employ that worked at Hartford Hall. I need to speak to her."

She shook her head. "I don't think so." Certainly what Flora had done there was not "work."

"She may have received a letter from my—my ward. Well, she's not precisely my ward, but a relation by marriage. She is of age, but I feel responsible for her, never more so than now." He met Iris's eyes.

His discomfort was acute. She kept her face passive.

"She's missing."

"I'm afraid I don't understand. Your ward is missing?"

"Yes. This whore may know where she is."

"I'm certain none of my goddesses ever were employed at your country estate, my lord. I should know if that were the case. I perform a very thorough interview before each girl is contracted here. You must be mistaken." She looked at her timepiece. "If that is all?"

"Please. Please ask them who received a letter. I need to find Miss Emery."

"It must be somewhat vexing to misplace a person, particularly one to whom you owe responsibility. What is this Miss Emery like?"

"She is above average in height. Too thin. Dark hair. Gray eyes."

Simple words, delivered with restraint, yet his passion was plain.

"I shall make inquiries, my lord. If I learn of anything, I will let you know." She rose.

Hart rose with her. He was dismissed. The woman had showed no recognition of Eden's name or description. There was nothing left to do but find Des at his club and get foxed to the gills.

* * *

Iris Brown stood outside Flora's door, listening to the girl's musical voice. She had very nearly convinced herself what to do, but wished to make absolutely sure. How fortuitous, then, to overhear Flora speak to the children about the man she desired but couldn't have.

"But, why, Miss Flora?" Francie asked. "You said he kissed you. Most gentlemen don't even bother with that. They just get down to business and poke it in."

Eden swallowed a laugh. "You little girls know much too much. Yes, he kissed me, but he didn't really want to."

"Pooh," Josie said. "How could he not? You're pretty and smart."

"Not smart enough," Eden said shortly. "He didn't like me. And now I'm here. Which is wonderful, yes? Because I can teach you and the other girls."

Oh, he likes you, all right, thought Mrs. Brown. She went to her parlor and penned the letter.

Chapter 11

When he finally lurched his way downstairs, the heavy vellum paper with the purple seal waited for him on a wooden tray in the hallway. He must have missed it last night in his stupor.

Purple! No one but a woman would use such a device, and no woman of his limited acquaintance would be sending him letters. For a split second he wondered if he held a missive from Eden, but she was not apt to use such a frivolous color.

He squinted at the seal. A tiny pantheon. Mrs. Brown! Perhaps her questions to her staff had provided answers. But maybe this was only an invitation to one of her special soirees. Hart laughed out loud. Obviously he was demented from worry and lack of sleep. And a hangover of classic proportions. He had only but to open the damn letter and all his questions would be answered.

When he did, all traces of laughter vanished. If he was too late, he'd kill Iris Brown with his bare hands.

* * *

Mrs. Brown entered in a swirl of silver skirts. "My Lord Hartford, how delightful it is to see you again, even at this very early hour. I trust we may accommodate you. How may I help you?"

She could see by the tension in his face he really was in immediate need of some sort of relief. She no longer saw to gentlemen herself, of course, except on the rarest of occasions. There was a rather elderly viscount who remembered her from her brief career on the stage, upon whom she bestowed some affection twice monthly for sentimental reasons. But, she thought, if she had to, she might be persuaded to break her usual rule.

However, she had a fair idea of why Stuart Hartford was in her private parlor, and it had nothing to do with the traditional pleasure he had previously sought at her establishment. For it was she who had sent for him, after a tiny bit of deliberation—although she had expected him last night, not to wake her from a very sound and well-deserved sleep at eight o'clock in the morning. She had kept him waiting a mere half hour. Her time treading the boards had made her quite the quick-change artist, but she wished to have full maquillage and every pewter curl in place before she faced his inevitable wrath.

"You said Eden was here," he ground out. "Apparently that fact escaped you yesterday afternoon."

"Lord Hartford, you were rather mysterious yesterday. I was uncertain whether divulging the young lady's whereabouts was prudent. Upon consideration, I changed my mind. Indeed, your Miss Emery is here. Although she's now known as Flora." She watched the utter despair wash over his face. Yes, she had done the right thing. She added gently, "She will make her debut in a few days."

"She will not!"

"Miss Emery has entered into a contract with me," she said smoothly. "Of her own free will, I do assure you. She has given me her services for a year. If you wish to see the document . . ." She made as if to go to her desk.

"I have no wish to see any damned document. You must release her from it. I'll pay you."

"Please sit down, Lord Hartford," she said, making herself comfortable upon the settee. "You quite terrify me, looming and glowering."

Hart looked reluctant, but he dropped to a chair and fidgeted with a cuff.

"I shall consider your offer, but it is Flora who must make the ultimate decision. If she does not want you as her protector, I shall not force her."

"I don't want to be her protector, damn it. I want to marry her."

"Then it is even more essential she agrees, is it not? I was under the impression you and she had a falling-out."

Hart's voice rasped. "What has she told you?"

"Only that you advised her to prostitute herself. Thank you for recommending my house. I expect her to be a great success." Perhaps she was going a bit too far, but Mrs. Brown was enjoying making the young baron squirm hugely. It was not as though he would ever seek her custom again after today, so she felt no need to flatter him. He'd be a fool of the first order to seek comfort anywhere but in the arms of his wife.

"I didn't understand. My uncle—"

"Yes, yes. While you were off winning wars, Ivor was busy losing his soul. You mustn't blame Flora."

"Eden."

"As you wish. Eden has alluded in only the barest way to what befell her. Do you know your uncle's history?"

"Bits and pieces." And he didn't really wish to know more. But he knew he was doomed to sit in this fairy-tale room with Iris Brown while she lectured him.

"He was always conventionally wicked, he and your father both. Then he noticed the fourteen-year-old daughter of his neighbor in Mayfair. They had connecting gardens, you see. By the time he was done with her, she had opened her legs for him and all his cronies at that club he belonged to. At his direction, of course. The girl was quite mad and would do anything he asked. Anything. There was a bastard child—a little girl, I believe—but I couldn't swear for a fact that she was Ivor's. The scandal was hushed up, and she was married off at sixteen to some rich old cit who was thrilled to get a viscount's daughter with an astronomical dowry. I'm afraid marriage has not mended her ways." She mentioned the name of one of the most notorious women on the fringes of the ton. "And she was certainly not the only girl who fell victim to him, just perhaps the most famous. I hear she still has your uncle's nude sketch of her in her boudoir."

Hart felt sick, not merely from last night's overindulgence. He remained silent, the drumming of Mrs. Brown's words enough noise for now.

"Your uncle bestowed his membership to my house upon your father after he was banished from town, you know. Charles was very informative, explaining all the prurient details of your uncle's disgrace. He seemed to think it was all a great lark, a bit of nonsense, though he was very happy to be in possession of my entry card. I was reluctant to admit him after recognizing what Ivor was capable of, but your father was not nearly as proficient in debauchery."

"Thank you, I suppose," Hart responded wryly. "While I find my family's history with the Pantheon fascinating, I have no wish to expand upon it. I know everything I need to, and I know Eden has to leave here."

"As I said, it must be up to her."

"No."

Mrs. Brown was startled by the violence of that one syllable.

Hart got up and slowly paced the room. "I'm afraid she won't leave. I don't believe she cares what happens anymore. She's—she's lost her way."

"And you truly think you know what path she should be on? You are very young to be so sure. My girls are extraordinarily happy here. I see to it personally."

Hart bit his tongue. He didn't think Mrs. Brown would appreciate his opinion of the possibility of happy whores. True, her goddesses were lovely and accomplished, but they could make no claim to be leading normal lives. But he was not here to argue morality. "Then why did you write me to tell me she was here?"

"I overheard Eden speaking to one of the maids after our interview. She has some feelings for you. I thought it might be a kindness for you to be her first gentleman."

"First and only. How much?"

Mrs. Brown named a figure.

She aimed high, an exorbitant amount really, but Hart would have met any price she decreed.

"I'll arrange for the funds to be transferred tomorrow. In the meantime, will she be safe here? It will take me a day or two to ready things for our marriage."

"I am a woman of my word. You will be in possession of the agreement, and her services will not be offered to any other gentleman until you collect her. I'll find something else to keep her busy. Is there anything in particular you would like her to be instructed in for your pleasure? She may as well avail herself of our expertise."

"Lord, no! She's had enough of that. She knows too much already."

"That makes you a very fortunate man, Lord Hartford. Don't discount her talents. It is not every new bride who can come to the marriage bed with such preparation. But you know," Mrs. Brown reflected, "I believe her sexual history was entirely devoid of love and affection. Your uncle was incapable of such feeling, and whatever she thought she felt at first came from the heart of a foolish child."

"Trust me, I know exactly how he manipulated her. I don't judge her."

"I should hope not. But you once did."

Hart flushed. "The most egregious misjudgment I ever made. I'll spend the rest of my life atoning for it." And it was not solely out of guilt and honor that he wanted to get Eden away from here, although they played a part. Hart wanted Eden as a woman, as a lover, not merely as a family responsibility. From the first time he held her, she had etched herself into his consciousness. There was no logical explanation for the driving force he felt to have her. He had fought against it long enough.

Mrs. Brown rose. "Very well then. We have a bargain." She extended a soft white hand to Hart and he shook it. "I shall wait to hear from you. I do hope I'm doing the right thing. Eden has suffered enough."

Hart could only nod in agreement.

* * *

Flora was unaccountably nervous. It wasn't as if what she was going to do was new. Cocks were cocks, some larger, some smaller, some even bent, the girls had said and laughed. They had made a grand party of her initiation night, spending much of the afternoon drinking a bit and teasing. There were thirteen girls altogether—a baker's dozen, laughed Athena, a tall brunette with a naughty mouth and the tiniest natural waist Flora had ever seen. Athena was excused partway through the festivities when a member of Parliament came to the door before the sun had even set.

Flora was assured that most of the gentlemen kept more regular hours, coming from their dinner parties or clubs somewhere after ten o'clock in the evening. Artemis preferred them foxed—"they're so much quicker that way"—so she could get back to her gothic novels or in bed with her lover Vesta if she were not busy.

But after a few days' observation, Flora knew that the girls were invariably busy all night, even until sunrise. Mrs. Brown encouraged stringent hygiene routines; even so, the girls were expected to service several customers a night, unless one paid a rather vast amount for the privilege of exclusiveness. Each girl had two evenings a week off from being on her back—or wherever a gentleman wanted her—one for her private amusement, the other to entertain the men waiting to get upstairs. Sexual congress was not required for the latter, but frequently there was a great deal of physical contact that stopped just short. The two girls on "parlor patrol" often had their hands full and their mouths busy with kissing and saucy conversation. Dinner and drinks were on offer for those who requested them. That left ten girls upstairs. Mrs. Brown kept a schedule that Wellington would have envied for its orderly routine. Each girl knew precisely what her duties were and where they would be performed.

Flora had taken the merest sip of champagne, but had given the girls free rein over her toilette. Although she had been taught how to enhance herself, she was relieved that other hands applied the sensual lines around her eyes and lips for her first night. Dressed in a sheer yellow robe embroidered with green ferns, she wore a crown of silk leaves and yellow roses in her wavy dark hair. Her body had once again been dusted with golden powder, her nipples and vulva dabbed with gold-flecked cream. When she looked in her bower mirror, she scarcely recognized herself.

There was no trace of bushy-browed Eden, no anxious girl waiting to feel the sting of the rod. In her place was Flora, a vision of honeyed seduction. The girls had assured her no man would be able to resist her, and Mrs. Brown had said she'd especially arranged her first gentleman for her as an exclusive. He would arrive at eleven, and Flora was expected to do just as he asked for the duration of the evening.

Eden had nodded. She was prepared to be obliging. For the first time in her life she was surrounded by gaiety and frivolity. She had *friends*. Mrs. Brown ran a well-ordered establishment. If a girl could not get along with her peers, if there was jealousy or pettiness, her contract was broken and she was free to seek other employment. The kitchen, staffed by two fussy French chefs, was open all day and night and stocked with tempting dishes fit for the regent's table itself. Exquisitely fashioned clothing, although more or less transparent, was provided at no cost. There were the latest books and newspapers to read in the upstairs sitting room, for Mrs. Brown prided herself on the intelligence of her girls.

Tonight would not be so bad. Eden could bear it. She might even enjoy herself. She wanted to. Needed to. It was essential she move beyond the hopeless dream of Hart. Beyond the orchestrated evil of his uncle. She had a year to drive both men far from her thoughts. After that—

Eden wondered if she would become a rich man's mistress. That seemed to be the goal of all the goddesses, to be set up in their own little houses with plenty of pin money. She'd heard tales of other girls' successes, how Mrs. Brown was ever so helpful in placing them in love nests scattered throughout the kingdom. Her generosity benefited her, too; her patrons expected variety, so it would not do to see the same girls year after year. Fortunately for Mrs. Brown, there were plenty of desperate young women who viewed employment at the Pantheon as preferable to starving or scrubbing floors.

Eden was not here because she was afraid of hunger or hard work. She was afraid of feeling. Of feeling anything. She was obviously a very poor judge of men. She had given her body to Ivor as a resentful, romantic child and look where that had led her. If she hadn't been so needy, she never would have believed one word from Ivor Hartford's lying lips. His nephew was vastly different—a good man, too good. Hart wouldn't lie, but would throw the ugly truth back at her. He unsettled her anyway and inflamed her skin.

But then he'd measured her and found her wanting.

She was as much a fool as she'd been at eighteen. It was time to detach. No one would get near her heart again. She would soon discover if her physical needs were met by the cream of English society. After the past several days' observations, she rather doubted it. But no matter. She had a roof over her head and other girls to ease her loneliness. She was beautiful for the first time in her life. She would simply take one night at a time.

*   *   *

Hart walked down the well-lit hallway, paying close attention to the carvings on each door. He was looking for a basket of flowers and fruit. Flora's bower. Beyond that door, Eden would be waiting for him.

What would she do when he entered her room? Would she smile in welcome or wish him to the devil? He had her contract in his pocket, so she was free, no matter what she did. He hoped she would consent to marry him, but if not, she need never submit to any man again.

He stood before the door and tapped softly. The cello voice within said, "Come."

The room was subtly lit by well-placed candles. Rose perfume filled the air. Reclining on a tufted chaise was the most exquisite harlot Hart had ever laid eyes on. Her eyes were downcast, but her sheer robe was parted to reveal pearlescent skin and the extraordinary adornment on her mons Venus. Her rouged lips and golden nipples promised endless satisfaction.

Without a word or a glance, the vision rose, then fell to her knees in supplication.

As he had last seen her. Only now, there were no tears, just a wicked, practiced little smile.

"Please get up, Eden."

Her eyes flew up to his face in shock, her mouth a silent *O*.

He extended his hand to her, but she refused it. To touch him was impossible, yet she must.

"Why have you come here, my lord?" she asked, wondering that her words could sound so even and dispassionate.

"I have come for you."

She shrugged. Such a casual gesture, meant to impart indifference. Within, her heart beat erratically. "Well, you have found me.

How may I pleasure you this evening, Lord Hartford? I recollect you were not in favor of fellatio on the last occasion we met. I am completely at your disposal. You need only ask and I shall be pleased to provide the solace you require."

Hart shut his eyes for a moment, as if he couldn't bear to see her, hear her, like this. It was time he faced her reality. She felt as though she had lived in this hellish room for years.

"Eden, please. We must talk."

"Very well. I am obliged to give a gentleman precisely what he wants. If all you want is conversation, I am sure I can manage it."

She rose with a grace and coolness she didn't feel and returned to the chaise. She had spent considerable time earlier arranging the folds of her robe just so. Now she was acutely aware that she might as well be naked. She noted that Hart didn't know where to look and was presently staring at the hideous wallpaper. Good. She hoped he was as uncomfortable as she was. The sooner he left, the sooner she could begin this new business. If he had paid Mrs. Brown so he could lecture her on her shortcomings, she supposed she'd just have to sit still and listen. She removed her silly crown and examined her painted nails.

He finally turned to her. She hoped he found her so desirable that he felt dumbstruck. Her mirror had told her there was no trace of the prideful, miserable young woman of Hartford Hall he'd last seen. She leaned back in relaxation so he would think he was with the most celebrated whore in London.

There was no place for him to sit but the bed and a spindly chair at the dressing table. He chose the bed, looking disadvantaged at once. "Come here."

She gave him a sultry smile, one she had perfected during the past days spent confined to her room. She could see its instantaneous effect. "I thought you merely wished to talk, my lord."

"I do. But I want you close."

She glided across the room. They'd taught her how to walk, a sensuous, effortless flow. She knew she radiated carnality, but she was not about to blush. Hart quickly pulled off the coverlet and wrapped her in it. She raised an eyebrow, but sat on the edge of the bed, waiting.

"I found the book."

Eden's heart skipped a beat. She didn't trust herself to speak, nor could she bear to listen to the disdainful diatribe that was sure to follow.

"I wanted you to know it's been destroyed. I've been assured it was indeed the only copy, so you have nothing to fear from it. Or me." He reached for a hand, but she slipped it beneath the blanket.

She straightened her spine. "When your uncle died, I stopped being fearful. I stopped feeling anything, really. But thank you for your effort."

"Words cannot express how I feel about what he did to you."

Eden nearly smiled. She'd somehow acquired a white knight. "Are you sure you read the whole of the book, my lord? I was every bit as guilty as he, right from the first."

"No! Don't think that. You were not the only girl he corrupted. He was evil."

Eden shook her head. "I have had years to think on this, Hart. I am not sure you can ever understand. I loved your uncle."

"No! A girlish infatuation—"

"Hear me out," she interrupted. "I was eighteen when I gave myself to him. And make no mistake, it was entirely voluntary. He did not rape me. I was as eager for him as he was for me. Many girls that age are married. I had—feelings. My mother was always ill and we couldn't go anywhere. I was angry at her. She didn't—she couldn't—" Eden sighed. "I was longing for something. I didn't even know what. Your uncle made my life bearable at first, exciting. I burned for him."

Hart shut his eyes. This was not what he wanted to hear, but she'd make him listen.

"It started conventionally enough, but then he tested me to see how far I'd go. He was not disappointed. I went far, Hart. Deeper than you can imagine. Or perhaps not. You've seen the book, after all. One thing led to another. If I could endure one thing, I could endure two. Or five. Or twenty-five. It's true he threatened me with reprisals against my sister, but I think now they were just empty words. He knew I needed to hear them so I would have no objection and do his bidding. They gave me an excuse to reveal my true nature."

"That isn't so."

"How do you know? We are barely acquainted. You've spurned me every chance you had after those two missteps. You were right to do so. I am not a normal woman, Hart. I don't think I ever will be. I—I wanted to be tied. Powerless. Ivor had me perform for a friend, Lord Blanchard. Do you know of him? No, a man like you wouldn't know a man like him. I did it gladly. It gave me a kind of thrill. I cannot even describe it. You can burn the book, but the deeds will be forever writ upon my soul." She reached for him now, feeling almost sorry. No doubt he wished to appear the hero, but she was past saving.

"I've come to take you away from this place."

Eden laughed. "Indeed? Why, it was you who sent me here. And I must thank you. The girls are very congenial and merry. I was anxious to undertake my first adventure this evening, but you've rather spoiled it. I was curious as to how I'd get on."

"Your arrangement with Mrs. Brown is at an end. I've bought your contract."

Eden felt the spiral of surprise to her toes. "What?" She knew it was the dream of most girls to be the mistress of a rich lord, but she had never expected Hart to keep a mistress. She knew he meant to marry soon. She would have to settle for second-best and, eventually, abandonment. Hart was simply too honorable to cheat on his wife with a courtesan.

"I am offering you a different life, Eden. When we marry—"

Eden stood up, shaking the blanket to her feet. "I must be losing my wits. You are offering me *marriage*?"

Hart flushed. "I've gone about this all wrong. Please sit down and cover up. I cannot think with you moving about like that."

Eden ignored him. "You cannot be serious! You cannot think to marry a whore."

"You are not a whore!" Hart shouted. "No one's seen you here yet. I made damn sure of it. Your Mrs. Brown is the canniest businesswoman imaginable. Why do you think you've spent the past few days with more 'lessons'? Locked in and hidden? I've made arrangements for our wedding. A special license. Furnished your bedroom." He sounded ridiculous, but he kept going. "Juliet had some clothes made up. A trousseau."

"Where does your aunt think I've spent the past week?"

"Your letter was just vague enough. I told her your new job didn't suit and you agreed to marry me. She was quite hurt, you know, when you ran off like that, but she's agreed to host the wedding breakfast."

A desperate laugh escaped Eden's mouth. "You are mad! Did you not consider what *I* might like? I am *not* going to marry you, Lord Hartford, no matter what you've done! We should not suit.

You are— You are— My God, do you know the girls here told me your nickname is Holy Hartford? You were a perfect gentleman, even with Fortuna and Aurora. I admit when I found out you had a subscription here I thought it might be amusing to run into you one day—but marriage? No, no."

Hart looked incredulous. "You are rejecting me because I am a gentleman?"

"Do but think. Right now you are imbued with some kind of reckless honor. You hope to make right the wrong done to me by your uncle. But I have explained, Hart—I wanted it. I needed it. There is a twisted emptiness in me. What would you say to your uncle's friend Lord Blanchard should he come upon you in some exclusive club and he tells you he's seen your shameless wife naked and on her knees? And Ivor's valet Kempton—he was blackmailing me. He knows everything as well. I can never be in one man's power again. I could not survive it. And I am barren," she said, spitting out the word.

"You don't know that."

Her lip curled. "I had almost four years of incessant sexual congress. Never once was there ever a suspicion of pregnancy. And during the course of their marriage, my mother miscarried too many times to count. The fault lies with me, I'm afraid." She wiped away an angry tear that blurred Hart's face. "You know my mother was never very strong, physically or temperamentally. She needed someone to take care of her and I failed her."

The ormolu clock on the mantel chimed the quarter hour, echoing other clocks on other mantels, the downstairs grandfather clock in Mrs. Brown's elegant hallway being the last to join in with its sonorous gong. Time was a valuable commodity here. Laughter and music drifted up the stairs, as well as the muffled sounds of pleasure.

Hart felt Eden slipping away as she drifted back into a place where he couldn't seem to reach her. "She had miscarriage after miscarriage. Dr. Canfield told Ivor to—to leave her alone. Of course," she said bitterly, "he refused. Just dosed her with laudanum until she didn't know day from night. All for an heir." She took a deep breath. Hart watched her try to master herself. "He would have passed off any child of ours as legitimate. My mother would not have had the courage to stop him. Nor I. But it never happened."

Hart took her hand in his, gently thumbing across her knuckles. "I believe we can agree that my uncle was a man of no principles and very little heart. What he did to your mother was unconscionable. What he did to you was unforgivable."

"I should have known better. I *did* know better. You don't want a wife who can't bear you sons. No man does."

"I was wrong to assume I knew what was best for you," Hart said softly. "Do not make the same mistake."

"Oh, go away!" cried Eden. "I'm sure Mrs. Brown will give you back your money."

"I rather doubt it. She strikes a very hard bargain." The woman never gave up, and neither would he. Eden had no idea of his determination.

And she was wrong. His marriage proposal was not based on mere chivalry. He'd fought against it, but he'd known somehow from the first time he held her in his arms that he couldn't let her go.

But it was equally true he didn't really know her. Didn't even know what her favorite foods or colors were. Whether she could sing or paint. If she preferred cats to dogs. He reckoned he needed to find out. He needed to court her. He needed to heal her, somehow fill up the emptiness she'd spoken of. He had the power to do it, and it was in his pocket. Switching strategies was simplicity itself after serving in the army for a decade.

"Well, if you don't want to be my wife, I'm afraid you'll have to be my mistress." He saw the shock on her rouged face. "Of course, that means I can't bring you to my house. Give me a day to rent a property for us. Get your things packed up and I'll see you tomorrow evening."

He kissed her benignly on the forehead, as though she was a child, and left her standing alone in the candlelight. He closed the door before she could find the words to call him back and argue.

Chapter 12

Mrs. Brown had expected some sort of fireworks, so was surprised to see a very subdued Eden in her parlor late the next morning. Well, as subdued as one can be wearing a sheer peach chiffon robe and smudges of last night's makeup, her hair a nest of tangled waves. Eden looked as though she had not slept a wink, and for that Mrs. Brown was sorry. She herself had passed a very profitable and peaceful night.

Eden attempted to reason with her, but she would have none of it. "Were you not pleased, my dear? The man was most insistent. Ordinarily, I consult with my girls before such a transaction is made, but I was quite convinced you'd welcome a marriage proposal. Those don't come along every day. Why did you refuse him?"

"I cannot marry him! I simply cannot! You must give him back whatever he gave you. Please," she added.

Mrs. Brown shook her head firmly. "I am a woman of my word. I should not have stayed in business these twenty years if I let a foolish, ungrateful girl dictate house policies. And your contract states in plain language than it—that *you*—can be sold at my discretion. We discussed all this the day you came to me. Surely a woman of your education and breeding cannot claim to have misunderstood the conditions of our business relationship. I did not give you to just anybody off the street, you know. You are acquainted with him. Lord Hartford asked for your hand in *marriage*, not a mere arrangement."

Eden fussed with the flimsy robe, attempting to cover more of herself, but it was a lost cause. It was just as well that she was leaving the Pantheon. Mrs. Brown could see she was a most uncomfortable courtesan. No matter how depraved her training at the hands of Ivor Hartford had been, he had not extinguished the vicar's daughter's modesty.

"He only thinks he wants to marry me. He's an idiot."

"A very handsome idiot, if I may say so. Such a splendid specimen, my dear! Tall, so commanding. All that fair hair, and those bright blue eyes. You will be the envy of all the goddesses when he takes you away. Why, you never even had to spend a minute proving yourself, did you? Lord Hartford left most abruptly. There was insufficient time to grant him satisfaction. Unless, the poor man—"

"No! He never touched me. That is to say, all he wanted to do was talk."

"A very expensive conversation. He had a word with me on his way out to explain the change in circumstances. He'll make you a fine protector. I believe he has quite a *tendre* for you."

"Worse and worse," Eden mumbled.

Mrs. Brown was amused. She liked Eden as much for the girl's spirit as the amount of money she had brought to her enterprise. Eventually she would come around and Lord Hartford would gain that satisfaction that had been so absent last night. Mrs. Brown thought him a clever man. If anyone could break through Eden's reserve, it was he.

"I am afraid," Eden whispered at last.

"That's only natural, my dear. I am sure he'll be kind to you."

"You don't understand. I will fall in love with him. Hell," she laughed bitterly, "I'm half in love with him already."

"Then why did you refuse his offer of marriage?"

"I'm not fit to marry anybody."

Mrs. Brown put her hand on Eden's shoulder. "Now who is the idiot? What has happened to you in the past is no measure of how your future will unfold. Give the man a chance. And if he tires of you, come back to me. I can find you a new protector or you may rejoin the girls if you wish. It will be your choice, but not for the next year. You must honor the contract."

Eden nodded. She had known it before she stepped foot into Mrs. Brown's elegant white world.

"If I do not see you before you leave, good luck, my dear. You've put me in a pickle, you have. I must find a new Flora posthaste." The madam impulsively kissed Eden on the cheek. "And do something about your appearance, love. Lord Hartford may be besotted, but I doubt he wants to see you in yesterday's dirt."

*   *   *

Calvert was a whiz. By noon he had found Hart a perfect little love nest, fully furnished and lightly staffed. Its owner was between mistresses and traveling on the Continent, happy to rent out the house for a short duration. By three Calvert had canceled the wedding arrangements and soothed Mrs. Cheverly. By dinnertime he had sent Eden's trousseau to the new house and Mattie to unpack it, swearing her to secrecy as he revealed her employer's plans. Mattie, a dreadful romantic, could not fathom her mistress's distaste for marriage, but allowed as how Lord Hartford would straighten her out in no time.

By midnight, Eden was in her own new bed. Hart escorted her to the premises, kissed her on the cheek this time and left her in the marble foyer. It was up to Mattie to introduce the butler and housekeeper-cook, a married couple who did not look down their noses at her.

Eden lay in her elegantly furnished room for hours, quite sleepless for the second night in a row. Hart had sent a simple black gown, bonnet and cloak to Mrs. Brown's yesterday so she'd not had to ride through the streets of London looking like a doxy. The mourning clothes hanging in her dressing room cupboard showed restraint and good taste.

Her underthings, however, were a different story. Juliet had ordered the most exquisitely naughty undergarments, perfect for a new bride. Or a new mistress. But Eden rather wondered when Hart would be helping her get out of them. So far he had treated her with kid gloves. Like a distant cousin. She had been resigned to do her duty by him last night, but he had not even entered the vestibule.

There was frost on the windowpane when she awoke, sweet rolls on a plate and chocolate in a pretty pot. Mattie had tiptoed in earlier and stoked the fire so the room was deliciously warm. The day stretched ahead of Eden with uncertainty. But there were books in the bookcase and the house to explore more thoroughly, so she rang for Mattie to help her dress.

Mattie blushed but shook her head. "Lord Hartford sent word he'll arrive at noontime, miss, and he'd just as soon you're still in your nightgown. But I'll help you with a bath and do your hair up pretty."

Dispirited, she let Mattie fuss over her. Eden had hoped to delay their union until it was dark. No matter. He'd seen all of her last night, seen all of her at Hartford Hall for that matter. Sunlight wouldn't grant him any more sense, and hours waiting wouldn't make her job any easier. There was a wealth of lacy peignoirs to choose from. She selected one the color of spring violets and waited in a chair by the fire with an unread book.

She heard him bound up the staircase, whistling, at noon exactly. He opened her door without knocking and removed his dark blue jacket, tossing it onto the carpet.

"Hello, Eden. You look lovely. Did you have a restful night?"

"Not particularly." *He* looked lovely in his shirtsleeves, the fitted gray waistcoat accentuating his long, lean torso. She pointed to the crumpled jacket. "Shouldn't you hang that up or fold it or something?"

"Now you sound just like the wife you didn't want to be. I don't believe I have time." He smiled at her rather mischievously. "Come here." He held out his arms.

She rose slowly from her chair and stood before him, waiting for instructions. Her eyes were on the carpet; she did not trust herself to meet the hopeful blue of his eyes. He seemed so impossibly, improbably *happy*. As though their arrangement had come to him free as a present tied with a big shiny bow. He lifted her face to him, his fingers slipping through her hair, his thumbs resting lightly on her cheekbones. He slanted his mouth over hers, barely brushing her lips before he drew away.

"I don't want you to be afraid. I don't want you to think of anything but your pleasure." She could see he was already thinking of his. His formfitting breeches revealed his arousal; he was larger than his uncle and most men she had seen in drawings or through Mrs. Brown's peephole. It had been an informative week.

Hart captured her hand. "Please touch me, Eden. I've dreamed of you doing so for quite a while."

As she had dreamed of him, night after night, in her cold bed. But now that he was here, inches away, she felt suddenly shy and nervous. All her instruction—all her experience—had not prepared her for the reality of Hart, the warmth of his breath on her cheek, the clean scent of his soap, the nearness of his lips to her own.

He jerked as her fingers curled around him. Emboldened, she pressed harder against the fabric. He was anxiously watching her touch him, as though he expected her to run fleeing from the room at any minute.

She would not. She could do this. Had done it countless times. But never with Hart, who had a vexing hold upon her emotions. She'd better master that, or else she was doomed to melt into a puddle of need and heat. Her breath hitched, betraying her.

"You are thinking," he said sternly. "I can see little elves with hammers and tongs racing about your brain. Tell them to take a nap, or at the very least a nice cup of soothing tea."

"I don't think there's enough tea in China to quiet them down."

"Perhaps a tot of brandy then. That usually does the trick for me."

Eden had stopped rubbing Hart, her fingers numb, her arms hanging loosely at her sides. All of her felt detached, remote, weak. She thought before long she'd have to sit down. Ah, yes. He was right. She was thinking too much, wondering when Ivor would appear and kill the budding pleasure between them.

"I can't do this," she whispered. She waited for what seemed like forever for him to rail at her.

"You don't have to."

"But I *should*. I should do *something*."

"You make it sound like an assigned duty, Eden, like tallying up a row of numbers or eating your spinach." He was smiling, no longer so happily. "We can take our time."

She shook her head. The sooner they began, the sooner she would know. She screwed up her courage.

"Please unfasten your falls. I don't believe my hands are up to the task."

"Are you sure?"

"Positive." She stepped back, watching him fumble with the fastenings himself. His cock sprang from the golden curls at the base. She bit her lip and began.

* * *

Her hand was perfection. There was something to be said for an experienced woman, however she had gained her experience. But if she didn't stop soon, he'd spend himself in her palm, and he had other plans for their afternoon.

"You are wearing too many clothes," he groaned. Somewhere along the way, she had pulled his shirt over his head and fastened her mouth around one of his flat brown nipples as she stroked him. He was in exquisite agony.

"Mattie told me I was to wear a nightgown. I shall do just as you wish, of course."

"No, you shall do as *you* wish." He reluctantly left the warmth of her hand and lay down on the bed. "And I do hope your wishes coincide with mine."

"And if they do not?" Eden untied the silk string of her robe. She went to the closet and hung it on a padded hanger. Her nightgown followed. Hart took a deep breath, hoping to find his voice.

"You are incomparable."

"And you, sir, are easily impressed." She lay on her side next to him on the bed, looking into his eyes. "Why, Hart? Why have you done this?"

Here was a question he had no answer for. It had bedeviled him for days. He should not want her—he should not even touch her. To atone for what his uncle did, he need only give her a generous allowance and chalk her fall up to the family curse. Was he about to fall with her? He was afraid so. He made his voice light. "Fate. The moon. The stars. I only know I have to have you, and I have to have you now. I fought against it, Eden, believe me. I don't want you hurt again. And I won't hurt you, I swear."

She leaned in to kiss him. He lay still, letting his lips be their sole point of contact. His arms ached to hold her, to flip her roughly on her back. His cock yearned to plunge and plunder, claim her for his own. But instead he let himself be kissed, an artless, nearly virginal kiss, which thrilled his soul and tested his resolve.

She broke away. "Am I not pleasing you?"

"You please me too much. I meant what I said. We shall do as *you* wish."

Her perfect eyebrows knit. "But I am your mistress. Surely it is up to you to tell me what to do."

"I think you'll figure something out."

"Are you serious? What if I just get up and walk away?"

"I do hope that's not your choice. I should be quite discomfited. In dire pain, actually."

"This is a trick," she said, rising from the bed. The sunlight behind her set fire to the gold strands in her brown hair. He longed to run his fingers through the waves, but perhaps not today. He had taken a risk, to come to her quickly today, to give her no chance to think or refuse him, to make their congress seem like the most normal, thoughtless, animal thing. The sooner they began this dance, the sooner he could set her fears to rest. And he really could not wait another minute.

"No trick. I am at your disposal. Surely you can see that."

Eden's eyes flicked to his manhood, which stood at rigid attention. "I may do anything?"

"Anything within reason." He hoped she would not subject him to the crueler games his uncle had inflicted on her.

"I must think on it."

To Hart's disappointment, she sat back down on her chair. At least she was still naked, so he could still admire her glorious body. That henna rose was intriguing. He hoped he might be able to inspect it at closer range sometime in the very near future.

Perhaps he'd been too precipitate. But he could hardly prevent the effect she had on him. He'd been rock-hard even before he picked her up at Mrs. Brown's last night. When she'd only exchanged monosyllables with him, he knew he was doomed to delay, but it seemed twelve hours was about all the time he could do without her. Surely once he made her his, she would see there was no choice but to marry him.

"Does your aunt know about this—this relationship?" Eden asked, startling him with the question.

"Of course not. She believes I sent you back to Hartford Hall with Mattie. That you decided it was too soon after all for a commitment such as marriage, but that you are thinking about it."

She shook her head. "I will never marry."

"So you've said. On the first day we met, actually." She was busy with her hands, smoothing her nails with a thumb. He wished she was smoothing him. "Should I get dressed?"

She bit her lip. "I don't know."

Patience, patience, patience, damn it. "Well, when you do, inform me of your intentions." He stretched, popping the tension in his neck. "My, this bed is comfortable. Perhaps I'll take a nap." He closed one eye.

"Don't you dare go to sleep!" She stalked toward him, her fists clenched. At least he'd gotten a rise out of her. She came a bit closer.

"That's a very interesting drawing you have on your—" Hart offered, not quite knowing what to call her feminine mound. "I don't suppose you'd object if I took a look at it while you and your elves are thinking?"

She lay back down on the bed, martyred, closing her eyes as if it hurt her to look at him. She was clearly not on the same page as he this afternoon. They were not even on the same chapter. Perhaps they were reading different volumes altogether.

Hart leaned on one elbow. When he touched the rose with a fingertip, she jumped a mile.

"Sorry. I didn't mean to distress you. I find it very difficult not to touch you, you know."

"Why don't you then? Let's just get this over with!"

He chuckled. "Hardly the words a gentleman wants to hear. You are depressing my ardor."

Eden opened her eyes and stared at his cock. His words were clearly not quite true.

"That's what I want. To begin and get done. You said we'd do as I wished."

"And what is it exactly you want me to do?" he asked, all innocence.

Eden clasped her hands tightly as if she wanted to slap some sense into him. Her irritation was amusing. "You know! Don't make me say it."

"This?" Hart asked, as he cupped her breast in his warm hand, thumbing her erect nipple. She shivered in pleasure. "Or this?" He nuzzled her neck, inhaling the rose fragrance on her skin. "Or perhaps this?"

The mattress shifted, and Hart's warm breath teased her rose. His tongue traced the artwork lightly, then slipped lower. Her legs fell open.

She made no argument. In fact, she said nothing of any note, just breathed in a satisfactorily rapid fashion. He limned each fold and crevice with his hands and his mouth, paying special attention to the hard little knot of her lust. He blessed the daylight as the tip of his tongue connected with her nub, each stroke darkening her flesh from pink to ruby. Her fingers laced through his hair, mindlessly mimicking the very movement of his tongue as he tasted her. When she stilled her hand, her fingertips pressing hard against his skull, he sensed she was about to come apart for him. He captured the bud in his mouth, sucking its sugared sweetness. Eden cried out, and he didn't stop, couldn't stop until she peaked again and his mouth was filled with her glory.

Just as perfect as he knew it would be. He held her close, fitting her to his body, skimming the surface of her hot skin with one hand. He wished he could say her satisfaction had satisfied him, but he wanted more. Much more.

But not today. If he didn't leave now, their moment might be spoiled. She wasn't ready. He knew it. He could wait. He had a week less than a year to make her his.

He rolled off the bed. When she opened her mouth to protest, he put one finger against her lips and told her to go to sleep, that he would see her tomorrow. That she must think of something she wanted him to do.

She watched him get into his disordered clothes as her body

adjusted to this latest marvel. She could think of a thousand things. But they all might remind her of Ivor. Eden allowed that Hart's technique was a considerable improvement over his uncle's, and she mercifully had not thought once of the man as Hart had kissed her senseless. But that didn't mean that tomorrow the ghost could not come between them.

But Eden did sleep; she was exhausted. When she woke it was dusk. When Mattie brought the supper tray, on it was a note.

It asked the simple question *How are the elves? Are you thinking?* Eden smiled and slipped it under her pillow.

* * *

Des had been hinting around all through dinner, but Hart pretended to be as thick as the beefsteak he was spearing into his mouth. He couldn't play the imbecile forever, though, and he thought he might just have the solution that would free him completely and make Desmond a very happy man.

"I've been thinking," he began. No elves were involved.

"Bad for your brainbox, Hart. Thought you weren't yourself."

"You know I must marry."

"Oh, not that again. A few weeks in the country and your head has gone to mush. Never tell me you met some dairymaid who's put down her bucket to become Lady Hartford."

"I have sheep, Des, not cows," Hart laughed, although he believed there were several head of cattle on the home farm for the usual butter, cream, cheese and milk. "But I *have* met someone."

Des threw his napkin down on the table. "I knew it! Who is she? Some squire's daughter?"

"No names. No details. I'm not sure of my suit yet, Des. I don't want to jinx it."

"Is the chit insane? Any girl would be happy to call you husband."

"Thank you for your vote of confidence. I am proceeding slowly. It is my hope that within the year—"

"A year!"

"I must be patient. She is worth winning. But I very much suspect she would not be happy to learn that I have a subscription to Mrs. Brown's."

Desmond had the grace to blush. He'd been angling all evening without much subtlety for an invitation there later. He'd probably found the last few weeks to be dead dull while Hart was visiting his estate. But Hart was about to dispel the dullness and make his friend's dreams come true.

"High in the instep, is she? A gel's got to know how to get on in the ton. Nothing wrong for a gentleman to have a bit o' fluff on the side. Her mother needs to tell her so."

"I'm afraid her mother is dead and it's certainly not a subject I wish to broach with her while I'm attempting to woo her. Anyway, I propose a solution which should suit all of us. I'd like to transfer my membership at Mrs. Brown's to you. I believe that has been done a time or two."

Major Henry Desmond looked massively disappointed. Not the response Hart had hoped for. But Des's next words explained his reaction.

"Gad, Hart, you know I haven't the blunt for it. I can't afford it. Too bad for you, old chap. Though no one's sorrier than I."

"You misunderstand. It would be a gift." Hart watched in amusement as light dawned on his friend's face.

"Oh, I couldn't. Well, perhaps I could, but Mrs. Brown might not like it. She's a dreadful stickler. Worse than the patronesses at Almack's."

"Nonsense. You're a war hero. You come from a good family and don't kick dogs and children. I'm sure the woman could be persuaded to take you on. She owes me a favor. Let's finish our dinner and go find out."

Des now looked like it was Christmas and his birthday combined. He ate a little faster than was good for his digestion, and shortly he and Hart were admitted to the Pantheon by a very stiff-necked butler.

Hart gave the man his card and whispered something in his ear. The butler moved rather quickly for a man of his age and returned shortly to invite the gentlemen to Mrs. Brown's private parlor. Hart had seen quite enough of that room, but Des was all agog.

They were left alone with two snifters of excellent brandy, the bottle handy on a silver tray. Mrs. Brown kept them waiting just long enough for Hart to become irritated, but he had to admit her appearance was almost worth the wait.

For a woman who was over forty, she radiated a serene sensuality that had caused regret in many a young buck that she no longer involved herself personally with her clientele. Tonight her pale hair was upswept with diamanté clips, and her snow white velvet gown's bodice skirted the limits of propriety. A single large teardrop pearl dipped into the cleft of her bosom, as if pointing the way to pleasure.

"Lord Hartford, I admit this is a surprise. I had not thought to see you so soon." She smiled, but was clearly puzzled.

"It is a pleasure to see you again, Mrs. Brown. I believe you know my friend Major Desmond."

"Of course." Mrs. Brown extended two gloved fingers.

"I don't know why this didn't occur to me when we last met, but perhaps I was distracted." And feeling somewhat robbed, Hart thought, although securing Eden's freedom had been worth every penny. More like pound. "I find I do not have need of my membership here any longer."

"Indeed? I hate to be the bearer of bad tidings, my lord, but we do not refund fees. Ever."

Hart laughed. The woman could run circles around the directors of the Bank of England. "So I should hope not. But I believe membership can be passed on. Didn't Viscount Wetherbury inherit his from his grandfather?"

"You know I never discuss my members, Lord Hartford," she said, smiling sweetly. "Surely you're not making out your will just yet?"

"I suppose I should. I'd like to marry."

She inclined her head. "A noble goal."

"I'd like to propose that my friend Major Desmond here take on the remainder of my year."

"That's a very unusual request. I am not sure I have ever done such a thing before." She placed a gloved finger on her chin and studied the distance, as if deeply lost in thought. She had told Hart herself that his father had taken his uncle's place here, but she seemed to have deliberately forgotten. Hart could see why she had been so successful on the stage and in so many boudoirs.

"You allowed my father to take my uncle's membership, I believe," he reminded her.

"Ahh. So I did. That was a such long time ago. The rules have changed."

Hart wondered how much more he'd have to pony up to complete the transfer. No doubt she'd advise him tomorrow in a purple-sealed letter. "Just think on it. Mrs. Brown. I would be grateful."

"I shall do so, Lord Hartford. How is our mutual friend?"

"Tolerable." Much better than tolerable, he hoped.

"Good. I trust Lord Hartford's recommendation is amenable to you, Major Desmond?"

Des swallowed. "Yes, ma'am."

"Well, rules are meant to be broken, or I wager I would not have a business. Come see me tomorrow afternoon for tea, Major Desmond. Your interview will begin at four."

"M-my interview?"

"Why, of course, sir. How do you think your friend Lord Hartford got into my good graces on such short notice? I owe it to my girls to make sure the gentlemen who patronize the Pantheon really *are* gentlemen."

As they made their way downstairs, Des muttered, "An interview. And *tea*. I can't credit it."

"Whatever will you wear?" Hart teased, only to feel the sharp end of Des's elbow in his ribs.

Chapter 13

The next day Hart lasted until all of two o'clock before he found himself knocking on Eden's door. He trusted he had made some progress with her and she was ready to assign him his next amorous task. Something that might relieve him as well.

He found her in the charming little sitting room writing a letter. She hastily shoved it in the drawer of the writing desk and rose to greet him.

"I understand from the girls it is quite the thing for a man to set a schedule with his mistress," she began, in a most distressingly businesslike fashion. "You know, Tuesday and Thursday afternoons, that sort of thing. I shouldn't like you to arrive and not find me at home."

"You're not planning on running away, are you?"

She was not a good liar, Hart thought, watching her expression change. If not actually planning to decamp, she certainly had thought of it. His uncle must have known every minute she was miserable. And derived perverse enjoyment of it.

"We have a contract, sir. I shall do my duty and honor it."

Damn, damn, damn. Where was the love-flushed girl of yesterday? "I hope you will eventually come to feel more than duty, Eden," he said softly.

"I shall give you no reason to complain, my lord," Eden said, a false smile on her face.

Hart sighed. There was no question she knew more about this business than he did, and a part of him grieved for her innocence.

"I have severed my connection at Mrs. Brown's, so I expect to be visiting you every day. Consider that your schedule." Hart hoped that if she had to see him daily, she didn't stand a single chance to guard herself against him.

"What time?" she asked with coolness.

He wanted to tell her his bags would arrive in the morning, that he'd wake up to her sleep-creased face every day and smooth it with kisses, that he'd catch her after luncheon and drag her back to bed, that he'd watch the candlelight flicker in her eyes as she arched against him in the dark. Instead, he said, "What time will be convenient for you? Remember, I am doing as *you* wish."

Eden drew her beautifully plucked eyebrows together. "You truly were serious yesterday."

"I was. I'm a serious man."

"It will do you no good."

"What do you mean?"

"I see what you are doing. You think because I was once a . . ." How to phrase it without using the words *slave* or *whore* or *slut*? ". . . player under someone else's direction that I shall enjoy having the upper hand. Doing the directing. Well, I won't."

"How do you know if you don't try?"

She hoped to shock him from his complacency. He had to know

right now what she was before this new game progressed any further. "Are you saying you'd lie there like a lump while I trussed you up and whipped you?"

Hart's face was carefully neutral. "To be frank, that sounds most unpleasant. I would much prefer what we did yesterday if it comes to that."

Eden blushed and turned away. She had dreamt of nothing else. "This will never work. Please send me back to Mrs. Brown's."

"I cannot. I have broken off my relations with her. As a non-member, I cannot even enter the Pantheon to sneak a peek."

"Damn it! Get a friend to take you! Write a letter! Hart, don't you see, this is wrong. I can never be what you want."

He came to her and put his arms around her. "I want you anyway. I need you. And whether you know it or not, you need me, too. Now may I kiss you?"

She looked up at him, her dark eyes welling with tears. "What?"

"I need your permission, Eden. I shall never take what you do not freely give."

Eden closed her eyes, shutting his beautiful face away. She had given nearly her soul away before. No matter how it had started, she had ended up in a hell of her own making. If her stepfather had not died, she knew she would have killed him. Or herself. The latter was more likely, so worthless had she felt.

She was coming to terms with what had happened to her, what she had let happen. She knew Hart would never hurt her physically, but he would tie himself so tight within her, she'd never be free of him. One day he would come to his senses, his ridiculous notion of her rescue unnecessary. She was not some gothic heroine to be pitied. She could forge her own future.

Yet she was in his arms. His warm lips were near. He smelled of lime and clean linen. And almost-love. So she lifted her face to him, risking her soul once again.

If he'd had time, he could have counted the tangle of dark lashes brushing the tender blue skin under her eyes, skin that told him she'd had as little sleep as he. He could have kissed the tiny beauty mark upon her temple and the spangle of freckles he discovered on her nose, which she had tried to cover with rice powder. He could have traced her perfectly imperfect mouth with the pad of his thumb until she captured it to suckle. He could have unpinned her hair and watched it fall in loose waves upon her creamy shoulders, breathing in its lush rose scent.

But he only had time for a kiss.

Each time he kissed her, he felt like an explorer navigating in uncharted waters. So far he had discovered her hesitation and her hope. He was grateful that her practiced arts deserted her when she was in his arms. He wanted to take her where she had never been, to learn where she wanted to be. And then he remembered. There was a great deal to learn.

"Do you like dogs?" he asked, breaking the kiss.

Eden sagged up against him. If he had not been holding her up, she would have been puddled on the carpet. "Pardon?" she asked in confusion. To her utter mortification she recalled her last mention of dogs to him. She'd been on her hands and knees, stripped of pride and desperate. It had been a shocking attempt to make him understand what had happened with his uncle, but perhaps that was how he meant to take her this afternoon. *The position of the dog.* "I—I will do anything you like."

"A dog would be good company for you here so you don't get lonely. Unless you prefer a cat. Which is it?"

"Um, I like them both." She'd had a cat when she'd come to Hartford Hall, but her stepfather's dogs hadn't always been toothless old things and had driven it off. How could Hart go from that miraculous kiss to a discussion about house pets?

"Cats are useful for keeping the mice at bay. I don't suppose Mrs. What's-er-name has said if they're a problem."

Eden untangled herself from Hart's arms and managed to get to the couch without falling. The man was mad. "Her name is Mrs. Philpott, and no, she has not."

"They fight, though." Eden's mind was still a blank as he chattered on. "Cats and dogs. It really should be one or the other. This house is probably not big enough for both."

The kiss had obviously addled his wits as it had weakened her knees. But a reply to this preposterous question seemed required. "A cat then. So it can be useful."

"Very well, then, a cat it is. I'll bring one back tomorrow." To her amazement, he bent down and kissed her forehead, then bounded out the parlor door and down the stairs. She never had a chance to tell him what she had been thinking about rather strenuously all night and morning long. This mistress business was not at all what she had expected.

She heard the door slam, then seconds later reopen. He must have taken the steps up two at a time, for he poked his head in the doorway rather quickly. "You never said. What time do you wish me to come tomorrow?"

Eden laughed. "You are impossible. Come for dinner. Eight o'clock. You and the cat may stay the night. I have been thinking."

* * *

This wooing business was dangerous. One would think in the teeming metropolis of London, the preeminent city of the world, one could find a well-behaved cat for a modest fee. Even a kitten would have done the trick, but apparently kittens, like lambs, were seasonal and November was simply not a good month for them. Both he and the estimable Calvert had combed the area pet shops. Had they wanted a parrot or a poodle or a goldfinch or a goldfish, they would have been spoiled for choice.

Instead, Hart found himself in possession of a young orange tomcat with a stunted, corkscrew tail, who took a dim view of his new situation and had clawed Hart right through his gloves. The cat was presently yowling his head off in a cage as Hart's carriage made the trip to Eden's house. Hart doubted Eden would get too terribly attached to the creature, and he had a substitute present in his pocket, a lovely pearl-and-diamond bracelet which would more than make up for the cat's shortcomings.

Hart allowed as his life had been completely upended these past two months. He had started as a soldier and ended a baron. His bills were now paid in full, he had two houses instead of modest bachelor digs, and he had fallen headlong in lust with a most stubborn, un-suitable woman. A woman whose honor made her refuse to marry him yet could abide being his mistress. A mistress he'd somehow forgotten to make love to when the subject of cats came up.

He reminded himself as the cat made its presence unmistakable that he'd vowed to go slowly with Eden. He knew she considered herself too damaged for decency. And how he regretted his own part in her feelings.

Hart wondered how many times he'd misjudged a situation. Not many, he hoped; he'd had a reputation of quick thinking that had saved his men and his own hide more times than he could count.

But he'd made a mistake with Eden Emery, the least likely femme fatale.

He'd spent his life running from the reputation of his family, but Eden had had no opportunity to run. His uncle had tamed, then trapped her. Eden had never known an ordinary life. She had been desperate enough to believe she should lose her identity entirely amidst the demimonde. How to persuade her to trade the name Flora for the Baroness Hartford?

My God. Even his title must be anathema to her. But there was nothing Hart could do about the patents dating to the fourteenth century.

His driver pulled up to the mews house and Hart grabbed the cage, getting swiped again for his trouble. The shop owner had tied a yellow bow on it, which was now sadly damp and chewed. "Little bastard," Hart muttered under his breath. Eden would probably choose a different name, but that suited the creature to the ground.

He was very tempted to pass the cat off to Philpott so it could begin its life in the kitchen, but he resolutely mounted the stairs.

Eden was reading a book by the fire. A branch of candles burned on the table at her elbow. She was dressed in one of Juliet's selections, a tasteful black gown trimmed with a smattering of gray pearls. She placed a ribbon between the pages and rose, curtseying. "Good evening, my lord."

"Please call me Hart. Surely we are on more intimate terms. I believe I've earned the right." Intimate did not even begin to describe what he'd done to her two days ago.

She nodded. "Very well. And what have we here?"

"This, my lady, is your cat. I shall not hold it against you if you release him into the streets at once. He seems to have a bit of a temper." As if to punctuate the remark, the cat howled.

"Well, of course. How would you feel if someone confined you in a cage? Poor little fellow." She bent to stroke his fur through the bars.

"I wouldn't if I were you. He's a perfect brute."

"Release him. I'm sure he'll be much more equable when he has his freedom."

Reluctantly, Hart lifted the latch, and the cat dashed under the sofa.

"If we're lucky, he'll stay there all night. But I have something else for you." He reached in his pocket for the jeweler's box.

"I know it's not my birthday." She took the case but didn't open it.

Another thing he didn't know. Her birth date.

"When is it?

"The eighth of October. You're a bit late." And there had been no celebration since the baron was scarce cold in his grave.

"And you are twenty-two, correct?"

Eden shrugged. "Alas, I am. An old maid."

"You needn't be." Hart brushed her cheek with a warm fingertip.

"Do not start in again, my—Hart. I have planned a pleasant dinner for us and I should not like us to disagree. It is very bad for one's digestion."

"Very well. I will endeavor to find topics of conversation to which you have no objection. Presents, for example. Look inside there. If it's not to your taste, I shall return it and get you something else."

Eden popped the box open. A delicate single strand of freshwater pearls interspaced with small diamonds lay nestled in black velvet. It was not the gaudy gift of a man to his mistress, but the kind of thing a man might give his wife.

"It—it's beautiful."

"Here, let me fasten it. The clasp is a shell. Isn't that rather clever? The jeweler has a matching necklace and earbobs, but I wasn't sure you'd like it."

She held out her arm. For a dizzying second she remembered other occasions when she had been in such a position, waiting to be bound. But she had never been tied by pearls and diamonds. She shook her wrist, watching the jewels catch the candlelight.

"How could anyone not like it? Thank you." Impulsively, she reached up to kiss him on the cheek.

He took advantage, quickly moving so his mouth connected with hers. He parted her lips with his tongue, stroking the edge of her teeth. Invading and tickling the plump padding of her lower lip, her palate, her cheek, until she couldn't help but do the same to him. He skimmed the beading at her neckline, then dipped a finger into the warm valley between her breasts.

Before she had a chance to push him away, he stepped back, straightened her bodice and smiled. "You are welcome. And I am starving. You have no idea how much trouble it is to catch a cat in London."

Eden frowned. "Do you suppose he'll be all right? I'll ask Mattie to put a sandbox in the scullery for him until he gets used to us. I wouldn't want to put him out in the garden and have him run off."

"Want to bet? What will you call him?"

"Why, Brutus, of course. The perfect brute. It seems he's already betrayed your kindness." She had noticed the long scratches on Hart's hands and had yearned to kiss them better. But she was determined to keep some sort of barrier between them until he realized this plan of his was pointless. Already he had flummoxed her by the kiss. Although she was perfectly prepared to sleep with him tonight, she would endeavor with all her might to distance herself from his charm. She feared she had a daunting task ahead of her.

He deserved someone else as a wife. She deserved not to have her heart broken. If she observed the terms of their contract, the latter was sure to happen. And really, she thought, would Holy Hartford ever go before the courts to sue his mistress for desertion? She thought not.

"Come, sir. I believe our dinner must be ready."

"What is on the menu this evening? I am famished, you know. Between the jewelry shopping and the cat conundrum, I did not have the opportunity to stop for lunch."

"My favorite. Roast chicken. I hope it will be to your liking."

Another question answered. Hart ticked it off his mental checklist.

* * *

Dinner had been a nearly normal affair. Hart realized that for the first time they were not arguing about the past or the future, but simply speaking to each other as friends. He had any number of nuggets of information about her preferences now, and was sure she knew more about him as well. He noted she drank very little of her wine, and knew why. He was pleased. He planned to make this a memorable night and wanted her to be cognizant of every kiss and stroke.

When he rose from the table and extended his hand, she clasped it. Looking down into her sober face, he asked, "Are you sure?"

"A poor mistress I will make if I deny you my bed," Eden said, attempting some levity.

"Eden, you know I want more from you."

"Hush. We will not walk that old ground. Let us just enjoy tonight."

He followed her up the stairs, watching the swish of her skirts. He dared not look up at her beautiful ass or the proud stiffness of her black back. Juliet had provided stylish clothing, but Hart was anxious to get Eden out of that fashionable mourning gown.

They entered her tastefully appointed bedroom, so very different from Flora's florid bower. Mattie had already been in to turn down the bed, but was nowhere in sight. She had left a basin of water and towels on the dresser and a tray with a bottle of port and two glasses on a side table near the fire.

"Some wine, my lord?" Eden asked, moving toward the table.

Hart shook his head. "I only want to taste you, Eden."

He watched her run her tongue over her lips unconsciously and felt a tightening in his groin. "Come to me."

Without a word, she complied and stood still as he worked at the devilish fastenings of her silk dress, finally draping it on a chair. Let Mattie hang it up tomorrow. Eden's chemise and stays were as black as night, festooned with tiny pink rosebuds and green stitching. "Very pretty, but wholly unnecessary." He untied the pink ribbons that laced up her back. He unbuttoned her shift and it drifted to the floor.

She was exquisite, standing in her beaded slippers and black stockings tied with pink rosettes. Hart envisioned her long legs wrapped around him, the whisper of silk against his skin. She stepped out of her shoes and bent to untie a garter.

"Leave it." His voice sounded harsh, even to him.

For an instant he felt her fear and cursed himself for his lust. He needed to return the control to her, no matter that she thought it calculated.

"Now," he said softly, "I require your assistance."

Eden blushed. She had never fully undressed a man before. Ivor had taken her clothed, or had come to bed in his dressing gown. She had welcomed the barrier of fabric between them, although she had always been stripped bare, powerless. It was as if his clothing distinguished him from her low animal nature.

"We shall see if your jacket is padded, my lord," she teased, trying to erase the unhappy image of herself cowering on the library floor.

"I can assure you, madam, that it is not. Nor are my inexpressibles." In fact, when Eden's eyes inevitably swept downward, she could see he was beyond aroused.

She eased him out of his tailored frock coat, placing it carefully next to her gown. His vest of figured satin came next. When she had difficulty with his cravat, she heard him mutter, "Damn McBride," and he tore it from his own throat. She pulled his linen shirt out of his pants and stepped back.

"Do not say you are done."

"I do not want you to get cold." Her own nipples were frozen berries, and her pale skin was all over gooseflesh.

"What an idiot I am. Get under the covers, Eden. I'll do the rest."

Gratefully, she slid under the quilted linens but did not close her eyes. She watched as Hart sat and struggled with his boots, tossed his stockings and shirt aside. When he stood to remove his breeches, she couldn't help but give an appreciative sigh.

He was golden in the firelight, the fair hair on his body shimmering like the powder she had worn at Mrs. Brown's. She thought of the men she'd seen during her week of lessons, pale, fat, lean, young, old. Hart surpassed them all, could have posed for a life study illustrating the Perfection of Man. And he was hers, for to-night. For a little while. Long enough, perhaps, to last her a lifetime of memories.

He sat on the edge of the bed. "Where would you like me to begin?" he asked, the mischievous crease on his cheek deepening.

Eden had been prepared for his deference. "You may kiss my toes." That would teach him. She still wore her stockings, after all.

His face betrayed no surprise. Gently, he loosened the coverlet at the foot of the bed and exposed her narrow feet. "Which side, madam, left or right?"

"Why, both of course." Two could play this ridiculous game.

Hart held her feet together, fingering one sole. Eden stifled her urge to giggle, then gasped as he somehow inserted both her big toes into the hot cavern of his mouth. A most peculiar sensation tugged in her lower belly as his tongue tricked and tickled. All the while he was massaging one foot, then the other. She felt an unfamiliar lassitude.

"That's quite enough," she said at last.

She felt his hands move up to her calves, stroking and kneading until her legs fell apart. The friction between his hands and her stockings unraveled her. He pushed aside the linens. The candles revealed the shadows on the planes of his face. Eden had never seen anyone with such earnest concentration before.

"I want to taste your rose again. May I?"

As if he needed to ask. She nodded and he parted her folds.

Bliss. The tip of his tongue swept slowly, remorselessly. She felt no embarrassment as she opened to him, urging him on with her thrusts. Two long fingers entered her while his mouth was busy feasting on her plump bud. She was drenched and filled with the certainty of his perfection. Soon she would edge beyond her boundaries, to the place where there was nothing but feeling and flying. In the meantime she lay dazed, almost thought-free, all focus on the morsel of flesh that was between his teeth and under his tongue. He was consuming her, devouring her. There would be nothing left but a flash of light as he made her disappear.

His fingers pumped in concert with her cries, bringing her to the brink and back. Teasing. Tormenting. And then he suckled, hard. Electricity crackled through her body, shock after shock. Heat spread from her belly to her breasts to her cheeks. He didn't stop. She didn't want him to. It was all too much, yet not quite enough.

When she was calm enough to speak rationally, she smoothed Hart's disheveled hair.

"I believe it must be your turn."

"And I believe I enjoyed that as much as you did." His finger traced the henna rose, skipping over odd ridges. He frowned. "Did they hurt you when they did this?"

"No, no. It's of no consequence."

"Hold still." Hart brought the branch of candles closer.

"Not the hot wax!" Eden cried. She scrambled into a sitting position and grabbed desperately for the blankets. Her bliss had dissolved in seconds, as though it had never existed.

"Eden. Love. What are you talking about?"

This, this was why it would never work between them. He could never understand. Her past, like white-hot flashes from a summer night's storm, would keep intruding. She shivered beneath the covers.

"N-nothing. I was nervous the wax would spill, that's all."

He put the candles down. "I will never hurt you. If I could bring Ivor to life again, I would kill him for what he has done to you. Eden, look at me."

Reluctantly, she raised her eyes. Hart looked like the fierce warrior he had been. She noted with some regret that his manhood was no longer standing at attention. Time spent with a debauched lunatic had a depressing effect, after all.

Her mix of shame and regret brought tears to her eyes. "I cannot do this, Hart. You must see that. When I'm with you, I cannot help but remember other times."

The muscle twitched in his cheek. "How did you plan to spend your nights at Mrs. Brown's?"

"It would have been different. Mechanical. My—my feelings would not have been involved."

She saw him surge with hope. She had revealed too much.

He sat next to her and took her hand. Absently he circled the soft pad of her palm. "Eden," he said softly. "Do you think me a murderer?"

"No! Why should I think such a thing?"

"Because I've killed men. I'm not even sure how many. I spent over ten years learning how to shoot, bayonet, bludgeon. How to use my bare hands if necessary."

He had conjured up a terrible vision for her. "But you were a soldier. And if you didn't know how to fight, you would not be here to tell me about it."

"Very true. I did what I had to do. And so did you."

"It's not at all the same."

"Is it not? What would have happened to you if you had defied Ivor?"

Eden knew too well. But God help her, at first she had been intrigued by the wickedness.

"I was not unwilling" was all she managed to say before he interrupted.

"Because he ensured that you were ripe for him, by all the devious steps he used to seduce you. You were little more than a lonely child, Eden. You had no idea of what he ultimately intended. I've seen the book. I've heard the tales. It was as if he made you his prisoner. Never tell me you were willing at the end."

No, she had not been. But she had no choice but to obey, or so she thought.

"What if he'd never planned to harm Jannah?" she asked in a hollow voice.

Hart snorted. "Oh, he would have. Only her illness prevented it. You did what you thought you had to do. And you must not let it ruin our future."

Eden felt the beginning of a pounding headache. She wished he would go away with his good intentions and honorable behavior. She could never change. "We have no future."

"Have you not been listening to a word I've said? I will stand by you until you come to me of your own free will. And you will." Hart flashed a grin. "I am told I'm irresistible. Now, come," he said lightly, "it is late and we are sitting on this comfortable bed. Perhaps we should lie down and try for sleep."

"J-just sleep?"

"Only that." He straightened the covers and slipped under them. "I shall hold you in my arms and watch you dream."

Eden joined him. He kept his hands on benign places, her elbow, her hip, but she could feel the heat of him. She had never been so comfortable or so miserable in her life.

* * *

Hart imagined he was the only man in London with a mistress whom he had pleasured twice but from whom he had received no reciprocation. His rod was absolutely rigid now, but he had no desire to disturb Eden in her sleep. She had been a devil of a bed partner, rolling, muttering, her slender body turning into one hundred sharp appendages that had poked him unmercifully all night long. Those tender toes he had kissed had kicked with abandon. He thought he might actually have a bruise or two.

But at this gray hour before sunrise, she seemed at peace, her dark hair tangled on the pillow. She'd had it cut at Mrs. Brown's. He missed the length of it as he remembered that rainy day when he saw her in the bath. It seemed like years ago.

He slid out of bed and stabbed at the ashes, finding a few feeble coals still useful. He tended to the fire as quietly as he could, then went into the tiny dressing room to relieve himself.

The cupboard stood open, and each of the black dresses that Juliet had selected hung neatly in the dark.

Hart wanted to see Eden in something other than black. Pale peach or pink or primrose, to contrast with her dark hair and eyes. Something normal. Girlish. She'd had no come-out, had never set foot in boring old Almack's or danced at balls or flirted with some foolish young blade. For the latter at least, he was grateful.

But she seemed to see no middle ground between being his uncle's concubine and being one of the Pantheon's jades. Eden had no hopes or aspirations for herself—certainly none that included him, even if she had admitted that her feelings were engaged.

He returned to his sleeping beauty. The covers had slipped, revealing her sinfully perfect body. She'd lost a pink garter in the melee of her night, but the black stockings stood out in stark contrast to the cream of her skin. Hart eased himself gently onto the bed and looked his fill, wishing the sun would hasten its appearance so he could see every glorious inch.

That flower adornment was incredibly erotic. He had never seen its like. He bent to study it, recalling the scarring beneath the petals. He stifled his oath. The painter had made every effort, but the straight angles of the letters had been difficult to conceal in the rounded petals.

The bloody bastard. Bile rose in Hart's throat, thinking of the cruelty of his uncle. Hart could imagine Eden, lying still, her tears ignored, waiting to be mutilated. He somehow must have skipped over this particular passage in the book. He was sure his uncle would have gloated over it.

For the first time in his campaign to court Eden, he felt a degree of despair. How could he counter with bracelets and cats what she had suffered? How naïve he had been. No wonder she had sought to erase one man under dozens of others. Perhaps she thought she could inoculate herself against ever feeling anything again.

He had spoken last night of killing with his bare hands. It had never given him satisfaction—it was simply expedient after his saber broke or his rifle had misfired. He'd not had to do it often, but how he longed to get his hands around his cursed uncle's neck.

Eden stirred, turning to her side. Hart saw more faint traces of his uncle's depravity. He closed his eyes, praying that his will to heal her body and her spirit would prosper. If not, he couldn't bear to think of her in Mrs. Brown's or some other place like it, no matter how superior it claimed to be.

With quiet haste, he dressed and let himself out of the little house. Eden might sleep the morning away, so exhausted she must be from her restless night. He had no idea how to spend his day, but knew a shave and a bath were in order. And a good, long nap.

Chapter 14

It was past noon when Mattie finally poked her head in the doorway. The baron had left before first light without even so much as a sip of coffee. Mrs. Philpott was quite put out after assembling what she hoped would be a proper postcoital breakfast to find the master missing and the mistress a slugabed. This couple was far different from the last lord and ladybird she'd served, Mrs. Philpott had said and sniffed. Miss Emery with her airs, her nose always buried in a book. The baron coming and going at all hours of the day and night. Mattie had to patiently explain that this couple was different, period.

Mattie was no fool. Something had been amiss at Hartford Hall, but she and Charlotte had had their hands full caring for the baroness and then Miss Jannah. There wasn't time to wonder why Miss Eden was sewing all those strange clothes or why she jumped at the sound of the master's voice. When young Lord Hartford enlisted Mattie in this scheme, he assured her he planned to make an honest woman of Miss Eden in the end. He'd better, or he'd have to answer to her.

Mattie set the breakfast tray down and opened the curtains. There wasn't much of a view, just a little patch of walled garden, but the house itself was a tidy little jewel box, everything up to snuff. Well, it had been until yesterday.

"Miss Eden, Mrs. Philpott wants me to talk to you about that cat."

Brutus. She'd forgotten about him completely, poor little mite.

"He's marking his territory, if you know what I mean. Mrs. P's having a fit of the vapors and Mr. P's got sticking plaster on his nose from when the cat tried to chew it off. They don't like him much."

"Oh, dear. Perhaps he should be shut in the scullery until he learns this is home. With plenty of cream and herring. Perhaps then he won't be so bad-tempered."

"I'm afraid you'll have to catch him then, miss. Mr. P would only strangle him if he got his hands on him again."

"That should give me something to do today," Eden said. "I do so hate being idle."

"I don't know what the baron was thinking. Seems to me the little devil is just an alley cat."

"Oh, surely not. He says he scoured the city for him. There was a lovely ribbon on the cage." But he'd never actually said he'd *purchased* him.

"Well, I'm sure you know best. You will ring for me when you're ready to dress?"

"Oh, yes." The wardrobe Juliet had supplied certainly required the assistance of a maid, vastly different from the dresses Eden had constructed for their maidless removal. Although Ivor Hartford had enjoyed watching her struggle before she'd had the wit to alter her clothing for his convenience.

Eden tore off a corner of toast and popped it in her mouth. She wondered if the girls were just rising at Mrs. Brown's. She missed the ribald chatter and easy laughter. And the little maids had been so earnest in the few lessons they'd begun. Impulsively, she pushed the tray away and rang for Mattie.

"Mrs. P won't be happy you didn't finish your breakfast."

"Pooh. Tell her that when I get back, I'll capture Brutus for her. And get Mr. Philpott to order me a hack in half an hour. I'm going out."

"Where are we going, miss?"

"*We* are not going anywhere. I have a private errand to run."

"You can't go out alone! The baron will have my hide!" Mattie wailed.

"He'll never know if we don't tell him, now, will he? And it will serve him right. I can't loll around here all day wondering when he'll turn up."

Mattie cleared her throat. "That's what mistresses do, miss."

"Not *this* mistress," said Eden with resolution.

* * *

She marched up the front steps. Even though she was veiled, the butler recognized her. He let her in, quickly escorting her upstairs to Madam's sitting room. Eden kept her lips firmly sealed as he scolded her. She wasn't Flora anymore. What was she thinking of, sailing in here in broad daylight? What if one of the gentlemen members couldn't control himself until darkness fell and found her lounging about in the vestibule? He all but said she was as mad as a hatter.

Mrs. Brown had been enjoying a demitasse in the kitchens, speaking fluent French with both her chefs, when Foster informed her of the disaster that awaited her upstairs. She calmly laid her cup aside.

"Claude, Henri, the midnight supper you have planned for the special event will be a triumph and long remembered. If you will excuse me."

Mrs. Brown was beginning to feel a bit like a player in a French farce. This Hartford business was taking up far too much of her time. The sooner the baron and Eden wed, the sooner they could sequester themselves in the country and stop involving her in their affairs. But if it was amorous advice Eden wanted, she had come to the appropriate source. Mrs. Brown took a deep breath and entered her sitting room.

"My dear, how chic you look," she said approvingly, noting the exquisite cut of Eden's dress and matching pelisse. She was pleased to see that Eden had at least had the sense to wear a veiled bonnet.

"It is Hart's aunt's doing. She thought she was ordering my trousseau."

"Then you have not changed your mind about marriage? I am shocked that Baron Hartford has not changed it for you. Does his lovemaking leave you cold?"

Eden blushed. "No. That is, we have not really done it yet."

Mrs. Brown sat down in some shock, inviting Eden to do likewise. "The girls told me he was perfectly capable. Accomplished, even."

"I really can't explain why he has failed to consummate our arrangement, but I expect he'll get around to it eventually. But I have come on a different matter."

"Oh?"

"The younger maids. Francie and Josie and the others. I should like to continue their lessons."

"What does Baron Hartford have to say about that?"

"I haven't mentioned it. I see no reason why I should."

Mrs. Brown considered. Eden looked determined. As much as Iris enjoyed working with her young charges, running her business and assisting the goddesses in their own educational endeavors took up a great deal of her time.

"You know I cannot spare the girls for more than an hour or so a day. Where did you think to instruct them?"

"Why, here, of course."

"Hartford won't like that."

"He won't know. I'll get him to set a schedule for his visits. Perhaps I'll tell him I'm helping with a charity school. It won't be far from the truth."

Mrs. Brown shook a manicured finger at her. "I won't have you putting ideas in their heads, Eden. They've all been whored out on the street, you know. That's how I found them. Katy was just six. These are not innocent little girls. A life here is more than they had ever dreamed of."

"I know. You are a generous employer and have a warm heart. I mean no criticism of you. Ceres told me she got her start here in just the same way, and I know she is happy. I was happy here myself." She looked down at her neat black kid gloves. "I miss my sister fiercely. Idle hands. I'm at loose ends."

"Perhaps you should volunteer at a real charity school then."

"I am a man's mistress. I hardly think I would be welcome."

Mrs. Brown knew Hartford meant to hide his intended bride until she was persuaded to make his intentions a reality. But if Eden was discreet, no one need remark on her visits. The maids could meet with her in the staff dining room in the back of the house. There was a private rear entrance that had been used a time or two when a gentleman had to make a hasty exit. Mrs. Brown recalled one very formidable dowager marchioness who had hunted her son the marquess down after months of fruitless letter-writing. She had not budged from the Pantheon's hallway for three-quarters of an hour. Mrs. Brown had to admire the woman's determination, although she'd had a depressing effect on business for the evening.

"Very well. The girls *were* disappointed when you left us. Work something out with Lord Hartford, and let me know when it will be convenient for you to come. I'll make sure your eager pupils are free." Mrs. Brown pressed Eden's gloved hand. "Do be careful, dear. I doubt very much whether Holy Hartford wants his future wife to have an association with an establishment such as mine. I shouldn't want you to ruin your chances with him."

"There is nothing to risk, Mrs. Brown. I expect before long I'll be right back here entertaining gentlemen."

Mrs. Brown's silver eyes narrowed. "Do you mean to break your contract?"

"No. But Hart will. He'll come to his senses and see how impossible this all is."

"Perhaps." But Iris Brown didn't believe it for a minute.

* * *

She should be happy. She was not, but she was at least comfortable. Perfumed and elegant, too. Eden sat on a parlor sofa awaiting Hart's return. The fire burned bright in the grate. Brutus purred in her lap. Another delicious dinner had been prepared, no thanks to the cat, who had gotten on Mrs. Philpott's nerves. But Eden thought the little fellow was simply misunderstood. He just needed some fattening up and the area behind his ears rubbed.

As she watched the hypnotic flames, Eden was somewhat stricken with the knowledge that she had sadly neglected Hart's pleasure thus far. She knew this interlude of theirs would not last, but she meant to derive every physical benefit from it. If she could steel her mind from her past, there was a chance she might enjoy the touch of a normal man.

She sighed. Hart was not normal. He was a paragon of virtue and honor. And unbearably handsome to boot. He'd make some young society miss an excellent husband. They'd raise an army of children to turn Hartford Hall into a real home at last, to banish the specter of sin forevermore.

She was startled from her reverie by the brush of warm lips on her neck. "Oh! You might have given me an apoplexy!"

"Stealth is just one of my skills. I didn't cause you to awaken this morning, did I?" He came around and sat down on the sofa next to her. Brutus opened one eye at the intrusion and promptly shut it. "I see you have civilized our little friend."

"The Philpotts are not very happy with you and your present, my lord. You may have to give them a raise."

"It is my opinion that the Philpotts are doing very well already. How did you spend your day? I confess after you kicked me into perdition all night long I went home and slept the day away. So I trust I shall be alert this evening for whatever you have planned."

Eden felt guilty on all counts—for being a restless bedmate and for her visit to the Pantheon. And she had avoided thinking about the matter of their intimacy. She tucked the cat into a corner of the couch and stood up. "May I get you a drink, Hart? Brandy? Sherry?"

"I'll have a finger or two of whiskey, if you have it."

Eden peered into the drinks cupboard. It seemed she had everything. She poured Hart a generous amount and returned to the sofa. As soon as she sat down, Brutus returned to the warmth of her lap.

"Nothing for you?" asked Hart after taking a sip.

"I shall have some wine with dinner."

They sat for a few minutes before the fire, the only sound in the room the hiss of the logs and the low rumble of the flames. Eden supposed they presented a charming domestic scene. But she felt the knot of worry at her neck. If her dress had not been so à la mode that it prohibited her from raising her arms, she might have rubbed herself as she had rubbed Brutus.

"You're very quiet. What are you thinking about, Eden?"

Perhaps now was as good a time as any. "I have heard of a school— a charity school. They are in need of volunteer teachers. You would not mind if I spent an hour or so working with young girls every day? I would of course be available to you in the evenings."

"That sounds very worthy." He looked into her face. Her gray eyes were huge with what appeared to be anxiety, as though she waited for him to forbid her. She had been forbidden from far too many things these past four years. He supposed she must be beyond bored waiting for his visits. If she only knew how he'd like to move in and spend every waking and sleeping minute with her. Well, perhaps not sleeping. He'd been devilish uncomfortable. "I have no objection. Is this your way of setting me on a schedule?" he asked and grinned.

"You have caught me out, sir. But I shouldn't like to inconvenience you."

"As long as you grant me a few minutes of your time every evening, I shall be a happy man." He had plenty to occupy himself with during the day. And now that Des's nights were spent in the arms of one goddess or another, company at his club was flat.

"Thank you, Hart."

"Come, puss."

Eden froze. But Hart merely transferred the cat from her lap to the floor.

"I need a kiss before dinner. I say, are you all right? You've gone pale as the moon."

"I-I am fine." Eden turned to him and closed her eyes, wishing she could close off part of her mind altogether.

She felt disembodied, floating. And his kiss didn't help, but sent her even further away. His lips were whiskey-warm. At first they simply pressed chastely upon her own, but then Hart's tongue teased the left corner of her mouth, swept in, invaded. She lost the battle for clarity almost immediately.

She should let him take her on the sofa now. Damn dinner. She had to know—

There was a knock on the door. Hart pulled back.

"Later," he whispered.

* * *

Eden had excused herself after a delicious dessert of meringues filled with bottled fruit to get ready for him. He was going to be deprived of all the unbuttoning and unlacing, and that was probably just as well. When one anticipated important events, one inevitably got nervous. Hart had to allow that he felt nearly as anxious as if he were preparing to go off to battle again.

And it was a battle. Somehow Hart had to erase the past. Not only had his uncle toyed with Eden's sensibilities, but he'd left an ugly reminder on her body that would forever scar her. And as seductive as the henna tattoo was, he was anxious that Eden's nether hair grow back and cover the symbol of her servitude. That was a simple solution. Far more difficult was erasing Ivor Hartford from Eden's mind.

Mattie knocked on the parlor door, blushing profusely. "You can go up now, my lord."

"Thank you, Mattie." He paused. "How would you say Miss Eden's mood is?"

"I think she's right nervous, sir."

"Well, so am I. We shall deal well together, or fall to pieces."

"I hope it's the first, sir. Miss Eden's had enough worry."

"Indeed she has. Thank you, Mattie."

When he entered the room, he was disappointed to find it in near darkness. But Eden had set the stage, and he was now an actor in her play. She lay in the bed, her hair a dark cloud upon the pillowcase, the quilted coverlet up to her chin. Without a word, he undressed efficiently. He thought of the other day, when he was as eager as a young stripling. When he thought the noon brightness would cast its light upon them. When he thought he knew the worst of her suffering and was prepared to tease and tempt her into pleasure.

His task ahead was more complex. Had greater chances of failure. Would lead to heartbreak for both of them if he did not find the way to ease her sorrow. A voice within questioned why he was so determined to have this particular woman, why his heart was at risk. Why did he want to marry her? For surely he had just wanted a comfortable, unexceptional wife. Some girl with a bit of education and a modicum of virtue. He had not even recognized Eden as the beauty she was when they first met, so he was not the victim of Cupid's arrow.

Hart knew Eden thought he was an unnecessary knight errant,

out to rescue a damsel who had earned every bit of her distress. He couldn't credit that. His was not simply a chivalrous quest for Eden's hand to somehow defend the family honor. To bury Ivor once and for all. True, he wished to do both things, but even more he wanted Eden to feel cherished. As she deserved to be cherished. For despite any pretense to reason or rationale, he believed he was falling in love with her, even though he knew only a part of her. She felt so right in his arms. He wanted to bring laughter to her eyes and joy to her soul.

But first, he wanted to bring her to climax. He could see the tension in her still body, mummified as she was by the covers. He wrestled the edge from her and slipped under.

"Eden," he said softly.

* * *

She was defenseless against him. He burned as brightly as an angel by the single candle.

"Yes, my lord."

A mistake. She saw the hurt on his face. "Hart."

"That's better." He pulled her to him, kissing a white shoulder. She thought if she looked, she would see the warm imprint of his lips on her skin.

"I will not hurt you," he promised.

Soon she felt his imprint everywhere. His mouth skimmed her neck, the valley between her breasts, each puckered nipple. When he licked the crescent under each breast, she thought she would expire of lust. She lay absolutely still, savoring each nip and graze.

He was conquering her, vanquishing her fears one inch of skin at a time.

His hand slipped between her legs and she gave a little cry.

She was ready. Slick and wet and oh so willing. Aching for him to enter her and make her feel whole again. Completed. Uncomplicated.

"Please." She could barely say the word. Her lips were numb, her mind a perfect blank. Her need was so great it was a wonder to her that she still breathed at all. But he did not seat himself within her, instead returning to the scene of her earlier rapture with his teeth and tongue to bring her to the brink. But no further. Tonight she knew they would come together, joined in body and spirit. She lay as his warm, rough tongue traced his pattern on her rose, parting her own petals and entering the dark recesses of her body. Tiny lights flickered behind her eyelids as he took her closer to the flame. He licked his way back up to her lips, drinking the nectar within her mouth with all the fervor of a starved man. She tasted her own honeyed decadence on his tongue.

"Look at me, Eden," he said, rising above her.

In the dark, he was so like his uncle it hurt. It was as though the devil himself was playing a trick on her, tempting her with the improved image of her foolish girl's desire and at the same time snatching away her future happiness with its reminder. How she wished he were darker or uglier. Instead he was her golden-haired angel.

"I want you to keep your eyes open when I make you mine," Hart said, his voice raspy. "I am not Ivor. I want you to see that, to know it with every touch, every kiss, every stroke. I will never hurt you."

Eden nodded. "I want to believe that." Her hand reached out to guide him home.

* * *

Effortless perfection. Sheathed heat. Liquid pleasure. His eyes remained on hers as he moved slowly above her and within her. It had cost him not to spill his seed the instant her hand first touched him. As much as he wanted to claim her quickly, Hart wanted to give her no discomfort. Their dance was languid, lazy even. At first she was as still as death, frozen in some sort of limbo. Gradually he felt her adjust to him, to meet his long thrusts with the rise of her hips. A sigh escaped her. Then a series of short cries. Her eyes closed, her mouth twisted.

Though he had been called Holy Hartford, he'd not been a monk. But this night with Eden was far different from anything that had come before. Whether it was simply a case of his patience being rewarded rather spectacularly, or something far more mystical, he had never felt so alive. He sensed she felt the same.

"Open your eyes, Eden." His voice was harsher than he'd intended. His actions harder. His breathing faster. He wanted to tell her, but couldn't find the words. Let his body tell her instead.

* * *

Eden watched him, fascinated that something she had experienced a thousand times could feel so new. His gaze was open and steady. He was smiling, not in triumph but pure happiness. She felt his hand cup her cheek and she turned to kiss it.

He thrust in steady rhythm, pulling her along to his music. His cock bumped against the tip of her womb and she arched, legs stiff, hands wild on his back. Urging him, crying, losing what little control she had. She was no longer capable of speech or thought, just pure driving sensation skittering from his body over hers and into her heart.

And then he flooded her, the wetness soothing the fire within her. He sought her mouth as he emptied his soul. Held her until their hearts quieted.

"You are all right?" he finally managed to ask.

"Perfectly." And it was true. Save for the initial fright, she had warmed to Hart's skill, savored his lovemaking. If she had been Brutus, she would have been purring, she thought ruefully. Her pleasure had been fleeting, yet intense. He had waited for her, and for that she was grateful.

He tucked her into him, his breath hot against her temple.

"Do you dare to sleep in this bed with me tonight?" she asked, attempting humor. She did not want a serious discussion of anything at the moment.

"I had not thought to sleep much," Hart replied, his voice a gravelly burr.

Eden smiled. "Because of my kicking, sir?"

"Because I will take you again tonight. And again, if it's possible. It is you who will have no sleep tonight."

"You are cruel." Eden could imagine nothing better.

"Cruel to be kind. Do you want anything? Some wine or a sweetmeat?"

"Only you." She kissed him briefly on the lips, then drew downward on the bed. She fondled his cock, sticky from their play.

Hart inhaled sharply. "You don't have to—"

"Hush. I want to." *I need to,* she thought.

Her lips and hands at first brushed his heavy sac. He twitched in delicious agony. When her tongue made contact with his shaft, she felt him relax and let her master him. She covered every square inch of skin systematically, cleaning him as a mother cat cleaned a kitten. She took him in her mouth and she felt his cock begin to stir again.

"Surely this is a bit of a miracle. I don't think I'm quite ready—"

"Do be quiet," she murmured, releasing him from the seductive prison of her mouth. "I will not stop until you are."

My God. Whether she'd learned these tricks from his uncle or her stay at Mrs. Brown's, he didn't know and didn't care. She guided him deep, her tongue stretched and dancing around him. She sucked and swallowed, each jump in her throat squeezing him in a delicious vise. It was almost the heaven of her cunny, hot and moist and wicked. Her dark lashes fluttered on her crimson cheeks, her brows knit in sensual concentration. She had never looked more beautiful to him, or more dangerous.

Then she opened her dark eyes, staring straight into his with bold purpose, her mouth lifting into a saucy smile as she took him even deeper. This, now *this* was true danger. He fell into the fathomless depths, taut and hard, drowning, about to spend himself in one endless wave. He couldn't hold out much longer against such luscious sin, floating at the edge of sanity. He attempted to withdraw, but she merely shook her head in impatience and suckled at him with another smile until he had absolutely nothing left. He lay dazed on the linen sheets, wondering if he was still alive. Lassitude crept over him as she nestled back beside him, pressing her white body close.

"God. I've never—that is to say—good lord. You've turned my mind to mush. I am incapable of any rational thought at present. Thank you."

"I merely returned the favor. I believe I owe you one more."

Hart groaned. "Please, not now."

"Very well. But don't be surprised if in the middle of the night—"

He silenced her with a kiss and drew the covers up over both of them.

* * *

"I am never moving. Never, not for all eternity."

"Unlikely. I would have to dust you if you stayed in bed forever."

"Is that what you would call it?" Hart chuckled, pulling her closer. "I'd call it something else entirely."

She pinched his arm. "Leave off, my lord, I beg you. Think of your future. Think of the loss to the world. The country would go into a decline should you fail to take your seat in Parliament. Here you'd lie in your own dirt. You would soon be bored. And, I fancy, smell."

"You could wash me again." She had done so just an hour ago, the two of them nearly tipping the copper tub over. Then they proceeded to negate all the soap by loving each other again until they were both slick with sweat. And very satisfied. Bright sunlight illuminated Eden's bedroom, yet they were still abed, after a futile attempt to be up and about. The breakfast tray still held a roll, which Hart popped into his mouth.

"Shall I order a luncheon?"

Hart shook his head. "As much as I truly wish I could stay here forever," he squeezed her hand, "and I do, Calvert is probably waiting at home for me, tapping his foot. He's an estimable young man."

"Young? You speak if you're an ancient one."

"Sometimes I feel old. Old-headed, anyway. Someone in the family had to take care of things." He saw the pained expression on Eden's face. "I'm speaking of my father. He was rather useless. And Juliet has needed my help these past five years since her husband died. I'm very fond of her boys. I can't wait for you to meet them."

"Hart!" said Eden, shocked. "I am your mistress. You cannot possibly think to introduce me to them."

Hart's little domestic fantasy was rent as Eden reminded him of their true, if temporary, relationship. He wondered how much longer it would take for her to cast her foolish objections aside. Surely after last night and this morning, there could be no doubt of their compatibility. If he had not totally driven the demon Ivor from the bedchamber, he felt he had come close.

"We'll argue over that at dinner," he replied, climbing out of bed. "How will you spend your day? At your school?"

Eden bit her lip. "Yes, perhaps. At least I'll make a visit and let them know I am available."

"I trust that they don't know you're my mistress." He knew those women hell-bent on charity were often the most judgmental.

"Of course not. They merely know me as a clergyman's daughter with a small independence."

"Well," he said, bending to give her one last kiss, on the cheek so he could actually make his way out the door, "I hope you enjoy the little angels."

"I will," she said, smiling. Little angels indeed.

* * *

The girls sat at a scrubbed table in the servants' dining hall. Claude could be heard in the distance cursing in French at Richard, the poor pot boy who was growing more bilingual by the hour, but the girls were paying no mind to him. They all knew Claude's bark was far worse than his bite. In any event, Eden had not gotten far enough with their French lessons for them to comprehend exactly what he was saying. They would not have been shocked in any case.

For the week she had been teaching them, Eden divided the paltry hour she had a day into quarters. The girls themselves had picked the curriculum. Josie was anxious to improve her speech, so for fifteen minutes the girls practiced reading poetry out loud. This had afforded Eden the opportunity to discuss definitions and symbolism with them. They had been agog to understand what Shakespeare had really meant by treasure; it had absolutely nothing to do with pirate booty or jewels. Mrs. Brown had found a globe and some maps somewhere for Francie, so four little heads, one golden, one red and two dark, pored over the world and tested one another on capitals and facts. Barbara insisted on learning mathematics, for she planned to take over Madam's business one day. Eden rather believed it might be possible. Barbara was taller, bolder and more beautiful than the rest, and Mrs. Brown's especial pet. Her younger sister Mary, the quietest, had wished to learn French and drawing. Drawing was overruled by the others as not a practical subject.

"What? Are we to have time to draw the gents' dangly bits? That's not what they pay for," said Barbara reasonably.

Eden was relieved. Drawing was Ivor's skill, certainly not hers. Eden suspected if Mary could, she'd try to escape her future and become a dressmaker. Mary was clever with a needle and possessed a keen fashion sense. The girls had been prostituted as a pair by their mother, who had herself died of the pox. Eden was nearly glad the woman had come to such an end for what she had done to her daughters. Eden knew how Mrs. Brown felt about her protégées, but perhaps she could be persuaded to make an exception in Mary's case. She seemed ill-suited to the whore's life, although Barbara at almost fifteen was champing at the bit to climb Mount Olympus and start her career as a goddess.

The short lessons seemed to suit them all. There was plenty of laughter mixed with the learning, and Eden wondered if she should not eventually seek a position as a governess, if ever her tainted background could be covered up. She could get the Reverend Christopher and his wife to vouch for her, she was sure.

Her life as it was couldn't last. It was too perfect. Somehow she had lost Kempton completely. Hart came home to her every night, almost like a husband. Better even. Many husbands of the ton were amusing themselves nightly upstairs, or in some other similar house like Mrs. Brown's, or with their mistresses. Eden knew her own little street was composed entirely of girls and women in exactly the same position she was, although she doubted they loved their keepers as much as she loved Hart.

He was a thoughtful lover and a charming companion. He seemed every bit as enthralled with her as she was with him. He brought her presents daily, although she was still fondest of Brutus, who had made himself indispensable as a mouser and had wormed his way into the good graces of the Philpotts. One night Hart brought her a cluster of hothouse violets, another evening a pearl ring, which he had placed on her left hand as though it were an engagement ring. Last night he had given her a diaphanous negligee, something that rather resembled what had hung in Flora's closet, a blush pink confection which caused him to remove it just moments after she had put it on.

And Ivor seemed gone—not totally forgotten, but his lingering presence did not mar the joy she found in Hart's arms.

Her attention was drawn to an argument the sisters were having over a French phrase, a rather naughty double entendre which Eden acknowledged would be regrettably useful with any number of gentlemen.

"Enough, girls." She looked at the timepiece that was pinned to her very proper black gown.

"Oh! It ain't time to stop for the day!" Josie wailed, careful to enunciate each word.

"*Isn't* time. I'm afraid it is. Lord Hartford will be visiting me earlier than usual today." Her dark eyes sparkled. "He says he has another surprise for me."

"You are so lucky." Barbara sighed. "A handsome, rich lord who's madly in love with you."

"Who gives you presents," added Mary.

Eden shook her head. "Don't romanticize, girls. Lord Hartford is very kind, it is true, but he is my benefactor, not my betrothed. We have a business relationship. When he marries, no doubt he'll give me his congé."

"What if it's you he wants to marry?" Francie asked baldly.

"That isn't possible. A gentleman needs a real lady for a wife, not a—"

She looked at the eager faces before her. If she considered that she had no chance for a normal life, what would happen to these young girls, brutalized as children? She wished she could take the lot of them home. New girls would only be too happy to get off the streets and replace them. Iris Brown had rescued them all from horror, but some horror still awaited them.

"Not someone like me, who has no wish to lose my independence and dance attendance on just one man," she finished.

"He's very handsome, though," said Francie. "I saw him here the night he took you away from us."

"Yes, he is very handsome," agreed Eden.

"What is he *like?*" asked Barbara. "Is he as big as Lord Radcliffe?"

"Barbara! A lady does not discuss such things."

"You just said you weren't a lady. It is not as if we four are children," Barbara said and sniffed.

"But you are! Or you should be."

Francie smiled, dimpling her freckled cheeks. Her hair was the palest red, quite curly and glorious, but she complained constantly that her freckles were the bane of her existence. Eden thought every inch of her was adorable. In a few short weeks, Mrs. Brown's gentlemen would think so, too. Artemis and Vesta were leaving the house to perform in a traveling theater company. Not much acting was involved, as the shows were erotic in nature, perfectly suited for the two lovers. They had been promised adventure and freedom on the Continent by one of Mrs. Brown's old acquaintances. Francie was destined to be the new Vesta, and was already receiving her courtesan training from the girls, which is how she'd come upon Hart that night. Mrs. Brown sent her junior maids off to bed before they could fall into her members' paths, but Francie had been observing. "Miss Eden," she said gently, "none of us were ever children, not that we can recall. I had a baby before I ever came here two years ago. A little girl."

Eden was shocked. "I didn't know. What happened to her?"

"She was taken away." Francie shrugged. "I was sick, but Mrs. Brown took me in, promised me a job when I got well. The men here are much nicer than what I put up with before. And if I get caught again, Mrs. Brown can help me."

Eden didn't want to think about how. Vinegar-soaked sponges were not always enough.

"You are sure this is what you want, Francie?" Eden couldn't help asking, despite Mrs. Brown's warning to her not to interfere.

"Oh, yes. I reckon I'll do very well. If the men can get past my spots. They are *everywhere*," Francie grumbled.

Eden gathered up her charts and books and put them into the cupboard. She resisted an impulse to hug each girl good-bye, for she would be seeing them in a mere twenty-three hours. She was well aware that each of them in her own way substituted for her sister— Barbara's ambition, Francie's bravery, Mary's quiet forbearance, and Josie's sunny good nature. They had all come to this house through trials that might have been fatal. Jannah would have quizzed them tirelessly in her attempt to "experience" everything. Eden was nearly grateful her sister had been spared the seamy side of life.

"I shall see you all tomorrow. If you have time during your duties, you should practice your multiplication tables. I shall test you tomorrow."

The girls groaned cheerfully and went back to their chores. Eden fastened her cape and dropped her hat's elegant veil over her face. She knew the hired cab would be at the end of the lane for her, and hoped her lover was not already impatiently waiting for her at home.

Chapter 15

LONDON, DECEMBER 1818

He would wake her in a few minutes to see this little Christmas miracle. The snow swirled in a slate sky, pure white at the moment. Soon it would be sooty, more inconvenient than enchanting. For now, it dusted the rooftops and frosted the lone tree in the little walled garden below, turning it into a fairyland.

But how foolish of him. She'd grown up in the north where the Cumbrian fells and moors were blanketed with snow for months on end.

And she needed her rest. Last night had been particularly harrowing, as she'd fought off an invisible attacker and cried out in her sleep. For every forward step he made with her, she dragged him back two.

He was fairly sure she loved him. She gave her body to him with complete unselfishness, perhaps even joy. There was no sense of Ivor's shadow in a dark corner, save at night, when her dreams drove Hart to wakefulness.

What he felt for her was more complicated. Desire, certainly.

Protectiveness. Something beyond simple affection. He thought if a gun was pointed to his head or a sword to his heart, he could not adequately explain why Eden was so important to him. It went beyond the physical. It went beyond pity for her past.

If he ever persuaded her to marry him, she would not make an easy wife. He marveled that in the month he'd kept her, she'd shed her hesitancy and was not at all shy in expressing an opinion or arguing a point. Sometimes he thought she was shrewish on purpose to drive him away, but he would not be so easily discouraged. He knew she chafed at the privacy he sought for them both, and reminded her that if they were married, they could move about in society as much or as little as she wished.

And then her face would pale. He knew about Kempton. He knew about Blanchard. She would never feel safe. A wedding ring would not change that.

"Merry Christmas, Eden."

She groaned and rolled out of his reach.

"Wake up! It's snowing! Let's get dressed and go out in the garden. I'll dash about and you may pelt me with snowballs." Hart imagined running in the tiny pocket garden. He'd injure himself on the brick walls with one good stride.

Eden stifled a yawn. She looked tired, and he wondered if she was coming down with something. "Tempting as that prospect is, sir, I shall have to decline." She stretched back in the bed.

"Are you feeling all right? You're a little pale."

"It's your fault, you wicked man. I shall have to give you laudanum in your wine so I may get a decent night's rest."

"Decency is vastly overrated," Hart said and grinned. "And besides, it was *you* who deprived *me* of sleep. Do you remember your dreams? They must have been particularly unpleasant."

Eden shook her head. "I'm sorry. Did I strike you?"

"Only once or twice. I'm made of sterner stuff. I can take the feeble fists of my mistress."

"Yet another reason for us not to marry. You don't want to be saddled with a pugilist for a bride."

"Come, I'll not start Christmas morning off with an argument. Shall we go down to breakfast?"

"Perhaps just some tea and toast. And if you don't mind, have Mattie bring it up to me. You go down. Mrs. Philpott will be upset if you don't."

Hart sighed but began to dress. "Yes, I must make sure she holds me in high regard. It's not as if I don't pay her enough. Eden, you know if we marry I can give up this house and put the avaricious Philpotts firmly behind me. I am not made of money, you know."

"Things are lovely just as they are. Why spoil it?"

"Because I want to spoil *you*," he said earnestly. "I want you as my wife, the hostess at my table, my helpmate."

He was careful not to mention mother of his children. He'd not forgotten her barrenness.

And it didn't matter. Not in the least. He must have some sixth cousin twice removed somewhere to inherit.

He looked at her in the early morning light. Despite her pallor, she was looking much healthier than she had when she fell at his feet the first day they met. She was no longer emaciated. Her plumpness was becoming, her breasts even fuller and more delicious than ever. So tempting that before he went downstairs he was forced to suckle at one, then the other, as Eden lay back in contentment.

"Tea," she said finally. "Toast."

"Your wish is my command, my lady. And when you are ready, I have your Christmas present."

When Hart left, Eden staggered to the dressing room to relieve herself. She did not faint. She never fainted, save the first time she saw Hart, but she was perilously close this morning. Dark spots floated before her. She tossed the wash water out the window into the garden and brought the basin back to bed. If she wasn't very much mistaken, she was going to cast up her accounts very soon.

She knew she was not pregnant. Her courses had arrived a few days ago. She'd never been regular, and was almost disappointed to discover that Hart was no more successful than his uncle had been. But it was for the best.

She'd have to send a message to the girls that she would not visit on Boxing Day tomorrow. Apart from feeling unwell, there was the snow to contend with. Eden didn't mind the cold, but she didn't want to walk all the way to Mrs. Brown's on slippery, slushy streets. Cabs would be hard to come by. The heavy, dancing flakes might not last until tomorrow, but they would be enough to sugarcoat the landscape and make foot travel difficult. Mattie would have to find an errand boy to deliver her note.

And there was roast goose and all the trimmings to contend with later. She wasn't sure how she'd manage tea and toast. But this was her first and only Christmas with Hart, and she'd have to rally.

* * *

Hart was a bit tired of leading his double life. By day he appeared in Parliament and worked on his affairs with Calvert. By night he was in Eden's bed. His aunt Juliet had become rather waspish as she berated him for his failure to attend musicales, dances and dinner parties. She had been hurt when he'd begged off Christmas luncheon. Guilty, Hart pecked Eden good-bye and gathered up his gifts for the Cheverlys. He could spare an hour on a frigid Christmas Day to smooth her ruffled, matchmaking feathers.

He wanted no one but Eden. But there were still times when he moved too quickly and saw her flinch.

When she stumbled over the words "Lord Hartford" as she was instructing the servants.

When she worried that somehow Kempton would find her, or Ivor's friend Lord Blanchard would recognize her.

Hart doubted the latter. He scarcely recognized her himself. Gone was the painfully slender, pale girl with the fierce brows and stiff lips. In her place, was a curvaceous, elegant young woman who smiled often and laughed easily. If she married him, he could take her back to Hartford Hall and make her safe there. As it was, he was concerned that somehow someone would discover she was his ladybird. He couldn't expect her to be shut up in her charming little house all day, but he worried about her teaching at the charity school, shopping in town with Mattie. If Eden bumped into his aunt, there would be the devil to pay once Juliet realized how Hart had set Eden up as his mistress.

It was time to make a penance call upon his aunt, and remind her that he still had every intention of marrying Eden. Let his aunt think a decent period of mourning was being observed. He mounted the marble front steps and was greeted by Juliet's very proper butler before his hand could touch the gleaming brass knocker.

"Good afternoon, Baron Hartford. Happy Christmas. Your aunt is already with Major Desmond, but I'm sure they will welcome your presence."

Hart nearly dropped his hat handing it off to the butler, who in turn handed it off to one of the footmen, Robert or Steven, he wasn't sure which. He shrugged off his coat, which was immediately dusted of its snowflakes. "Des is here? How on earth did he know that I was going to pay my aunt a visit?"

The butler smiled thinly. "I'm sure I couldn't say, my lord."

Clutching the gifts, Hart followed the man up the Turkey-carpeted stairs to his aunt's drawing room. The doors were firmly shut, but Hart could hear the tinkle of his aunt's laughter. Old Des could be a charmer if he wished. The butler Gerrard knocked.

"Come."

"Mrs. Cheverly, Baron Hartford," Gerrard announced, as though Juliet didn't have eyes in her head.

Juliet blushed prettily, matching the soft rose of her Swiss muslin day dress. Hart bent to kiss her cheek.

"Merry Christmas, my absent nephew! I thought you refused my invitation. Gerrard, have another place set for lunch."

"I'm afraid I can't stay, Juliet. I just brought presents for you and the boys. Where are they?"

"Upstairs somewhere playing with the soldiers Hen—Major Desmond was kind enough to procure for me. What do you mean you can't stay?"

"I can make no excuses, only apologies. Des, I'm astonished to see you here. How did you know I missed my old aunt?"

Juliet pushed him away. "Old! If that is how you apologize, Gerrard can see you right out."

Des stood as stiffly as if he were about to go on parade. "I believe your aunt is but a year or two older than you yourself, Hart. If anyone is old, it is I. I shall be thirty on my next birthday."

Hart grinned, knowing full well his aunt had celebrated her thirtieth birthday nearly two years ago. "Yes, you are virtually decrepit. General Tavistock will see you out on your ear any day now. How is the old Tartar?"

"As short-tempered as ever. There's talk that we shall go to India."

"Oh, no!"

Both men turned to Juliet, whose rosy blush had now turned to crimson.

"Ah. For a moment I had forgotten you sold out, Hart." Juliet twisted her rings, a sure sign she was prevaricating.

Hart looked to his friend. Des was turning a rather alarming color as well. What the devil?

"Mrs. Cheverly, I've taken up enough of your time. No doubt you have family business to discuss with Hart."

"Th-thank you for bringing the boys such a fine Christmas gift, Major. You are too kind."

"I thought you didn't want to encourage the bloodthirsty little devils in their war games, aunt." Hart watched in amusement as both Des and Juliet looked stricken. Never in a million years would he have imagined that his determinedly unmarried best friend and the Mad Matchmaker would make a match of it. But he still had some of his wits about him, despite his own love-struck state. However, if he knew Juliet, she would not for one minute put up with Des's patronage of Mrs. Brown's. Nor would Hart.

"You know I'd do anything for my boys," Juliet said, her tone more brisk. "The major found the perfect set."

"Lucky, that. Des, I'd like to have a word with you. I'll walk part of the way home with you. Juliet, don't go anywhere. We have some catching up to do."

Des looked even more rigid than before as they went down the stairs. Gerrard helped them with their outerwear and they went into the street and the storm.

Hart lifted an eyebrow. "When were you going to ask my permission to court my aunt?"

"Don't be ridiculous! You are not her guardian and she's not a child!" Des blustered.

"Indeed she is not. She is, I believe, a few years older than you are."

"What of it? She's a very handsome woman."

"With a substantial portion. One might even say she is filthy rich."

Des looked like he'd enjoy throttling Hart in the middle of the sidewalk. "Are you implying I am a fortune hunter, Lord Hartford?"

"Stand down, Des. I am implying nothing of the kind. But Juliet and her boys are my only living family. I feel responsible for them. Cheverly named me their trustee. I should have thought you'd speak to me before undertaking a friendship with her."

Des removed his hat and ran his fingers through his hair. It was cropped so short there was little point, but Hart recognized his friend's nervous habit.

"Juliet is expecting you back."

"I imagine she's going to develop a headache and will be unable to receive me. How long has this been going on?"

"Not long. A month or so. We met by accident on Oxford Street."

"And you didn't think to tell me?"

"I didn't want . . . You weren't . . . She said . . ."

Hart laughed. "Good God, man! You do have it bad." To his surprise, his friend sat down upon the snowy marble steps of a town house, having no care for his uniform.

"I love her, Hart. Can you credit it? I, who've escaped her schemes for years, have fallen for *her* instead of all the silly chits she's thrown in my path. Gad, do you remember Araminta Shirley?" Des shuddered.

"What of her boys?" Hart asked quietly.

"Araminta has no children," Des said in confusion.

"My nephews, you dullard. Raphael and Sebastian."

Des's face lit up. "Capital young fellows, but I don't need to tell you that."

Hart sat down next to his friend. In minutes he supposed Lady Fullham's butler was going to throw scalding water on them. They were already attracting the attention of passersby out for a Christmas stroll in the snow on the fashionable street. Hart turned and looked at the dark green door behind him. The knocker had been removed. Good. Lady Fullham must be wintering in the country. But that didn't mean he wished to lounge about on her icy marble steps for very long.

"What are your intentions, then?"

"I've asked her to marry me."

Hart frowned. "And?"

"She hasn't accepted. She hasn't refused, either," Des said hurriedly. "I know she'll never get over her husband. She's made that plain."

Hart kept his opinion of Juliet's glorification of her late husband to himself. Cheverly had been perfectly worthy, but far from the paragon Juliet thought him. Des was certainly more than his equal, if not in finances, then in bravery and spirit. "It's not like you to be contented with second best, Des."

"I know she cares for me. In time I think I can make her happy. Not forget Cheverly, of course. But I could be a good father to his boys. I'll sell out if she accepts."

"And then what? Carouse your evenings away at Mrs. Brown's?"

Des shot up from the steps. "Of course not! I haven't been there in weeks, if you must know. Not since Juliet and I—" He broke off and flushed crimson.

"Good God!" Hart stood as well. "Don't tell me you've taken her to bed!"

"As you yourself pointed out, we are both of an age. I refuse to discuss this any further."

Hart grabbed his friend's arm before he could stalk off down the street. "We are not enemies, Des! We both have the same goal, to make Juliet happy. I'll not stand in the way of your suit, you must know that. And if you carry on a discreet affair, I've no objection to that either. Juliet has been in widow's weeds long enough."

Des shook his head and began striding down the block. Hart had to hustle to keep up with him. "I don't want an affair, Hart. I've told you, I want to marry her. I know my prospects are nothing much to brag about. But I have some prize money put aside. And my great-aunt left me a bit in her will." Des stopped walking. "I don't even know where I'm headed. Juliet invited me for Christmas lunch."

"Your aunt Mary is dead? I'm sorry, I didn't know." Hart and Des had long complained to each other about interference from their aunts, although Mary had been at least ninety and rather resembled an ancient reptile.

"Two weeks ago. You've pretty much disappeared from the face of the earth lately, Hart. I haven't had the opportunity to tell you. I've nothing compared to Juliet, but I'll make sure hers all goes in trust to the boys should we marry. That's only right."

Hart laughed. "Perhaps right in your eyes, but Juliet is very expensive. I doubt she'd be happy with a normal wife's pin money."

Des's face darkened. "It won't come to that." He quoted the amount of his recent inheritance, and Hart whistled. "So you see, you should have no objection to my financial status."

"I have no objection to anything!" Hart assured him. "I was just somewhat surprised. I never thought you'd fall victim to Cupid's arrow. And with Juliet, of all people. It's almost fantastic."

"Why? Are you the only man allowed to fall in love in London? Who is this mystery woman who takes up all your time? I thought you were mixed up with some little country miss."

"I'm still persuading her to marry me."

"Perhaps she's not worth the effort, Hart."

"Would you say the same about Juliet?"

"No, no. Women! They do live to devil us, don't they? Come, it's too cold to tangle on the street. I should go back. Juliet is all alone."

"Merry Christmas, Uncle Henry," Hart laughed.

* * *

Eden was waiting in the hallway when he came home, ready to brush the snow from his coat.

"What are you doing out of bed?"

"I got bored. How was Juliet?"

"Come sit down in the parlor. You're dead on your feet, aren't you?" He pushed her through the doorway into the cheerful room. A fire crackled in the grate. Her book lay facedown on the sofa, and the afghan she had wrapped around her feet had fallen to the floor when she sprang up to greet him.

"I'll be fine." She poked at the holly in a vase on the mantel. "This is a very odd Christmas, isn't it? You should be with your family."

He picked up the blanket and folded it into a neat square. "*You* are my family now, Eden. You're all I want. Besides, my aunt has taken a lover."

Eden opened her mouth in shock.

"Yes, it's true. The entire family is steeped in sin. And it feels marvelous." He patted the cushion beside him.

She settled next to him, examining his mischievous face. "Don't joke."

"I assure you, I'm not. Juliet has taken up with my oldest friend, Henry Desmond. I've mentioned him."

"The man you gave your subscription to?"

"The very one. But he, too, has abandoned Mrs. Brown. She won't care. She'll keep the money and have the last laugh."

"But how wonderful for Juliet. Jannah said——" She broke off. It was still almost impossible to speak of her sister without dislodging the frog from her throat. "She said Juliet needed a man of her own, and now she has one. Do you approve?"

Hart shrugged. "It's really none of my business, but yes. Des is a good man. He'll steady her. And he cares for the boys. I suppose they'll marry."

"How nice." Eden felt a bit wistful. Hart would remind her she could marry, too, if she would simply say yes.

He fingered the brightly wrapped parcel on the table. "I think you were really hanging about downstairs because you wanted to open your present. Have you shaken the box?" he asked, stern.

"I have. It rattles."

"You vixen. You're not to be trusted."

"I have told you that a thousand times."

"But I pay no attention to you. You say a great deal of nonsense."

"I don't!"

"You do. All this business about never marrying, for example."

"Not today, please, Hart. It's Christmas."

"All the more reason to discuss it, Eden. How long will it be before I wear you down?"

"I am impervious to your entreaties, my lord," she said, trying to turn her refusal into a jest. "You may climb the tower or slay the dragon. Get in league with the dwarfs if you must. I shall not change my mind."

"Maybe this will help." He tossed the box to her.

She reached below the sofa and pulled out a present of her own. "You first."

He looked inordinately pleased, but the gift wasn't much, just a small framed watercolor of Buttermere she'd found in a shop, with Fleetwith Pike in the background. "It's not too far from Hartford Hall, you know. I've never seen it myself, but the views are considered very fine."

"Thank you, Eden. This will remind me of home. I haven't really had one, you know. Not since I was a little boy. Now you."

She unfolded the paper carefully, lifting the lid of a square box. Nestled in tissue was a smaller box, and inside a box smaller still. Eden laughed. "Appearances are deceiving, I see. I expect there will be a speck of dust in the last one."

"Keep going."

She came to a tiny box about an inch all around. Within was a round diamond-studded wedding band, quite the most beautiful piece of jewelry she'd ever seen. "Hart!" She couldn't stop herself from picking it up between her fingers.

"Say yes, Eden."

"I cannot," she whispered.

"Eden," Hart said quietly, "how long will you make yourself suffer for the past? It is over." He settled her up against his chest, inhaling the clean rose scent from her hair. Her demons might just be too entrenched to banish for good. He cursed his uncle, and himself for good measure. "I wish I could change your mind. I wish I could change a lot of things. I'd dig up Franz Mesmer himself if I thought he could convince you to let go of your pain."

Eden squeezed her eyes shut. She couldn't bear to see the concern in Hart's face. She felt as though she were going mad. She shook her head, placing the delicate ring back in its container. "I-I really am awfully tired."

Hart leaned back on the sofa, his playfulness gone. "I suppose we've only known each other a few months. Keep it until you can make a decision. Let me take you upstairs."

Slightly dizzy, she let him guide her to the bedroom and set her back onto the pillows. Brutus chose to hop off the bed rather than defend his territory.

"Please don't leave."

Hart lifted a brow. "Are you certain?"

"Yes," she said, her voice edged with desire. She couldn't give him the answer he wanted, but she could show him how she felt. Soon Hart's hands and mouth were busy, skating over each new curve, and her body gloried at his touch.

She lay back as he gently pushed her legs apart, felt the solid warmth of his hands stroke each thigh.

"Are you sure—?"

"Hush." She kissed away any protestations he could muster. His fingers sought her sheathed heat. Lazy desire rippled through her limbs, dancing slowly beneath her skin as he slipped within in tender, tortuous increments. He thumbed her clitoris unhurriedly, almost carelessly as their tongues touched and tangled. Eden trembled at each welcome invasion, wondering how she had borne the few hours from his last touch. This was so right. *They* were so right, for Christmas Day.

Reluctantly she broke the kiss and stilled his hand. Hart's disappointment was clear as daylight. "Are you uncomfortable?"

"No. But what if you get sick, too?"

Hart grinned. "We'll both be trapped in bed together. Won't that be a shame?"

He turned her gently, to delight in the curve of her back and buttocks, spelling words upon her with a fingertip for her to guess. Soon he was hard and hot against her back, grazing her throat with his teeth, raining kisses upon her shoulder, cupping her full breast, brushing her belly lightly. She impatiently pushed his hand into her lengthening curls, heard his sharp intake of breath, then a chuckle. If he hadn't believed how much she wanted him, the slickness of her passage made it plain.

His arm draped over her belly, one finger, then two entering her, his thumb circling the swollen center of her pleasure. She gave herself up to the sensation, rocking and sighing against him. Soon his skillful fingers were not enough. She reached behind her to grasp his velvety cock, so hot, so hard for her. She swirled the thick drop of moisture at his tip with a finger and it was his turn to sigh.

"Please." She angled her arse to allow him entry, and he glided in from behind even as his fingers plied her folds, continuing his languorous assault. He was all gentle iron, each stroke almost painfully slow as she tilted back to meet him. He touched her as though she were a fragile porcelain doll, a treasure, a cherished prize too delicate for the world beyond the bedroom door.

When the waves of pleasure came, she held fast to Hart's hand so she wouldn't spin away in the torrent alone. He followed soon after, his lips pressing against her ear, her whispered name a prayer. She shivered despite the heat and damp, not trusting herself to say a word.

Chapter 16

Brutus the cat was in the doghouse. Poor Philpott had tripped over him on the kitchen stairs, resulting in a fractured leg and an enormous lump on his balding head. The butler was holding court from a bed in the basement, Mrs. Philpott even more irritated than usual since her every action was now subject to her husband's advice and opprobrium. Hart had arranged for one of his young ex-soldiers to serve as a footman for the household until Philpott's leg mended or his wife killed him, whichever came first.

It was one thing to slip away from Mattie to teach the girls, but now that Hart had installed Jeremy, she had a new difficulty. Hart insisted that if she went abroad, she be accompanied by the maid *and* the footman. There had been a rash of attacks in Mayfair not far from the house. Of course, Hart would really prefer if Eden never set foot outside her pretty blue door. The threat of discovery worried him, although Eden assured him she wasn't apt to visit any fashionable place his aunt might. Though she didn't specify them to him, her needs were far simpler: She had to get to Mrs. Brown's.

There was nothing for it but to take a horrified Mattie into her confidence and Mattie to take the footman to the heights of flirtation. While Eden spent her hour at Mrs. Brown's, Mattie and Jeremy wandered arm in arm in the streets of Mayfair.

It was the merest chance that Hart learned about this arrangement. Coming home one afternoon from an appointment, he noticed the pair of servants on the street and hailed them. Mattie lost all color to her blushing cheeks and Jeremy seemed embarrassed, as well he should be. Hart was not paying him to moon over maids. After listening to Mattie's halting explanation of how the pair spent their time after escorting Eden to her school, he was curious. When his mistress was unusually subdued at dinner after he questioned her activities, he became uneasy. And when he surreptitiously followed the trio the next day, a part of him died.

* * *

Eden was in her best negligee, as though that had the power to improve her temper. Hart had not come home for dinner, not even sending her word of his whereabouts.

She was angry at his absence, now that she'd finally decided to confess her sins. She wanted to get it over with. It was time she told him of her bargain with Mrs. Brown. He'd asked her very pointed questions yesterday, and she hated lying to him. The last years of her life had consisted of one enormous lie after another, some designed to protect, some designed to pretend. No doubt he wouldn't like her teaching the children and order her to stop. If she could persuade him otherwise, she would make sure he wasn't sorry. She was prepared to argue the case, but knew better than to fight a fighter.

As the clock on the mantel chimed the hour, Eden could not help but yawn. Perhaps she would nap before he came to her and joined her in bed.

Hours later, she woke to the slam of a door. She waited, but the house was silent. Worried, she slipped into her dressing gown, lit a candle and went down the carpeted hall.

There was movement behind one of the guest room doors, a stifled oath, a thud. Eden tapped on the door and was rewarded by a full-on curse.

Hart pulled the door open. He was stripped of his shirt and one boot, a perfectly blank expression on his face.

"Hart! I am glad you're home. I was worried. Why are you undressing in here?"

"I plan to sleep here."

"Wh-what?"

"Is your hearing deficient, madam? I shouldn't like to raise my voice and awaken the servants."

Eden took a step backward, her candle flickering. She could almost feel his fury. "I don't understand. What have I done?"

"Let us just say that you have been yourself, Eden. Tomorrow you and Mattie will return to Hartford Hall. Calvert has hired the coach and made arrangements for your financial needs. I am most weary. Good night." He shut the door in her face.

She turned the handle. To her surprise, it opened. "Why are you here if you're getting rid of me?"

"To make sure you go."

She could strike back. "Of course I'll go. I've wanted nothing else but to be free of this ridiculous arrangement."

"You have your wish. Unlike you, I'll abide by our contract. Support you until November. After that, you can go anywhere. Back to Mrs. Brown's if you choose, and I expect you will. You can't seem to stay away from the place, can you?"

"Have you—have you been *spying* on me, Hart?" Eden asked.

"*Spying.* You make it sound so sordid. Like *fucking.*"

"I was going to tell you. Explain. Tonight. But you never came home."

"I thought you cared for me, Eden. I thought that part of your life was over."

Eden felt nauseous. "You think that I—"

"Oh," he said, his eyes bleak, "you'll deny it. You'll get weepy, and squeeze your hands until they bleed. Say you went there for tea, I expect. Another lie."

"I never lied!"

"Every time you move your lips, Eden." He tossed an extra pillow to the floor.

"You stupid man! I have been at my charity school!"

His mouth curled in disgust. "In a whorehouse? Come now."

"Go ask Mrs. Brown!"

"Ah. Iris. The woman who picked my pocket and made me like it. A pillar of rectitude. Yes. Well." He cleared his throat. "Go to bed, Eden."

"I have been teaching the little girls who live and work there," Eden said slowly, as if the speed of her voice could penetrate the curtain of his disdain. "Iris takes them in off the street. What has befallen these girls is not of their own making. They are *children*. One of them even had a child herself. So many little girls—they have no choice. They are forced, become infected. They are left in ignorance. Uneducated. Unloved."

"You can't be serious."

"I am deadly serious. How can you be so sanguine when men

like you use these poor girls and then toss them back into the alleys to starve and die?"

"Men like me? Enough!" Hart roared, forgetting his vow of quiet. His cheek muscle twitched in anger. "Do not cast me in that category. Even if what you say is true, you cannot think to save the world."

"But I can save a small part of it. I have just been teaching, Hart. French. History. Mathematics. I was going to tell you. I was going to stop if you didn't like it."

"Like it?" Hart laughed without mirth. "Have you not seen enough degradation, Eden? Must you root around it like a pig sniffing out truffles? I gave you a chance. A new life. I wanted to marry you, for God's sake."

Eden felt the icy fist clutch her heart. She'd known from the first that Stuart Hartford was beyond her reach. Untouchable. He'd been slumming himself when he took up her cause. No matter what he said or what he gave her or what his perfect cock did to her body, they had begun badly and would end badly. She really could not have expected anything different.

"As I've said over and over, my lord, I will never marry. You've had a lucky escape. Count your blessings."

He pulled her toward him. "You were giving lessons? That's all?"

Now she *could* lie, and finish it once and forever. But he looked so hopeful, the fool. As if the truth would matter in the end. "That's all."

"Then you'll stop."

She shook her head. "No, I won't. But I *will* leave tomorrow."

"If I was wrong—too harsh—"

"Too holy? You can't help it, can you, Hart? We are done."

He held her fast. "Damn it, Eden! Don't make me out to be the one who's in the wrong. You lied to me!"

"I told you I never lied."

"Withheld the truth, then. What was I to think? You can't deny you were sneaking around, enlisting my servants in your scheme."

"Don't punish Jeremy. He only did my bidding."

He looked down on her, his face a rigid mask. "No, I'll not punish him. I'll punish you. Punish us both."

She tried to pull away. "Wh-what do you mean?"

"Oh, don't worry. I won't hurt you. Not really. But I'll give you something to remember me by. You really, truly want to leave?"

Her tongue stuck to the roof of her mouth. She nodded.

In a second he was kissing her, his mouth nearly brutal. He flattened her against the wall, one hand pinning hers above her head. The other was untying the ribbons at her waist and shoulders until her robe was open and nightgown fell. She tried to shift away but only felt the burning friction of his body against hers as he pressed against her, the golden hairs of his chest taunting her skin.

This would be the last time Hart would ever touch her.

Gone was the Hart who had been gentle and considerate. In his place was a rough warrior, a man who took what he wanted because he could. Eden sagged against him as he palmed a breast, her nipple trapped between his fingers. She stiffened as he left her mouth and nipped his way down her throat, fastening his lips around one beaded peak. She felt the pull to her womb and groaned as he suckled, wishing she could touch him as he was touching her. But she was fixed in place, open to his war on her senses, a war she had long dreamed of. A war she wanted to lose. She brought herself closer to his to feel his rigid manhood. This, at least, had always been remarkably simple between them.

He might think he was forcing her, but he was not his uncle. He was not detached or distant, but as affected by their entanglement as she was. More so perhaps, because he had always wanted what she could not give.

It was not because she didn't love him. She did. Who could not? She'd looked in vain for the chink in his armor, but found nothing but bright polished mail, forged by will, securely linked and impervious to tarnish. By contrast she was mended lace, too fragile to withstand the sunlight. He might be driven by his odd mixture of lust and family honor now, but in time he would need a different woman to stand with him.

She shivered as he tore down the lilac silk from her hips. In seconds he had freed his cock and pushed her legs apart. She had brought him to this frenzied state, her wickedness finally corrupting him. As much as she wanted it, she pulled back. "Hart. Not like this."

"Just like this."

She willed herself to yield to the storm in his eyes. Somehow she had brought him to desperation and her delight. She wanted to thread her fingers through his hair or cup his cheek or stroke his chest, but her hands were still imprisoned above her head. She lifted a leg and wrapped it around him, making it easier for him to fist his cock and impale himself within.

Their eyes met. Eden couldn't bear it and dropped her lids. He released her hands, the better to lift her hips and she covered his mouth with hungry kisses. The scrape of the wall against her back was nothing to the sensation on her lips and her center and her heart. She'd never been so aware of his strength or every iron-hard inch of him as he crushed her to his body. She held fast, both legs now locked around him as he thrust into her, over and over until the tense

spring inside her stretched into waves of wicked pleasure. Her hands
were free now to scratch and soothe, to stroke the golden bristles on
his cheeks, to squeeze his broad shoulders as she lost herself. With a
cry, he pumped his seed deep, then, still connected, carried her to the
bed, where he pitched them both down on the mattress.

They were slick with sweat and still half-dressed, their bodies
seizing. When at last the spasms were over and their heartbeats almost regular, he pulled out of her and worked off his boot and
breeches. She lay in her tangle of damp silk, trying to think of anything she might say to end this folly on a grace note. Her mind was
blank, her body betraying her even now with its yearning for one
more encounter with the naked bronzed god in the guest bed.

He bent over her, sweeping a strand from her forehead, combing
through the knots in her waves with his long fingers. "I want you
to be transparent as glass from now on. No more secrets. No more
lies."

He thought they had resolved the difficulty between them, with
one good fuck. Oh, not good. Exquisite, even up against a wall like a
Covent Garden prostitute in an alley. She shook her head away from
his attentions and sat up, bunching her robe closed in a trembling
hand.

"You will always doubt me, Hart. I suppose I deserve it. I've
earned it."

"No, I—"

"You would not have even told me why you were banishing me
to Hartford Hall if I hadn't barged in here. And when I told you the
truth, you didn't believe me. There's no trust between us."

"I've given you no reason to distrust *me!*"

"Oh," she said sadly, "but you have. At the first opportunity, you
thought the worst. Deep down I will always be your uncle's whore.

That's what my collar said, you know, inscribed inside the silver. Whore. He thought it a great joke."

"Oh, God, Eden. Don't."

"I'm not afraid of the truth. And contrary to what you believe, I've given up lying."

"I'm sorry," he whispered.

He looked sorry, too, looked almost as miserable as she felt. But she had to salvage her pride and leave before the tears fell and her resolve wavered. It wouldn't take much. "I'm sorry, too. Good-bye, Hart."

He reached for her, but she was too quick. "Please don't go, Eden."

"I must, for both our sakes. I'll never measure up, Hart. Not that I still think of myself as worthless. I don't. You've helped a bit there." She allowed herself a small smile. "I can't undo what I did, and I won't be that girl ever again. But I am not the right woman for you. For anyone right now."

"If—"

She shook her head. "No more. I'll go to Hartford Hall until November. Then we'll see where the future lies."

"You won't go back to Mrs. Brown's."

"Very probably not." Not after what she and Hart had shared. There was no obliterating it under the heaving body of some perfume-scented lordling. "Thank you for everything, Hart. For the chance you gave me. I am grateful."

"I don't want your gratitude," he said, his voice bitter.

She leaned down and kissed his forehead as he'd first done to her when he meant to gentle her into submission. Fortunately, he made no move to pull her back down into the bed. "Take care of yourself."

He said nothing. She picked the nightgown up from the carpet and left the room without a backward glance.

* * *

She heard him leave at first light, barking orders to the drowsy servants. A tearful Mattie came to her room with a breakfast tray. "I'm to pack your trunks, Miss Eden," she said, sniffling. "The carriage is already here. Oh, what has happened?"

Dully, Eden shrugged. "It's over."

Mattie rubbed her eyes. "Lord Hartford's sending my Jeremy with us. He has some heart, at least," she said, trying to smile.

"He has gone then?"

"Yes. He said he won't be back."

"Very well. No maudlin good-byes. Let's make haste, then. There is one stop I wish to make before we leave town, however."

When Mattie heard the destination, her eyes were round as saucers.

* * *

The carriage was slightly overcrowded and very busy, Eden observed with a smile. Jeremy had taken one look at Eden's little party and fled up top with the driver. Despite her initial misgivings, Mattie seemed to have made peace with the idea of traveling north with four ramshackle young girls and one very irritated cat in a cage. She had already braided Josie's taffy hair and was now set on repairing the one more-or-less respectable bonnet the sisters Mary and Barbara had shared between them. Barbara had insisted Mary take it with her, as Barbara was not going to be respectable very much longer. Helen and Jane chattered like the city children they were, exclaiming over every rook and rock and tree. They kept themselves to a corner of the squabs, but Jane's unfortunate fragrance was unmistakable.

Before leaving London, they had made a detour to a seedy section of town to gather up an astonished Jane. Helen, Mrs. Brown's newest reclamation project, had begged Eden to find her old friend and take her away, too. Eden did not have to negotiate with anyone to remove Jane from the street. The child had nothing and no one.

Mrs. Brown had proven to be harder to convince of the wisdom of Eden's scheme. "After my life experiences, I consider myself immune to surprise, but you have truly shocked me. What shall I do when you spirit my girls away, Eden?" she'd asked, querulous. "The Pantheon shall be at sixes and sevens."

"Mrs. Brown, you know you need only snap your fingers to find their replacements. I only want to take a few of them, after all. Two or three. Only if they wish to come."

"And I suppose you want me to supply their wardrobes? I am not made of money, you know. They may take the clothes on their backs and two changes, that's all."

Eden smiled. For all Mrs. Brown's bluster, she had not fought very hard to keep the young maids. And Eden couldn't help but see her press coins into the girls' hands as they lined up to say good-bye. Then she turned to Eden and gave her a brief hug and an air kiss.

"I think you are quite mad, Eden. Lord Hartford will not like this when he learns of it."

"Lord Hartford did not restrict whom I could take with me to Hartford Hall. I see no reason why he should even find out." Eden examined her feet, unable to meet her former patroness's eyes. "It's only until November. Then we'll be back." At least the girls would. She hoped she would have secured proper employment by then.

She nearly shied away as Iris reached out and patted her shoulder in pity. "He has settled something on you, hasn't he? The girls are always hungry."

"Oh, yes. His man Calvert has taken care of the details. Never let it be said that *this* Lord Hartford is clutch-fisted."

Mrs. Brown squeezed her hand. "I am so sorry, my dear."

Eden shrugged and retied her bonnet strings. She had suffered worse. "Well, girls, it's very chilly out, but we shall be snug together under the carriage blankets," she said with false brightness.

Indeed, they were snug. The warm little bodies radiated excitement and heat. When they tumbled out at a posting inn for the first night, they were awed by the sweep of stars above in the clear sky.

"Just wait," assured Eden. "Hartford Hall is the most beautiful place. There will be snow—pure white snow, not all sooty as it is in town. The mountains are taller than anything you've ever seen. By spring you will all be country girls." And perhaps Brutus would be happier freed from his wicker bondage.

If the innkeeper wondered why Miss Emery kept such odd company, her coin and a dark glance from Mattie held his tongue. A bath was brought promptly for Jane, and Helen volunteered a dress. Eden insisted on a private parlor for her wards' dinner. The fare was not quite up to Mrs. Brown's standards, Josie declared. Certainly there was no French chef in the modest kitchen of the White Birches Inn. Eden decided it was time to set a few ground rules.

"Now, girls," she said over the pudding, "it will not do to mention Mrs. Brown or her house. This trip is a fresh start for all of us. No one need know any of the sad things that have happened."

"Mrs. Brown's weren't a sad place!" Josie objected.

"No, of course it wasn't. But ordinary people will not understand how kind she was to you. The servants at the Hall are forgiving of much, but I do not think you need to unburden yourselves with your previous employment. When we get there, I am going to put it about that you all were in a charity school training to go into service. Do you think you can remember that?"

Jane shook her head. "It won't do, miss. I can't read. I ain't never been to school."

Eden laughed. "We shall soon fix that. You may depend upon Helen to help show you the ropes, I'm sure. We all learn by example and learn by doing."

Helen nodded in assent and swallowed another mouthful of apple tart, being not half as fussy as Josie. Jane had already finished two pieces. Eden wondered if the child had had a decent meal recently. She thought not.

Eden picked up her teacup and took a sip. "I've known the people at Hartford Hall half my life. Shall I tell you about them?"

The girls nodded. Mattie rose and put another stick on the fire. Everyone had napped half the afternoon away as the carriage bumped along, and none of them were especially anxious for bed in a strange inn. The little parlor fire crackled cheerfully.

Eden folded her napkin and waited for the girls to do the same. They might not be ladies born, but she would try to civilize them as best she could. "Mattie, where shall I start?"

"I should think with the dragon," Mattie said, grinning in mischief.

"Yes, you're quite right. It's always best to get the unpleasant tasks done first. We'll save the best for last."

"A dragon?" Mary said in a small voice.

"Indeed. The dragon's name is Mrs. Burrell. She is the cook, and she *hates* children."

"Coo! Does she roast and eat them?" Jane asked.

"She hasn't yet, but you must mind her well. I'm thinking our Josie is the one to sweeten her up."

Josie gaped. "Me?"

"Yes, dear. You know a bit about food. Henri and Claude were quite fond of you and taught you a bit, *oui*? I imagine Mrs. Burrell could use a new hand in the kitchen. She runs through kitchen maids like water. I think you've got the bottom to weather her out."

Josie's chin rose in determination. "All right. I'll give the old bat a try."

"Good. Then there is Collins and his daughter, Charlotte. He is the butler and she the maid of all work. Collins has been at the Hall forever, since my stepgrandfather's time. Charlotte will be thrilled to share her chores, I'm sure."

"Lazy, she is." Mattie's lips curled in contempt.

Eden knew Mattie thought Charlotte sometimes got lighter duty because of her father. Charlotte had come late in his life with a surprising and brief marriage and was the apple of his eye. Mattie and Charlotte were of an age, and there had always been a bit of a rivalry between them. Footmen, cast-off clothes, the last heel of bread. Eden hoped Charlotte wouldn't think Jeremy was fair game. Mattie would scratch her eyes out over her man. "Hush. Mrs. Washburn is the housekeeper, though I do wonder how much longer she'll stay. She's getting up in years. But she's kind."

"That's it? That's the best?" Jane asked. She didn't sound as impressed as she should, considering she'd been swept off a street corner, a rather homely urchin in rags.

Eden's eyes twinkled. "No. There are some stable lads. And Billy, who is a *very* handsome footman. I don't want you girls fighting over him."

"Pooh," Mary said. "I'm not going to get mixed up with another man."

"Very wise," murmured Eden. She wished she had gone with her first instincts regarding Hart. She looked up at the tap on the door. The landlord's wife curtseyed briefly.

"The rooms are ready upstairs, Miss Emery, if you and the children are done with your dinner."

"I think, if you don't mind, we'll stay down here a bit longer and enjoy the fire. This is a lovely snug room you have, Mrs. Packer, and the meal was delicious, wasn't it, girls?"

There was polite nodding and murmuring. "But we don't want to keep you up late, Mrs. Packer. Perhaps the girls can help clear the table?"

Mrs. Packer looked dubious, but allowed as she could use the extra help. In minutes, under Mattie's supervision, the girls gathered up the crockery and disappeared into the kitchen. Eden found she had the parlor to herself.

She'd better get used to being alone.

She was going back to the home of her shame, where people suspected if not knew what had transpired between her and Ivor Hartford. But it *was* home. She would have the companionship of her pupils, and Mrs. Christopher and other people in the village. She would make a family blanket of torn patchwork squares, stitch by careful stitch. Until November.

When they arrived at last, after rutted and snow-sprayed roads, at her rugged corner of Cumbria, the girls were frightened of the emptiness and the stiff, cloud-shrouded peaks. But they exclaimed over Hartford Hall, standing gray and blocky on a field of snow, the bare creepers looking like fine spiderwebs on the stone.

"Cool!" cried Jane. "It's a castle!"

"Fiddlesticks. Castles got towers," Josie said. "But it's a fair-sized house. Who washes all them windows?" She squinted at Jane meaningfully.

The door opened and Mrs. Washburn bustled out. "Miss Eden! We've been looking for you. Lord Hartford wrote and—" She stopped. Four youngsters had alighted from the carriage and were giving her the once-over. A desperate, alarming yowl came from somewhere inside the conveyance.

"Is that the dragon?" came a whisper, then a squeak as fingers pinched her quiet.

"Mrs. Washburn, let me introduce you to my new wards. I have been teaching in a charity school, you know, and these girls came to my particular attention. They have come to take lessons here and help with household tasks, so that they may go into service when they're a little older. Josie, Mary, Jane and Helen."

Eden was pleased to see each girl smile and bob when her name was announced, even Jane, whose edges were going to require thorough and continuous sanding.

"Come inside, girls. It's cold," Mrs. Washburn said, quickly recovering. "Miss Eden, Lord Hartford made no mention of these children. I'm afraid we haven't prepared—"

"Oh, don't worry about a thing, Mrs. Washburn. The girls can settle themselves. It will be excellent training for them. I thought, actually, that we could put them in the nursery instead of the attics."

"I made up your mother's room and your old one, not being sure . . ." The housekeeper trailed off.

Neither room held good memories for Eden, but she could imagine having a tea party with the girls, teaching them manners and conjugating verbs in her mother's sunny sitting room.

Eden gave the woman an impulsive hug. "My mother's room, I

think." Eden looked around the foyer. Everything gleamed, except her charges, who stood fidgeting on the flagstone. She turned to Mattie. "Do you think once Jeremy brings the luggage we might get some bathwater sent up? The girls and I need to get out of our travel dirt."

"A bath!" protested Jane. "I had me one when we stopped at that inn the first night."

"And it's time for another," Eden said firmly. She rather suspected it was going to take more than one dip to properly cleanse the little wretch. Mrs. Brown's girls were models of godliness in comparison. "Let me show you to your rooms. We'll get an extra bed or two moved up there as soon as the men are able. Mattie, could you see to the linens? And there is the matter of Brutus."

Mrs. Washburn looked confused.

"My cat," Eden smiled. "A gift from Lord Hartford. He may be a bit surly to start. Travel has not agreed with him. But I expect he will settle in. We are home now."

And so, with just a few words, Eden took control of her unconventional household and took one step from her past even as she returned to it.

Chapter 17

Hart had tried every amusement available—except, of course, for going back to Mrs. Brown's Pantheon of Pleasure. Des still held his membership voucher in any case, not that he was using it. Hart was positively nauseated to watch his old friend and his young aunt in their courtship ritual. Juliet was blazing with sexual satisfaction, and Des—footloose, feckless Des—was now the epitome of a quiet gentleman of the ton. Juliet had supervised his new wardrobe, arranged for an opera subscription—Opera! Des!—and trotted about town with him on an invisible yet very real leash. Des seemed to have no objection to his neutering. In fact, Hart thought him the happiest he'd ever seen him. Certainly an affair with Juliet was preferable to the wet trenches, shooting and starvation the army had provided for entertainment, and the deadly dull postwar billeting they had both chafed under.

It was near midnight. Hart sat in his dressing gown, a decanter of brandy at his elbow. McBride had lifted one woolly eyebrow some time ago but had had the sense to hold his tongue and put himself to bed. The bedroom was warm enough without a fire. In fact, spring had come without Hart's invitation or interest. People were at this very moment waltzing and supping, trysting and tupping.

He opened the window overlooking the back garden and breathed deeply. All his fortune could not erase the smell of the city, but there were daffodils below. A gardener had come today to cut the patch of lawn, too. He was happy here, living a life he'd never truly expected, with not a care in the world—

Hart frowned into the dark. He'd never touch Eden again. Not after the last time.

Nor, it seemed, touch any other woman. He'd found himself unable to perform for the first time in his life, on the one misguided occasion he'd sought to erase her from his mind. He was eight-and-twenty, not some doddering oldster. The whore had pitied him and he'd wanted to snap her neck.

My God, what was happening to him? He poured himself another glass and listened to the night noises. Somewhere down the street came strains of music and laughter. A carriage passed, the horses' hooves clipping smartly on the cobblestones. The world was out enjoying itself, and he was unshaven, undressed and more than half-drunk.

He could remedy some of that. He tossed his robe aside and rummaged through his drawers. It was a fine spring evening. He was going out on the town.

* * *

Iris Brown's face betrayed no emotion when her butler whispered in her ear. She excused herself from the gentlemen in her parlor with a flirty air kiss.

"I took the liberty of putting him in your parlor, madam. He objected—quite vociferously—to the green room, and he wasn't fit to stand in the hall for any length of time."

"Barrel-fevered, is he?"

"I should not go quite so far as to say that, but he is not himself."

"Are any of us?" Iris muttered as she made her way to her little inner sanctum. "Foster said you wished to speak with me. You are forever turning up on my doorstep, Lord Hartford," said Iris Brown sweetly, closing her parlor door behind her. She arranged her ivory skirts and relaxed back in a chair. "But am I mistaken? I believe you resigned your membership. And now I understand I've lost the custom of Major Desmond as well."

She could tell he had not come to discuss the unlikely love affair between his aunt and his best friend. She could not remember when she had seen a gentleman quite so acutely uncomfortable, except when one requested a brisk caning, of course. Lord Hartford refused her offer of libation—she thought he'd already had enough somewhere—but did sit down.

"Eden—" he began, then examined his gloved hands as if he'd never seen them before.

Mrs. Brown waited. When no more was said, she prompted, "Ah. Eden. How is she faring?"

"Well enough, I suppose. She's in the country." He lurched up off the gilt chair. "I have to know. Are you a woman of your word, Mrs. Brown?"

"I have always thought so." She looked directly at him. His blue eyes were still clouded with doubt.

"When she was here in this house . . ." He stopped. No amount of brandy had silenced the thoughts in his bedeviled brain. It was clear he was in some kind of torment. "Was she—was she untouched?"

"Did she tell you otherwise?"

"Answer me, damn it!"

Mrs. Brown looked the baron over. He was disheveled, stubbled, and, if she was not mistaken, much the worse for drink. But she knew Foster was stationed nearby. He had probably asked Tim to come upstairs, too. All of them had some experience with unruly patrons. To threaten the loss of membership would not work in the baron's case, however.

"Lord Hartford, you and I came to a business arrangement. There was no deception on my part. The week that Eden was a guest in this house, she was an observer only."

"But after," Hart rumbled.

"After?"

"I know she came here after I set her up as my mistress. To teach the children. She explained it all, not that it makes a bit of sense. I followed her, so do not bother lying."

Iris didn't let his offensive words offend her. She was not the one at fault here. She lifted a silver brow. "Stop roaring at me, sir. It is true she came every day without fail for several months and worked with them. You and your mistress, it seems, are both very foolish. You need to sit down and have a cozy chat with her, preferably when you are not foxed.

"Eden is softhearted. While she was here as a guest, she formed a friendship of sorts with the girls I rescued." Mrs. Brown shook her head ruefully. "Well, that makes me sound like a saint, and I am far from that. But I have been known to take in child prostitutes and employ them. Get them safe off the street. The pretty ones only, I'm ashamed to say. Some of them stay on as they get older. It is their choice to remain servants or become whores. Most opt for the latter capacity." She gave an odd smile. "Far less work is involved." She looked at her timepiece. "I have many other things that need my attention just at present, some of which I can lay directly at Eden's door. I have been egregiously short-staffed for the past few months. No," she said, watching his mounting color, "it is not at all as you suppose. Eden came to my house to tutor my young maids. And now she has stolen them, and one more besides."

Hart felt as though a swarm of bees were buzzing in his head. "What?"

"The girls adored her, and when she left, she begged me to let her take some to the country with her. Helen, the newest maid, wouldn't go unless Eden promised to take a little friend, not a very appealing child. She did not meet my requirements. The last I saw Eden, she was on her way to the stews to pluck up Jane."

Deliver me, thought Hart. "I don't understand."

"Eden wanted to continue their education. I have a feeling she used to play schoolmistress with her sister. Eden is a very bright young woman, you know."

Hart nodded. He did know. How often had he come across her in their little parlor, books spread out upon the divan? He had thought her a bit of a bluestocking, which was preferable to being enamored with some empty-headed little nitwit. It seemed that *he* was the nitwit, however.

"She took whores to Hartford Hall?"

"She took abused children to Hartford Hall," Mrs. Brown corrected. "Josie, the oldest, is no more than fourteen."

Hart felt the bile rise in his throat. He loosened his already loose cravat. He needed air. He needed a drink.

"You look very unwell, sir. May I get you anything?"

"Nothing." He deserved nothing.

"They all write to me several times a week. It is part of their lessons. I know how many new lambs were born, and that your cook Mrs. Burrell dislikes children in her kitchen. Josie is trying to change the woman's mind, with little result I'm afraid. Eden has repapered the parlor in a blue stripe that reminds her of the color of your eyes. Jane cannot spell or read very well as yet, and was never in my employ, but she writes as religiously as the rest of them."

"How many are there?" asked Hart, progressively more alarmed.

"Only four. Josephine, Mary, Helen and Jane. I had high hopes for Josie," Mrs. Brown added, sighing.

The world had run mad. He didn't begrudge the hiring of extra staff. Hartford Hall had been run in rather a slipshod fashion for years. His uncle had spent his money on inventive ways to terrorize Eden instead.

But girls from the street, being trained for Mrs. Brown's—his mind failed to understand what Eden was thinking.

"Thank you for your time, Mrs. Brown. I shall see that the girls are returned to you."

"I shouldn't mind that, if Eden can spare them. But not Jane. She will not do at all."

Hart was nearly out the door when she stopped him. "Eden is the most naturally sensitive, sensual girl I've ever encountered. She has a wild streak which Ivor sensed and damaged. She may think to tame it, but I don't think it's possible. And wholly unnecessary. You may need to go beyond a man's conventional weaponry with her if you want her back."

Hart's head was nearly split in two. "What do you mean?"

"Show her that some of the things Ivor taught her can be pleasurable."

His head officially broke. "You want me to *whip* her?"

"Of course not. You would never be so cruel, although your kindness to her has not served you well, has it? I suspect," Mrs. Brown said, resting a cool hand on Hart's scruffy cheek, "that she likes to be dominated. It gives her permission to feel as strongly as she does."

Hart shuddered. Eden had made allusions to that side of her nature, but he'd been convinced he could bring her happiness without that sort of thing. And he'd been more or less successful, before he'd bollixed it up with his distrust. "I couldn't."

But he could. That night when he'd taken her against the wall was etched in his mind. She had been pliant, her arms pinned above her head, her eyes shining. He had been rough, brutal—and she'd come apart more quickly that she ever had. He'd temporarily lost his mind in anger, but perhaps that was the key to finding hers.

And to be honest, it had thrilled him beyond reason to control her . . . except that afterward, she'd left him anyway.

"We're not talking chains or canes or anything uncomfortable. A silk blindfold. A soft rope. See if I'm not right. You'll both enjoy it."

Hart had to get out of there before he lost his mind altogether. Iris Brown had been a font of information, none of it welcome. He hoped by morning he'd forget half of it. He'd head for Hartford Hall at dawn and get his life in order. Come to some sort of accommodation with Eden, no matter what it entailed. He'd tried to live without her, and he just could not do it.

* * *

He had come, without warning. Mattie fussed over her but it was a futile hope to bring order to her person. She and the girls had been sketching the morning away, high on a windy hill, when Mattie made the breathless climb to tell her that the master had come home. There was time now for the pursuit of art, music, languages, all the pretty accomplishments expected of a well-brought-up young lady, advantages that Eden had to teach herself. Her girls would be fit to serve as exclusive ladies' maids, companions or perhaps even governesses once their education was complete. Eden even hoped, if they so desired, that suitable marriages might be arranged somehow. She was perfectly willing to suborn the truth, or fashion it to suit the needs of her charges.

The art lesson was abandoned. The measured tumble to the bottom of the hill had done nothing but bring more color to Eden's face and wildness to her hair. She could spend hours in her bedroom with her maid and still not tame herself.

The children had been thrilled with Mattie's news. It was their fondest wish for Eden to reconcile with her lord. The past months had been the happiest of their young lives. Their London cheeks had long ago lost their pallor, and each had grown a bit stouter. Mrs. Burrell claimed she didn't care for children, but she fed them well enough. They were, however, sufficiently wise to know that Eden did not share their joy.

"Leave off, Mattie. It's hopeless." Eden's hair refused to stay smooth, and her dress was a rusty black leftover let out at the seams, not one of Juliet's selections. She had at least removed her apron.

"Don't you move." Mattie went to the dressing table and rummaged through the drawer.

"Now what? He won't like to be kept waiting any longer. Collins said he refused to even clean up and change." Eden bit her lips, both out of worry and the attempt to bring some vibrancy to the surface. "I hope something is not wrong with Juliet or her boys."

As well as writing to Mrs. Brown weekly, she also wrote to

Juliet, to preserve the fiction that all was normal with her and Hartford Hall. She had come back to a pile of letters that Juliet had been sending since before Christmas. Eden lived for Juliet's letters, which always contained some small news of Hart. Eden suspected the woman did not know that her notes were the only communication of Hart's activities she received. His aunt was still under the impression that one day Eden and Hart would be married, and each letter contained suggestions for the wedding that would never be.

Mattie brandished the tweezers.

Eden waved her away. "Oh, we don't have time for this!"

"Now, Miss Eden, it's the least you can do to look respectable. You've become a right barbarian again."

Because it didn't matter.

Perhaps she should submit to the plucking, change her clothes from the skin out. Not that she would ever let herself love him again. She was done with that futile exercise. She closed her eyes and nodded. "Very well. And I think I will change after all. You pick something. Ouch!"

* * *

As the minutes ticked by, Hart became increasingly impatient. He had expected Mattie to fetch Eden and bring her directly to the parlor, but most of an hour had passed. She must have entered from a side or kitchen door and gone directly up the servants' stairs to her room.

He knew she was back. He had caught the sound of girlish giggling, and one bold little baggage had poked her head around the door frame and stared at him with undisguised curiosity until she was finally frightened away by his glare. He was most tempted to join Eden upstairs just to get the confrontation over with. If he had to wait any longer, he might fall asleep on his feet.

The blue wallpaper was an improvement, but the stripes were making him dizzy. Perhaps he'd go into the library and wait for her there. Have something bracing to drink. He nodded to Collins, who was hovering in the hallway. "If Miss Emery ever deigns to come down, I shall be in the library."

He walked down the dim hallway and opened the door. He was shocked at the transformation. Most of the shelves were now empty, thanks to the quick trip to the country Calvert had made last fall. Hart's pockets were considerably plumper after the man had arranged a book auction for connoisseurs with tastes similar to Ivor's. A large new globe had been placed on one corner of the library table. Surrounding it were some maps, carefully drawn in colored pencil. There were small jars of spring flowers, some of the shriveled blossoms picked apart on paper, each part labeled. A set of child's letter tiles was stacked neatly on top of a primer.

And there was not a drop to drink. The drinks cabinet was empty. Hart rang for Collins.

"Where is the brandy?" he asked curtly.

"Miss Eden uses this room as a schoolroom, my lord. She wished to remove temptation from the young ladies."

Hart snorted. Young ladies indeed. "I assume you still have some hidden away somewhere?"

"Certainly, my lord. I'll go fetch you a glass."

"Bring the bottle, if you please."

Collins looked at Lord Hartford with hesitation. Hart had refused the offer of a bath and had not sought the comforts of his bedroom or the contents of his saddlebag. He knew he radiated irritation, perhaps something even more disturbing. The butler probably thought poor Miss Eden would be in for it and wanted to come to her rescue. Eden did inspire rescuing, although it was infinitely too late.

"Would you perhaps care for a pot of coffee as well? Some luncheon? Mrs. Burrell could prepare a tray, sir."

"Just the brandy."

Hart walked over to one tall window. Here was last fall's vision come to life. The grass was a new green, the trees and shrubs were budding and flowering. His sheep dotted the hillside. Puffy clouds as white and fat as they floated across the sky. He had passed the home farm on the ride up the lane to the hall, its fields newly tilled and neat. John Pinckney kept him informed of the estate's business, but somehow he had omitted to tell him his house was now a foundling home for underage strumpets.

There was a tap at the door. A solemn dark-haired girl bore a tray with his bottle and glass. "Your brandy, sir. Lord Hartford," she said, bobbing quickly. "Shall I light the fire? The room is chilly."

Hart shrugged. It was much cooler here than in the city, the mountains still snowcapped. He drank a glass of brandy in one long pull, poured himself another as he watched the girl set a taper to the kindling. It wouldn't do to be foxed when he saw Eden, but he enjoyed the punishing burn right down to his gut. He decided to punish himself further.

"What is your name?"

The girl startled and turned. "Mary Bonner, my lord."

"You're new here."

"Yes, my lord."

"Come from the village, do you?"

"No, sir. From London."

"Ah." He simply could not imagine this Friday-faced, flat-chested child in anyone's bed. But some men in their wickedness would be tempted by anything, he supposed. "Thank you, Mary. That will be all."

She scurried out of the room, no doubt to impart his description to her compatriots. He wondered how she'd convinced Collins to let her bring in the brandy. His house was upside down and must be set to rights. He looked at his watch again, then at the clock on the mantel. The portrait of the previous Lady Hartford that had once hung there had disappeared. Hart was suddenly struck by the fact that this picture had been on the wall all the while that Eden and Ivor engaged in their complicated games. If only her mother had been truly present, Eden might not have come to such grief.

Hart shook the sympathy from his head. Eden was a consummate liar. She had lied to her mother, even if in his opinion the woman had been next to useless. She had lied to him. She had not trusted him enough to tell him what she was really up to, because she knew he would have forbidden her. He rubbed his eyes in exasperation, then took a moderate sip of the brandy. She thought so little of herself that she was more at home in a brothel than anywhere. He knew she mourned her sister, but to transfer her affection for Jannah to bawdy house housemaids was really beyond belief.

But if it made Eden happy—somehow made up for the suffering she'd endured—he could probably allow her anything. He would do—be—what she needed. These weeks without her had been torment.

He heard the rustle of her skirts and turned slowly from the window. There was no mistaking the faint hope on her rouged face or the depth of her considerable décolletage. She was certainly no longer the reed she had been when he first met her those months ago.

If she thought to trap him with her womanly charms, she was sadly mistaken. He was already trapped. He set his drink upon the desk, keeping his expression neutral.

"Good morning, my lord," Eden said, curtseying quickly.

"Is it still morning? I vow I believe you've kept me waiting through the afternoon. But it was worth the wait, Eden. You look well."

"Thank you. I feel well. What brings you to Hartford Hall, sir? If you had let me know that you were coming, I would have greeted you at the door and not kept you kicking up your heels. Surely you wish a bath and some refreshment."

"Not as yet. Sit down, Eden. I have matters to discuss with you."

She spread her skirts, beginning almost immediately to twist her fingers. "How may I help you, L-lord Hartford?"

The name came so naturally to her in this library, and he heard the tremolo of fear. From her lips, it was not his name now, but his uncle's. He had somehow returned her to her past. Here she was again, weak. At a disadvantage. He was just another imperious man dictating.

He hated every inch of the library. It was here Eden had suffered. It was here where her mind broke, allowing her to become disordered enough to come up with this insane scheme with the children. If Iris Brown was right, Eden had been driven across the boundary from her natural inclination to submission to total degradation by his uncle. Hart would not take the same path.

"Eden," he said, attempting to keep his voice level, "you must see this is not an appropriate place for your charity. Hartford Hall is my family home. I'm going to make arrangements to transport the girls back to London."

"You cannot!"

"Mrs. Brown wants them back. Except for—" For the life of him, he could not think of the name.

"Jane," Eden said. She jumped up and flitted about the room for a few moments like a black butterfly. It was easier for him to drink his brandy than to watch her agitation. She finally came to rest against a French door, her hand flat against the pane as she stared at the rugged landscape. The only sound in the room was the pop of dry wood in the fireplace.

"Do you feel there is no hope for redemption, my lord?"

Her voice was scarcely above a whisper. He was well aware how Eden had struggled with her past transgressions, how strictly she held herself accountable for much of them. They had spent hours in each other's arms as he had tried to assure the clergyman's daughter that she should not abandon hope of heaven. God could not be so cruel when she had already suffered so much. "Of course. I believe as you do."

"I very much doubt it. The one thing I have learned since I returned here is that I cannot escape my past, but I do not have to be forever scarred by it." He remembered her body's hellishly unique adornment. Ivor had left scars outside and in.

"What happened to me was mostly my fault. I accept the responsibility. But what has happened to my girls was never their fault, not for a moment. Their parents sold them for coin. Helen's own father raped her, then abandoned her when she became pregnant. It was a mercy she lost the baby. These girls might be dead had they not come to Mrs. Brown's attention. I told you she employs children like them as maids, and eventually they are old enough to take their place in the Pantheon. If they are willing, and most of them are. It's quite a step up from what they're used to." She paused for breath. "You talked of offering me a chance once. If you do not permit me to keep the girls here and school them, I will go back with them to Mrs. Brown's."

"That's blackmail."

"You do not own me."

"That's where you're wrong. We still have a contract. You agreed to be my mistress until November."

"I agreed to nothing! Take your complaint up with Iris Brown."

"She is inconveniently far away. I've missed you, Eden."

He shocked himself. This was not what he'd planned to say at all. He was here to remove those wretched children from his house and set some guidelines for his mistress. Instead he wanted to tear down her bodice and lick the white globes of her breasts until they flushed pink and she begged him for more.

He had shocked *her*. "You've come all this way to bed me?"

Yes, he had. And he could barely wait. "I've come to check on the estate as well."

"I assure you, things are running smoothly. Mr. Pinckney must have written. I've ridden out myself to visit the tenants."

"Very lady-of-the-manor of you, Eden."

"I know I have no right."

"You could have had," he said softly. He drained his glass.

"Oh, not all this nonsense again! I'll sleep with you if I must, but I will not marry you. I see a few months of solitude have not improved your wits."

"How do you know I've been alone? Perhaps my aunt Juliet has found me a bride," he shot back.

He was gratified to see Eden blanch beneath her rouge. "Are congratulations in order, my lord?"

"Not quite yet."

God, he'd been an ass. He was the son of a libertine who'd hung on to his pretensions far longer than was practical. He knew he would never be satisfied by anyone but Eden. She was his light and his dark. With her, he was finally himself, all his imperfections soothed between her thighs. She would never deny any of his urges, whatever they might be, just as he'd been unable to discourage hers. She thought him above her, but she was so wrong. How to convince her?

Despite everything she'd endured, she had an innocent heart.

Like the little girls who were working their innocent hearts out for her.

Once more he had made a mistake. It was getting to be something of a habit.

"Eden," he said, his voice sounding foreign even to himself, "can we begin again?"

Eden looked across the room at him. She could smell leather and horse from where she stood. His boots and clothing were mud-splattered, and he hadn't shaved in days. He appeared as though he'd slept in a ditch or not at all. He was beautiful.

"I don't know," she said, and walked out of the library.

Chapter 18

Hart sat alone in the dining room, the sconces lit, the silver shining, dish after dish arriving to tempt the fussiest palate. He might as well have been served dog and rat. He politely ate what was put in front of him, staring down the long table at the place where Eden should be. Was not.

As Collins served him personally, he had informed Hart she was taking a tray in the nursery with her wards. This was their evening off from household duties. His unexpected arrival had changed nothing except for unprecedented haste to get his dinner preparations done in time.

"Miss Eden is one to stick to a schedule, sir," Collins said, looking slightly embarrassed. "The orphans rise and breakfast early, do some chores, then break for some hours in the schoolroom with a luncheon. Afterward they return to their assigned tasks. Hard workers, Lord Hartford, all of them."

"Yes, the hall has never looked better," Hart said vaguely. He hoped Collins wouldn't hear it as an insult.

A bath and a nap had not been able to reverse the effects of the brandy and the encounter with Eden. It seemed he was saddled with Eden's charity project and her disappointment. But "I don't know" was far better than "No." He had some groveling to do but didn't know where to start. He was Holy Hartford no longer, certainly not in his own eyes. Even that damned cat had spat at him and clawed at his leg.

He pushed himself away from the table. The decanter of port, like the wine before it, sat untouched. The last thing he needed was a repeat of his state these past months—bedeviled with brandy and uncertain temper. Even at war, he'd been a paragon of control. One dark-eyed woman had undone years of self-discipline and order.

Hart opened the French doors to the lawn beyond and stepped outside, relishing the nip of fresh, cool air. There was no moon to show his way, just a scattering of silent stars. His eyes looked up to the second floor for the nursery windows. The curtains were drawn, but were edged by a sliver of light. He would not be welcome there.

Hart walked farther into the night, his vision honed by necessity and experience. The clipped boxwood walls of the modest formal garden loomed before him. Somewhere within was a stone bench where he could sit and feel sorry for himself. He'd had plenty of experience lately with that, too.

It was time to examine the muddle of his life. Well before he reached his majority he had been driven to scrub at the stain of his family's reputation. He'd been, he realized, something of a prig, looking down his handsome nose at fellow officers who fell short of moral perfection. It was a wonder Des was still his friend. Although now, of course, Des himself had lost his wayward ways, thanks to Juliet. The man was becoming a dead bore.

Hart had served his king and his God well. Then Eden had dropped to her knees in front of him. How he wanted her there again.

He didn't want an ordinary woman. He wanted Eden—Eden as she was before, when their nights were filled with exploration and discovery. When she lay in his arms and talked of her life in the vicarage, a little general bringing order to her hapless mother's household. When she worried over the disappearance of the wretched cat he'd given her, and her joy when the beast returned, somewhat battered but apparently victorious. He had watched her grow in confidence, blossoming like a stubborn rose in winter.

A flicker of light through the hedges caught his eye, and he straightened on the bench. Someone was coming. He hoped he was not to be surrounded by Eden's little army, pinned like a butterfly to blotting paper. He started to rise, but stopped when he saw Eden herself, the lantern she carried illuminating the pale muslin beneath her shawl.

"Don't be afraid," he said, his voice sounding hollow in the shadows.

"Oh!" Her lantern swayed. "What are you doing out here?"

"Same as you, I imagine. Thinking." *Regretting.*

"I shall leave you to it then." She turned, causing the golden glow to vanish behind her.

"No. Wait. Please stay." He rose from the bench. "Come sit with me for a moment."

Hart had spoken those same words to her the day they'd met. He could sense her hesitation in the dark, then saw it as the light cast its shadows on her face.

"Please. Do you remember when we met out here that first day, all those months ago?"

She nodded, placing the lantern in the center of the bench, the better to keep him at a distance lest he singe himself, and sat. She was as still and stiff as the marble beneath her.

Hart took his place, stretching his long legs in the damp grass. "Are you cold, Eden? You may have use of my coat."

He watched her wrap herself more firmly in her shawl.

"I am warm enough."

He doubted it. The shawl was too flimsy for the chill of the spring evening. What could she be thinking of, wandering around like this in the dark? He shrugged himself out of his coat.

"Take it. I insist."

"Is that an order, my lord?"

Hart thought he'd heard the humor in her voice, but it was impossible to see if she was smiling.

"Yes. You know what an overbearing ass I am. I've proven that to you time and time again."

Now he did hear a slight burble of laughter, a most welcome sound. He felt his wire springs within unwind just a bit. "I missed you at dinner," he ventured.

"I keep the girls to a strict routine. They depend upon it. And me."

"I have no wish to interfere. Hartford Hall seems to be thriving under your management." It was true. The whole house seemed brighter somehow. Even old Collins stepped more lively.

"Mr. Pinckney has been very helpful."

"I doubt Mr. Pinckney picked out the new wallpaper." Wallpaper that, according to Iris Brown, matched Hart's eyes.

"You once said you hated the pink. He assured me that the expenses incurred were reasonable. I have not exceeded your allowance."

"I am not criticizing, Eden. I am complimenting. The house looks wonderful. The acreage as well. Even at night I can tell you've done something different to this garden."

"Yes. The girls and I have been busy."

Hart wanted to take her in his arms and carry her across the lawn and up to bed. He cleared his mind and then cleared his throat. "I hope you are not tiring yourself out."

"Not at all. I seem to be full of energy. How long do you plan to visit, my lord?"

He clapped a hand over his heart. "Ouch. I am wounded. No longer Hart, no longer anything but a visitor in my own home."

"I did not mean—"

"Let us be honest, Eden. Of course you want me gone. I cannot blame you. Since the first day I met you I've done nothing but misconstrue your every action."

He heard her silence, could almost touch it, as tangible as the lantern between them. He let it hang about him, blocking his hope until he could bear it no more.

"If you will permit me, I should like to stay."

"Permit you! Surely I have no say in the matter. As you have pointed out, this is your ancestral home. I am sure we can reach some accommodation."

Hart envisioned her hiding out in the nursery with her charges, sliding just out of range around corners, locking herself in her room at night. She would make it impossible for him to woo her, for woo her again he must. This time he wouldn't be gentling her body but her mind.

He shifted on the bench, saw her worrying her long white fingers in the lamplight.

"Your terms, Eden. I have no wish to interfere in your running of the household."

"The girls can stay?"

Impossible to miss the surprise in her voice. "You were quite impassioned and eloquent in their behalf, Eden. Worthy of a speech in the House of Lords," he said teasingly. "I am sure they will be of comfort to you for the time being."

"And after?" she asked sharply.

His first step. She had to believe him. "Hartford Hall is their home for as long as you wish it."

She rose from the damp chill of the bench. "I think we have agreed enough for one night. I am going back to the house."

"May I accompany you?"

Eden picked up the lantern. "I'd rather you didn't. Can you find your way back in the dark?" She was not about to lean on his arm and wind up in his bed.

"I'll manage. Good night."

Eden crossed the lawn unsteadily. So much for a quiet think under the stars. Her heart beat rapidly as she slowly climbed the back stairs to her room. Her first order of business was to check the bolt between her dressing room and Hart's. When she had taken her mother's rooms, she had not anticipated Hart would ever be beyond the walls. All traces of Ivor had been packed up long ago and assigned to the attics. Should Hart have any interest in his uncle's personal effects, he'd have to do the rummaging on his own.

But while Ivor's earthly possessions were safely boxed, he'd left his mark on Eden, even on Hart, who had never known him well. Her heart contracted in bitterness. A few months ago Hart had assumed that she was the sort of woman who could spend an hour on her back at Mrs. Brown's for the pure hell of it. The seeds of distrust had been planted so early on between them that Eden doubted they'd ever be thoroughly weeded. Even if she turned into a paragon of absolute virtue, Hart would always see something missing within her. It was why she had refused him all those months, why she had to refuse him now.

Mattie tapped at the door and entered. "Can I help you get ready for bed, Miss Eden?"

"No. I'm fine."

"What are you going to do now that Lord Hartford's here?"

"He says the girls can stay. We'll just go on as we have."

She dismissed Mattie and brushed the tangles out of her own hair, wishing she had a brush for her mind as well. It was pointless to grieve for the past. She'd been more than instrumental in disposing of her innocence with Ivor. No matter that he'd played masterfully upon her own insecurities, she had been aware of every step, so eager for his kisses and compliments. What came later was only what she deserved.

If Hart wanted her to be his mistress again, she could do it. He would tire of her soon enough and long for city life again. She punched the pillows up to help her get comfortable. Eden had just settled herself when the door handle to the dressing room rattled. She would feign sleep. She couldn't bear to see Hart's earnest, handsome face until tomorrow.

* * *

He had expected nothing less. Hart cursed himself for a fool. Eden probably thought he had designs upon her body, which, unfortunately, he did. Even if only to just pleasure her as he first had when he won her over slowly from her fear and reticence in the early days. But tonight he had only wished to talk.

He had time. If he were to remain at Hartford Hall, he'd have the opportunity to make amends. He cast his mind back to the first time he had truly bedded her. It had been in November. They'd had but a few months together before his trust shattered and she left him. In some respects, he'd been crueler than his uncle, for he knew just how fragile Eden was, should have realized she would never betray him. He had blundered. Badly.

Hart stripped himself, tossing the covers aside. The room was warm from an unnecessary fire, probably laid by one of Eden's girls in order to make him as comfortable as possible. Hart doubted very much he'd be comfortable again until he held Eden close. In the meantime, Hartford Hall would be under siege as he sought to win the battle for Eden's affection once again. And he had a fair if frightening idea how to go about it.

Chapter 19

Hart woke up, late, with a renewed sense of purpose. His thoughts had kept him awake much of the night, as well as the knowledge that Eden was lying next door in her fragrant bed linens, as untouchable as if he were still in London.

After a quick, lonely breakfast of coffee, muffins and baked eggs, he made his way to the library, only to find the room deserted. All traces of the schoolroom had vanished, from globe to experiments. The liquor cabinet was once again stocked and tempting even at this hour. Eden had restored the room to a manly haven as if by magic. More likely, many little hands were involved at an unconscionably early hour.

Hart had never given much thought until last fall to what it took to run an estate. He had been preoccupied keeping himself and his men alive under perilous conditions too long to think of the soft life the future might hold for him upon his uncle's death. But his life was blessedly cushioned now due to the ministrations of servants, tenants, John Pinckney here and the inestimable Calvert in town. He'd done nothing lately but view the world from the bottom of a brandy bottle.

Hart took the stairs up to the nursery suite two at a time. He stood outside the schoolroom door listening as the girls took turns conjugating verbs in English, then French. Eden murmured encouragement over their accents, with special emphasis on driving the poverty out of their native tongue. It was clear to Hart she had aspirations for these girls beyond training them as housemaids. But whether it was the subtle shadow he cast or their sensitivity to male invasion, the chatter ceased. Eden came out into the hallway, looking beautifully irritated.

"How may I assist you, my lord?"

"I thought I would observe your classroom lessons. Perhaps discover how I might assist *you*."

Eden gaped up at him. "You wish to tutor the girls?"

"Why not? I expect my responsibilities here are not so onerous that I shall not have any free time. Between you and Mr. Pinckney, I daresay the estate hardly requires my presence at all."

"Now that you're here, there will be no need for my oversight," Eden replied, her back stiff.

"Nonsense. The tenants and servants obviously hold you in high regard. I shouldn't wish to interfere." He'd been stopped for what seemed a hundred times yesterday afternoon as he rode aimlessly over his land.

"Don't be ridiculous! I've only filled in for you in your absence. You are more than welcome to take up the reins."

Hart smiled. "Well, then, perhaps we shall share the responsibilities. Of everything. You may tutor *me* on your improvements, and I can help you with the education of my wards."

He watched as Eden processed his words. She appeared totally confounded. Out of the corner of his eye, he saw four faces, eyes goggling, as the girls eavesdropped from behind the door. "Girls," he said smoothly, "come out. Don't be shy. Have you any objection to having a gentleman teach you some subjects? Riding, for example? Perhaps some archery? History is a passion of mine, too. I've traveled quite extensively in His Majesty's service and could bore you senseless with my anecdotes."

"Coo! A cove like you could never be boring," said Jane, earning her a shove from Helen's elbow.

"We're very satisfied with Miss Eden's instruction," Mary said loyally.

"Oh, I should not like to usurp her role as your primary teacher. I would be merely a bonus. Rather like pudding after a hearty meal," Hart said, his eyes twinkling in mischief. He noted almost immediately that Josie looked as though she might like to devour him on the spot with or without a spoon and regretted his choice of words.

"You cannot be serious," murmured Eden.

"Indeed I am. I haven't the experience you have with children—young ladies, really—but I'm sure we could work out a schedule to everyone's satisfaction. It is far too lovely to be trapped indoors in a musty schoolroom."

"The schoolroom is not musty! And just yesterday we were outside sketching!" Eden said hotly. "Until you came back and turned everything upside down!"

"I have no intention of making anyone stand on their heads, least of all you, Eden." He squelched the amusing mental image of Eden with her skirts down and long legs pointed to the ceiling as he saw her thunderous expression. This foray into wooing was not going as he planned, but then nothing seemed to go right for him with his prickly mistress. He watched as she tried to get hold of her emotions. But perhaps that was the last thing she should be doing. She had been ignoring her own needs and desires, indeed her very self, trying to please others, for far too long. Hart half hoped she'd tear his head off.

"It's most irregular. We have a routine already in place."

"I expect you do. But it's time you looked after yourself, had a bit of fun. I'm sure the children wouldn't mind doing without you this morning."

"I would!"

Hart put a hand on Eden's round bottom and swept her up in his arms. "You girls stay here and study until whenever you would normally finish. I'm counting on you to supervise yourselves, then go about your regular day. We'll talk later."

The girls were too surprised to say anything. Eden was not so shy. "Put me down!"

"Not a chance." He carried Eden down the hall.

"What on earth do you think you are doing?"

"I reminded you yesterday we had a contract. The terms, should your memory need refreshing, are this. I paid a pretty penny to secure your services as my mistress until November. A mistress, as you recall, is at the mercy of her master. That would be me."

He snatched her wrists together before she could pound him. "Careful. We're on the stairs. I wouldn't want to drop you."

She stilled in his arms but couldn't still her tongue. "It is the middle of the morning!"

"The perfect time to undress you and see the benefits of country living. You're getting heavy."

"Oh! You odious man!"

He grinned. "I am, aren't I? I've decided that virtue is vastly overrated. I'm prepared to be an utter villain. Number one on my list is to fuck you until you cannot walk."

Hart was growing into this role, his arms full of a writhing Eden, her every curve etching itself on his body. He shouldered his way into the bedroom and shut the door with a slam. As soon as he deposited Eden on the bed, she scrambled up. He got to the door before her, locked it and pocketed the key.

"Too bad you've bolted the door to your room. There's no escape."

"I'll jump out the window."

"It would be a shame to break your pretty neck."

Eden looked as if she wanted to get her hands around his. "Hart, you are being ridiculous."

"Am I? You're probably right. I haven't gone about this the right way at all."

"Good. I'm glad you're coming to your senses."

He examined the carved oak posts and took a playful bounce on the feather mattress. It had seemed vast and lonely to him last night, but the thought of having Eden next him gave him hope, even if she kicked him to kingdom come.

If he was wrong, he'd ruin everything.

But he'd tried it the good way, the Hart way. He had not been able to convince her he was what she needed. And perhaps he hadn't been. She was still afraid of living, of loving. Eden could surround herself with all the children in the world and decline verbs until the end of it, but there was something missing.

She had haunted his dreams for weeks no matter how hard he had tried to drink them away. Now Iris Brown's words haunted him. "I'll be back," he said abruptly.

He'd have to warn off the servants and the girls. The pound-

ing and the screaming—and, my goodness, the inventive cursing—
were rather deafening as he took the stairs. Hart had no intention
of turning Eden loose anytime soon. He was on a rescue mission,
but had to make sure no one else rescued Eden before he had his
chance.

After some brief instructions to Collins, he went into the blue
and white striped parlor. New soft blue silk curtains hung on the
windows, looped back with smooth gold cording. How clever of
Eden's redecorating to provide just what he required. He untied
the lengths from the curtains and, leaving the room in sudden
dimness, stuffed the lengths in his pocket. There would be no
blindfold. He wanted her to watch him as he took her with the
utmost care.

He'd never tied up anyone but prisoners of war. Eden might be
considered such—she was fighting him, wasn't she?

He found the path to the stairs blocked by Eden's four charges,
their bony little elbows linked. Up above came a steady thud on the
heavy oak bedroom door.

"Now, see 'ere, guv," Josie began, sticking her dimpled chin out,
"Miss Eden's been good to us. Better'n our own mums. Don't you
do nuffink to 'urt 'er."

"Anything," murmured Mary.

"'E knows wot I mean." All of Eden's elocution lessons had
vanished.

"You have my solemn oath. May I pass?"

Four sets of eyes bored into him. If Eden didn't kill him after
this, the girls would. Reluctant, they stepped aside.

Maybe he should have waited until dark. Maybe he should have
waited until tomorrow. Next week. Next month.

He'd waited too long already. He had so hoped her misgivings had long been put to rest. Foolish of him, to be sure. They had spent hours in the early days, Eden whispering in the dark, as though voicing the words in too loud a voice would bring the horror back to life. He had held her and shown her in the only way he knew how that she had nothing to fear anymore. When he doubted her, all the wounds reopened. Doubts and fears had had plenty of time to fester in the months they had been separated. No wonder she had thrown herself so wholeheartedly into so many reclamation projects with the girls, the house and the local people.

She was standing at the open window when he entered the room, a stiff breeze blowing at her starched white apron. He hoped that in her deep pockets she didn't have a pair of scissors with which to stab him.

"It's a long way down."

"I told you I would resume—" She bit her lip. "There's no need to force me. You'll get your money's worth."

"This is not about money. It's about trust."

Eden snorted. "You've made it plain you don't trust me."

"I was wrong. It doesn't happen often, but when it does—" He pulled the tie of her apron string and tossed the apron out the window. It jerked like a white kite in the wind before it settled on the gravel path below.

"Please don't throw the rest of my clothes out the window."

She stood still as he unfastened the tiny buttons at the back of her dress. "I hate to see you in black."

"I'm in mourning, remember? People would think it very odd if I gave up my blacks."

"I don't care what people say." He nuzzled her back, right where her wing would be if she were an angel. She smelled of roses and starch. He pulled the dress down her arms and then to where it puddled at her feet. Her corset and shift were not the naughty French confections Juliet had ordered but plain, serviceable garments he made quick work of. She wore nothing now but rough cotton stockings and black slippers. Her nipples peaked. "Come away from the window. You'll get cold."

"It's spring."

"Yes, when everything becomes new again." He cupped her cheek and kissed her.

Ah. Wondrous. A taste of tooth powder and rose salve on her lips. She held her mouth open for him, permitting invasion without a skirmish. Her straight dark lashes dipped to the dusky blue beneath her eyes. She had slept as little as he. Her hands still hung at her sides, when he wanted them to touch him—anywhere.

But no. He broke the kiss and reached for the cording in his pocket.

Her eyes flew open, one hand going to her swollen lips as though she wanted to make sure the kiss had truly happened. He pulled her close.

"We talked of trust a few minutes ago. Do you trust me, Eden?"

"I used to."

"I want to tie you up." He realized with a shock that he meant it. The image of Eden, open and waiting for him, swamped him with longing.

"Wh-what?"

"We can take turns. Tomorrow you can tie me."

"You are absolutely mad!"

"I want this, Eden. Don't deny me."

"Just because I am your mistress doesn't mean I've completely lost my mind!" She struggled against him, but he held her tight.

"But I want you to lose your mind," he said softly. "I want you helpless with need. Unable to stop me from what *I* need."

"And what is it that you need, Hart?"

"I want to feast upon you, kiss every inch of skin. Starting from those pretty toes, to the curve of your calf. Work my way up your white thigh to here." He cupped her mound of Venus, covered again with dark brown curls. They were damp with her dew from just one kiss. "Lick you. Taste you. Put my tongue in your pussy, then my fingers. Fuck you. Hard." At his crude words he felt her shiver and his own cock rise. "But never hurt you. You need do nothing except receive pleasure. And make no mistake. There will be plenty for both of us."

He saw the doubt in her eyes. Saw, too, the interest. Her eyes darted to the bed. "Oh, yes. We'll do it on the bed this time, although you liked it up against the wall, didn't you? I know I did. I had you pinned. Trapped. There's nothing wrong whichever way we try it, Eden. There never will be anything wrong between us. And whatever I do to you, you may do to me. If you want to."

She looked up at him, her eyes black. "You know that's not how I like it. There's something wrong with me."

"Hush. There's nothing wrong with you. Nothing in this world. Come."

He led her to the bed. "Lie down."

She did as she was bid, her hands covering her breasts. Gently he eased her fingers away. "Do you want your arms together over your head or each tied to a bedpost?"

"Together," she whispered.

More helpless. More exposed. He looped the cording around as tight as he dared, anchoring her to the finial on the headboard. A delicious flush was spreading from her cheeks to her throat to her chest. Hart pushed her legs apart, pulling her shoes off and stockings down. Eden watched him, licking her lips nervously as he weighed one cotton stocking in his hand.

"If I place this across your mouth, it means I won't be able to kiss you. But it also means you may cry out as loud as you wish and no one will hear. Which is it?"

"Constrain me." If Hart felt disappointment, he must not show it. This was her choice, her fantasy. He would only benefit in the end. Lifting her head from the pillow, he knotted the stocking, wishing it was silk and not common cotton. Her legs were already open to him, spread even farther. He wrapped her ankles and lashed them to the bedposts.

He sat beside her, taking the pins from the untidy knot in her hair, fanning the waves across his pillow. "Open your eyes, Eden. Do not be ashamed. I'm honored by your trust in me. I won't ever betray you." A tear slid from the corner of one dark gray eye and he bent to lick it away. "If I don't please you—if you become uncomfortable, you must tell me. Ah," he said, laughing, "and how can you do that when I've muzzled you? Blink once for yes, twice for no, five times if you want me to stop at anytime. Agreed?"

She lowered her eyes slowly, then raised them. There was no trace of fear, just curiosity. He wondered if he could remember to ask permission and notice winks when he wanted so very badly to impale himself inside her and never get out.

"I believe I said I'd start with your toes. I hope you had a bath this morning, as foot odor is not my favorite thing. Believe me, in the army I smelled more than my share."

She blinked once.

"Excellent. But what am I thinking? I'm overdressed, aren't I?"

He stripped, freeing his rampant cock from its confines. It would be a while before the fellow got its reward, but it couldn't be helped. He then did exactly what he had said, sucking each toe and stroking the pad of her foot. She groaned beneath her gag as he kneaded and licked first one leg, then the other. He set to showering kisses on the sensitive flesh under her knees, then traced his tongue straight to her center. The rose scent was strong here, mixed with her own distinctive fragrance. He buried his nose in her silky curls as his fingers busied themselves parting her labia to expose her bud.

And then pure instinct took over. Oh, there was nothing pure about it. His tongue was wicked, his mind blank of everything except to devour the morsel of flesh between his lips. As his fingers slid into her heat, she began to convulse under him, her muffled cries ensuring there was no blinking "no" up above. Her walls clenched and rippled around his fingers, her clitoris swelling and pulsing in his mouth. He brought her over twice more before leaving reluctantly.

"Do you want me to stop?"

Two rapid blinks. As if he could anyway. He kissed her belly, rounded now, her body as beautiful as the first pictures of her in his uncle's book. Before he turned her submission into slavery. Hart would never cross that line, but the power she had given him over her made his blood sing. He doubted he'd ever been harder or more desperate, but he had inches more to cover.

Each darkened nipple, so perfect, so delicious. Each creamy breast, too full for his hand. The ridge of bone beneath her throat, so kissable. Her smooth neck. Her stubborn chin. An earlobe. A rosy cheek. Her eyes were wide as he worked his way up to her damp forehead, tasting her salty surrender. She struggled with her bonds at each nip and stroke. He hoped beneath the stocking she was smiling.

"I want to fuck you now, Eden."

Her lashes fluttered down, then she met his eyes with naked invitation.

* * *

Every ghostly scrap of emotion she possessed was battering her. For the longest time, she had buried her feelings in the routine and mundane chores that were heaped around her. She'd ignored her fatigue and loneliness. Ignored her hunger.

Yet now Hart was over her, a place she never expected to find him again. Inside her. He had tied her securely with unbearable tenderness, then made love to every place he could reach with his mouth and hands. Just yesterday she'd convinced herself she was immune to his capricious charm. Had to be, for his sake. He had thought he knew all her shameful secrets, but she knew better.

She did not understand it herself. A part of her was strong. Independent. She had managed miraculously since she came back to Hartford Hall.

But the other part, the darker part—the part that had allowed Ivor Hartford absolute control over her body could not be ignored. Though in the end he had gone much too far, in the beginning she had been so willing a victim.

She'd thought a man like Hart could never understand. She'd tried so hard to hang on to the image of Holy Hartford. Sneering. Cold. Dismissive. He was so much easier to hate that way.

Not hate. Never that, she admitted to herself. She could trick herself into thinking a lot of things, but hating Hart was not one of them. She had built up those barriers against him so he would stay safe from her. So she would stay safe from him.

She had never felt safer than now, tied to his bed, exposed to his hot gaze, cherished. He was not repelled by her desire to be dominated, to give herself totally. True, she'd enjoyed what he did to her in London. Who could not? He was an attentive and accomplished lover. But this morning was entirely different. She was on a new plane of passion, her skin sensitive to every astonishing graze of his fingertips and teeth. Each thrust sent her spiraling to a place she'd never believed truly existed. Heaven. Nirvana. Paradise. Whatever it was called, the risk of honesty was worth this reward.

He tore down the stocking. It didn't take much to turn the gentle brush of their lips into something far deeper, darker, more elemental than a simple exchange of affection and power. The kiss was a pledge of trust on her part, a promise of tenacity on his. His mouth was warm and tasted of coffee. Sweet with a touch of spice. What their life together could be like. The final orgasm with their lips joined shook them both with its ferocity.

They lay entwined, the slick heat between them a living thing. Eden trembled with aftershocks, still edging into bliss. Hart finally found strength enough to withdraw, fumbling with the stocking that was now around her throat.

"I've tied a devilish knot."

She smiled. "Yes, you have. Thank you for this. I have never—"

What could she say? That the sex act had never been so perfect for her? It was true, but she doubted he'd believe it, or even welcome the information.

He put a finger to her lips. "And neither have I, Eden, believe me. You should have told me."

"I couldn't." Her voice was raw from her silenced shrieks.

He rolled off the bed, the slice of cool air between them both a balm and a pity. He went to his boot, pulling out a rather deadly-looking knife with which he sliced the curtain cords. "The parlor is rather gloomy at the moment. We'll have to invest in a lot more roping."

"You needn't do this again, Hart. It's not—it's not natural."

"Don't be a goose. Do you know what you looked like beneath me? I felt like some savage god. It's a wonder I didn't spend at once like a schoolboy. Eden, who is to say what is natural? What is normal? I want to give you pleasure, no matter what you ask for. I told you that months ago when you made me kiss your toes."

"But—"

"No buts. No more conversation whatsoever. I want you to rest now," he said, his voice rough, too. "We'll talk more later. Right now, I think I'll give my first lesson to those little hoydens upstairs."

She didn't turn as she heard him gather up his clothes and go into the dressing room, but instead shut her eyes, imagining him splashing cold water upon his golden body to wash away the evidence of their decadence. When he bent to kiss her good-bye, she feigned sleep and didn't move until she heard the door click shut.

Hart was simply too good to be true. He couldn't possibly bear to live with a woman like her forever, no matter how much she wanted him to. No matter how much she loved him. His care of her today was nothing like his uncle's, and it was everything she had ever dreamed of.

He would leave eventually. But while he was here, she'd see exactly how much pleasure he could deliver.

* * *

Before he went anywhere near the schoolroom, Hart went into the library and opened the pair of French doors that led to the back garden. The boxwood hedges beyond ruffled with the wind.

All the fresh air in the world could not clear his head. The past complicated hour had been a revelation.

How easy it must have been for Ivor to mold Eden to his will. For all that she was a managing sort of female when it came to her family, she had an unspoken need to be passive. To lose herself completely. Hart thought back to their months in London. It was he who initiated sex, although she had been more than enthusiastic. She was as responsive as any man could wish. He knew he had pleased her, watched her sensual pink flush and heard her cries. But today—

Today she had been incandescent. And he had felt a surge of power he'd never known. He'd never suspected the family curse could thrum so pleasantly in his blood. Now that he knew what he was capable of, he could not wait to exercise his authority again.

He'd told her that nothing was taboo between them. Now he'd have to make it true, every single day for the rest of his life.

He chuckled wryly. He was Holy Hartford no more.

But he was not his uncle. He could never bear to see for himself the bleakness in Eden's eyes that his uncle had drawn with such accuracy. Hart had thought the man monster enough, but now that he knew Eden's vulnerability, what the man had done was somehow even more evil. Eden had been pushed far beyond her limit. It was no wonder she thought to escape her past beneath the bodies of Mrs. Brown's patrons.

What had he said? Spring was when everything becomes new again. This was their chance to begin again, on a slightly different footing. Months ago he had attempted to save Eden from her unhappy history. He'd been so confident that he could by using his conventional, gentlemanly methods. But Eden wasn't conventional, and he'd have to learn to be less of a gentleman.

He realized he'd relish this new task, stretch his own limits a bit. And first up was a trip up the stairs to the four saucy little girls whom Eden had rescued. They were bound to open his eyes, and perhaps even cross them.

*   *   *

After a lesson where all parties learned something valuable, Hart spent the rest of the day reacquainting himself with the duties of the lord of the manor. When Mattie informed him she was bringing a tea tray upstairs—for two, she said with a wink—Hart shut the ledger he was perusing away in his desk and told Mr. Pinckney to go home to his family.

Eden was sitting up on a bank of fluffed pillows in his bed, her dark hair down and curling around her shoulders. Her color was fresh, but Hart suspected it had more to do with a tinge of anger than health. Books were strewn all over the coverlet. Brutus was chewing on a corner of one of them. She was now in a pristine white night rail, a pale peach muslin shawl draped around her. Hart yearned to unwrap it and hold her close.

"Mattie tells me that you ordered me locked in here and practically naked for the day."

"You looked tired, Eden. I thought some time without your usual responsibilities would be restful."

"I must insist, my lord, that I return to my own rooms," she bit off, before Hart had a chance to seat himself on the chair that had been drawn by her bedside.

"Oh?" asked Hart innocently. "No doubt you miss your personal things. I'll instruct Mattie to bring them."

"Do you mean to keep me in here forever? I need my privacy!"

"I believe you've been alone all afternoon. No one has bothered you, save for this disreputable creature." Brutus stretched out on the counterpane and resolutely ignored him. Hart hoped he wouldn't find fleas in his bed later, or that the fleas wouldn't find him. "How did he get in?"

"Through the window. He's a daredevil. He prowls the rooftops every chance he gets, hunting for birds and taunting the dogs below. You can't keep everyone away." She looked so mutinous Hart had to stop himself from laughing.

"Now, which is it, Eden? Alone in this not inconsiderable splendor or surrounded by the staff? You can't prefer it both ways." Hart picked up a biscuit and popped it into his mouth in its entirety, then another. "May I pour you tea?"

"Seriously, Hart, you can't imprison me and expect me to drink a bloody cup of tea."

"You're not imprisoned. I truly was only thinking of your health." He poured some tea anyway, into a china cup painted with violets. "Two lumps, correct?"

"Yes. And poppycock. My health is perfectly fine. You were just as sleepless as I last night. I heard you at the door."

"Indeed. I wanted in quite desperately."

"After this morning—" Her cheeks deepened in color. "Just because I let you—you know—doesn't mean I want to be hidden in here like a concubine in a harem."

He pictured Eden covered in silk veils, him removing each layer and binding her to the bed with them. Yes, the new Hart's horizons had definitely expanded.

"It's only been a few hours, Eden. And you did sleep, didn't you?"

"What else was I to do?"

"Precisely. I taught my first lesson in your stead. I didn't want the girls to fall behind." In truth it had been he who was left behind, trying to follow their excitable Cockney chatter. "They are blood-thirsty little wenches. We discussed Waterloo in all its fearsome glory."

"You'll be a bad influence on them."

"I think the reverse may be true, Eden. But I can see why you enjoy working with them."

She looked surprised. "You can?"

"Yes. Schooling is important, even for young ladies." He winked at her before she thought to throw a pillow at him.

She toyed with her hands instead. "My father always thought so. He taught us himself. And a few of the village children. There still is no school here at Hartford. The vicar and his wife do what they can, but—" She shrugged her shoulders, then turned her shining dark eyes hopefully on him.

Hart was aware of the idea forming in Eden's head and felt his pocketbook lighten considerably. But the proceeds from the sale of his uncle's infamous books would go a long way in providing education to the local children in this sparsely populated place. Back of beyond, as Des had termed it so long ago. *His* back of beyond, how-ever, a region that had been sadly neglected by his uncle, and now himself, for far too long.

"Tell you what," Hart said, swallowing a bolstering sip of tea. "I'll support a school here—well, not at the hall, but in Hartford village—if you promise me you will not try to teach in it. You will not have time."

"And just what will I be doing?"

"My bidding, Eden. Seeing to my pleasure. Yours as well."

"Please stop."

"There is but half a year allotted to us, Eden. I'll not waste a second more of it. I want you beneath me as often as I can manage. Or perhaps you above me. And this harem idea of yours is very intriguing."

Eden nearly dropped her cup. "You won't invite other women into our bed!"

"Of course not. You are more than enough for any man. But I was thinking of veils—yards and yards of rainbow silks to wrap you in and tie you fast."

"Oh." That seemed to satisfy her. Hart wondered what other creative entertainment he could provide to pique her interest. It was a challenge he was more than happy to undertake.

"I'll ride over and speak to Mr. Christopher in the morning."

"Ab-about veils?" She blushed.

"No, silly. About starting a school."

"Hart! You would do that for me?" Her face lit with joy, and Hart decided he would do just about anything to see that expression far more often.

"Of course. It's long past time. Maybe our girls could even attend once it's established. I suppose we'll need some sort of building. A teacher. *Not you*," he added and grinned. He hoped she didn't miss his saying "our girls." He meant to do right by them, after spending an hour in their exhilarating if exasperating company. He had even more respect for Eden now that he knew the challenge she faced every morning promptly at nine. He, like Mrs. Brown, had severe doubts about little Jane. The others seemed to have actually benefited from being partly raised in a brothel; they at least knew some semblance of decorum and demeanor. He was quite certain Jane would have picked his pocket had his hand not been in it.

"So," he said, helping himself to another tartlet and feeling rather heroic, "tell me about your lessons as a child."

"Well, we studied the Bible, of course. Eli was keen on all the battles and bloodshed and made little maps of the Holy Land. I preferred the poetry."

And how lacking in poetry her life had been. Hart gave an encouraging nod. As he listened to her talk about her brother and then, more hesitantly, her sister, he grieved anew for her lost innocence. But she seemed to derive pleasure from reminiscing over happy childhood times. He remembered his first attempts at getting to know her, and then remembered the cat, who was curled beneath the table.

He dropped a bit of sandwich to the floor and was amazed at the speed and efficiency with which the creature devoured the tidbit. "I suppose Brutus regards this room as his own now?"

"Oh, no. He's too restless to stay in one place."

"Good. I shouldn't like to share my bed with him."

"Then, sir, you shouldn't share your food with him. He'll become quite spoiled."

"I don't mind spoiling him if it will please you. I intend to spoil you, too, you know. Every night, all night, right here." He reached for her hand.

"Are you saying you want me to stay in your room? To—to sleep in here with you?"

"Yes. Will you?"

Hart smiled as she struggled with framing her desire. Excellent. He was one step closer to winning her over. He marveled that he had ever thought her plain, for her radiance was near blinding. The soft fall of her chocolate hair, her thick-lashed eyes shyly seeking his own, her wondrous mouth moving to form the right words enchanted him utterly. But beyond her beauty was her spirit, strong and stubborn. She had survived what few would have, and he would spend the rest of his days making sure she had nothing whatever to fear. God save him, he loved her.

Chapter 20

Hart's determination to protect Eden was called upon when he least expected it. Spring had given way to summer, yet Eden had not quite given way to him. She still refused his proposals, only with much less certainty than before. He might stop asking, but he'd never stop wanting.

It was as if they were married, however. She slept in his room. They made love, with and sometimes without the silken bonds and blindfolds they had both come to crave. They bickered. They played cards with the girls and divided their lessons. They read books of an evening in the parlor as the light faded across the sky, talked of tenants and ordering schoolbooks and slates for the school in the village Hart had promised her. Life was as close to perfect as it could be without the blessing of the church, and Hart was sure by summer's end Eden would finally agree to marry him, if only to set a good example for the girls.

A willow-work chaise piled with enough pillows to satisfy a sultan had been set up under the shade of a tree so she could teach them outdoors on fine days. She lay now in the deep shadows, half a glass of lemonade and a novel on an iron table at her side. Following another night of bad dreams, she was dozing after their luncheon. Her bare toes peeped out from under the hem of her dress. He had sent her to sleep with tiny kisses to her eyelids, the lobe of an ear, the sweet corner of her lips. Hart thought he could spend the entire afternoon watching her and the busy butterflies, although lying on his desk was a list of tasks to do as long as his arm. His attention was diverted, however, as Collins stepped quickly through the clipped passage in the hedge. At his advanced age Collins never pushed himself unless there was a good reason, and Hart felt immediate alarm. When the butler stood at some distance and motioned, Hart knew he had reason to fear.

He crossed the lawn in a moment. "What is it?"

Collin's color was high, his collar askew. "We have a visitor, Lord Hartford. And his damnable valet." He drew a breath. "There is a Lord Blanchard here. An old friend of your uncle. And in his employ is your uncle's man Kempton. Miss Eden dismissed him. He—he—"

Hart watched the man struggle with his words. "He knew," Hart said quietly.

Collins flushed and nodded his head. "I want you to know, sir, I never really understood all that transpired here. I didn't *want* to know. My Charlotte—" He broke off, looking embarrassed. "I do know that Miss Eden was hurt, and this Blanchard fellow paid us several visits. He's a randy old goat. And looks down on his luck, too. His cuffs have been turned, his breeches are shiny, and his boots aren't. Kempton is a blackguard, but he always knew his job.

He was an army man. Served at Waterloo, or so he bragged. They want money, I'll bet."

Blackmail again. Eden mustn't be disturbed by this now. She had feared the disgrace for Hart, but he cared nothing for what these men might say. Hart raised an eyebrow and moved behind the hedge with Collins.

"Get rid of them. Send them to the Plough and Plunder." The ramshackle inn was to no one's standards, but it was the best and only one Hartford village had to offer. "Tell them I'll pay the shot and come see them tonight."

Collins swallowed. "I already tried that, my lord. They won't budge. Kempton threatened to show Lord Blanchard to the best guest room, smirking like he owned the place, but I've put Lord Blanchard in the library with a bottle of your best. Not that he deserves it. Shouting about a spot of lunch, he is, but he's not going to get it. Kempton's in the stable seeing to the horses. I sent the stable lads packing. Remembered an emergency." Collins managed a grin. "Billy and all your boys have gone off somewhere, too. Poor Kempton. What a come-down for him."

"Collins, you're a wily old bastard. What about the women? And the girls?"

"Those two won't find anyone to bully to make their stay comfortable or to tell their tales to. Mrs. Burrell and Josie are keeping to the kitchen with orders not to cook a thing unless you or Miss Eden ask for it. My Charlotte and Mattie have taken the other three youngsters into the village. Mrs. Washburn is visiting her niece, you know, and will be back tomorrow noon."

Hart placed a firm hand on the old man's shoulder. "You've done a superb job, Collins. He cast his eye back to Eden, who was still in blessed repose. "Perhaps we'll have all this sorted out before she wakes up."

Collins looked uncertain but nodded loyally. Hart reminded himself to sweeten the butler's salary once this day was done. "Stay out here with her, will you? And when she wakes, bring her directly up to our room. The kitchen way's quicker, and she's less apt to be seen. Tell her I have unexpected business and cannot be disturbed until dinnertime. Tell her I very much regret I cannot spend this afternoon with her. I'll make it up to her later. All night."

Collins actually blushed. The sight made Hart laugh, even in the face of the unpleasantness that was to come. "You say I'll find this valet in the stables? Perhaps he'd like a drop of my brandy, too."

Hart's first stop was to find Kempton amidst some very unprom- ising nags. He recognized the horses as belonging to Peter Holly, the owner of the Plough and Plunder. Blanchard and Kempton must have come to Cumbria by mail coach then. Not a very comfortable journey in all this heat. Hart would send them back to whatever hotter hell they came from in his own conveyance at the earliest opportunity.

"Good afternoon," Hart said as genially as he could muster. "Let me give you a hand. It seems I'm sadly short-staffed at the moment."

Kempton looked up, a sneer on his thin face. "Things were a sight different when I worked here."

"Yes. There is not a doubt in the world I am not my uncle." Hart didn't speak again but dealt with the horses as efficiently as an army officer was trained to do. When he was done, he turned. "You and your employer have fallen upon hard times, I understand."

"What makes you say— That old fool Collins!" Kempton blus- tered, his face reddening. "Thinks he knows the way the wind blows.

You'll hear what his lordship wants and then we'll see who's fallen on hard times."

"That seems very much like a threat," Hart said, careful to keep his voice mild. Hands clenched in his pockets, he watched the dust motes drift down in a shaft of sunlight. The stable was cool and calm, unlike the current pace of his heart. One of the horses whickered and set to drink from the trough.

"No need to threaten." Kempton's sour smile was a travesty. "We've got the proof!"

Hart raised his golden eyebrows. "Indeed. But proof of what? Perhaps you should join me in the library then when I meet with Lord Blanchard and you both will enlighten me."

"It's to do with your whore. Eden," Kempton all but snorted.

Hart felt the muscle leap in his cheek. "You forget yourself. If this is how you plan to proceed, you'd better let Blanchard do the talking or you'll be facing the business end of my pistol."

Kempton laughed and reached into his saddlebag. "I don't think so." He produced a gun of his own. Hart recognized it as old military issue. Unpredictable but dangerous all the same. And at this range—

"You'd best not shoot me before you try to get what you've come for." Hart moved forward slowly out of the building, heading toward the set of French doors to the library, the gravel of the path crunching under his boots. One door stood open to the breeze of what had been a perfect day. He prayed Eden was still asleep. What would she think of him being frog-marched into the house, a gun in his side? He pictured her flying across the lawn to his rescue. He smiled to himself.

"Think this is funny? You won't in a while."

Hart said nothing. He thought he might be able to take Kempton, gun or no. The man was close to his size, a bit leaner. But far more desperate. Hart could smell it over the scent of horse and unwashed clothing. For some odd reason, Hart didn't feel desperate at all.

He noted the polished brass door handle as he stepped through the open door. Whose job was it to keep the knob gleaming so? He'd have to find out. Blanchard sat behind the desk, clearly trying to stake his territory. To show he was in control. Spread out on the surface were two yellowing sheets of linen art paper, their edges uncurled by the ink pots and some books. Hart was fairly sure what was depicted on them. He looked at Kempton for the first time. "Where do you want me?"

Blanchard half rose out of the leather chair. "Here, here, Kempton. What's the meaning of this?"

"Thought he might try some funny business, my lord."

"We are gentleman, Kempton. Put that gun away. Very fine brandy you have, Hartford. Just as I remember it." The man actually extended a hand. Hart declined to take it and sat down across the desk in the chair usually occupied by Mr. Pinckney when he made his weekly accounting.

Viscount Blanchard appeared to be in his late fifties, what hair he had left still dark but peppered with silver. He might once have been a handsome man, but years of hard living had left their mark. Deep pouches bracketed his basset brown eyes, and his teeth were stained with decay. Hart repressed his revulsion thinking of that mouth anywhere near his wife. He hoped his uncle had been too possessive to share.

"I'll come right to the point then," Blanchard said, returning his unshaken hand to the desk. He smoothed one of the drawings with it and smiled. "I was one of Ivor's best friends. We enjoyed many of the same interests. The training of young ladies to our tastes, like your lovely mistress, for example."

Hart fixed his eyes to the right of the viscount's head and wondered what the price for their silence would be. Whether there were any more samples of his uncle's hellish handiwork. He'd gone through each of the books in the library himself months ago, ensuring that no extra drawings were tucked away in the bindings before they went up for auction. Apparently his uncle had passed out pictures as souvenirs. Somewhere behind him, Kempton chuckled.

"I was his guest here for several—ah, demonstrations. Eden is a delightful girl, unusually biddable. Perhaps not a great beauty, but she has other talents, wouldn't you say? I do hope you're receiving the benefits of her education. Kempton tells me she was quite frantic to keep her past a secret."

As if waiting for his cue, Kempton stepped into Hart's line of vision and seated himself on the edge of the mahogany desk. He let his eyes linger on the images beneath Blanchard's fingers. "She gave me her baby cup. Solid sliver. Some jewelry and money," Kempton said, smug. " 'Twasn't enough. I knew his lordship the viscount could do better."

"Yes. Kempton sought me out once he was so rudely released from service here. Fortunately my valet had just met with an accident and died and I was able to employ him." Blanchard wrinkled a brow. "Ah, that sounds heartless. I'm sure old Russell was a good man in his way."

Something passed across Kempton's face during this ridiculous homage. Hart felt quite certain Russell's accident was no surprise to Kempton. "How did your man die?"

"Shot by a footpad. By chance, Kempton turned up on my stoop the next day. It was Providence."

"If you say so," murmured Hart. Kempton shot him a warning look, which Hart ignored. "Whose grand plan was this to accost me in my home and defame my fiancée?"

Blanchard leaned over the desk, an elbow obscuring one of Eden's thighs and Hart's uncle's head. "If you must know, it was Kempton's. Bright lad, he is. Had the presence of mind to remove these two drawings, and several more, from the premises before he was tossed out. Remembered me from my last stay here. Your uncle always gave me a jolly time. And really, you know, defamation is not at all accurate. You cannot deny Eden did the things in these drawings. I saw her with my very own eyes. Ivor always said he'd bring her to town one day to show the world, but I was the only one of his old friends to know about the tasty peach he had tucked into his back pocket. Most of our little secret society are too reputable for words now anyhow. Wives, sons and grandsons at Eton," he said in disgust.

"What do you want?"

Kempton laughed harshly. His thin face was triumphant. "Why, money, you dolt. Pots of it. Or we'll go to your auntie and your nephews and anyone else you care about with these."

"Go ahead."

"What?"

"Go ahead. Tell anyone you wish. I love Eden. It doesn't matter what she did, what she was forced to do. I'll marry her anyway. If she'll have me."

Blanchard's mouth hung open like a landed fish. "Perhaps you don't understand. I know people. I have influence. They'll write about you in the newspapers. You won't be able to show your face in town. Your children will be outcasts."

"I'll manage somehow if I have her by my side." He'd never spoken truer words.

"But—but—" Blanchard sputtered.

"He's bluffing," Kempton sneered.

"Am I? I don't think you know me well enough to judge me."

"Won't matter what I think. Society will judge you. You'll be a laughingstock, dipping your wick in used goods. She wanted me, too, you know. Offered to fuck me, but she wasn't worth it. I wanted the money instead. She's a hot little piece, I'll grant you that." Kempton swept his hand over the desk like a conjurer and Hart saw his chance.

Somehow the inkpot tipped as Hart and Kempton crashed onto the desk, rivulets of deep blue running across the papers. Blanchard gave a sharp cry as his chair tipped and he scrambled away from the flying elbows and feet. "Get my gun!" Kempton screamed. "On the table!"

"Careless of you not to put it back into your pocket," Hart said, snapping the man's wrist neatly. Kempton let out an unearthly howl. "Right-handed, are you? Or left?"

"Right! Right! Blanchard, you fucking fool! Shoot him!"

Hart looked straight in the devil's eyes as he broke his other wrist. He rolled Kempton off the desk. The ink-stained drawings fell with him, stuck to the back of his coat. Hart kicked Kempton over, regretting having to touch him with even his boot, peeled off the papers, then crumpled them in one fist. He lobbed the ball into the empty fireplace.

"There are more. Lots more," Kempton ground out between clenched teeth. "Tell him, Lord Blanchard."

Blanchard was frozen, but his eyes darted to the table. Hart stood between him and the gun.

"Your—your uncle was a prolific artist," Blanchard began, sweat beading over his upper lip. He wiped it with the back of his hand.

"We have enough pictures of your little whore that we could paper St. James Palace. Tw-twice over."

Hart took a long stride backward. He picked up the gun and was pleased by its reassuring heft.

"There's nothing that bitch wouldn't do. She even offered up her pretty white arse. Ivor buggered her till they were both blind," Kempton added with some effort from the floor. "We've got drawings."

Hart found himself grinning. Who would imagine such a subject would bring him such joy? "You are both lying, but I believe I'll have to shoot you anyway."

Blanchard was as good as his name. He turned absolutely white. "You'll hang."

"I doubt it. I was attacked in my own home. And I've recently discovered I'm the magistrate in these parts, a duty I've sadly neglected." He cocked the pistol and Kempton sat up clumsily, his useless hands flapping at his side. "Who wants to go first?"

"It was *his* idea," Blanchard said, pointing rather unnecessarily. "He stole the drawings. There were just the two. Gone now. I'll never say a word, I swear it. Kn-known for my discretion. Ask anyone." He inched toward the French doors.

"You blubbering buzzard! Hang me out to dry, will you?"

In a flash, Kempton was on his feet. He butted the viscount with his head and knocked him backward into one of the doors. Both men fell in a rain of glass and blood. Despite the fact that Kempton's wrists were broken, he savaged Blanchard with his head, his knees, his feet, even after Blanchard lay still beneath him, a jagged piece of glass lodged deep in his neck.

Hart fired a warning shot into the empty bookshelves. "Stop! He's dead already, Kempton, or close to it."

"You'll pay." Kempton spat out the blood from his mouth.

"I might have. But it's you who'll hang now."

"I'll tell them! I'll tell them everything!"

Hart showed his teeth. "The word of a murderer."

"You broke my wrists! *You* killed the viscount."

"Then why are you covered in his blood? No, it won't do." Hart tugged the bellpull, remembering too late that he'd left Collins in the garden. But then the butler stepped through the open door, his face pale as he took in the disarray.

"Find my lads and a stout bit of rope, Collins. And send for Dr. Canfield." He tossed the gun aside.

Kempton howled in rage again and charged at Hart. Before he could reach his quarry, another shot rang out and Kempton dropped to the carpet, silenced forever.

Hart looked at his butler in surprise. Yes, a raise was very definitely in order.

Collins carefully placed the revolver back in his pocket. His voice shook only a little. "I thought it wise to be prepared, my lord."

"Were you bluffing?"

Both men turned. Eden stood on the gravel path outside the shattered window. Her eyes were fixed on Blanchard's body.

Dear God. She had been outside the whole time, hearing every filthy thing those bastards said. "Stay where you are, Eden."

He had to get her away from the scene. This room. When he had time, he'd have the whole wing torn down. He left Collins alone with the bodies and used the other door to the gravel path. She was as white and still as a marble statue, her hair half-down from her nap in the shade. He put his arms around her.

"Were you?" she whispered. "Did you just say you loved me to get rid of them?"

"No, Eden. You know I love you. You must know. I asked you to marry me a hundred times."

"Out of guilt. Duty."

"Yes. Maybe at first. But duty be damned! You're the only one who doesn't realize I can't do without you. And I tried."

"You love me."

"Eden. It's just three words. You make it sound like you do not understand their meaning."

"You've never said them."

He stepped back. "What?"

"You've never said them," she repeated.

"Would you have believed me?"

"No."

"Well, then. It's all your fault. Why should I waste my time saying I bloody love you and I bloody want to marry you when you bloody won't believe me?"

"Your language. The girls might hear."

"That's all you have to say?" Hart asked, incredulous.

"No. I mean, yes. I'll marry you."

"Yes?"

Eden looked up at him, her lips twitching. "My lord, it's just one word. You make it sound like you do not understand its meaning."

"You'll marry me." Hart wanted to flop down onto the gravel path and take Eden with him. But that was bound to be uncomfortable. He settled for a kiss.

Not just a kiss. The perfect kiss. A kiss of promise and protection. A kiss of sweet seduction. A kiss of innocence and wickedness and trust.

Well, Eden thought, perhaps it was not the most romantic proposal in the annals of history, but it was timely. And very, very welcome, she acknowledged to herself. More than she had dared to hope, despite the fact it was merely the latest in Hart's offers of marriage. Eden felt a key tumble and turn within. It wasn't a smooth sensation, but rather an uneasy fit into a rusted lock. But the lock was opening—she was opening. Somehow Hart valued her, perhaps even loved her as much as she loved him. He offered her a chance to forever close one door and open another. He had made it clear he would be with her every step of the way. When she stumbled. When she looked back in spite of her good intentions. She knew that together they would be able to go forward.

She had been too proud *for* him before to accede to his wishes, thinking she'd never, ever suit as his wife, but the flutter within her now led her to believe otherwise. The past lay beyond the scattered glass and blood. But it was not only because her villains were dead. Her hero was alive, and she was in his arms, right where she belonged. It was time to be happy.

Epilogue

Her son lay, perfect, in her arms, each spidery gilt-tipped eyelash, each tiny wrinkled finger counted. His nose was pressed against her breast, his plump cheeks pumping as he suckled. It was altogether a different sensation from when Hart had been similarly occupied in that particular location. Eden allowed a small giggle to escape. John's baby brows knitted for an instant, then relaxed as he fell into a milk-induced stupor.

"I'll take him, my lady, and be back to help you dress in a trice." Mattie held her hands out, and Eden reluctantly passed the infant to her maid to return him to the nursery and the girls. It was still something of a scandal that Eden had refused the wet nurse Hart had engaged, but she was determined to be a presence in John's life. Her son was not to be left to the care of strangers. Was never to be ignored, his future marred by mischance as hers had been. There would be no one to induce him into debauchery, even if she had to protect and teach him at home herself.

Eden worried at her lip. Hart would want the future Baron Hartford sent away to school. It was expected amongst the ton after all,
even if Hart didn't lend much credence to society ways. He had vol-
untarily absented himself from London all these months, seemingly
with no trouble. He'd become quite the country gentleman, riding
all over the estate, even helping his tenants with their harvests. Hart
had become an expert in roofing, reaping, gossiping. He knew who
had kissed Molly the miller's daughter behind the hedges at the
church fete and why the brewer's wife had left him and with whom.
He had regaled Eden with such tales when she became too cumber-
some to leave her bed at all the last few weeks of her pregnancy.

And he had undertaken the education of the girls. By all accounts, they were now well-versed in Napoleon's and Wellington's
battle strategies, had a smattering of Italian to go with their fractured French, and were rivaling Diana the Huntress herself with
their archery skills. Eden suspected her romantically inclined charges
found him a far more appealing instructor than they did her.

Her bemused smile was still in place when Hart found her abed
a moment later. He entered without knocking, and she straightened
up. Two unexpected visitors so early in the day left her at a disadvantage. Her hair was still a bit of a mess for all that Mattie had
fussed during Dr. Canfield's visit, and she had a great longing for
some tooth powder. Fortunately young John's standards of hygiene
were focused solely on his food source.

"What did the doctor have to say, Eden? His mouth was too full
of his free breakfast to give me the time of day, the old codger."

"He *was* a bit early. I expected him later in the morning."

"He knew Mrs. Burrell would fatten him up, I reckon. Well?"

Eden blushed. She heard what he was really asking. "He's very
pleased with John's development."

"You are deliberately toying with me, madam." He plunked himself onto the blankets and captured her hand. "I should like to resume my marital rights. If it is safe and you will let me."

Her face was fiery now. "There is no impediment."

"Ah, but there is." His blunt fingertips brushed her chin, and she raised her warm face to him. "Do you still love me, Eden?"

"More than I can bear."

"Excellent." Hart's face split with a naughty boy's grin. "I shall come to you tonight."

Eden kept his hand firmly in her grasp. Recklessly, she asked, "Why wait until tonight? John will not need me for another few hours. I believe I have time to spare for you, my lord."

Hart raised an eyebrow. "In the daylight? How absolutely shocking." He looked absolutely delighted.

"You knew when you married me I was a sad rip. Do lock the door. Mattie will return any minute."

She watched him stride across the room, the exquisite cut of his coat melding with every muscle of his back. Before she knew it, the coat was on the floor along with the rest of his clothes, and his long, lean body was beside her.

"That is a lovely bed jacket, madam wife, but I believe you must be too warm."

"Yes," said Eden, her voice a sigh.

"Let me help remove it."

Eden lifted her chin as Hart pulled the satin strings open. His fingers neatly dispatched the nightgown's buttons from their buttonholes and soon both garments were tossed aside. He opened the bedside table and took out the skeins of velvet ropes.

Eden kept close watch on her husband's face. Her body was a girl's no longer. And Mrs. Burrell was busy fattening *her* up so John would continue to thrive. The breakfast delivered to Eden had been enormous, and to her shame she had eaten every last crumb. Perhaps it would have been wiser to wait until tonight. Candlelight was every woman's friend.

"I haven't even cleaned my teeth," she remembered.

"It's of no consequence. It's not your teeth I'm interested in."

And Hart began his amorous assault, making her forget any objection she might have had to the hour and the circumstances. He only paused at the rattle of the doorknob, to growl, "Come back later. Much later."

And thus their marriage entered its next chapter, bound by their love and the little miracle in the nursery, guarded by earthly angels.

Keep reading for a preview of
the next title by Margaret Rowe

Any Wicked Thing

Available in January 2011 from Berkley Heat

*If he thinks he can come here and lord and master it
over me, he is much mistaken.*
—FROM THE DIARY OF FREDERICA WELLS

"No and no and no."

"Frederica, you can't refuse to see him forever. This is his house, after all." Mrs. Carroll preened in front of the pier glass, retying the strings to her widow's cap for the third time. Sebastian Goddard, the new Duke of Roxbury, was apt to make the most devout of widows toss up their black petticoats for a blissful tumble with the ton's most revered, most thoroughly unrepentant rake. Mrs. Carroll was devout only when considering her own pleasure, and Sebastian its possible provider.

"I can do anything I like. And this is hardly his home. I doubt he knows an inch of Goddard Castle—he's only been here once, and that was ten years ago. I imagine he'll get lost and fall down the garderobe." Frederica pictured Sebastian, stained and stinking. Some brave souls had once stormed Chateau-Gaillard through a latrine drain in 1204, if she remembered her history correctly. But mentally it was much more satisfactory to push

Sebastian down than to picture him climbing up, conquest on his mind.

"He *is* your guardian."

"I don't need a guardian! I'm a grown woman, for heaven's sake." The terms of his father's will had been explicit, however, and Frederica was stuck with him. She had dreaded the day he would come here again.

"You may be long in the tooth, but not in possession of your fortune just yet."

"It's hardly a fortune," Frederica said. Well, she supposed it was. She could live quite independently until her hair was silver, and she didn't have a long tooth in her head. The old duke had made wise investments on her behalf. It was a shame he'd been unable to do the same for himself. The financial climate at the castle was chilly at best.

Frederica stabbed at the fabric in her embroidery hoop with a vicious stitch. "Duke or not, I won't have Sebastian Goddard bully me for the next two years. Whatever was his father thinking?"

"If only you had married when you had the chance, you wouldn't find yourself in this predicament."

Frederica tossed her sewing aside. "Oh, stop! Not that again." Living with her eccentric uncle Phillip had been no picnic, but it had not been bad enough to marry the lisping, lecherous Earl of Warfield, one of several suitors who, at the duke's invitation, had come to court her like she was a Yorkshire Rapunzel in her tower. The ensuing attentions had been most unpleasant, Warfield leaving to blacken her name after she brandished a fourteenth-century sword at him in defense of the virtue she had already parted with. Frederica was content to be left alone, although lately she had begun to wonder if independence was all that it was cracked up to be.

Sometimes Frederica thought that the old duke had invited the least suitable men on the planet to Goddard Castle. She suspected in his heart he hoped she was still carrying a sputtering torch for Sebastian. If she was, she planned on dousing herself in very cold water before she saw him again.

Mrs. Carroll adjusted a suspiciously bright red curl and turned from the spotted glass. "Very well. All my nagging doesn't seem to matter anyway. But now you are about to pay for your stubbornness. I shall enjoy watching the new Duke of Roxbury torment you."

Frederica stayed her impulse to stab the woman with her sewing scissors. "You really are the most odious companion."

The woman gave her a nasty smile. "I am a necessary evil. You wouldn't want to be left all alone here with him, now, would you?"

Frederica shuddered. Trapped between a bitch and a bastard. Her late guardian had been oblivious to Mrs. Carroll's waspish nature, but he was dead now, and Frederica had suffered long enough.

"All right. I will see Sebastian. And the first thing I shall ask him to do is to dismiss you."

Mrs. Carroll blanched, revealing suspiciously bright red circles of rouge as well. "You wouldn't dare!"

"I believe I would. When he discovers you helped yourself to his mother's jewels after Uncle Phillip died, I think he'll see reason."

"How did you—?" Mrs. Carroll bit her tongue and her face mottled to match her paint.

It had been a guess—an educated one. Mrs. Carroll always locked her rooms behind her. Why be so secretive when one had nothing to hide? "I'll write you a reference if you go away today—I can lie as well as you can. But leave the duchess's things behind."

"*Today!* You little brat! I will go, and good riddance to you. Sebastian Goddard will have you in his bed before the week is out, not that you deserve him. But I hear he fucks anything, so even an antidote like you stands a chance."

"Get. Out. Now."

Frederica picked up her embroidery, not flinching when the heavy door slammed. She was *not* an antidote.

And she'd been in Sebastian's bed before.

Well, she had not been precisely in his *bed*. But the consequences were the same and she was ruined. He'd been much the worse for drink and drugs, and she had been in disguise and tipsy herself, so eager and enthusiastic to divest herself of her virtue that she couldn't even blame that footman who passed her those extra glasses of apricot ratafia. What happened afterward made the night unforgettable for all the wrong reasons.

Frederica had been a remarkably stupid girl the night she'd taken advantage of Sebastian so he could take advantage of her. She wasn't sure she was much smarter now, for the thought of Sebastian's long, dark body anywhere near hers gave her palpitations. But he couldn't stay up here forever. A few days would bore a man like him senseless.

The late duke had purchased the castle on a whim almost a dozen years ago. It had sucked up the Roxbury treasury and was still a drafty, dangerous place, the moors beyond it even worse with their sinkholes and fierce winds. Sebastian would soon go back to London or Paris or wherever there was sufficient amusement to be had and leave her alone.

Frederica removed her spectacles and rubbed the bridge of her nose. She didn't want to see her embroidery anyway—she was making a dog's dinner of the vines and flowers on the pointless pillowcase. Why embellish something that was to be drooled on? It was not as though she'd ever have a man in her bed to impress with her

neat French knots and chain stitches. And if that's all he'd be looking at—

A perfectly wicked thought crossed her mind. True, she had
pledged to herself to never marry. She planned on hiring a much
nicer companion than Mrs. Carroll in two years when she came into
her funds, and living modestly on her inheritance, with a faithful
dog or a cat. Men were disappointing creatures who cared for nothing but their own comforts, and often had fleas besides. Sebastian
was the very model of such a man—selfish, careless, reckless. But
the play upon the family name—he was known as God of Sin by the
chin-wags—was surely deserved.

Frederica's paltry attempt at sexual experience a decade ago
should probably not even be counted as such. While she had undoubtedly lost her virginity, she'd never been transported to heaven.
Over the years, she had achieved that for herself without going insane or blind, but how lovely it would be to be brought to abandon
by a skillful lover.

A Sebastian who was not dead drunk or full of poppy smoke. A
Sebastian who had ten years to hone his skills and earn his disreputable reputation. Of course, he might have picked up something far
less desirable than knowledge—gentlemen were dying off left and
right from debauchery. But if Sebastian didn't have the pox or nasty
little insects nesting in his nether hair, he just might do again.

How very shocking. She was considering making a second
mistake with Sebastian. In a real bed this time, with embroidered
pillowcases and clean linens and candles scattered about the room
illuminating his masculine perfection.

Of course, there was a considerable impediment to her plan. Sebastian Goddard hated her.

She *would* see him. But not like this, not in a worn-out dress with her hair every which way. She would bathe and ask for apple cider vinegar to bring out the shine in her light brown hair. She would powder her face and chest to conceal her unfortunate freckles, perfume herself from top to toe, find a dress that revealed just enough of her skin. And then, if she could figure out a way, she would seduce Sebastian all over again and see if God of Sin was a misnomer or the God's honest truth.